Soundings Edge

CHAPTER ONE

The wind rattled the leaded panes of the study with a persistence as methodical as the slashing rain. A meagre fire muttered in the grate, doing little to repulse the moist chill that insinuated itself into every crevice of the room. Nicholas Cruwys, seated upright on a chair that had known better centuries, stared at the letter before him as though it were an object of theological importance. The script was formal and upright, with an Admiralty seal.

Opposite him, in the half-light thrown by a candle that guttered with each new draught, sat his father, Mr. Richard Cruwys, barrister of Exeter and sometime scholar of Gray's Inn. A man of economy in purse, word, and affection, he considered his younger son with the dispassion he might apply to an equity dispute or a flawed title deed.

Nicholas read the letter again. Despite the frugality that governed the household, his father had engaged tutors for both his sons, holding that a gentleman's education was indispensable. Nicholas could read and write with ease, possessed a serviceable Latin and the rudiments of Greek, and could work through a page of Euclid with unflinching clarity. He had taken naturally to figures and showed an early inclination toward maps and sea-charts, a tendency his tutor—a retired curate with maritime leanings—had fostered with grave and private pleasure. His hand was small and exact, his orthography conservative, and his reading had extended far into the literature of voyages—factual and fanciful alike, from Dampier to Defoe.

At length, his father exhaled through his nose—a sound suggestive of an overtaxed bellows—and inclined his head by a precise and deliberate degree, as though issuing a verdict rather than a benediction.

"You will note," he said at last, "that many lads of your age who aspire to His Majesty's commission have long since gone aboard as midshipmen, and now learn the service from the deck. The old school has its merits, to be sure." He paused, his gaze resting a moment on the boy's face. "You, by contrast, are to attend the

Academy—not universally esteemed in the fleet, with some claiming it turns out mathematicians rather than sailors. But my cousin Captain Trevenen speaks well of its instruction in navigation, and his nephew James will be joining you. It is an opportunity few are afforded—and not one to be squandered."

"Yes, sir," said Nicholas, his voice emerging through a throat unaccountably dry, his tone properly solemn. Yet in truth every fibre of him throbbed with a scarcely contained elation, the breathless wonder of a boy of fourteen standing at the threshold of his dream.

His father was silent a moment longer, then steepled his fingers in thought. "There was a time," he said, "when salt water ran not so thinly in our blood. Admiral Sir Josias Cruwys—my grandfather—was a man of the old navy: hard as cannon-shot, and no friend to waste or whim." He glanced up, eyes remote. "Lowestoft, Bergen, the Channel actions—he rose to his flag before King William's wars were done. The name of Cruwys bore weight in the service then." He nodded toward the letter. "Whether it shall do so again lies with you."

A sigh stirred the air in the doorway, and Mrs. Cruwys entered, her gown of faded silk whispering faintly with each step—a garment once elegant, now merely respectable. The candlelight caught the fine creases at her mouth, the long-set furrow between her brows etched by years of quiet strain. She placed a hand upon Nicholas's shoulder—a touch light, deliberate, and very brief.

"You will write," she said.

It was not a question, nor did he take it as one.

"Of course, Mother," he replied," though he suspected the letters would be few and hurried, snatched between drills and study, and perhaps too dull or brief to satisfy.

No port was poured, no toasts offered in the drawing-room. Supper proceeded as it always had—measured, indifferent, bounded by remarks on the weather and Mr. Cruwys's view of a recent judgment from King's Bench. Edward excused himself early, his indifference as plain as the gesture itself. Nicholas, though stung, had long ceased to expect fraternal warmth.

Later that night, abed beneath the sagging rafters of his chamber, Nicholas stared upward into the dark. Memory stirred of its own accord: a summer's day three years before, the salt tang in the air, the black-and-yellow hull of a frigate riding at her moorings, her pennant snapping smartly in the breeze.

The journey to Plymouth had been undertaken at the instigation of a cousin in Cornwall, for reasons of familial obligation, thinly veiled as a visit of courtesy. But it had served another purpose. Nicholas Cruwys, then but eleven years of age, sat beside his father in the jolting interior of the chaise, his boots not yet reaching the floor, his hands folded neatly in his lap, his silence broken only by the occasional monosyllable, as decorum required. Beneath that composed exterior, however, his thoughts ran elsewhere. He had brought two books—*Anson's Voyage* and *Gulliver's Travels*—though he had read both before, and certain passages more than once. The old woodcut of the *Centurion* off Cape Horn remained vivid in his mind: spars rimed with ice, the deck awash. He admired Dampier too, though the prose was dry in parts, and had read *Robinson Crusoe* with the usual boy's fascination—though less for the goats and palisades than for the notion of command: the making of one's own world aboard a wrecked hull or on a desolate strand.

They had quitted Exeter early in the morning to finish the journey in one long summer day the road passing through the fixed, enduring world green of the countryside, as English as the Book of Common Prayer, its bounds as familiar and unaltered as the parish lines.

But late in the afternoon, as the horses drew them up the long shoulder of a rise, the world changed.

The land fell away as though swept from the board by some vast, invisible hand. Beyond, the sea: vast, restless, unknowable. It caught the light like hammered pewter, shifting and alive, moving with a life that defied all domestic metaphor. Not the stillness of ponds, nor the idle chatter of brooks. This was motion unbounded, deep and elemental. Nothing in his books had quite prepared him for it. The sea, not imagined, but real: pale in the distance, streaked with light, moving under a wind he could not yet feel. His breath caught, though he showed no sign.

His father, too, had taken in the view, but made no comment. He merely adjusted the set of his hat and gave the driver a curt nod to proceed. Nicholas, however, stared at the ocean until the road descended and the hedges closed about them.

As they rumbled into the cobblestone streets of Plymouth, the mingled scent of salt, tar, and cordage, that unmistakable perfume of seafaring places, seemed like an old friend from his books, yet awakening something long dormant, or perhaps always present. By the time they reached their lodging—a cheerless inn several streets back from the harbour edge—Nicholas found himself breathless with anticipation.

As they climbed down from the coach, he made to walk with his mother, but his father's hand came down with the finality of a writ on his shoulder. "Your mother will go in," he said. "Edward, see that she is made comfortable."

Edward, turned with mild surprise. It had been his assumption given the habits of their lives that any undertaking of note would include him. "But—"

"No arguments," said their father, in a tone that admitted none. "Nicholas. Come."

They stepped into the street. The air, salt-laden and sharp, moved about them with a quiet insistence. Mixed into it was the smell of horse and hemp, fish offal, tar, and woodsmoke: the unmistakable breath of a working port. Mr. Cruwys paused, casting a glance at his son as though weighing him against the scene before them. There was something in that look—regret, perhaps, or resignation. Then, with a squaring of the shoulders that seemed to conclude some private calculation, he began to walk.

"Come," he said again, not unkindly.

As they came down through the town toward the water's edge, the full sweep of the anchorage opened before them, a confusion of spars and pennants, and sailors, boatmen and fishermen calling out. Nicholas stared—there were brigs, cutters, fish-laden luggers nosing in under sail, and the squat shapes of victualling hoys offloading flour and beef to the wharves by derrick. Coopering yards rang with mallet-strokes, barrels rolled on iron-shod rims toward the sheds.

Farther out in the Sound lay the ships of the line, anchored in two proud tiers, their black and striped lines of gunports hulls solemn above the pale swell. Naval tenders and barges moved ceaselessly between shore and ship, their oars flashing in the late afternoon light.

One of the nearest warships caught and held his gaze. She was tethered to a heavy buoy, sleek, black-hulled, with a single yellow stripe running the length of her side, broken only by the square rhythm of closed gunports. Her beakhead bore gilt scrollwork that caught the late afternoon sun like captured flame. Beneath her bowsprit, a pale figurehead—a woman, or perhaps a goddess—gazed out toward the open sea, serene and fierce at once, her blue painted eyes staring forward over the water.

A boat was putting off from her side, pulling steadily through the harbour chop, the oars rising and falling in near-perfect unison. As it approached the quay, the coxswain gave a sharp command, and the blades lifted vertically together. The boat came in smooth and sure, and a man in the stern rose to his feet. Nicholas knew, without needing to be told, that this was Captain Matthew Trevenen.

He stood with the ease of long habit, a man of perhaps forty, tall and broad shouldered, but wiry. His coat was faultless in its turn; the gilt on his cuffs caught what remained of the light, and the linen at his throat was crisply tied. He did not smile, nor offer ceremony, but gave the impression of one for whom this was merely the next in a long succession of unremarkable landings—some better, many worse.

"So, cousin Richard," he said, stepping lightly ashore. "This is the boy."

Richard Cruwys inclined his head with judicial economy. "Indeed. May I present my younger son, Nicholas."

Nicholas removed his hat and bowed, not floridly, but with a decorum suited to the occasion. "Sir," he said, with all the steadiness he could muster. "It is an honour."

The captain regarded him a moment, his gaze narrowing. "You've an interest in ships, I'm told," he said. "But no sea-time?"

"No, sir," Nicholas replied, the words catching slightly. "But I have long wished for it."

Trevenen gave a low grunt, neither assent nor dismissal. "Have you, indeed?"

Trevenen turned without further word and resumed his place in the sternsheets. "Come along. You shall see her properly."

Nicholas's heart gave a sudden bound, but he contained it. He descended carefully between the oarsmen, moving with all the composure that excitement would allow. The boat pushed off, and the coxswain ordered, "Give way together." The oars rose and fell in practiced unison with a swish of blades through water, the creak of thole pins. It was a kind of music, strange yet stirring, that seemed to draw the frigate closer with each stroke. She grew, her masts and yards forming a lattice of rigging against the fading sky.

As they rounded her stern, her name became visible in gilt: *Pallas*. Nicholas felt the word strike some deep and resonant chord within him. The goddess, of course. He had been right about the figurehead. His tutor would have been pleased.

He craned his neck upward as the boat came alongside the port side. The ship was alive—lines creaking in their blocks, sailors moving up and down the rigging, a boatswain's pipe trilling somewhere out of sight. Trevenen gestured Nicholas forward. "Mind your step," he said, and without further word, grasped the man ropes and went up the side. Nicholas followed, his hands clammy on the ropes, his feet pushing up from the battens in the hull, movements cautious but competent.

He reached the deck and looked around at a different world—ordered, self-contained, precise as a watch's movement. His gaze lingered on the sweep of the deck, the polished curve of the capstan, the taut lines that vanished aloft into rigging like a drawing in air.

Trevenen waited a pace away, his arms clasped behind his back.

"Well, young Nicholas," he said. "What do you make of her?"

Nicholas hesitated, not from doubt but from the sheer weight of the moment. "She's beautiful, sir," he said at last, the words falling short of all he felt.

Trevenen gave a grunt—not displeased—and turned to lead him aft. As they passed down the quarterdeck, men moved aside with the unconscious grace of long practice. A marine stood sentry in his scarlet coat, ramrod-straight. A midshipman ducked below, a slate tucked under one arm. Everywhere, men moved with the silent assurance of long habit, their tasks as natural as breath.

The great cabin aft surprised Nicholas with its breadth and quiet refinement. The bulkheads were painted a deep cream, the overhead beams and doorways shone with a varnish the colour of honey, warm against the darker patina of the planked deck. Two whale-oil lamps swung gently in their brass gimbals, their light catching the stern windows where the last of the daylight filtered in, dappling the broad mahogany table. A Hadley quadrant lay there, beside several rolled charts, the corners held flat by brass dolphins that gleamed like old coin.

It was a room of practical elegance, neither straitened nor showy. The desk chair, upholstered in faded blue wool and studded in brass, matched the small settee along the forward bulkhead; both bore the quiet marks of long usage at sea: salt-threaded nap, the worn curve of elbows. A wine-dark Turkey carpet covered part of the deck, its pattern dulled by use. These were the quarters of a man who inhabited the narrow but honourable space between naval discipline and gentlemanly cultivation—one who prized utility, but did not scorn comfort when it could be justified.

And then, near the weather-glass, hung upon pegs set into the beam, Nicholas saw the captain's sword.

It was a hanger, plainly kept but far from ordinary. The grip was of darkened shagreen, bound in twisted brass wire dulled with age, and the guard—though simple at a glance—bore the faintest vestige of hand-chased scrollwork along the knuckle-bow, worn soft at the edges. The scabbard, leather and brass, bore the kind of polish that comes from habit rather than show. It was not the short, brutal cutlass of the lower decks, but something older, longer, finer.

Nicholas stared a moment longer than was strictly polite.

"Something catch your eye?" asked Trevenen from the far side of the cabin, his tone dry.

Nicholas straightened. "Your sword, sir," he said. "It looks... very well balanced."

Trevenen turned slightly. "That so?"

Nicholas nodded, his voice steady despite the moment. "Yes sir. My tutor—Mr. Pennant—has taught me some fencing. He has a pair of blades for demonstration. But nothing like that one." He hesitated, then added, "Is it... very old?"

Trevenen studied him for a beat longer than usual. Then, perhaps amused, perhaps something else, he crossed to the pegs, lifted the hanger down, and drew it partway from its scabbard.

"It was my grandfather's," he said. "Cartagena, 1741. Worn through three wars."

The steel was dark with age, the edge just visible. A trace of faint patterning, nearly lost to time, shimmered briefly in the shifting light.

Nicholas leaned forward slightly—not to touch, but to look. "It's beautiful," he said, reverent without awe. "Not showy. But it looks fast."

Trevenen gave a sound that might have been approval. "Fast enough, if the hand behind it knows how to use it."

He slid the blade home with a soft, final hiss, and returned it to its pegs. "Better than a pistol at close range," he said. "But not something to play at."

"No, sir," said Nicholas.

Trevenen looked at him again, measuring, perhaps. "The Navy is no easy life, but it is an honourable one. A ship's deck is no place for idlers. But for those with resolve, it offers purpose—and the chance to make one's mark."

Nicholas said nothing, though the words had set a quiet blaze within him. The boat returned him to shore as dusk fell, gulls wheeling overhead in long, slow arcs, the tide slapping gently at the quay. His father met him and though he said no more than a few words on the walk back, Nicholas marked, with a flicker of pride, that he did not walk ahead. That night he lay awake beneath a thin coverlet in a narrow bed, listening to the life of the harbour beyond in the distance: the groan of cordage, the faint clang of a bell, the muffled voices of men. It was no longer the stuff of boys' tales, and he wanted it more than anything he had known.

Three years later, the family's Exeter house in Cathedral Yard was still in shadow when Nicholas Cruwys departed on an early April spring morning. Its draughty rooms and worn furnishings were as indifferent to his leaving as they had ever been to his presence. No candles had been lit, no servants summoned. There was no farewell, only the continuation of a routine that would carry on without remark.

In recent years, Nicholas had come to understand that his father's household ran on the same principles that governed his work: precision, economy, and a certain hard clarity of purpose.

Frugality had not been forced upon Richard Cruwys by ruin or folly; it was a matter of principle. He was third son of the late Squire of Cruwys Morchard, a parish about sixteen miles northwest of Exeter with several small hamlets, including Pennymoor, Way Village, and Nomansland, with the church and the Cruwys manor house situated at the center of the parish.

Richard had long since carved out a life as a barrister in Exeter, measured, self-contained, and anchored in the law. His elder brother held the manor now. There had been no quarrel, no resentment—only the quiet economy of a landed family: the house and estate to the heir, who had a son of his own, a career in the Church for the second, and the law courts to the third. The middle brother held the living at Morchard Bishop, respectable and assured. His daughters, though well-mannered, would inherit nothing. The entail was sure and unbending, and Nicholas, second son of the third son, might as well have been born a stranger to the land.

Nicholas' mother kissed his cheek, her lips cool against his skin. Her fingers brushed his sleeve and lingered there a moment, then fell away.

His father stood waiting in the front hall, where the cold pooled on the stone flags beneath the door. Richard Cruwys extended his hand, but no embrace. The grip was firm and carried, beneath its austerity, a faint suggestion of pride. No grand words were spoken; only a brief nod, and a deliberate once-over, as though confirming that

Nicholas stood straight, bore himself well, and would not bring shame to the name. That was Richard Cruwys's benediction: exacting standards met, and—silently—approved.

Nicholas' sea chest, new-made of oak and banded in iron, stood beside the hired post-chaise, its brass hasps catching what little light there was. It had been well provisioned. His father, though no trafficker in sentiment, had ensured his son was sent out neither gaudily nor meanly turned out. The uniforms were of proper navy wool, plain, but well cut; the cocked hat stiff, serviceable, and without ornament. Even the octant, procured through a legal acquaintance, had been tested and found sound, though the case bore another man's initials, and the screw on the limb had a tendency to loosen.

Each item bore the same tacit message: you are sufficiently begun. What follows is your own affair.

The morning lay hard with frost, the hedgerows rimed in silver, the city's towers veiled in a slow-drifting mist. As the chaise jolted over the cobbles and turned eastward out of Exeter, the cathedral's spire faded behind them, tall and grey against the thinning light. Somewhere to the northwest, beyond Tiverton, lay the family's historic land, and a grey-fronted manor of long wings and mullioned windows, set among fields that folded like cloth over the mid-Devon hills. The house stood low and square upon its land, not grand in the modern style but dignified in its age, with stone gateposts carved in weathered arms and a small deer park. Nicholas had been there only twice, as a boy—once for a cousin's christening, once for a funeral, and had wandered the box-edged walks behind the house feeling not so much unwelcome as unnecessary. Though the name carried weight in the county, it brought him no consequence. His name was a proud inheritance, yes—but not a future.

Nicholas looked back only once, then turned his face to the road ahead.

The post-chaise rattled down the narrow lanes and out through Eastgate, past shuttered shops and the black bulk of the old Guildhall. By the time the sun cleared the trees, they were well beyond the town and climbing into the cold folds of the countryside.

The Portsmouth stage met them at Honiton, a lumbering vehicle whose flaking red paint and harness scored with age bespoke long service on indifferent roads. The guard, swathed in green baize to the chin, balanced himself behind with the dignity of a man guarding treasure, while the driver blew into his hands and muttered about frost on the downs. Nicholas climbed aboard with his satchel; his sea chest, heavy with damp and brass-bound, had been roped onto the roof with the others, canvas thrown hastily across it as if in vague concession to the weather. His own place within was narrow: hemmed between a grocer of ponderous girth who steamed faintly, a narrow-chinned clergyman absorbed in Fordyce's *Sermons*, and a widow of such imposing carriage that she sniffed audibly at the state of his boots and thereafter addressed her remarks to the air.

The pace was all it promised: seven miles an hour when the road allowed, rather less when it did not. The horses were changed with professional haste at Axminster, where Nicholas took a slice of venison pie and a weak cup of ale at the inn. Supper was boiled beef and dumplings at The George, heavy with suet and served in a common room thick with the smell of damp wool and tallow. Nicholas said little, observed much, and noted a few spare lines in his journal before turning in. His chamber was narrow, his mattress thin and hard, and the window frosted over from within.

The next day brought worse roads. Near Bridport, the lane had half dissolved after a week's rain, and the coach wallowed in every rut. At one incline, the driver asked the gentlemen to descend and walk the better part of a mile lest the wheels bog entirely. Nicholas trudged beside the clergyman, his boots caked in clay. The widow, triumphant in her seat, remained unmoved throughout.

At Dorchester, they dined on sliced ham, coarse bread, and pickled cheese. Thereafter the road improved somewhat, and by evening they reached Blandford Forum. Nicholas was at last given a square, clean chamber with a bed both dry and decent. He slept soundly despite the midnight racket of mails changing in the yard below.

On the final morning, the coach rolled into Salisbury beneath a sky of thinning cloud. The cathedral spire, tall and improbable, pierced the grey above the rooftops like a ship's mast seen from afar. At the White Hart, the yard seethed with carts, mail-coaches, and liveried post-boys. Nicholas snatched a meat pasty from a pie-woman beneath the arch just as the guard's horn sounded.

The last leg passed in a blur: chalk-white hills, thatched villages, sheep pressed behind low stone walls—and then, cresting a rise, a first glimpse of the Solent: grey, vast, and shining.

The dockyard spread out below them like a tapestry of rigging and smoke. The clink of hammers on copper rang out across the morning air, mingled with the sharp tang of pitch, tar, and brine. Sailors moved with bundles slung over their shoulders, boys shouted from skiffs, and a Marine drummer tapped out a cadence in some inner yard. The coach rattled down the slope, past the gates and the press of carts, and drew up at the George Inn. A porter grunted as he hauled down Nicholas's chest, and the boy stepped onto the cobbles—stiff-legged, but alert.

He had arrived.

The next morning dawned sullen, the air thick with brine and the faint, metallic tang of the dockyard. Nicholas presented himself at the gates of the Royal Naval Academy, his letter of appointment folded with care in the breast of his coat. The watchman admitted him without ceremony, and moments later he stood in a stone-flagged courtyard among a dozen other boys—each stiff in a new uniform, each striving not to look overawed.

The Academy's walls were high and pale with age, its corridors echoing with the clipped tread of instructors. His bedchamber was a narrow cell with two bunks, a tin basin, and the persistent scent of chalk dust, salt, and old wool. That first night, he dreamed not of Devon, nor of ships, but of the sea itself—dark, heaving, filled with a voice just beyond hearing.

CHAPTER TWO

Nicholas' arrival at the Royal Naval Academy marked the beginning of the life he had long imagined but scarcely apprehended. Though he wore the proper colours and his sea chest sat square on the stone floor of his quarters, he was yet untested, his learning theoretical, his courage unproven. Still, something in him thrilled at the hardness of it all: the stark walls, the clipped commands, the echo of discipline in the quadrangle below.

The Academy, housed within the fortified bounds of Portsmouth Dockyard, was at once a school and a symbol, though what it symbolised varied according to the observer. To its founders, it was the answer to chaos: a place where mathematics and navigation might steady the service. To many officers of the old school, it smacked of French theory and genteel presumption: a manufactory of drawing-room midshipmen who had never reefed a topsail in a rising gale.

The buildings, raised in the reign of King George the Second, were of Hampshire stone and Portland lime, solid, unadorned, and plainly meant to endure. Windows marched in rigid rows like gunports, admitting the pale southern light in parsimonious shafts. The flagstones of the forecourt led to a heavy oak door marked only with a brass Admiralty anchor.

Within, the corridors held the mingled scent of chalk dust, ink, tallow, and the unshifting damp of a coastal winter. Wooden benches lined the walls, their surfaces dulled to a waxen sheen by the press of blue serge trousers. Notices in copperplate hand adorned the boards above. The stairwells were narrow and steep, as in a ship of the line, and the classrooms austere: long desks, dark slate, and chalk boards with the smeared calculations of celestial trigonometry.

His first days passed in a blur: formalities, drill, lectures, and a schedule of inspections that left no margin for idleness. He rose before dawn to the beat of the drum, washed in cold water drawn from a basin, and dressed by candlelight before hurrying to muster.

The instructors were former lieutenants, master gunners, warrant officers, and naval mathematicians, each with his own method, and his own imperious intolerance for error. There was no gentle acclimation; cadets were expected to keep pace, or be left behind.

Mr. Davis, the mathematics master, was a tall, hollow-cheeked man with a voice like rigging in a squall. "A single degree of error," he announced on their first morning, "and you won't merely miss your port, you'll strike a lee shore, and drown with your reckoning. A careless navigator is a murderer by another name."

To his own quiet surprise, Nicholas found he had a head for it. Declinations, hour angles, lunar distances, the arcana of latitude and arcminute—these nested in his mind with ease. For the first time in his life, he was not simply competent; he was proficient.

But the school was not mathematics alone. Seamanship, gunnery, swordsmanship, signals, and the conduct befitting a gentleman were all drilled into them—sometimes at the blackboard, more often through sweat, shouted orders, and the thump of bruised knuckles. Gunnery loomed largest. Though the Academy lacked a ship of its own, cadets were taken in rotation to one of the old hulks moored nearby, still armed for the purpose where cannon waited in grim alignment along her lower deck, their black muzzles mute and menacing even in peace.

The gunnery master was Hawkins, a stocky man with a voice like iron and a temper to match. A veteran of the Seven Years' War, he had left two fingers at Louisbourg, and most of his forbearance off the Grand Banks. "A well-drilled crew wins the battle before the first shot," he would bellow, pacing the gundeck while cadets fumbled with sponge and rammer. "A sloppy crew dies before they fire again."

It was during one of those early drills that Nicholas met James Trevenen.

They became fast friends. Trevenen, slight and quick-limbed, could scale the ratlines with the ease of a natural climber, moving as if the ship's rigging were stitched into his bones. Nicholas, taller and still growing into his reach, brought a steadier form—economical, grounded, precise. They sparred together most evenings, honing their swordsmanship with a kind of cheerful severity: Trevenen favouring speed and flourish, Nicholas a measured discipline. Outside the salle, they were seldom apart. Trevenen had a keen eye for mischief and opportunity; Nicholas, more reserved, tempered impulse with calculation. Each sharpened the other.

Together they explored the dockyard's vast machinery of war and maintenance, from the mast pond, where Baltic pine seasoned in slow, brackish silence, to the ropewalk, where hemp was spun into the cordage that gave ships their sinew and reach. The air was thick with the bite of Stockholm tar, the sweetness of sawn oak, and the musk of the sail loft, where canvas was marked and stitched with methodical care.

They lingered by the dry dock, where a seventy-four lay stripped to her copper sheathing, her massive rudder propped and waiting for the joiners. Teams of shipwrights swarmed her hull, hammering caulking into seams with a steady percussion that echoed off the timber walls. Above, the shrill whistle of bosun's pipes cut through the din, signalling orders no less urgent for being routine.

They watched the marines drill near the victualling yard, scarlet-coated and rifle-straight—and wandered the warehouse lanes where casks of salt beef and hard biscuit were loaded by hand and pulley. From the seawall, they studied the ships anchored in the Solent, not by counting gunports as landsmen did, but by the rake of the masts, the shapes of the sterns, the quiet clues that marked a Slade design from others.

Not all was camaraderie. Among the cadets was Edward Fanshawe, son of an admiral and no stranger to his own consequence. Fanshawe took a particular dislike to Nicholas, perhaps due to his quiet competence, or perhaps merely from instinct. He seldom addressed Nicholas directly, preferring to belittle him before others or deliver his slights with the smooth cruelty of inherited rank.

James, for his part, had little patience for him. "If he ever falls overboard," he muttered after one such encounter, "I shall wait a full three minutes before throwing him a rope, and even then I may aim to miss."

Among the many disciplines taught at the Academy was practical swordsmanship—not merely the elegant forms of the salle, but the brutal efficiencies required in boarding actions. The naval cutlass was their primary weapon: shorter than a cavalry sabre, heavier than a smallsword, and meant for close quarters. They drilled with wooden wasters, their jackets padded but never thick enough to prevent bruises. Fanshawe excelled in these lessons, having been trained from boyhood by his father's master-at-arms.

Their first real clash came during cutlass drill. Fanshawe, paired with Nicholas, pressed his attack with more force than the exercise required. When the instructor's eye turned, he abandoned the sequence and landed a sharp cut to Nicholas's ribs, one that left him breathless and bent.

"Mind your guard, Cruwys," he said, his tone smooth and faintly mocking. "At sea, there's no master to cry halt."

Nicholas said nothing. But a fortnight later, when they were paired again, he was ready. Fanshawe came on hard—too hard—his blade low and fast, the sort of stroke that might have cracked a rib had it landed clean. But Nicholas had anticipated it. He pivoted, slipped the blow, and brought his hilt down sharply behind Fanshawe's knee, turning the motion into a sweep drawn not from the salle but from the close-quarter work of a boarding-pike. It was not elegant, but it was effective.

Fanshawe went down with a thud that silenced the salle—his breath gone, his pride more so. For a moment he lay stunned, his cutlass clattering against the floor with a noise that rang louder than any applause.

Nicholas stepped back, blade still raised, his breath steady. "Footing is treacherous at sea," he said, just loud enough to carry.

Their next encounter was with the smallsword, the lighter weapon preferred by officers for duels and personal defence. Here, speed and precision triumphed over weight, and Nicholas found himself unexpectedly at ease. Fanshawe fought with textbook form, all measure and flourish. Nicholas, by contrast, honed an economy of movement, nothing wasted, nothing forecast.

The tension came to a head during the winter examinations. Fanshawe, confident past caution, overreached in a lunge. Nicholas parried and riposted in a single, fluid motion—the buttoned point of his blade landing squarely against his opponent's ribs. Fanshawe flushed scarlet, his knuckles whitening on the hilt. Nicholas only lowered his blade and gave a proper bow. No word passed between them.

Their practice bouts continued through the term, and though the instructors must have noted the particular charge they carried, none chose to intervene. This was, after all, a naval academy: a place where boys trained to become men who would one day fight real enemies, in close quarters and without quarter. A certain edge was expected.

By spring, the Academy held its annual Prize Contest in Arms—a tradition nearly as old as the institution itself. The event drew officers from the fleet, Academy governors, and now and then a member from the Admiralty Board. For the cadets, it was more than a contest; it was a proving ground, where a clean victory might carry further than any report of scholarly merit.

The competition opened with a series of preliminary bouts that swiftly thinned the field. Nicholas advanced cleanly through his bracket—his footwork balanced, his movements spare and exact. Fanshawe, too, dispatched his opponents with ease, though more than one observer noted his preference for flourish over function.

When the finalists were announced, an unexpected pairing emerged. Though from different years, Nicholas and Fanshawe would face each other for the overall prize—a senior cadet against his junior. The rules allowed it, but such matches were rare, and never without consequence.

The final bout was held on the central floor of the salle d'armes before the entire student body, and more than a few men of consequence. Among them were Rear Admiral Winthrop of the Admiralty Board and two post-captains lately returned from the West Indies. Lieutenant Hardcastle, the fencing master, recited the rules in clipped tones: five touches to win, no time limit, only clean points counted.

Fanshawe saluted with a flourish, his confidence manifest in every measured gesture. Nicholas's salute was simpler and unadorned, but entirely correct. As they took their marks, the contrast between them sharpened: Fanshawe tall, immaculate, assured; Nicholas a shade shorter, but still as a loaded spring, his expression unreadable.

At the command to begin, Fanshawe came on at once—quick, complex, and theatrical, clearly intent on settling matters early. Nicholas parried with restraint, giving ground step by measured step. A murmur passed through the watching cadets as Fanshawe landed the first touch with a textbook lunge.

"First blood to the favourite," someone murmured at the edge of the crowd.

Nicholas adjusted his stance with a slight shift of weight. When Fanshawe attacked again, he met it with a pared-down parry and a swift riposte, his blade striking home before Fanshawe had fully recovered. One-one.

The next pass came fast. Fanshawe attempted a feint, too clever by half; Nicholas read it cleanly and countered with a touch to the shoulder. Two-one.

Fanshawe's expression darkened. His next attack came on with a force better suited to a cutlass than a smallsword. Nicholas slipped aside rather than meet it, letting Fanshawe's momentum carry him forward unchecked—then touched him lightly between the shoulder blades. A few cadets chuckled. Three-one.

Anger now plain on his face, Fanshawe abandoned finesse for fury. He pressed Nicholas with a flurry of blows that drove him steadily toward the edge of the floor. For a moment it seemed the younger cadet would be forced off his ground—and then Fanshawe's blade struck home. Three-two.

As they stepped apart to reset, Nicholas glanced into the crowd and caught James's eye. His friend offered an almost imperceptible nod.

In the final exchange, Nicholas altered his approach entirely. No longer reactive, he took the initiative with a flanconade followed by a coupé-dégagé, an elegant sequence Lieutenant Hardcastle had pressed upon them only weeks before. The combination demanded perfect timing, and was rarely attempted by junior cadets. Transitioning cleanly from seconde to tierce, Nicholas executed it with a quiet exactness that belied his age. Fanshawe, anticipating another retreat, was left wholly unprepared.

Nicholas's blade struck three times in swift succession—shoulder, chest, throat—each touch light, deliberate, and perfectly placed. There was no flourish, no waste: only precision, and control.

"Match to Cadet Cruwys," said Lieutenant Hardcastle, his voice cutting across the stunned hush of the room.

Nicholas offered the customary salute, then extended his hand. Fanshawe, his face set and pale, took it with the reluctance of a man who had never been bested where it mattered. As they shook, Nicholas leaned in just a fraction.

"I believe that concludes our lesson," he said, low enough for Fanshawe alone.

Admiral Winthrop presented the small silver cup, his weathered face showing the faintest trace of approval, a brief tilt of the head, a glint behind the eyes. Nothing more.

Fanshawe stepped aside, unmoving, as the hall broke into polite, almost perfunctory applause. The look he directed at Nicholas was cold, but beneath it lay something more enduring than resentment, a promise that the matter, in his view, remained unresolved.

As the cadets began to drift into knots of chatter and analysis, Trevenen sidled up beside him, his eyes bright with mischief.

"I do believe you've committed the unforgivable, Mr. Cruwys," he murmured. "Not merely bested Fanshawe—but left him no excuse. That sort of thing tends to linger. And for the record, that final sequence, damned near poetry. I feared your spherical trig had dulled the edge."

Nicholas permitted himself the faintest smile. "You might have warned me you were wagering on the result," he murmured.

"And spoil the spread?" Trevenen grinned. "No, my friend. But I knew."

By May of 1776, Nicholas had been two years at the Academy. Though short of the full three-year course, he had distinguished himself in navigation, gunnery, comportment, and, most memorably, in arms. His instructors described him as steady, capable, and, in the parlance of the service, "fit for advancement." He had turned sixteen that month.

One morning, without preamble, he was summoned to the commandant's office and handed a sealed letter bearing Admiralty markings. Later that same day, James received his own. Both were to be appointed to *HMS Resolution*, under the command of Captain James Cook.

Nicholas turned the letter over in his hands, reading it twice. Even then, it scarcely felt real. Cook's name was spoken in tones of admiration throughout the service—an explorer, a navigator, a fighting officer with the restraint of a scholar. To sail with him was a stroke of fortune so great it felt nearly mythic.

James, reading over his shoulder, let out a low whistle. "Cook's ship," he said, grinning. "That'll be something. And I'm going too!"

Nicholas nodded, still dazed. "We've been given a chance that most only dream of."

James clapped him on the shoulder. "Well, Mr. Cruwys," he said with mock solemnity, "it appears our education is about to become extremely practical."

CHAPTER THREE

She lay to anchor with her bow canted slightly to the tide, a broad-beamed vessel with low freeboard and a bluff, unadorned bow. From a distance she lacked all elegance. Her lines were simple, almost sullen, thick through the waist, square in the stern, her black hull broken by a yellow strake and shuttered gunports that seemed less martial than practical.

"A collier," James murmured as they approached in the launch. "Whitby-built, by the look of her."

Nicholas nodded. He recognised the lines from their drawings at the Academy—broad-beamed, deep-bellied, slow to answer the helm. Cook had chosen her for strength, not speed, and her design showed it. She was no man-o'-war, no sleek sloop. She was a vessel built to endure. And despite her plainness, or perhaps because of it, Nicholas felt a prickling respect.

"She'll not win a race," said James. "But I fancy she'll reach ports others wouldn't dare attempt."

The launch drew up alongside, and Nicholas craned his neck at the towering masts above. Whatever her origin, she was his ship now—his world, for the months and years to come.

The wind stirred uneasily across the bay, but it filled *Resolution*'s canvas well enough as she slipped out of Plymouth Sound on the

12th of July 1776, her consort *HMS Discovery* close astern. Nicholas stood at the larboard rail, his fingers tight on the salt-scoured wood, the wind sharp with brine as the ship heeled to starboard. Behind them, England receded into mist—green hills softening into grey, as though withdrawing by design.

For weeks the ship had been a hive of motion: provisions hoisted aboard, the magazine stocked, casks secured against heavy weather. Captain Cook moved among it all with tireless precision, lean, composed, and seemingly omnipresent. His manner was quiet, but his disapproval, when incurred, was formidable. He had no need of raised voices; his silence did the work.

Those who had served with him before spoke of his habits with a mix of awe and caution: how he would test for dust along a beam with his fingertip, or descend to the bilges to inspect their state himself, no matter how detailed the report.

Lieutenant Clerke, Cook's trusted first officer, offered the necessary counterbalance—translating orders, tempering the edge, and delivering direction with a steadiness that softened nothing but soothed much. Where Cook was spare, Clerke was clear.

Together they reviewed every detail of the preparations, Cook recording his observations in a neat, compact hand in the leather-bound journal he carried everywhere. Nothing escaped him—not the quality of the salt beef, nor the construction of the new chronometer boxes, nor the stowage of the scientific instruments entrusted to the expedition. The midshipmen saw little of him outside these inspections, but his reputation preceded him: a master navigator, relentless in discipline, and possessed of a meticulous concern with scurvy and cleanliness.

Stories circulated of midshipmen who failed to name a brace correctly and were placed on additional watches until every rope and shroud was learned by heart. Yet for all his rigour, Cook was known to be scrupulously fair. He judged by competence, not birth. A seaman who did his duty received praise without embellishment. A gentleman who shirked received silence colder than any reprimand.

James stood beside Nicholas at the rail, his grin dulled by the solemnity of the moment. "It's different now, isn't it?" he murmured. "All those lectures, the drills, the books—it all felt like a rehearsal. But this... this is the play."

Nicholas nodded. "Now it's the world before us." He turned to glance at his friend. "Are you afraid?"

"Only of the captain's methods," James replied. "And those, my dear Cruwys, are no small matter. For it is said in the service that God may command the seas, but Cook has charted them to the last fathom."

The early days passed in a flurry of routine: sail drill, gun drill, mess arrangements, noon observations, log-line readings, and the unending maintenance of a wooden world afloat. Nicholas was assigned to the middle watch. The hours felt unnatural to his land-bred body, yet in the stillness of the darkened deck—the creak of timbers, the gleam of phosphorescence in the ship's wake—he found an unexpected peace.

The midshipmen's berth was cramped and airless, lit only by the lightwell above the gun deck. Twelve midshipmen were borne on *Resolution*'s books for the voyage. An unusually high number for a ship of her size, but reflective of the Admiralty's intent to furnish experience to promising young officers. Hammocks hung cheek by jowl; sea chests wedged under benches; every inch contested by boots, elbows, and muttered oaths. Yet there was fellowship in the closeness, and Nicholas slipped into its rhythm more readily than he'd expected.

Little was said of home. Most had learned that silence travelled better at sea. In his off-hours, Nicholas practised with his octant, finding the precision of the instrument no longer so simple when the deck pitched beneath him. Still, he copied each observation into his logbook with careful pride.

At night, he read by the stub of a purser's candle, the flame rising and falling with the motion of the hull.

After nearly four weeks at sea, *Resolution* made her first landfall in the Cape Verde Islands, anchoring at Porto Praia on Santiago beneath a ridgeline of bare, sun-blasted hills. Cook approached the anchorage with due caution, sending men aloft to watch for shoals while the leadsman in the chains called out fathoms in a steady chant. At last, they found six fathoms over black volcanic sand and let go the anchor to a splash and a thunder of cable. The heat descended like a physical blow—heavy, airless, and far beyond anything Nicholas had known in England. Pitch bubbled between the deck planks; the brass grew too hot to touch. The air was thick with salt, dust, and a lingering stench of dried fish that seemed to soak through the rigging.

"So this is Africa," James murmured at the rail, sweat darkening his shirt though it was not yet mid-morning. "Or near enough. It don't look much like the maps, does it? All those neat lines and careful shadings. Nothing to prepare a man for this."

Nicholas nodded, his gaze fixed on the shore. A scatter of whitewashed buildings huddled near the waterfront, their flat roofs and faded walls dulled by wind and dust. The settlement looked poor, makeshift, with little sign of Portuguese wealth after nearly three centuries of colonial rule. A low stone fort overlooked the bay, its flag limp, its walls sun-cracked and beginning to crumble. Beyond, the land was barren and bone-dry. The drought, Cook had said, was now in its third year.

"It looks..." Nicholas began, faltering.

"Godforsaken," James offered, with a glance toward the cracked earth beyond the ridge.

"No," said Nicholas, still staring. "Harsh, unyielding. As though nature herself has set herself against man's ambitions here."

Within the hour, local traders began to put out from shore in a scatter of boats, some narrow fishing craft patched with sailcloth and twine, others dugouts hollowed from African hardwood, low in the water and steered by paddle. A few bore signs of hasty repair, their planking mismatched or their seams caulked with tar and cloth. Their crews were a varied lot: some black Africans, others of mixed Portuguese and African descent, their dialect a shifting blend of Kriolu and old Portuguese.

"Trade, English! Good trade!" they cried. The boats rocked gently in the swell, holding oranges and limes from exhausted orchards, dried bananas, a few withered watermelons. Several carried goats— scrawny, long-legged creatures with their legs bound in fibre cord.

Others offered gourds and stoppered bottles of aguardente, the raw sugarcane spirit of the islands, and a sharp local wine drawn from vines that had weathered generations of dust and heat.

Captain Cook had authorised trade for fresh provisions, and the purser, Mr. Bentham, came down to the entry port with a tally book and a careful eye. Nicholas watched from above as each offer was appraised. At a port like this, where coin was scarce, and few goods could be spared, iron nails, coarse cloth, and tools were currency enough.

The citrus, though small and bruised, was valued above all—not for taste, but for what it prevented. Scurvy was the sailor's quiet death, and Cook, who had lost no man to it on his last voyage, meant to do no worse on this one.

"We shall go ashore tomorrow," said Lieutenant Clerke, appearing beside Nicholas. "The captain will pay his respects to the Portuguese governor and arrange for watering. You and Mr. Trevenen will accompany the shore party. Six bells in the forenoon watch."

"Aye, sir," said Nicholas, unable to keep the eagerness from his voice. His first foreign soil, an occasion he had long imagined. Clerke allowed a small, dry smile.

"Keep your wits about you," he added. "These islands are not what the charts might suggest. There's been drought for years, and much poverty. The Portuguese hold their authority, but lightly. Their governor's a military man of middling rank, small garrison. Stick together, follow orders. And remember: they've seen a great many sailors pass through, few of them improving the impression left behind."

"And mind the fever," James added after Clerke had gone. "The surgeon says the miasma rises from the marshes near the watering place. Water's to be boiled, unless you fancy the bloody flux."

That night, as he lay in his hammock, Nicholas found sleep elusive despite the day's exertions. The unfamiliar sounds of a foreign harbour drifted down through the hatches: the bark of a dog, the distant thrum of a drum from somewhere within the settlement, the soft slap of water against the hull. The air remained thick and warm, barely stirred by the faint offshore breeze that carried with it a scent of dust, ash, and the sea. It was not the world of books or maps. It was something else—something real.

The launch was lowered at six bells, the oarsmen taking their places with the smooth precision that came of long practice. Nicholas sat beside James and kept his hands folded, his posture careful. He was aware of the uniform on his back, of the polished buckle at his waist, of the slight stiffness in his new shoes. The boat moved steadily through the chop, the sun already hot on their shoulders.

The landing stairs were worn smooth, salt-eaten at the edges. Two Portuguese soldiers lounged at the quay, their coats sun-faded and their posture indifferent. A boy led a limping goat past them without comment. The town behind seemed scarcely awake, whitewashed houses low and blank-faced, their doors shut against the heat to come.

The governor's residence stood a little higher on the slope, square and undecorated, a building more military than civic in design. Inside, the walls were pale and empty save for a crucifix and a fly-blown print of the King of Portugal. Cook and the governor conversed in halting French, their tones polite but pared to essentials. Nicholas stood at attention with the others, saying nothing, his eyes on the cracked tiles of the floor, his mind recording everything.

When the formalities were concluded, the shore party returned to the quay. A pair of stevedores passed with baskets of dried fish, and somewhere nearby a woman shouted at a mule that would not move. Nicholas descended the same worn steps, boots scraping the stone, and climbed into the launch without comment. The boat pulled away with the same practiced ease, oars rising and falling in steady rhythm.

Back aboard *Resolution*, the glare gave way to shadow as they stepped below decks. Nicholas peeled off his coat in the midshipmen's berth, his shirt soaked through and his collar limp with sweat. He said little over the midday meal, content to listen to the rhythm of others' talk. James filling the gaps with cheerful mimicry of the governor's stiff French and one of the younger boys speculating, without basis, that the aguardente might be flammable enough to cook with.

That evening, Nicholas stood again at the larboard rail, the sun low behind the ridge. A fishing boat drifted near the stern, its single sail patched in three colours, its hull bleached grey by sun and salt. The land behind seemed unchanged—dust, stone, shuttered windows—but Nicholas understood it differently now. It had been seen, not read. Stepped upon, not merely sketched.

He felt no thrill in it. But there was a weight, an anchoring sense that he had crossed something invisible but real. His world had been small, once: bounded by study, expectation, and the contours of Devon lanes. That world had begun to fall away.

The next morning, *Resolution* and *Discovery* took on their final casks of water and stores, and the ships stood out to sea under full spreads of canvas, shaping an east-southeasterly course that would carry them well clear of the African coast, avoiding the sluggish northerly set of the Guinea Current on their long passage toward the Cape.

The days fell into a rhythm shaped by the ship and the sea. The doldrums brought with them heat and stillness that made the sails sag and the pitch bubble between the deck planks. Shirts stuck to backs; tempers shortened. Then came the squalls—sudden, violent, drenching—followed by a flat calm again, as though the sky had simply forgotten itself.

Nicholas learned the feel of a watch by its weight on the body: the slack-limbed fatigue of the middle watch, the slow drag of the forenoon after a restless dawn. He could now climb to the masthead without thought, his time at the Academy having trained him to manage the height without undue dread—though it was quite another thing to do so with the deck pitching beneath, the rigging alive beneath his hands. He could read the trim of the sails from the angle of the shadow on the deck, kept his log with precision, tested his octant against known stars, and plotted noon positions on a chart that slowly curved south and east.

There were nights when the moon rose huge and yellow out of the sea, and the water shone with fire as the bow wave curled back from the cutwater. Nicholas would lie awake in his hammock and feel the ship flex with the swell beneath, creaking and breathing like a living thing. He did not dream of Devon. He dreamed of lines and rigging, of points on a chart, of something vast and unknowable ahead.

As they passed the equator, the ceremonies began. The older hands prepared with relish: whiting their faces, fashioning tridents, stringing up ropes across the deck. Neptune came aboard in a wig made of spun yarn, and even Cook allowed a faint smile as the men were ducked, shaved, and roared at in good humour. Nicholas took it in stride, submitted to the ritual with soaked dignity, and came up grinning through a mouthful of brine.

South of the Line, the air turned colder by degrees, and the sea began to heave with a longer, deeper swell. The wind settled into the west and began to build, steady and vast. Captain Cook took her far down into the forties of southern latitude, not to run straight for the Cape, which lay farther north, but to catch the great winds that circled the globe unbroken from west to east. The Roaring Forties took them in hand, and the sails stretched full under grey skies.

By late October, they sighted Table Mountain rising out of the haze, flat-topped and immense. The wind dropped as they approached, and *Resolution* and *Discovery* ghosted into Table Bay under shortened sail. The water was calmer here, but the air smelled of cattle, woodsmoke, and distant cooking fires. Nicholas stood at the rail, watching as the great shoulder of Africa rose before them, dry hills striped with vineyard and track, the white-walled buildings of the Dutch settlement bright in the sun.

Resolution took on fresh water, firewood, and livestock. Her weathered rigging was meticulously overhauled, each spar inspected for rot or strain. Though not careened, she was brought as near to readiness as the Cape's modest facilities allowed, with the hull scraped clean of barnacles and trailing weed along the waterline. The cooper hammered brass hoops tight around the staves of leaky casks, while the sailmaker's needle flashed in the sunlight as he patched worn canvas on the wharf side, his fingers calloused from years of such work.

Nicholas accompanied Clerke ashore to negotiate a shipment of salted beef and ship's biscuit. The Dutch East India Company's influence pervaded the Cape Colony, evident in the Company's distinctive monogram emblazoned on warehouses and official documents. Malay laborers in broad-brimmed straw hats moved cargo under the midday sun, while Khoikhoi herders, whistling low and rhythmic, drove lowing cattle along dusty lanes that wound between whitewashed buildings. Dutch merchants in somber long coats and buckled shoes conducted their business beneath shaded porticos, haggling with animated gestures over casks of Cape wine and bundles of exotic spices from the East.

At a Portuguese cookshop near the market square, Nicholas savored a bowl of stewed game and coarse bread, seated adjacent to a group of weathered seamen from a Spanish brig. They spoke in hushed tones, their conversation punctuated by significant pauses as they glanced frequently toward the Company men passing outside the open doorway. Nicholas maintained his solitude, attending more to listening than speaking, noting with interest how one officer meticulously counted silver coins beneath the rough-hewn table before passing them, concealed within a folded napkin, to a dark-clothed merchant. The market's air hung heavy with the competing scents of ground pepper, vinegar-preserved goods, and the omnipresent Cape dust that coated everything by day's end.

The stop at the Cape lasted five days, and though the air was fresher and the food better than they'd known in weeks, Cook kept the liberty tight. Shore leave was granted in shifts, the work constant. Still, Nicholas found time to walk the perimeter of the bay alone on the final evening, watching the sun sink behind Lion's Head, the sky streaked orange and violet above the masts of anchored ships.

From the Cape they struck eastward, running before the westerlies at the edge of the Roaring Forties. The wind held steady and cold, and *Resolution* bowled along at her best speed, her hull rising and falling with the long, grey swell. Weeks passed without sight of land—only sky, sea, and the endless hiss of water along the strakes. The decks were constantly awash with spray; ice formed on the windward rail in the morning; hands moved with their collars up and speech kept brief.

As they went south the sky grew lower, and the wind more insistent. There were few distractions now, only the rhythm of duty and the care of gear. Nicholas found comfort in precision, tight knots, clean log entries, the quiet satisfaction of marking a correct lunar distance.

The sea had ceased to feel strange, and he was not the boy who had first stepped aboard in Plymouth, but something leaner, steadier.

By late December, they were far below the known routes. Ice began to appear in the sea—first small fragments, then floes, then ghostly bergs that loomed out of the mist without warning. Lookouts were doubled, sails were reefed more often. On the twenty-fourth, a dark shape broke the horizon—land, low and jagged, under a sky thick with rain. It was Christmas Eve.

The island Cook had come to examine was Kerguelen, though he would name it otherwise. Its coasts were raw and inhospitable, the cliffs black and the bays choked with kelp.

On Christmas Day, *Resolution* anchored in what Cook would christen Christmas Harbour, yet the name was the only cheerful thing about it. The wind howled through the rigging even in the anchorage, and the rain seemed to come from every direction at once. There were no trees. No people. The cold was unrelenting; the decks slick with sleet. Seals bellowed from the rocks. The men gathered for a hasty meal—salt pork, biscuit, and a dram—and sang a verse or two of a carol before the wind smothered the sound.

"Lord save us from a holiday in this godforsaken place," muttered James, as they stood on the quarterdeck. "I would sooner dine on the Devil's own table than pass Christmas here."

"It will make for a bold entry in your journal, at least," replied Nicholas, though he could not help but share his friend's sentiment.

"Bold, is it? Aye, and so would hanging, but I'd prefer to avoid the experience."

Nicholas stood at the rail, peering through the damp mist as the rocky shoreline revealed itself, strewn with jagged boulders and slick with endless sheets of rain. The sea, black and churning, foamed hungrily against the crags, as if eager to claim any who dared step ashore. There was no sign of human habitation, no trees, no welcoming signs of life—only the ceaseless wind and the distant cries of seabirds. The sky remained a heavy, leaden grey, the clouds rolling endlessly from the west, bringing a constant drizzle that soaked through every layer of wool and sailcloth.

Ashore, the ground was hard and barren, composed of dark volcanic rock, slick with damp, treacherous underfoot. The hills beyond were covered only in patches of moss and lichen, with a few stunted clumps of grass struggling to take root in the wind-blasted soil. There was nothing here for permanent settlement: no wood for fires, no fruit, no fresh water that did not come from half-frozen streams trickling weakly through the rocks.

Yet the necessity of replenishment demanded that the men go ashore. Seals lay in great lumbering clusters along the shoreline, their mournful cries rising eerily above the waves. Penguins, unlike any birds the crew had seen before, waddled in vast colonies, their black and white bodies comical and dignified at once, utterly fearless of men. The work parties butchered the birds with ruthless efficiency for barreling; the seals, too, fell easily, their thick blubber a source of vital oil and meat. As a midshipman, Nicholas did not join in the slaughter, but oversaw the loading of carcasses into the longboat and recorded what he could: weather, bearing, kill sites, quantities. He kept his face expressionless, his hands busy, and his thoughts to himself.

That night, the crew gathered for a meal of salted pork and fresh seal meat fried in pork fat. It smoked the galley, its scent heavy and strange. Someone played a few bars on the fiddle, but the air was too wet for song. Even Cook kept to his cabin, drafting bearings and sketching coastlines by the flicker of whale-oil lamps.

On the second full day, as Nicholas stood beside Quartermaster Markham near the longboat, preparing to go ashore again, a shout went up from the rocks. One of the officers had found something strange: a half-rotted post of driftwood wedged between the stones. Carved into it, faded by salt and time, was a line of letters barely legible in the grain: F. MARION 1772.

The name meant nothing to the sailors, but Cook, upon hearing of it, frowned in thought. It was the mark of the French explorer Yves-Joseph de Kerguelen-Trémarec, who had discovered this island just four years before. There had been rumours in London of Kerguelen's misfortunes, his discovery of an inhospitable land, his disgrace upon returning home, and his eventual imprisonment. His men had left their sign here, a lone scrap of evidence that they had come, seen, and left this place behind, as the English now meant to do.

"The French have been here, sir," said Lieutenant Clerke, as Cook examined the post.

"So it would seem," replied Cook. "They have found nothing worth claiming. Still, we shall make a thorough survey. It may be that our French friends overlooked something of value."

He took Nicholas along most often to help in this work, having noticed the lad's quick mind and navigational skill.

"Mr. Cruwys," Cook had said on the third morning, his voice precise and measured, his face revealing nothing of his thoughts, "you will accompany me in the launch. Bring your octant and notebook. We shall take bearings of the western headland."

After a few days, Nicholas' steady manner in assisting with the hard work in the freezing conditions of the boats and shore, his careful accuracy with the octant and other instruments, and the precise script in his survey notes, pleased Cook. Nothing in the captain's manner indicated his approval, for he was not a man given to unnecessary praise or conversation, and he remained remote and formal with all the junior officers. Yet it was noted by the other officers that Cook called for Nicholas with increasing frequency for the survey work.

By the end of the week, the casks of seal oil were stowed, the decks cleaned of the offal, and the men stood ready to be rid of the place. Cook gave the order to prepare for sea. Anchors were weighed with visible relief, and the ship swung to her heading once more, pointing east into the grey. Nicholas stood at the rail as the jagged peaks of the Isle of Desolation slipped back into the mist. He did not think any man would return there willingly.

These last months had scoured him like wind over stone: the cold, the storms, the silence of icebound coasts. He found himself thinking less of duty, and more of survival, of endurance—of charting not just coastlines, but something within himself.

By early 1777, they reached Van Diemen's Land, anchoring in Adventure Bay. The land was strange and untamed, with towering eucalyptus trees, odd animals glimpsed in the underbrush, the air sharp with the scent of unfamiliar vegetation. The bay was well-sheltered, the water calm after weeks of hard sea. The ship settled to her anchors with a creak and a groan, and the men stood a little straighter just to feel the stillness beneath their feet.

"This is more like it," said James, as they went ashore to help supervise the watering party. "No more of your blasted frozen rocks, but a proper land, with timber for the taking and a bay so fine a fleet might anchor in it."

"Yes, but mind you do not venture too deep into those woods," cautioned Lieutenant Clerke, overhearing them. "The savages here are not to be trifled with. They have killed Englishmen before, and would do so again, if given the chance."

Nicholas said nothing, but the words settled in his mind. It was the first time he had heard Clerke speak so plainly, and it gave the place a different weight. The trees no longer looked simply tall, but watchful.

The shore party moved cautiously inland, marking trees for felling, collecting samples for the naturalists, and watering from a cool stream that spilled down through the brush. The birds were raucous and strange. Once, a creature like a large rat bounded upright through the undergrowth. No one knew what to call it.

Cook had charted this coast before, but there was more to do: bearings to refine, new anchorages to confirm, signs of habitation to record. Smoke had been sighted once, curling faintly above a distant ridge, but no people appeared. Nicholas took notes on the terrain, measured distances with a surveyor's chain, and recorded compass bearings while Clerke worked the alidade.

New Zealand followed. Cook had charted much of it before, and the Māori received him with a mixture of wariness and recognition. Nicholas watched from the deck as the great war canoes paddled out to meet them—long, sleek vessels, their prows carved with fierce, open-mouthed figures, their paddlers moving in perfect rhythm. The sound of their chanting, deep and guttural, carried across the water like a challenge.

The encounter was formal. Trade was conducted: flax, fish, and kumara for iron tools and nails, but there was an undercurrent to it all, a kind of careful tension that Nicholas could feel even without understanding the language. Cook did not forget what had passed on previous voyages: the skirmishes, the misunderstandings, the dead.

The Māori warriors were tall and powerful, their faces marked with the intricate tattoos of moko, each line and curve a record of lineage, battle, and standing. Their eyes met those of the English without flinching. Their chief came aboard in a cloak of fine flax adorned with dog fur, his staff topped with a greenstone blade. He pressed his forehead and nose to Cook's in the traditional hongi, and the captain, though visibly stiffened by the contact, bore it with the gravity such ceremony demanded.

"They are a martial people," Cook was heard to say that evening to Lieutenant Clerke. "Proud, fierce, and not to be underestimated. We shall trade with them, but we keep a close watch. Their memories are long. And they have not forgotten."

Their departure from New Zealand's Queen Charlotte Sound came on a morning of shifting mist, the wooded heights fading into grey as *Resolution* stood out to sea, *Discovery* close in her wake. The Māori who had paddled out to bid them farewell, whether from genuine affection or simple curiosity, were soon lost in the gathering haze, their war canoes dwindling to specks. Cook had chosen to steer directly for Tahiti rather than by way of the Friendly Islands, having received intelligence from the Māori of islands lying eastward, unmarked on any chart.

The Pacific, that vast and enigmatic ocean Cook had now traversed more thoroughly than any European before him, showed its capricious nature at once. A week out from New Zealand, the barometer fell steadily and the sky thickened to a uniform pewter. By nightfall the wind had veered northwest and freshened to a full gale, the sea mounting with a long, rolling fetch. They reefed down and bore away before it, her timbers groaning with the weight of the weather. For three days, *Resolution* laboured through heavy seas. The ship's company, softened by the comfort of harbour, had to find their sea legs anew. Many turned green-faced and miserable, though few officers would admit it.

"This is nothing," said Thomas Edgar, gripping a backstay as a violent roll sent a cascade of water over the lee gunwale. The master's mate stood with the easy balance of a man who had seen worse, his weather-beaten face impassive beneath the spray. Edgar was a different breed from the younger midshipmen: nearly thirty, ruddy of complexion, with the scarred hands of a man who had hauled himself up from common seaman rather than entering service as a gentleman volunteer. His practical seamanship was beyond question. Though formal navigation rested with the ship's Master and Captain Cook, even Cook at times asked Edgar's opinion.

"You should have seen the blow we weathered off the Horn in '72," Edgar went on, tightening his grip against another roll. "Three men washed overboard in a single watch, and the old *Endeavour* shipping water through every seam. This?" He gestured dismissively at the heaving sea. "Mere channel weather." He tied the knot of his tarred queue with practiced fingers, his deep-set eyes constantly scanning the horizon, habitually checking the trim of the sails against the wind's direction.

Nicholas nodded, concentrating on keeping his footing, and his dignity. He had learned quickly to respect Edgar, despite the man's rough speech and easy contempt for "young gentlemen." Edgar carried an encyclopedic memory of coastlines and harbours, could splice a cable faster than any bosun's mate, and had the uncanny knack of reading the weather hours before it declared itself—all skills Nicholas quietly aspired to master in time.

Cook had set a punishing schedule for the midshipmen: celestial navigation, signal drill, and lectures on Polynesian customs filled their days, leaving little time for seasickness, or idle talk. He had recognized Edgar's value immediately, promoting him to master's mate despite his humble origins, and often assigning him to oversee the midshipmen's practical education. Edgar was relentless during daily practice with the octant and azimuth compass. He tolerated no shortcuts and demanded a standard of precision few could meet.

"Five minutes of a degree might be the difference between a safe landfall and a coral reef," Edgar would say, tapping a scarred finger against their workbooks. "And I doubt any man aboard fancies explaining to the captain why the ship is pounding her guts out on a reef because he thought the sun too hot or the sums too tedious to mind his numbers proper."

By the second week, the trade winds had steadied, and *Resolution* fell into her pace. She made a solid six or seven knots across a sea of deep, unfathomable blue, her wake trailing behind her like a road drawn across water.

She was no frigate, no ship built for speed, but a Whitby collier—handpicked by Cook for her strength and capacity. Her bluff bow and broad beam gave her a stubborn look in the water: a vessel made not for swiftness, but for survival. Even under a full spread of sail and with a favouring wind, she rarely made more than seven knots.

Her former life as a North Sea coal carrier had bred into her timbers a stubborn indifference to heavy weather. Where finer-built vessels might labour and strain in a blow, *Resolution* rose heavily to each swell and settled again with the same imperturbable rhythm. Her broad holds, once packed with the black diamonds of Newcastle, now bore the weight of provisions, scientific instruments, trade goods, and stores enough for years, not months. Her shallow draft—only fourteen feet when fully laden—let her creep close to unknown shores where heavier ships dared not follow. And her stout framing could better endure the grinding scrape of a shoal, should the charts prove false, or more usually on voyages of discovery, absent.

Cook had demanded further modifications before accepting her into service. Her bottom was sheathed with copper to resist marine growth and the boring of the teredo worm in tropical waters. Her interior was reconfigured to house the natural philosophers and their cabinets of specimens. Additional gunports were cut, not to add weight of metal, but to drive air through her decks in the dead heat of the tropics. Most critically, her rigging was thickened, her spars reinforced, to stand against the violence of southern seas

"She's a creature of compromise," Lieutenant Clerke had remarked to Nicholas during a quiet middle watch. "Not the fastest, not the most weatherly, not the most imposing. But perhaps the most suitable vessel ever sent out for discovery. When you've sailed as many miles as the captain, Mr. Cruwys, you learn: endurance matters more than speed, and reliability outweighs elegance."

They crossed paths with no other vessel; indeed, they might have been alone in all the world, sailing across an ocean vaster than all

Europe, the nearest Christian soul thousands of miles distant on some lonely Spanish settlement along the South American coast.

As they approached the equator, the heat remained heavy, but the steadier trade winds tempered its worst effects. The pitch softened between the deck seams, and canvas awnings were spread to shelter the watch from the sun. Cook, practical as ever, adjusted the ship's routine to the new conditions: heavy work was shifted to the early watches, and men were permitted to sleep on deck, where the moving air eased the nights. Below, the midshipmen's berth was close and foul, but life above was not the stifling trial it had been in the Atlantic calms.

It was during this passage that Nicholas Cruwys first began to distinguish himself as a navigator. Noon sights, simple and reliable, had long since become routine aboard *Resolution*. The real test lay in the finer arts: working lunar distances for longitude, reducing double altitudes, and correcting for parallax, semi-diameter, and refraction. Among the midshipmen, a quiet competition took root—not for the fastest figure at noon, but for the cleanest solution across a full set of observations. Working the spherical triangles by hand, their only help the laborious logarithmic tables, many faltered. While others struggled with slippery tables and misread octants, or a few the more expensive sextants, Nicholas worked steadily and with care, often completing his reductions while others were still fumbling to finish their first sight reduction. Lieutenant Clerke, glancing over his figures one afternoon, gave a rare approving nod. Even Captain Cook, who gave compliments as sparingly as he gave leave, allowed that Mr. Cruwys's observations were "tolerably precise." From such a quarter, there was no higher praise.

Twenty-five days out from New Zealand, they encountered something extraordinary: a pod of whales so vast that it stretched from horizon to horizon, their spouts rising like distant geysers, their broad flukes slapping the surface as they sounded. Cook ordered the ship hove-to while the naturalists gathered at the rail, notebooks and glasses in hand. Nicholas stood nearby and watched in awe as the creatures passed—some nearly as long as a frigate—their sighing exhalations carrying clearly across the still water. It was a sight few Europeans had seen, and he recorded it carefully in his journal, sketching the distinctive markings along their dark, heaving backs.

The only interruption to their steady passage came with a sudden tropical squall, descending with scarcely an hour's warning. To the north, the sky darkened from clear azure to a livid purple-black, and the wind veered sharply, tearing at the canvas with violent hands. Cook, pacing the quarterdeck with his habitual restlessness, gave the order to shorten sail without delay. Nicholas found himself aloft with the topmen, clinging to a thrashing yard as the canvas beat like a drumhead under artillery fire. The rain came down not in drops but in rods, stinging the skin raw and cutting visibility to a few yards. For three hours the storm raged, then passed as swiftly as it had risen, leaving *Resolution* rolling in a flat calm beneath a vault of stars so brilliant they seemed close enough to touch.

On the thirty-second day of their passage, the cry every sailor waits for rang down from aloft: "Land ho!" A smudge on the horizon slowly took form, resolving into a low-lying island girdled by a white fringe of surf. It was not Tahiti, but one of the lesser Society Islands—Meetia, as Cook named it. The captain gave orders to pass along the western shore, close enough for observation but well clear of the treacherous reef. Nicholas, along with others not on watch, brought his glass to bear, making out swaying palms, a curve of beach, and what might have been thatched roofs, half-lost in green shadow.

Rounding the northern point of Meetia, another cry rang down from aloft: Tahiti. Its high, volcanic spine was unmistakable even at twenty leagues. A ripple of relief ran through the ship's company. Tahiti meant more than a landfall on a chart; it promised fresh water, fruit, shelter, and the ease of known shores. Even Cook, usually spare in such displays, allowed himself a small nod of satisfaction as he brought his glass to bear on the island.

"Make a note in your journal, Mr. Cruwys," he said, still observing. "Thirty-three days and fourteen hours from Queen Charlotte Sound to the Society Islands. A fair passage, considering the wind's temperament."

"Aye, sir," Nicholas replied, already setting down the bearing and estimated distance in his precise hand.

Their final day's run brought the land nearer with each hour. By late afternoon, the island's flanks stood clear: green highlands rising steeply from the sea, the twin peaks of Orohena and Aorai standing like sentinels above the ridgelines. Narrow cataracts veined the slopes, flashing white against the foliage before vanishing into the trees below. Along the shore, palms bowed inland above a broad sweep of pale coral sand. The ocean beneath them shifted hue as they neared—deep indigo giving way to a brilliant turquoise that betrayed reefs and shoals lurking just below the surface. From miles off, they could hear the dull, rhythmic thunder of surf breaking on the outer reef—a sound like distant thunder, low and constant.

Beyond the coral's edge, the lagoon shimmered, impossibly still in the lee of the breakers. Cook, who knew these waters well from his earlier voyages, conned the ship with steady care, his glass trained along the reef until he marked the channel: a narrow passage of deeper blue, quiet amid the surf, leading inward to Matavai Bay.

Resolution slipped through the reef opening into stiller water, with *Discovery* close astern. It was the 13th of August, 1777. The anchor splashed down, the cable roared out, and the ship settled against her ground tackle for the first time in more than a month. Even as the men furled the final sails and coiled down the rigging, canoes were putting out from shore—voices raised in greeting, branches lifted in token of peace. The long run from New Zealand was ended. One chapter of their great Pacific voyage had closed; another, of different weight and expectation, was about to begin.

The lush green hills and the brilliant blue lagoon struck Nicholas with awe. They had heard so much of this place, of its ease and beauty, but the reality overwhelmed expectation. The sweet scent of tropical blossoms drifted across the water, mingling with the salt spray. Beneath the ship, the water was so clear that Nicholas could see coral heads sprawling beneath the keel, fish flashing in brilliant colours far below. The crew lined the rails, staring with undisguised wonder at the paradise before them. Even the hardened sailors, men who had seen ports across the globe, seemed moved by the sight. The beach was pure white, lined with coconut palms swaying in the gentle breeze. Beyond, the land rose in lush, verdant slopes, dotted with breadfruit trees and flowering shrubs, a vision of Eden made manifest to their eyes.

CHAPTER FOUR

The following morning broke clear and warm, the lagoon inside Matavai Bay lying still as polished glass. Nicholas stood among the appointed shore party, his coat brushed, salt-dulled buttons properly fastened, his journal tucked into a leather satchel beside a compass and pencil case. Lieutenant Clerke had given his orders quietly but firmly: full uniform was to be worn, for they carried not merely their ship's name, but His Majesty's.

Beside him, James stood equally straight, immaculate in dress, though a familiar glint of mischief flickered in his eye, and he muttered out of the side of his mouth, "Mind your bearing, Nick. You're about to step into paradise, if the accounts are true. Try not to look like Crusoe on his first landfall."

They landed without difficulty. A small cluster of Tahitians awaited them on the beach. The men bare-chested, women draped in patterned cloth, some modestly across the shoulders, others only at the waist, their bearing natural and untroubled. The sight, though innocently offered, caused more than one midshipman to glance away with awkward haste, and a few of the older hands to grin behind their hands before schooling their expressions. Several bore offerings: fruit heaped in baskets of plaited fibre, small bouquets of blossoms, and, in one case, a live pig neatly trussed in woven matting. They spoke in a lilting tongue Nicholas could not follow, though he caught the rhythm of welcome in their tone and the repeated word *haere mai*.

Lieutenant Clerke, more seasoned in such encounters, stepped forward and returned a courteous bow, accepting the proffered gifts with due gravity and offering beads and small iron tools in exchange. The transaction was conducted with the smoothness of long practice. Nicholas, watching intently, noted how Clerke neither smiled overmuch nor stiffened into hauteur. It was a performance of balance, and Nicholas resolved to emulate it.

They were guided inland beneath an avenue of palms, the ground springy with fallen husks and leaves. A warm breeze stirred the fronds overhead, carrying the mingled scents of flowers, damp earth, and woodsmoke. Children darted among the trunks, laughing, while an older man, perhaps a priest or chief, walked beside them with deliberate solemnity. Nicholas did his best to observe without gawping: the huts raised slightly above the ground, their walls slatted, their thatched roofs dark with age; the carved figures that stood at crossroads; the footpaths bordered with white coral stones.

They were received with formality at the settlement by a man introduced as Tu, a chief of considerable standing. Tu was tall and broad-shouldered, bearing a quiet dignity that required no embellishment. He wore a cloak of tapa, dyed a deep red and fastened at one shoulder with a polished shell. Through an interpreter, Clerke conveyed the captain's greetings and intentions: a friendly visit, a request for fresh water and supplies, and thanks for past kindnesses shown to English ships.

Tu responded with slow nods and a short speech, his voice even and measured. Nicholas could not follow the words, but he recognised the cadence of diplomacy: welcome granted, terms acknowledged, peace affirmed. A feast was proposed for that evening. Clerke accepted on behalf of the officers. There was a pause, and then the mood lightened—children reappeared, musicians struck up a soft rhythm on drums and pipes, and a girl not much older than Nicholas placed a flower behind his ear, giggling as she vanished before he could stammer out a word.

"That, Mr. Cruwys," said Trevenen, appearing at his side, "is diplomacy, South Seas-style."

Nicholas touched the flower behind his ear, uncertain whether to remove it or let it be, and turned his gaze seaward. *Resolution* lay at rest in the bay, her rigging dark against the pale sky. Beyond her, the reef shimmered in the morning sun, and farther still, the Pacific stretched vast and deep. For the first time in many days, the world did not feel like motion. It felt like arrival.

It had been only ten days since their arrival in Matavai Bay, and already Tahiti seemed a place outside of time—a world so far removed from England that it might as well have been imagined. The days were warm and unhurried, heavy with the scent of frangipani and the soft rhythm of surf breaking on the reef. At night, the stars pressed close above the lagoon, and the air grew thick with music, laughter, and a language that seemed made for ease rather than urgency.

Tahiti was unlike anything Nicholas had known. England, even in summer, seemed pale and measured by comparison—its hedgerows trimmed, its skies reluctant. But here, colour was sovereign: the green of the steep volcanic slopes, the brilliant white of coral sand, the luminous blue of the lagoon. Outrigger canoes skimmed across the water, their paddlers moving with effortless, almost unthinking grace. The people, too, moved lightly, their dark hair often crowned with flowers, their garments of tapa dyed in hues of ochre, crimson, and indigo.

"I begin to wonder," said James one evening, as they sat beneath a tree heavy with blossoms, "whether anything in England will ever seem as fair again."

Nicholas smiled, watching the breeze stir the palms. "Perhaps not," he said. "But better to have seen it, than to have only read of such places in books."

As midshipmen, they were afforded more liberty ashore than the common seamen, though Cook's expectations remained clear. He did not forbid interaction with the islanders—he knew the futility of such orders—but his disapproval of excess was quiet and unmistakable. The crew were left largely to themselves; the gentlemen were expected to comport themselves without needing correction.

Nicholas and James had, for the most part, honoured that understanding. Yet Tahiti was a kind of invitation: feasts and songs, dances held beneath the moonlight, and walks along the beach in the scented dusk. The people gave freely, without calculation or artifice, and to young men newly come from hardship and cold seas, it took no effort at all to be enchanted.

It was on such a night that Nicholas left a gathering early, walking along the shore with a girl named Tehani. She was sparing of speech but quick to smile, with eyes like polished obsidian and a sidelong glance that made him feel as though they shared a secret. Without ceremony, she took his hand and led him along a narrow path between the palms, where the ground was soft with fallen blossoms and the night air smelled faintly of woodsmoke and salt. They came at last to a small hut woven of matting and leaves, its doorway open to the breeze.

What followed was not conquest, nor even indulgence, but something quieter and less easily named. He had imagined it often enough—awkwardly, in distant abstraction—but the reality was neither awkward nor remote. It was not grand; it was simple and kind. The dark was warm around them, the hush broken only by the faint stirring of the trees. He felt altered by it, though he could not yet have said how.

Later, Tehani paddled him back across the lagoon in a small canoe, her strokes light and soundless in the moonlit water. Nicholas sat quiet in the stern, the night pressing soft and warm around them, his mind still turning on what had passed. When he climbed aboard *Resolution* at the entry port, a fellow midshipman caught his eye, grinned, and gave a slow, knowing nod before returning to his duties.

The officer of the watch, leaning by the gangway, cast him a sidelong glance and said, not unkindly, "Furthering our diplomatic mission, Mr. Cruwys?"

Nicholas straightened, smoothing his coat with unconscious formality. "Studying their customs and language, sir."

"I've no doubt," the lieutenant replied, dry as ship's biscuit. "I trust you found their vocabulary... instructive."

Nicholas had murmured a suitable reply and made his way below, his cheeks warm despite the breeze.

But now, standing outside Captain Cook's great cabin the following afternoon, Nicholas Cruwys felt none of that warmth. He adjusted his coat, brushing an invisible speck of dust from his sleeve, his heart beating a steady, measured rhythm. He had been summoned without explanation, and though he could name no clear offence, he could not help but wonder if the Captain had learned of his late return the previous night.

The marine sentry knocked once, and a voice from within called, "Enter."

Nicholas stepped into the stern cabin and removed his hat, standing rigidly at attention. The space was immaculate: the instruments of Cook's trade—sextant, parallel rulers, logbooks—were arranged with almost mathematical precision. A large chart was spread upon the captain's table, the ink still glistening where the latest soundings had been set down. From the open stern windows drifted the mingled scents of blossoms, seawater, and the ever-present tang of tar and hemp.

Cook looked up at last, his keen eyes weighing Nicholas with a measured gaze. The flickering light from the stern windows threw shifting shadows across his weathered features. He was tall and strongly built, the strength of his frame evident even in stillness; yet it was not size that lent him command, but something harder to name: an authority of bearing so natural and so complete that it seemed to alter the very air around him. His face, bronzed by years beneath pitiless suns, was deeply lined by wind and salt—the very texture of long watches at sea. The gaze he turned on Nicholas was calm and grave, the gaze of a man accustomed to truth, impatient of pretense. His habitual severity was evident now; yet there was, just discernible at the corners of his mouth, the faintest flicker of what might have been amusement, as he studied the young midshipman before him.

Nicholas was well-knit and already tall for a young man, standing an easy six feet, his frame shaped by years of motion: climbing, riding, and working aloft at sea. His hair, thick and nearly black, was tied back with a plain black ribbon, though a few strands had come loose in the humid air. His grey-green eyes, sharp and clear beneath dark brows, might have looked cool and confident under other circumstances; but now, set in a face darkened by weeks of sun and salt, they betrayed a flicker of unease.

Cook had seen it before, that quiet tension in the presence of command, the careful attempt to maintain composure under a superior's gaze. The young man had a strong bearing, and a face that, in time, might settle into something truly distinguished; but for all his steadiness, he was still young enough to feel the weight of the summons. And Cook, who had summoned many such young men across many years, knew well enough the cause of his discomfort.

Cook was well aware of Nicholas's late return to the ship. It was a familiar story: young officers venturing beyond the narrow compass of England, discovering, some with more discretion than others, that the world held wonders no tutor could prepare them for. Earlier that day, he had spoken with his first lieutenant regarding the men's behaviour ashore. Clerke, who had sailed with him on two voyages already, was a steady hand and a shrewd judge of character. As *Resolution* swung quietly to her anchor, the light slipping across the stern windows, Clerke had mentioned Cruwys's tardiness with a wry glance and a dry remark, but no true disapproval.

"A good lad, sir," Clerke had said. "Quick, diligent, keeps his books close. A finer hand with an octant than most of twice his time afloat." He had paused, the wind stirring the chart on the table. "Moves well on deck—none of that loose-jointed awkwardness you see in some of them. Strong-built, but light-footed. Carries himself like a young officer already, not a boy playing at it. The hands respect him."

Cook had grunted—his usual economy of assent. He recalled Cruwys's quiet steadiness amid the sleet and biting winds of Desolation Island, the way the young man's figures were set down neat and true when older hands fumbled. "I'll not have my midshipmen playing the rake ashore," he had said, more from principle than real displeasure. But in truth, his mind was already made up. The young man had shown judgement enough to merit risk and perhaps, in time, something finer still.

Cook let the silence stretch a moment longer, allowing it to settle like a weight across the room. Then, shifting slightly in his chair, he spoke at last, his voice calm and deliberate.

"Mr. Cruwys," the captain said at last, his voice level, his manner precise. He motioned him a pace forward. "You have acquitted yourself well on this voyage. Your skill in navigation and surveying is noted, as is your steadiness in conduct. I have need of such ability."

Nicholas felt a flush rise to his face. It was the first unqualified commendation he had received from Captain Cook in all the long months since they had left Plymouth Sound. He straightened instinctively, aware of the weight behind so few words. "Thank you, sir," he said, his voice firm despite the hammering of his heart.

The captain inclined his head, the movement so slight it might have passed unnoticed. He tapped a finger on the chart spread before him, the ink barely dry upon a scattering of islands to the northwest of Tahiti.

"I intend to dispatch you to survey the island of Bora Bora before we proceed north," Cook said, his voice as measured as the lines he drew across his charts. "The Tahitians speak highly of their neighbours. On my previous voyages the islands were sighted, but there was no time for a survey. We may find safe anchorages there, or harbours yet unknown. You will go and see."

Nicholas blinked, uncertain at first that he had understood. "Ashore, sir?"

"More than ashore, Mr. Cruwys," said Cook, tapping the chart with a finger steady from long habit. "You will travel with a native canoe, under the guidance of one of their navigators. You will take observations, record bearings, and set down soundings as best you can. You will see how they navigate, how they read this ocean as a man reads a familiar page. There is wisdom here, Mr. Cruwys, if a man has the wit to learn it."

Nicholas felt the weight of the assignment settle upon his shoulders. This was no idle task. It was a great responsibility, surveying an island independently, trusted to carry out the very work that had made Cook famous. The idea both thrilled and terrified him in equal measure.

"Their methods of navigation are unlike our own," Cook continued, his voice taking on a rare note of contemplation. "They read the ocean: the swell patterns, the flight of birds, the colour of the water at dawn. I say to you again there is wisdom in this, Mr. Cruwys, wisdom that may yet be of use to the Navy, if properly understood and recorded."

"Yes, sir. I shall endeavour to learn all I can."

Cook inclined his head, his expression returning to its usual severity. "You will have Markham with you—an experienced quartermaster, and steady with the instruments." He turned to the chart, his finger tracing the line from Matavai Bay northwest toward Bora Bora. "It lies some hundred and forty nautical miles distant. With fair winds, the passage should take two days. The pahi canoe is well-suited to these waters; Tu, the paramount chief, has assured me of it himself."

He tapped a specific point on the chart where Bora Bora lay. "Tu's cousin, Puni, rules there now. He secured his authority some years past, after a season of conflict with neighbouring islands. I am told by Tu that he would be well-disposed toward British ships, though wary of the Spanish, who passed through these seas in '72." Cook spoke as though reciting a ledger: calm, factual, but precise. "Puni has agreed to provide smaller outriggers for your coastal survey. He will assign his son, Mai-o, to assist you. The young man speaks a little English, having spent time among traders at Huahine. The large voyaging canoe must return to Tahiti as soon as you are set ashore. Tu requires it for ceremonial matters connected with the approaching Matahiti festival."

Cook turned back to the chart, measuring the distance anew with his dividers. "*Resolution* will collect you when we are bound northward toward the Sandwich Islands, approximately three weeks hence." His voice remained clipped, the weight of precision in every word. "In the meantime, your journals are to be complete, your calculations exact. Pay particular attention to the western and northern approaches; we know little of the reefs there, and such knowledge may prove invaluable to the Admiralty, and might yet serve us, if fortune should drive us back this way."

He snapped the dividers shut with a decisive click. "I expect soundings, current observations, and precise bearings of every prominent landmark. The Tahitians navigate by the stars, by the flight of birds, by the set of the sea, but the Admiralty requires numbers, Mr. Cruwys. Precise numbers. Learn what you can, but set it down properly."

"Yes, sir. I understand."

"Very good," said Cook, his tone softening by no more than a hair. "This is an opportunity few young officers are given. In most commands, you would be thought too green for such a trust. But I have observed your work at Desolation, and your bearing since. You are methodical, clear-eyed and, so far as I can judge, possessed of that rare quality: discretion. I am prepared to take the risk."

Cook paused a moment, the weight of command settling over his features again. "And remember this: while the inhabitants of Bora Bora are said to be friendly to British interests, they are not without their own politics and ambitions. Treat Puni and his people with respect. We cannot afford misunderstandings in these waters, particularly as the French and Spanish press their influence ever farther across the Pacific."

Nicholas straightened, squaring his shoulders with quiet resolve. "Aye, sir."

"Very good," said Cook, returning to the chart with the finality of a man closing a book. Then, almost as an afterthought—though one weighted by experience—he added, "Take care with their canoes, Mr. Cruwys. They are not built like our ships, but they are better suited to these waters than any Englishman would suppose. You would do well to observe their construction, and their handling."

Nicholas inclined his head, understanding that this was not merely advice, but part of the larger charge entrusted to him. "Aye, sir."

Cook regarded him a moment longer before giving a short nod. "Good. Report to Lieutenant Gore for additional instructions. That will be all."

Nicholas stepped back, bowed with crisp formality, and let himself out. As he emerged onto the quarterdeck, the sudden brilliance of the sun struck him like a blow. The warm air, laden with the scent of salt and blossoms, wrapped around him, a reminder that the world he was about to enter would be very different from the ordered decks of *Resolution*.

Bora Bora. The name itself seemed to hum with promise—a land charted only faintly, a venture beyond the ship's known horizon.

The beach was alive with activity. Tahitian men moved with practised ease, securing provisions: bundles of dried breadfruit, gourds sloshing with fresh water, woven mats for sleeping. Women wove garlands of bright-scented flowers, pressing them into the hands of departing sailors with soft smiles and low-spoken words. The air was thick with salt, damp earth, and woodsmoke, and from farther inland came the slow, steady thrum of drums.

"Well, Nicholas," said James Trevenen, crouched beside a sea chest, carefully stowing the precious surveying instruments in oilcloth, "it appears you've drawn the King's ticket in our little lottery. A voyage to a new paradise with a crew of islanders, while the rest of us labour aboard until we sail north."

"It is no holiday, James," Nicholas replied, though he could not quite keep the smile from the corner of his mouth. "The captain expects charts he can rely upon, and so does the Admiralty."

"Oh, to be sure," said James, his face grave but his eyes dancing. "And I've no doubt you'll produce charts of Bora Bora to astonish even Their Lordships at the Admiralty. But spare a thought, if you can, for your poor shipmates, toiling in the heat while you explore new shores and feast on fruit."

"You have a singular gift," said Nicholas, fastening the octant's case shut with deliberate care, "for making duty sound like indulgence."

"It is a gift, I grant you," James said, laughing softly. Then, after a beat, his voice turned more serious. "But take care, brother. These seas are not always as gentle as they look. And those canoes, for all their cleverness, are no *Resolution*."

Nicholas nodded, sobering slightly. "I shall be careful."

As Nicholas stepped into the canoe, Tehani pressed a garland of tiaré blossoms into his hands, the petals cool against his skin, their scent sharp and sweet on the salt laden breeze. "To remember," she murmured, her fingers lingering a moment longer than custom required.

A heaviness settled in his chest, not grief, but something near it. She had given him kindness, and something more difficult to name: a first intimacy, a first farewell. He had not found the words that morning, and he did not find them now. He only knew that a part of him would remain behind, and that it mattered, though he could not yet say why.

He touched the garland, now resting in his lap, and said nothing.

"I am gratified to see the natives hold you in such high esteem, Mr. Cruwys," said Markham, the weathered quartermaster assigned to accompany him. A faint smile creased his leathery features as he regarded the young officer, who by his reckoning could not be more than seventeen.

"Though I'd wager it wasn't your skill with an octant that won the lady's favour," he added, his voice dry as old canvas.

Nicholas felt his face warm beneath his tan and busied himself with checking the lashings on his sea chest. "These blossoms are said to bring luck to voyagers," he said, keeping his tone even. "It would have been discourteous to refuse."

"Oh, aye," said Markham, with a knowing look. "Very discourteous indeed. Well, here's hoping they bring us fair winds and following seas, for we've a fair stretch of water to cross."

The canoe itself was unlike anything Nicholas had ever seen. It was no mere skiff, but a great double-hulled *pahi*—a voyaging canoe built for the open ocean, its twin hulls joined by a framework of lashed crossbeams and platforms, bound fast with sennit cordage braided from coconut husk. The hull planks, shaped from breadfruit wood, were fitted edge to edge with such precision that no iron was needed—only wooden dowels and the patient strength of fibre lashings, hardened by salt and age. Above, a great crab-claw sail, fashioned from strips of pandanus leaf, was rigged between twin spars that rose in a sharply angled V, its creamy surface curved like a gull's wing to catch the wind. This was no rude contrivance; it was a vessel of consummate skill, light yet strong, shaped for blue water, and fast enough to leave any European longboat wallowing in its wake.

"She's a clever piece of work," murmured Markham, running a calloused hand along the smooth hull. "No keel to speak of, yet she'll run before the wind like a Thames wherry—and make a decent cast to windward if a man handles her right. There's seamanship in these people, no question of that, whatever else a man might think."

The journey ahead was no mere paddle along the coast. Bora Bora lay more than forty-six leagues to the northwest, across open sea beyond the shelter of the nearer islands. Although sighted by the Dutch explorer Roggeveen in 1722 and later charted by Cook in 1769 when *HMS Endeavour* sailed past, there was no clear record that Europeans had yet set foot on its shores. While Captain Cook had claimed the island for Britain along with other Society Islands, his men had barely made landfall there, contenting themselves with observations from the water. For Nicholas, stepping onto its beaches would be treading ground perhaps not yet touched by European boots—it might as well have been a blank space on the map.

Tua, the navigator leading the voyage, stood barefoot at the stern, his chest marked with the intricate dark lines of tatau, his broad hands resting lightly on the steering paddle. He would find Bora Bora by the stars, by the set of the sea, by the colour of the water at dawn, by the scent of land borne on a breath of wind. As the crew pushed off, the canoe slid free of the shallows into the deep water of the lagoon. Nicholas turned once to look back. Tehani was still there, small against the green of the palms, one hand raised in farewell, the other resting lightly at her side. The breeze stirred her hair against the pale cream of her tapa cloth, and for a moment, she seemed part of the island itself, rooted, still, and shining in the sun.

"There's no turning back now, Mr. Cruwys," said Markham quietly, his voice almost lost beneath the lift and slap of the waves. "We're in their hands until we reach Bora Bora, or *Resolution* comes to fetch us."

"I've no wish to turn back," Nicholas replied, feeling the spray on his face as they gathered speed toward the reef passage. "This is an opportunity few officers will ever have."

"That it is, sir," agreed Markham. "That it is."

Then, with a sudden lift, they cleared the reef. The change was immediate, the gentle lagoon gave way to the deep, heaving swells of the Pacific, rolling vast and endless to the horizon. The water turned from transparent blue to a deep, unknowable indigo, the scent of land falling away on the breeze.

Nicholas gripped the wooden gunwale, adjusting his stance as he felt the unfamiliar motion beneath him, smooth, swift, and unlike any ship he had ever known.

"She rides different from our boats, don't she, sir?" said Markham, settling himself amidships with the easy balance of a man who had spent half a lifetime adapting to strange vessels.

Tua, the navigator, stood poised at the stern, his bare feet planted wide, his hands resting lightly on the great steering paddle that guided their course. His gaze, sharp and unblinking, searched not for land, still leagues beyond sight, but for the subtler signs written upon the sea itself.

"Do you know, sir," said Markham quietly, watching Tua with undisguised respect, "I've sailed with men who couldn't find their way from Portsmouth to Plymouth even with the coast in plain sight, and a compass under their noses. Yet this fellow will carry us straight to Bora Bora with nothing but the stars and the feel of the sea beneath him. There's a kind of seamanship here we might do well to study."

"The captain believes so," Nicholas said, drawing out his journal and setting it carefully upon his knees. "He spoke of it before we departed—the wisdom in their methods, if a man has the wit to learn it."

Tahiti slipped away astern, the steep green slopes fading into haze, until they were no more than a faint smudge against the sky. Around them, the deep blue of the open ocean closed in, immense and alive. The swells grew larger, no longer broken by the shelter of reefs, and the canoe rode them with an effortless grace, rising and falling like a seabird carried on the wind.

The Polynesian crew moved with quiet efficiency, adjusting the sail, tightening lashings where needed. These men had crossed such distances before, Raiatea, Maupiti, Taha'a, each part of the Society Islands that lay strung across the vast blue waters, known by heart and reached without error. Bora Bora lay two days away under fair conditions, though the islanders spoke of reaching it in a single day when the winds were strong.

The wind held steady through the early evening, the stars kindling one by one as the sky darkened into a deep, violet-blue vault. Nicholas marvelled at how lightly the canoe skimmed the surface of the sea. There was no groan of timbers, no rhythmic creak of yards overhead—only the whisper of the wind through the sail, and the occasional soft slap of water against the twin hulls.

Tua called softly to the crew, gesturing toward the western sky where the constellation *Matari'i*—the Pleiades—was rising. Then he pointed to the swell, indicating the subtle shift in the long, rolling waves. Nicholas watched as Tua placed one hand flat upon the deck, feeling the ocean's pulse through the hull. *He is reading the sea as a man reads a map,* Nicholas thought. No compass, no octant—only the instincts and hard-won knowledge passed down through generations.

"Ask him how he knows our course is true," Nicholas said, turning to Maui, a young islander who had once served aboard European trading vessels and spoke enough English to make himself understood.

Maui crouched by the steering paddle and conferred with Tua in low, rhythmic Tahitian. The older man answered at some length, gesturing to the stars above, the dark sweep of the sea, and the faint line where sky met water.

"He say this star, *Matari'i,*" Maui translated, pointing to the rising cluster, "she stand there when Bora Bora ahead. He say wave come from there," he added, nodding toward the east, "always same. He feel wave under canoe, know where land is."

Nicholas nodded slowly, making careful notes in his journal. The explanation, to his academically trained mind, seemed almost maddeningly incomplete: no angles, no bearings, no measured altitudes. And yet, he could not deny the certainty with which Tua steered, nor the quiet mastery that had carried his people across these seas long before any European ship dared venture so far.

"Remarkable," murmured Markham, who had been listening. "Cook would value this knowledge greatly, though I wonder if we shall ever truly comprehend it. It's not something taught in books, is it? More something passed from father to son, through centuries of living upon these waters."

The night passed in slow, steady motion, the canoe moving northwest beneath the glittering sweep of the Milky Way. Now and then, one of the crew would call out softly, pointing to the dark sea where a flying fish broke the surface in a silver flash before vanishing again. Nicholas, lulled by the steady rise and fall of the hulls, felt sleep tugging at him, but he forced himself awake. He would not miss a moment of this voyage—not for the world.

By dawn, the wind had freshened, filling the sail with renewed force. The canoe leapt forward, the twin hulls skimming the waves with a speed that astonished Nicholas. At the stern, Tua lifted his chin and spoke a single word in Tahitian. The crew murmured in answer, and Nicholas followed their gaze. At first, he saw nothing but the endless blue of the ocean; then, as the morning sharpened, he caught the faintest smudge on the horizon—a darker blue, too steady to be cloud, too fixed to be dream.

Bora Bora.

It was still hours away, but the sight of land sent a ripple of energy through the crew. The canoe surged forward with fresh purpose, the men tightening the lashings, shifting their weight, adjusting the sail by instinct as much as command. Nicholas, shading his eyes against the rising sun, watched as the shape of the island grew clearer: tall peaks lifting steeply from the sea, their slopes cloaked in dense green and streaked with gold where the morning light caught the ridges. Above it all rose a single jagged summit—dark and abrupt against the sky, like the prow of some vast, broken vessel—ringed by coral shallows that flashed white and turquoise in the swell.

It was more dramatic, more unlikely even than Tahiti: a place that seemed half-born from cloud and sea, too bold and beautiful for the world he had known.

And for the first time, he wondered if the people of England, with their powdered wigs and city streets, their parlours and their dockyards, would ever truly understand what he had seen.

"A beautiful sight, sir," said Markham, stepping up beside him. "Though I'll not mind feeling solid ground under me again. These canoes are wonders, no question, but there's still something to be said for the stout planking of an English ship."

Nicholas nodded, though in truth he had come to admire the graceful efficiency of the Polynesian vessel.

Less than an hour later, the southeast trade wind began to shift, backing slowly toward the east. Nicholas, scanning the horizon, noticed how the once-clear sky had begun to bruise in the northeast, the edge of a low bank of clouds tinged with an eerie, sulphurous yellow. The Polynesian crew, who had moved with easy rhythm moments before, stiffened almost as one; then, without needing a word, they set to work reefing the great sail, hauling in the sheets and gathering the woven mat close to the yard. Some glanced aloft, gauging the mast, and Tua barked a sharp command, an order to lower it altogether if the wind freshened further.

But even as the crew scrambled to obey, Nicholas felt a prickle of unease. He turned toward Markham, who was already securing their instruments and charts, wrapping them carefully in oilcloth against the coming rain.

"What do you make of it, Markham?" Nicholas asked.

Markham hesitated before answering, his lips tightening. "Squall, Mr. Cruwys. A heavy one." He sniffed the air, as if tasting it. "She'll be on us fast."

Nicholas looked out at the clouds, now thickening into a mass of bruised purple and grey, dragging shadows across the water. "A hard blow?"

"Aye, sir," Markham said grimly. "And not a friendly one."

The first gust struck without warning, a violent slap of wind from the northeast that sent the reefed sail shuddering and luffing wildly before the crew could bring it under control. The ocean's surface, glassy moments before, darkened to a sullen grey as the squall bore down upon them, the swell turning sharp and broken as if the sea itself had risen in anger. Then the rain came, hard, blinding sheets that lashed the deck and reduced the world to a blur of water and noise. The canoe shuddered under the first real weight of the storm, the great steering paddle trembling in Tua's grip, the mast groaning ominously aloft.

Tua shouted over the storm, but his voice was torn away by the wind. The crew struggled to keep the canoe steady and to bring the mast down—but the sudden fury of the squall made it impossible. A second, heavier gust roared out of the northeast, caught the sail, and with a splintering crack that seemed to tear the very air apart, the mast gave way. Nicholas barely had time to throw himself aside as it crashed down, striking the gunwale and shaking the hulls before plunging into the sea.

The canoe lurched hard to starboard, the deck tilting steeply beneath Nicholas's feet. For a moment, he thought they would roll clean over, the world spinning sideways as the hulls heeled under the weight of wind and water.

"Hold on!" Markham bellowed, gripping the gunwale with both hands as a surge of seawater rushed over the deck.

The world dissolved into chaos: rain lashed their faces in blinding sheets, the wind shrieked through the torn rigging, and the canoe yawed wildly in the broken swell. Lines snapped taut, then went slack with each heave, the wreckage of the mast dragging against the twin hulls, threatening to pull them broadside to the waves and capsize them with every surge.

"We must clear away the wreckage!" Nicholas shouted to Markham, his voice half-lost in the roar of wind and rain, even as he lurched forward to help the Tahitians struggling with the fallen mast and tangled cordage. "If it drags against the hull, we'll broach!"

Markham nodded grimly, pulling his knife from his belt. Together, they worked alongside the Polynesian crew, slashing at the rigging, freeing the broken spar, their hands raw and bleeding from the effort. The rain beat down mercilessly, reducing visibility to a matter of yards, the world beyond a grey curtain of wind-driven water. A wave crashed over the bow, sending a rush of seawater across the deck. Nicholas felt it tugging at his legs, threatening to sweep him overboard. He clung to a lashing, his heart pounding, knowing that to be lost in such a sea would mean certain death.

After the first violent squall, the wind backed rapidly around to the north, then the northwest, then west and blew less but still very hard. The mast was gone, the shattered stumps of its two parts of no use, and several of the paddles had been lost. Two men had gone overboard and disappeared swiftly into the swirling darkness, one moment there, the next swept away by the relentless sea, their cries fading into the howling wind with a terrible finality.

"Poor devils," Markham muttered, crossing himself as the canoe was carried onward, leaving no mark upon the churning waters where the men had vanished. "May God have mercy on their souls."

Nicholas, exhausted and sodden to the bone, nodded without speaking. He had seen men die before, for the Navy was no gentle service. Two had fallen from the rigging in bad weather, another had succumbed to fever off Desolation Island. But there was something uniquely terrible about this loss—no burial, no last word, only the silent, implacable swallowing of life by water.

Something within him shifted then, quietly and without flourish. The sea, once a promise, now revealed itself as a reckoning. It was not malevolent, but it was immense, unheeding, and utterly without memory. He would serve upon it, yes, but never again would he mistake it for a friend.

The storm raged through that first terrible night, the rain so heavy it seemed the very air had turned to water. They bailed without cease, using anything that would serve: gourds, wooden bowls, even cupped hands when nothing else remained.

By dawn, the worst had passed, but the sea still ran high: great, rolling swells that lifted the battered canoe and dropped it with sickening regularity. The sky cleared by slow degrees, revealing a pitiless sun that seemed to mock their misery with its cheerful brilliance.

Three days later, though the canoe still floated, they were adrift, the wind having settled back into its usual course, steady from the southeast. The ocean stretched endless in every direction, the rolling swells still breaking in long, foam-streaked crests.

Bora Bora, so near before the storm, was nowhere to be seen.

"How far do you reckon we've been driven, sir?" Markham asked, his voice hoarse from thirst. Their water supplies, though carefully rationed, were dwindling alarmingly.

Nicholas shook his head. Without his octant, lost overboard in the fury of the storm, he could not fix their latitude, let alone even estimate a position. "The storm and the current have carried us eastward, away from the Society Islands. But by how many miles, I cannot say."

"And which way lies the nearest land?" Markham asked, though he knew there was no certain answer.

"That I cannot say either," Nicholas admitted, feeling the weight of responsibility press heavily upon him. "But Tua may know better than we."

Tua sat near the stern, silent, his expression unreadable as he studied the sea. His dignity remained undiminished, despite the loss of his men and the damage to his vessel. He had spoken little since the storm, but now, as Nicholas pulled himself upright, the navigator turned and pointed steadily toward the horizon.

"*Avei'a*," he said, his voice steady despite their circumstances.

Nicholas followed his gaze and recognized the Southern Cross, its distinctive pattern hanging low above the horizon like a celestial beacon in the deepening dusk. He had heard the name before—knew it was one of the key markers Polynesian navigators used to chart their way through these southern waters, its position relative to the horizon telling them how far north or south they had traveled. It was reassurance: they had not strayed beyond the belt of islands.

"What does he mean?" asked Markham, his parched lips cracking as he spoke.

Nicholas turned to Maui, who crouched nearby. "Ask him."

Maui spoke briefly with Tua, then turned back. "He say we drift far," Maui explained, his own face drawn with fatigue. "Not go Bora Bora now. Too far. He say we near *Paumotu*."

The stars told them they were still within reach of land in a similar latitude. But the set of the swell beneath the canoe, confirmed what Tua must have known for some time: they had been carried eastward, into the fringes of the *Paumotu*, what Cook had named the Dangerous Archipelago, and what the Tahitians called the Tuamotu, the Long Skirt of Islands. A vast, scattered chain of coral atolls, low-lying and treacherous, surrounded by reefs that had claimed countless vessels. Even Cook, with all his skill, had treated these waters with the utmost caution.

"Are you certain?" Nicholas asked Tua directly, though he knew the man would not understand his words. But the navigator merely nodded, his eyes never leaving the horizon, his expression grave but composed.

"If he's right," muttered Markham, "we're in a fair pickle. Those islands lie so cursed low in the water they're devilish hard to spot till you're nearly upon them, and their reefs extend for leagues. Captain Cook himself marked them as hazardous on his charts after we passed their western edge in '69. Captain Wallis nearly came to grief there with the *Dolphin*, and I've heard the Frenchman Bougainville counted himself fortunate to escape them. Scarcely any vessel has sailed among them and lived to tell the tale."

"Yet they may be our only hope," replied Nicholas. "Without water, without provisions, we cannot survive long at sea. And if we see one island, there may be others near enough to reach."

Markham nodded grimly. "Aye, sir. Better the devil we know than the one we don't, I suppose."

For three days, the wind and current bore them steadily westward again, their supplies dwindling, their water rationed with increasing stringency. The sun beat down, the glare off the water blinding; and at night, the thirst that gnawed at them found no easing. The men took turns bailing, for even in the calm of the open sea, the ocean pressed in, creeping through the worked lashings and loosened planks, strained by the violence of the storm.

Nicholas found his thoughts turning, more and more, to England: to green fields and cool streams, to rain-dampened earth and morning dew, the waters he had once taken as his due, little reckoning their worth until now, when the lack of them might mean his death.

On the fourth day, a school of flying fish flashed across the canoe, some striking the woven mats with soft, wet thuds. The crew seized them with practiced ease, plucking the silver bodies from where they fell. They ate them raw, the flesh salty and slick, each mouthful a vivid shock against parched tongues. After so many days of sun and thirst, the taste was like a gift wrested from the sea itself.

"Not the finest dining at the George in Portsmouth," said Markham, chewing carefully on the slippery flesh, "but I daresay I've never had a meal more welcome." His attempt at humour was undercut by the deep lines of exhaustion and thirst etched into his face.

Nicholas nodded, too parched to waste words. The raw fish gave some slight relief, but not enough. They needed fresh water — and soon.

By the fourth day after the return of the trade winds, Nicholas began to fear they were truly lost, adrift in the immensity of the Pacific, with no hope of rescue. *Resolution* would have no way of knowing where to seek them; the ocean was too wide, their frail craft too small, invisible against that endless blue. If they were to survive, it would be by their own efforts, or by the grace of God.

The sun dipped lower, staining the horizon in bruised shades of purple and gold. Nicholas watched it sink with grim fascination, knowing that another night adrift awaited them, another slow erosion of strength, another wager against thirst and despair.

Beside him, Markham shifted and winced, his movements stiff and deliberate. The others lay sprawled where they could, husbanding what little strength remained. It was not fear that gripped them now, nor even pain, but a hollowing, as though the sea, patient and implacable, was whittling them down to nothing.

Night fell with the swift certainty of the tropics. Stars pricked out overhead, fierce and innumerable, wheeling slowly as the canoe rocked beneath them. Nicholas lay on his back, the woven mat rough against his skin, and counted constellations by habit, clinging to the order they offered.

Somewhere aft, a man murmured a *karakia*, the ancient prayer rising and falling like the swells beneath them; another coughed, the sound dry and ragged. The sea whispered against the hull, a ceaseless murmur that Tua and the other islanders seemed to understand as one might understand the voice of a respected elder. To Nicholas, the ocean seemed patient, endless, and not unkind, merely indifferent. But he noticed how the Polynesian sailors regarded the vast expanse with a different awareness, as if conversing with a living ancestor whose moods might be respected but never fully predicted.

Then, just before dawn on the fifth day, Tua straightened where he sat, his head tilting slightly, nostrils flaring as though catching a scent on the wind. His sudden alertness caught Nicholas's eye at once. Tua said something in a low voice, urgent but controlled. The others roused themselves, their heads lifting, their bodies tensing with the brittle hope of men who had too often been betrayed by it. Nicholas strained his ears, but at first heard nothing beyond the low slap of water against the hull.

Nicholas watched him carefully. "What is it?"

Then, faint but certain, Nicholas caught it too — a low, steady rumble, unlike the familiar slap of the sea. It came and went with the lift and fall of the swell, a sound felt almost as much as heard: the long, distant roar of surf on rock or reef.

He turned to Markham, who had lifted his head with a slow, painful movement. No words passed between them; none were needed. There was land nearby, or some treacherous shoal lying in wait beneath the horizon. Hope, long starved, stirred uneasily in Nicholas's chest.

Tua did not speak at first. He sat motionless, his gaze fixed on a point beyond their sight, nostrils flaring as if tasting the air. Then he rose, moving with a sudden certainty, and pointed seaward with a steady hand. "*Manu*," he said, his voice low but sure.

Nicholas followed his gesture, straining his burning eyes against the pallid light. At first, he saw nothing but the endless seam of sea and sky. Then, a shape. A bird, dark against the brightening east, circling high above the water. And another. Seabirds, their wings catching the first gold of the rising sun.

Hope surged through him so fiercely that he felt light-headed, giddy. Tua called out to the others, and within moments, every eye was turned west and north, searching.

Markham, still half-dazed from thirst and weariness, pushed himself upright with a grunt, shading his eyes with one shaking hand. He squinted at the sky, then turned to Nicholas with a broken, weary grin.

Nicholas exhaled slowly, his heartbeat beginning to steady as he gripped the gunwale. The morning sun, climbing over the eastern horizon, caught a distant shimmer on the water, faint, wavering, perhaps a mile away, perhaps more. At first, it seemed nothing more than a trick of the light, a mirage conjured by desperate hope. He narrowed his gaze, forcing tired eyes to focus, heart hammering.

"No," he said, almost to himself, his voice stronger than it had been in days. "Not yet."

As the canoe drifted closer, carried by the current and the weary strokes of the paddles, the shimmer resolved itself into a narrow, gleaming line of white: surf breaking upon a reef. Beyond the foam lay a low smudge of green, barely distinguishable from the sea, palm trees, thin and wind-bent, but unmistakable. Land. Shelter. Life.

Tua was already on his feet, issuing sharp commands, his voice urgent but controlled. They would have to navigate the reef with extreme care; one misjudgment, and the canoe would be dashed to pieces on the coral. Nicholas steadied himself, every muscle trembling with exhaustion and the fierce, almost unbearable surge of hope.

The morning of the 2nd of September 1777, dawned bright and clear, the air unusually still over Matavai Bay as *Resolution* and *Discovery* prepared to weigh anchor. The three weeks spent in Tahiti had been productive: water casks filled, firewood stowed, fresh provisions brought aboard in quantities sufficient to last weeks, if properly managed. But Cook's mood had darkened with each passing day since the storm's fury had been witnessed even from the sheltered waters of Matavai, his concern for the missing midshipman and quartermaster growing more pronounced.

"The pahi should have returned no more than five days ago," Cook remarked to Lieutenant Clerke as they stood on the quarterdeck, watching the boats make their final trips to shore. The captain's spyglass was trained on the northwest horizon beyond the reef. "That pahi canoe was stout enough, but the gale we felt here would have been twice as severe in the open water between islands."

Clerke nodded, his own face betraying concern for the young midshipman who had shown such promise. "He had Markham with him, sir, a steady hand if ever there was one. And the Tahitian navigator, Tua, knows these waters better than any European."

"Indeed," said Cook, collapsing his glass with a sharp snap. "But knowledge counts for little against a full gale in open waters, particularly in a vessel without a proper keel. I had intended to proceed directly to explore the islands further north, but now we must first search for our missing men."

Word of *Resolution's* impending departure to search for the survey party had spread quickly through Matavai Bay. That morning, as Cook prepared to give the order to weigh anchor, one of the island's leading men paddled out to the ship with a final offering: a gift of fresh breadfruit and a small carved figure, a gesture of goodwill for the journey ahead.

"He says the figure will guide us to our men," translated Lieutenant William Anderson, the ship's linguist, who had become remarkably fluent in the Tahitian tongue during their stay. "And he offers three of his own men to accompany us, if you wish it, sir. They know the waters around Bora Bora well." Cook studied the carved figure, a stylized representation of a sea deity, its features worn smooth from handling. Though not a superstitious man by nature, his years in the Pacific had taught him respect for local knowledge and customs. "Thank him for the offer. We shall take two men, one aboard each ship, if they are willing. Their knowledge of the local waters and language may prove valuable."

Resolution and *Discovery* weighed anchor with the morning tide, a Tahitian aboard each vessel. *Resolution* led the way, passing through the reef opening into the open sea beyond, where a moderate southeasterly wind filled her sails. The sea ran fair, a gentle swell from the southeast with a small cross swell from the west—the lingering breath of the storm that had raged days before, now reduced to mere ripples upon the vast Pacific.

Cook had laid his course with customary precision. Bora Bora lay to the northwest, across open sea, a voyage of some two days with fair winds. But his intent was not merely to make landfall there. First, he would sweep a broad arc through the waters between Tahi and Bora Bora, searching for any sign of the missing pahi canoe or her occupants.

In the great cabin that afternoon, Cook spread his chart upon the table, Lieutenant James King and Sailing Master William Bligh studying it alongside him. The islands of the Society Group were marked with the meticulous precision that had made Cook's name as a hydrographer: Tahiti, Mo'orea, Huahine, Ra'iātea, and Bora Bora, with some rendered in greater detail than others. Bora Bora was among the less detailed, its volcanic silhouette sketched in broad strokes rather than the fine lines that defined Tahiti's coastline.

Cook traced the island's outline with a weathered finger, feeling a familiar weight of responsibility as he thought of his decision to send young Midshipman Cruwys there to remedy that deficiency. The lad had shown promise—perhaps too much promise.

"If they kept to the eastern approach," Bligh offered, indicating the channel with his divider's point, "they would have had the prevailing wind to their advantage."

King nodded, his expression grave. "And if weather forced them to seek shelter?"

Cook studied the fragmentary coastline, the blank spaces where reefs and shoals might lie unmarked. Each empty patch on the chart represented not just unknown geography, but potential peril, the very reason he had dispatched the survey party in the first place.

"We shall follow this track," said Cook, tracing a line across the waters, "keeping toward the leeward side of the islands, where a distressed vessel would most likely have been driven. Mr. Bligh, organize a watch rotation. Glasses will be issued to the lookouts for the duration. Every man aloft is to scan the horizon continuously. If they took to a small boat, or are clinging to wreckage, we might easily miss them."

"Aye, sir," said Bligh, making a note in the master's log.

"And Mr. King," Cook continued, turning to the lieutenant, "you will work with our Tahitian guest. He may know of small islets or reefs not marked on our charts where survivors might have found shelter."

King nodded, his expression grave. At twenty-seven, he was one of the younger officers, but Cook had come to value his methodical approach and scholarly mind. "I shall prepare a list of questions, sir, with Mr. Anderson's help for translation."

As the afternoon wore on, *Resolution* made steady progress to the northwest, the green heights of Tahiti gradually receding astern. The routine of the ship continued: watches changed, men took their stations, meals were served with the precision of a well-ordered floating community. But an undercurrent of tension ran through the vessel. Nicholas and Markham were well-liked among both officers and crew; their absence was felt keenly. James Trevenen had taken up a position in the bows, his glass trained steadily on the western horizon.

"Mr. Trevenen," said Bligh, "you will remove yourself from that station at once."

Bligh stood squarely on the deck, his hands clasped behind his back, his tone flat.

"You have been at that glass five hours without relief."

"I cannot leave it, sir," said Trevenen. He did not lower the instrument. "Not while Mr. Cruwys may be within sight."

"Your sentiments do you credit," said Bligh, not varying his tone, "but they have no place in the search. Captain Cook has laid a pattern. We are to follow it precisely. You are due the middle watch tonight. Exhaustion serves no man. Half an hour to eat and recover. Then you will report to the quarterdeck."

Trevenen said nothing. His jaw tightened, but he bowed stiffly and turned away. The glass weighed heavy in his hand now, and his shoulders burned with fatigue he had not felt before.

Bligh watched him go, offering no further comment.

James made his way down from the forecastle, his tread careful on the wet planks. He thought, with a tight grimness, that Nicholas would have handled it better: would have nodded, smiled perhaps, and defused the master's iron formality with a word or two. It was not merely that Nicholas was liked, it was that he had known, instinctively, how to move between the quarterdeck and the lower deck, between those born to command and those who had climbed there.

A rare skill. Rare, and missed.

By dusk, they had made some thirty miles from Tahiti, the island of Moorea now visible to the west, its jagged peaks etched against the setting sun. Cook ordered the ship hove-to for the night, unwilling to risk missing anything in the darkness. Lanterns were hung from the yards, their light feeble against the immensity of the night, but a signal nonetheless to any who might be searching for salvation.

Dawn on the 3rd of September saw renewed activity. The winds had freshened overnight, swinging more easterly, allowing for a quicker passage, and Cook took full advantage, ordering all canvas spread as soon as the light was sufficient for safe navigation. *Resolution* surged forward, her wake a ribbon of white against the deep indigo of the Pacific depths.

From his position on the quarterdeck, Cook methodically swept the horizon with his glass, pausing occasionally to study some irregularity in the distance that inevitably resolved into breaking waves or the shadow of a cloud upon the water. The Tahitian navigator, perched near the forecastle, pointed occasionally to subtle changes in the sea's color or the pattern of swells.

The day passed without sight of the missing men, though they encountered floating debris: palm fronds, branches, and near midday, a shattered canoe paddle that brought a shout from the lookout. For a moment it raised a flicker of hope throughout the ship, men gathering at the railings as the object was brought aboard. Cook examined it carefully, turning it over in his hands, noting the worn lashings and the wood bleached gray by sun and salt.

"Not recent," he pronounced finally, the brief animation in his features settling back into lines of concern. "This has been adrift for weeks, perhaps months."

He returned the paddle to the Tahitian, who confirmed with a solemn nod what Cook had already surmised. The debris was merely the Pacific's flotsam, offering no clue to the fate of the pahi canoe. As the sun began its descent toward the western horizon, Cook made a terse entry in his log and ordered the course maintained through the night under reduced sail, lanterns again to be hung from the yards.

At dawn Cook ordered the course altered for Bora Bora. By midday on the 4th of September, the island stood clear: steep green peaks, a ring of *motus*, the sea flashing turquoise over the reef. A Tahitian pointed out a channel; Cook nodded. Bligh conned *Resolution* through, *Discovery* in her wake.

Once anchored, Cook sent four boats to sweep the coast. King's party went to the main settlement. By nightfall, there was no trace: no wreckage, no word.

That night, in the great cabin, King made his report. Cook listened in silence, tracing the Tuamotus on the chart before him. If they had not made landfall before the storm, they would likely have been blown far to the east. A full search would take weeks they did not have. The voyage had a greater purpose, and the season pressed against them. Delay could mean the loss of the northern exploration altogether. The Tuamotus, too, were treacherous waters.

"We shall remain one more day," Cook said at last. "Sweep the nearby islands. Send a boat to Raiatea. If nothing by tomorrow evening, we sail north."

The next day brought no better news. The islands yielded nothing; the boat to Raiatea returned empty.

As the sun began to set on the 5th of September, Captain James Cook stood alone on the quarterdeck, his hands clasped behind his back. The lagoon lay still, the island rising lush and green beyond.

Lieutenant Clerke approached and halted a few paces off.

"The men are all aboard, sir."

Cook nodded slowly, not turning. "Weigh anchor with the morning tide."

Clerke hesitated. "And Mr. Cruwys, sir? And Markham?"

Cook was silent a long moment. His gaze rested on the far horizon, where the sea darkened into night.

"We have done what we could, Mr. Clerke. The Navy cannot risk a ship and her company, let alone two, even for the worthiest of men."

He turned at last. The red light of sunset caught the deep lines of his face, the weariness that duty could not wholly hide.

"Note in the log: Midshipman Nicholas Cruwys and Quartermaster Thomas Markham, missing—presumed lost at sea. I shall write to their families myself."

"Aye, sir."

Cook's voice, when it came again, was firm. "And have Mr. Trevenen report to me. I would speak with him privately before we depart."

He stood a while longer as Clerke withdrew, his silhouette dark against the last flush of sky, the ship lying at anchor, the island sleeping beyond the reef. A breeze stirred his coat as he clasped his hands behind his back and straightened with naval precision.

Later that evening, James Trevenen stood before his captain, his young face showing the strain of the past days. Cook gestured for him to be seated, an unusual courtesy that betrayed nothing in his countenance, but spoke volumes about the gravity of the moment.

"Mr. Trevenen," he said, "I understand you and Mr. Cruwys were close."

"Yes, sir," said James, his voice tight. "Since our days at the Academy."

Cook nodded, the lines about his eyes deepened by the lamplight. "I have commanded ships for many years, Mr. Trevenen. In that time, I have lost men to storm, to fever, to accident, and to the hazards of our calling. It never grows easier." He paused, choosing his words with care. "A captain must weigh the lives of a few against the welfare of many, or against the duty entrusted to him. These decisions — they are the true burden of command."

He rested his fingers lightly on a sheaf of papers beside the chart table — Nicholas's coastal soundings from Desolation, neatly inked in that tidy, measured hand Cook had come to recognise at a glance. For a moment, he ran his thumb along the margin, though the page lay perfectly flat. Trevenen said nothing, watching with the sharp perception of youth.

"He had a clear eye, your friend," Cook said, with a rare half-smile that came and went like a distant flash of light. "And a steady hand. I had thought he might go far."

He moved a brass divider carefully into place, a small habit of order born from years at sea.

James looked up, meeting his captain's gaze directly. "You are abandoning the search, sir."

"I am continuing our mission," said Cook, his voice measured but not unkind. "There is a difference, though it may not seem so to you now." He turned to the stern windows, looked out a long moment into the dark, then back. "In '56, during the war, I was master's mate aboard *Pembroke*. We lost a skiff off Louisbourg , three good men. I fought to continue searching. But the duty lay elsewhere."

He shook his head slightly, as if brushing away the memory. "The Admiralty has charged us with a greater task. The northern season is brief. Delay now could lose it altogether."

James bowed his head slightly. "Nicholas would understand, sir. He always understood duty. But I... I find it harder."

"As do I, Mr. Trevenen," said Cook, a rare frankness in his voice. He adjusted the inkwell on his desk with a small tap that echoed in the quiet cabin. "As do I. But I will tell you this: if your friend lives — and we must not abandon hope — he is resourceful, well-trained, and he has Markham with him, a steady sailor. The Tuamotus hold fresh water and food for those who know how to find them. And the seas are not so empty as once they were."

He hesitated. "I have known men given up for lost who found their way back from the very ends of the earth, Mr. Trevenen. The sea takes its tithe, but not always when we expect it."

James nodded, though the comfort was thin.

"One more thing," said Cook. "When we reach our next port, I shall send letters by the first homeward vessel. One will be my report. The other a private letter to the Admiralty, commending Mr. Cruwys' conduct and recommending his promotion, should he return."

He said it with a hint of gruffness, as though caught in an act of sentiment.

"That will be all, Mr. Trevenen. We sail with the morning tide."

The following morning, *Resolution* and *Discovery* weighed anchor and stood out through the reef, setting a course to the northwest. As the island fell away astern, James Trevenen stood at the rail, his glass trained on the diminishing land.

Edgar found him there, standing motionless long after the island had vanished beyond the horizon.

"He might yet be alive," said the master's mate, his gruff voice uncharacteristically gentle. "Men have survived worse at sea."

James nodded, his gaze turning from the empty horizon to the ship around him, the familiar bustle of men at their stations, the complex web of rigging above, the solid deck beneath his feet. This was his world now, a world where duty continued regardless of personal loss.

Far to the east, beyond the scattered reefs and the long empty miles, a small vessel moved across the Pacific. It bore no pennant, no gun, no polished timber, — only a handful of men, and the stubborn thread of a voyage not yet ended.

Ten days later the pahi canoe slipped through the reef passage into Bora Bora's lagoon, its repaired mast and fresh sail catching the late afternoon breeze. Nicholas Cruwys stood at the bow, watching the island's towering volcanic peak grow clearer with each stroke of the paddles. Beside him, Markham squinted into the setting sun, his weathered face marked by strain.

The island rose steeply from the sea, its green slopes dotted with breadfruit trees, pandanus, and the tall, swaying palms that fringed the lagoon. Inland, jagged ridges caught the last of the golden light, their outlines sharp against the deepening sky. Here and there, thin wisps of smoke curled upward from unseen fires, faint threads against the still air.

Their journey had taken a circuitous path. Blown far to the east by the storm, they had reached a small atoll in the Tuamotu Archipelago, where for twelve arduous days they worked alongside the surviving Tahitians to repair their shattered vessel. Tua had proved a master shipwright, overseeing the felling of two suitable trees for a new mast and the intricate weaving of replacement sails from pandanus leaves. When the work was judged sufficient for sea, they set out first for Tahiti, seeking more complete repairs before continuing toward Bora Bora.

It was there, in Matavai Bay, that Nicholas learned the crushing news: *Resolution* and *Discovery* had searched for three days around Bora Bora before resuming their northward voyage. Cook had departed nearly two weeks earlier, sent messages back to Tahiti to chief Tu in case the missing Englishmen should return.

"From what the Tahitians told us, Captain Cook was thorough in his search," Markham had said, as they made ready to depart Tahiti.

Nicholas had merely nodded, accepting the vagaries of fate. "What matters now is completing our mission," he had replied. "The captain expected a survey of Bora Bora, and a survey he shall have, even if we must deliver it ourselves upon our return to England."

Now, as they approached the white-sand beach of Bora Bora, where a small crowd of islanders had gathered to watch their arrival, Nicholas took stock of his tools. His octant was lost, but in Tahiti with Markham's help he had contrived a makeshift quadrant. His pocket compass had survived, sealed in its waxed leather case. For charts, he had acquired sheets of tapa cloth—the fine bark paper of the islands—and ink made from octopus fluid and charcoal. Not the precision instruments of a Royal Navy surveyor, but enough for a determined officer to complete his appointed task.

"We shall manage admirably, Markham," Nicholas said, as the canoe's hull grated on the coral sand. "First, we pay our respects to Chief Puni, as the captain would have done. Then we begin: every bay, every reef passage, every safe anchorage. By the time we find our way home, we shall have complete and full charts of Bora Bora."

He said it with the confidence of a young officer determined to fulfill his commission. Yet a strange unease stirred beneath the surface of that resolve. England seemed very far away, less a destination now than a memory. He turned from the shore and followed Mai-o up the path toward the village. The work lay ahead, and he would do it well. But something in him—he could not yet have said what—had already begun to change.

That evening, seated cross-legged beside the chief's household, Nicholas declined the place offered him at the centre and chose instead to sit among the canoe-builders and chart-bearers. He laid his chalk and compass alongside their adze and shell-drawn lines, not as demonstration, but as inquiry.

He asked questions slowly, haltingly, in the Tahitian he had begun to absorb more by ear than by rule. And when he made mistakes, as he did often, they corrected him without condescension.

He did not know yet what they thought of him. But that night, a small boy brought him a pandanus-leaf bundle of roasted fish without being asked, and two older men invited him to watch the stars with them from the headland.
It was not quite acceptance. But it was a beginning.

CHAPTER FIVE

The days at Bora Bora unfurled in a rhythm absent from any shallow measure, guided only by the quiet, unhurried certainty of the sun's course across a vault of endless blue, where each hour passed as lightly as a breath upon the water. Here, time had no weight and seemed apart from the familiar world.

The island rose from the water in perfection that seemed beyond the work of mere nature, a vision formed before the world had learned sorrow. At its heart Mount Otemanu soared to nearly three thousand feet, its high sheer flanks dropping towards the sea. Lower ridges descended in a quiet tumult, clothed in green upon green: breadfruit, pandanus, groves of palms swaying with a grave and silent grace. At dawn, the mountain's spire caught fire in the rising sun, casting colours across the sky that no palette could contain, rose deepening to gold and violet. By evening, the sea held the sky so faithfully in its surface that it became impossible to say where earth ended and heaven began, and the world seemed briefly without limit or boundary.

The reef encircled the island in a ring of living coral, broken here and there by small *motus* of dazzling white sand and crooked palms, scattered like pearls upon the sea. Within the translucent lagoon, fish of all colours darted far below, and the vivid hues of coral seemed just within reach, though fathoms deep. The waters shifted their hues with the changing light of each passing hour, from the palest turquoise to the deepest indigo, yet held in a harmony so perfect that it seemed a living mirror of the heavens themselves. On the stillest nights, when the wind had fled and the lagoon lay like glass, the stars and the silver sweep of the Milky Way were reflected there so purely that it seemed the island floated between two heavens: the one above and the one beneath, both strewn with countless brilliance, a vision lost to all but the earliest ages of the world.

Here was a world entire, untroubled by ambition, uncorrupted by want; a place where the harmony of sky, land, and sea was so perfect, so complete, that even Nicholas, who did not easily turn his mind to the divine felt, with a certainty beyond words, that he was gazing upon the very hand of God.

Amidst this Eden, Nicholas applied himself to his survey with the disciplined precision that Cook had instilled in all his officers, though he found himself adapting naval methods to a world for which the Admiralty had provided no specific instructions. Each morning, as the eastern sky began to lighten and while the village still slept, he and Markham would launch one of the narrow outrigger canoes provided by Chief Puni. They were often accompanied by Mai-o, the chief's son, a youth whose knowledge pointed to subtle variations in the water's color that revealed hidden shoals or safe passages with an accuracy no chart could improve upon. The makeshift quadrant yielded readings of surprising reliability when checked against landmarks of established position. Nicholas's naval eye, trained to measure distances across open water, soon adapted itself to the enclosed world of the lagoon, developing a facility for estimation that, while perhaps not satisfying the exacting standards of the Admiralty's hydrographers, proved both consistent and adequate for their purpose. Reef passages were sounded with lines weighted with coral fragments, each measurement recorded in his log with meticulous attention. The *motus*, those perfect jewels of sand and palm scattered along the reef, were sketched and named, their outlines inked upon stretched tapa cloth with a steadiness of hand that belied the primitive nature of his implements. Come evening, when the day's work was done, Nicholas would transcribe his notes by the golden light of a coconut-oil lamp, arranging his instruments—quadrant, compass, and slate tablets—with naval precision beside bowls of breadfruit.

"The Captain would give his approval to your methods, I believe," remarked Markham on their fifth day, observing with the quiet satisfaction of a mariner who had served under many lesser officers as Nicholas traced the sinuous outline of a treacherous reef passage onto his tapa-cloth chart with a precision that would not have disgraced the Admiralty's most accomplished cartographers. His weathered face, already taking on the bronze patina common to European men who had spent time in these latitudes, creased into a smile of professional appreciation. "He values nothing so highly as this, the ability to adapt oneself to circumstances while maintaining the standards of one's profession. I have known officers who, finding themselves without proper instruments, would declare the task impossible rather than improvise as you have done."

Nicholas nodded, pleased with the quartermaster's assessment. These words from Markham, a man not given to idle praise, meant more than any commendation from a less experienced man might have done. "We shall give him a survey worthy of the Navy, even if our instruments are somewhat unconventional. Captain Cook would expect nothing less." He ran his fingers lightly over the chart, feeling the texture of the tapa cloth beneath the ink—so different from the stiff vellum of Admiralty charts, yet serving its purpose with a certain native elegance that he had come to appreciate. The thought of Cook examining their work upon their eventual reunion sustained him through the more tedious aspects of their task, though he found, to his mild surprise, that the tedium itself was of a different quality here. There was something in the rhythm of the days, in the perfect union of work and place, that rendered even the most exacting measurements a kind of pleasure.

The western approaches to Bora Bora, where the barrier reef lay close to the island and the great Teavanui Pass opened toward the unbroken Pacific, proved the most treacherous to chart. Here, the ocean swells, having crossed thousands of miles of open water without impediment, rebounded around and struck the reef with a violence that transformed the gentle blue of the lagoon into a chaos of white foam and flying spray, shooting thirty feet into the air. On their first attempt to survey this rugged stretch, Nicholas and Markham very nearly lost both their canoe and themselves when an unexpected set of waves surged through the pass, catching them in a cross-current and driving them toward a submerged coral head—a black mass just visible beneath the churn. Only Mai-o's quick reaction, his powerful arms driving the paddle with a precision that Nicholas could only admire, saved them from disaster. Even so, they reached shore with their canoe half-swamped, their instruments drenched with salt water.

"Perhaps we should enlist more experienced help for this section," Nicholas suggested, as they bailed seawater from their half-swamped vessel. The salt water had already begun to work its mischief upon his clothing, and he wrung out his shirt with the resigned air of a man who had long since accepted such discomforts as part of his profession. He examined their instruments with care, relieved to find that the compass, at least, had suffered no apparent damage. The chart, hastily elevated above the incoming water, showed only minor spotting along one edge.

It was Mai-o who introduced them the next day to Atea. "My cousin," he explained, gesturing toward the slim figure who approached along the beach. "She knows western reefs better than any. Her father was great navigator, brother to Chief Puni." Nicholas looked up from his chart to observe the young woman walking toward them. His practiced eye, accustomed to evaluating distances and proportions with naval precision, noted that she stood nearly five foot seven - unusually tall for a woman of the islands - and moved with a natural grace that suggested complete harmony with her surroundings. Unlike many island women, who wore only a simple pareu wrapped about their waists, Atea was dressed in a more elaborate tapa cloth garment that draped from one shoulder, secured at the waist with a belt of woven pandanus. The rich reddish-brown of the fabric complemented her copper skin and gave her an air of quiet dignity that commanded respect.

But it was her face that arrested Nicholas's attention most completely. High cheekbones and a straight, delicate nose gave her profile a perfect harmony. Her mouth was full and expressive, and broke into a quick to smile yet tempered by a certain seriousness of bearing. Her eyes, large and widely spaced beneath gracefully arched brows, were so dark as to appear black in certain lights, yet in the bright sunshine revealed themselves to be a deep brown, flecked with amber near the pupil. Unlike the more elaborate styles favoured by many women of the islands, she allowed her hair to flow freely down her back in waves as dark and lustrous as polished obsidian, catching the sunlight as she walked and swaying like sea grass in a gentle current.

Her form possessed the toned resilience that comes from a life lived in constant movement upon both land and sea. Her shoulders, burnished copper by the sun, bore the clean lines of a swimmer's strength; her bosom, modestly covered by the upper fold of her tapa cloth, rose and fell with the measured breathing of one accustomed to diving in the lagoon's depths. The graceful narrowing of her waist and the strong, shapely lines of her legs, glimpsed in motion beneath the hem of her garment, spoke of countless hours spent paddling and clambering up the island's verdant slopes. She stood with the natural poise of one wholly at ease within her own skin: dignified, unselfconscious, and possessed of a confidence that came not from rank or ornament, but from absolute mastery of her world.

"My cousin says you wish to make..." She paused, eyes narrowing slightly as she searched for the word. "A drawing? Of the reef passages?"

She was more striking than he had expected, though he could not have said what, precisely, he had expected. There was something in the shape of the eyes, in the calm of her bearing, that unsettled his sense of equilibrium for a moment. Then the question caught up with him, and he found his voice.

"Not quite a drawing," he said. "A chart, of sorts, but also a record of depths, bearings, bottom composition. If it's done properly, it may help others through the reef."

Her gaze lingered, not coy but searching, the look of someone who had learned early that silence often yielded more than speech. "So it is for the next ship," she said, "not only for yourself."

And with that, she turned and walked away. Her back was straight, her stride unhurried, and something in the ease of it lingered in Nicholas's mind, unnamed, but not easily set aside.

True to her word, Atea arrived at their dwelling the next morning as the first light broke over the eastern horizon. She did not come on foot, but paddled a small outrigger canoe with quiet efficiency, the vessel perfectly balanced beneath her sure, deliberate strokes. Nicholas and Markham were already waiting, their instruments wrapped in oilcloth and packed for the day's work.

"The western reef is dangerous," she said without preamble as they approached. "But there are three passages safe for small boats at certain tides. I will show you."

The next weeks fell into a rhythm. Each morning, Nicholas and Atea set out in her canoe—sometimes with Markham, sometimes alone if the quartermaster was occupied with other sections of the coast. Atea proved not merely a guide but an indispensable source of knowledge: she knew which passages were passable only at high tide, which currents shifted with the seasons, and which reefs were growing and which had begun to die.

As the days passed, Nicholas's facility with the Tahitian language improved steadily under Atea's tutelage. She was a patient but exacting teacher, correcting his pronunciation with quiet persistence until he began to master the subtle distinctions that often eluded European ears.

"How do you know all this?" Nicholas asked one morning in Tahitian, as she guided the canoe through a narrow channel that, to his eye, looked no different from the dangerous reef on either side.

She glanced back at him, half amused, half surprised, as if the answer should have been self-evident. "The sea is our mother," she said simply. "We learn her moods as you learn your mother's face."

He told her stories of England, of Devon's green hills and the quiet, rain-softened lanes of his childhood. He described London not from experience, but from books and the recollections of others: the great dome of St. Paul's, the endless chimneys, the roar of carriage wheels on wet stone. He tried to shape these foreign images into something she might see.

"It rains there often?" she asked one day, as they sat in the shade of a breadfruit tree, taking refuge from the midday heat.

"Almost constantly in winter," he replied.

She considered this, her brow furrowing slightly. "And yet you leave this place of cold rain to sail across the great ocean?"

"It is our way," he said, finding no better explanation. "As the sea is your mother, ships are our home."

She accepted this with the same quiet gravity with which she received all his accounts of English life, neither judging nor dismissing, but filing them away like a navigator assembling a chart: not of reefs and passages, but of a foreign world.

By the fourth week, Nicholas had completed a rough draft of the eastern and southern coast surveys. His uniform, soaked regularly with seawater and bleached by the sun, had begun to give way despite his best efforts. The wool, never intended for such a climate, had stiffened with salt, and the brass buttons were turning green.

"You should wear proper clothes," Atea told him one morning, eyeing his bedraggled uniform with frank concern. "The sun burns your skin, and the salt rots your English garments."

The next day, she returned with a bundle wrapped in leaves: a man's pareu and a short tunic of finely beaten tapa, the kind worn by Chief Puni and other men of rank. The cloth was soft against his skin and far better suited to wading through shallows and scrambling over rock.

Markham regarded the transformation with raised eyebrows and practical approval. "More suitable to the climate, sir—without question. And it will preserve what's left of your uniform for more formal appearances."

Nicholas soon discovered other advantages to adopting local dress. The islanders, who had shown him cautious respect but a measure of reserve, began to treat him with greater ease, inviting him to communal meals and ceremonies that might otherwise have remained closed. He learned to handle the outriggers with growing confidence, mastering the subtleties of wave patterns and the subtle shifts in water color that indicated reefs or currents below.

Atea's role grew beyond that of a guide. She became a cultural interpreter, explaining the island's complex social structure, the ties between Bora Bora and its neighbours, the old rivalries and enduring alliances that had shaped the politics of the Society Islands for generations. Through her, Nicholas came to understand the island not only as a place, but as a society—layered, intricate, and fully formed.

"Since the time of Taaroa," she said, naming one of the great gods of her people. "Many, many generations. Our oldest songs tell of the long voyages that brought our ancestors here from Havai'i, far to the west."

Nicholas made careful note in his journal. Cook had long suspected that the Polynesian peoples had spread across the Pacific through deliberate navigation, not accident, and Atea's words lent quiet weight to the theory.

She looked at him with a small smile. "Long enough that the sea remembers our names," she said. "And long enough that we remember hers."

He said nothing for a long while. There was nothing to add, and no need. The surf rolled across the coral shallows, and the stars turned overhead. For the first time in many weeks, he felt completely at rest.

Another time, they sat beneath the broad fronds of a breadfruit tree, where the tide whispered along the shore and the air cooled with the hush of coming dusk. Atea watched the horizon in silence, her arms wrapped loosely about her knees, the light catching faintly on the curve of her cheek.

"You ask many questions," she said at last, not reproachfully, but as one noting a habit.

"Because I want to understand," Nicholas said, careful not to press.

She turned then, her gaze level, unreadable. "Then you must learn that here, we do not always speak all that we know. Some things belong to the heart, and speaking them too often makes them less. Or alters them in ways we cannot recall."

She looked back to the sea. "The sea understands this. It says nothing. Yet it remembers everything."

Nicholas said nothing, but the words stayed with him.

As the weeks passed into the end of a second month, Nicholas found himself looking forward to each day with Atea with an eagerness that went beyond the requirements of his survey. Her quick intelligence, her quiet humor, the grace with which she moved through her world—all of these had woven a spell around him that he neither could nor wished to break.

They spoke now almost exclusively in Tahitian, and he found that the language, with its flowing rhythms and subtle inflections, allowed him to express thoughts and feelings that somehow seemed constrained in English. In her presence, he no longer felt the awkwardness of a guest, nor the posture of an officer. He simply was.

It was during their survey of a small *motu*—one of the tiny islands dotting the outer reef—that something shifted between them. The work complete, they sat in the shade of a coconut palm, sharing the sweet meat of a freshly opened nut. A comfortable silence had fallen between them, punctuated only by the gentle lapping of waves against the shore and the distant cry of seabirds.

"Why do you not have a wife in England?" Atea asked suddenly, her direct gaze meeting his.

The question caught Nicholas off guard, though he had grown accustomed to the Polynesian frankness about such matters. He gave a quiet laugh.

"I'm seventeen. Still considered young in my country—especially for marriage. At home I'd be expected to be at sea, or in study. Not building a house."

She looked at him with faint amusement. "You are not too young here. A man of your age would have children already."

He tilted his head slightly. "And you? Why are you not married?"

A shadow passed across her expression. "I was to marry the son of the chief of Raiatea. He died in the same fighting that took my father. That was last year."

"I'm sorry," Nicholas said, and meant it.

She shook her head gently. "It was the will of the gods. But now…" She hesitated, then continued with the same frankness. "I am eighteen. There have been others. Some I chose because they were kind. Some because I was curious. Not all were wise. But none were forced. That matters more."

Nicholas looked at her—not surprised, but steady. "There was someone. In Matavai. Tehani."

Atea smiled and nodded. "I know her from my visits. She chooses those who are gentle."

"You knew?"

"I did. It is no shame to be chosen."

He was quiet for a moment. "This feels different."

"It is," she said. "You ask questions no boy would ask. And you listen."

She reached out then and placed her hand over his, calmly, deliberately. Her fingers rested with quiet certainty atop his, and in that stillness he felt a current more powerful than any he had known.

Her eyes held his, and in them he saw not merely beauty, but intention, a steadiness that asked for nothing but presence.

He looked away for a moment, toward the reef where the sea met the sky in a haze of white gold. Once, just weeks ago, he might have imagined himself returning to the quarterdeck, his name entered in the ship's log, his charts laid before Captain Cook with quiet pride. But that life now felt curiously distant, blurred at the edges by time and the intense beauty around him.

There were no sails on the horizon, no bells to mark the watch, only the hush of surf in the shallows, the scent of warm breadfruit on the breeze, and the soft press of sand beneath him.

He thought of duty: of Cook's measured gaze, of Bligh's sharp eye, of Trevenen's laughter, and felt a pang. But it passed like a gust through the palms.

Here was another kind of clarity. A life unmeasured by uniform or rank, shaped instead by tide and gesture, by silence and presence. And beside him sat Atea, poised, radiant, and utterly herself. She did not beckon, did not claim. She simply was. And her presence, like the island, required no justification.

Something in him loosened, some quiet resistance, long held. He felt himself unmoored, not by storm, but by stillness.

And in that stillness, he turned to her.

Without conscious thought, he leaned forward, and their lips met.

The world seemed to pause, the endless rhythm of the waves suspended for a heartbeat. When they parted, something fundamental had changed between them, a boundary crossed that could never be restored.

"Atea," he began, not entirely certain what he meant to say.

She placed her fingers gently against his lips. "Do not speak yet," she said softly. "Some things need no words."

The days that followed were touched with a new radiance. The survey work continued, for Nicholas was still, first and foremost, an officer with a duty to complete, but now the hours with Atea held a deeper significance.

She took him to sacred places on the island, sites not usually shown to outsiders: ancient *marae* platforms where ceremonies had been conducted for centuries; hidden valleys where certain sacred plants grew; a small, perfect cove on the western side of the island where, she told him, the spirits of departed navigators came to guide their descendants.

In the evenings, he would often stay in her family's compound, a collection of well-built *fares*, thatched dwellings, set in a grove of breadfruit trees near the lagoon. Her mother, a dignified woman who bore a striking resemblance to what Atea herself might become in thirty years, welcomed him with a reserved warmth. Her younger brothers treated him first with suspicious appraisal, then with the rough acceptance accorded to a potential brother-in-law.

They asked questions with the directness of boys, tested him with mock-challenges of strength and skill: climbing trees, hurling spears at drifting coconuts, racing barefoot along the packed shore. Nicholas, tall and muscled, held his own awkwardly but well enough. They laughed at his accent and admired his knife.

After supper, they would sit outside, the air soft with dusk, firelight flickering against the broad leaves overhead. Atea's mother would weave pandanus mats by the glow of a small lamp while the younger children dozed or played quietly nearby. Occasionally her uncle would visit from the next *fare*, a tall, soft-spoken man with grey at his temples and the calm presence of a canoe master. He asked Nicholas careful questions about the ship, the voyage, the purpose of the charts, and nodded at the answers without comment. His gaze, when it passed between Nicholas and Atea, revealed nothing—but it lingered.

Nicholas spoke rarely during these evenings, understanding that presence meant more than performance. He listened to the rhythms of their speech, caught the flow of stories whose full meanings were not always clear, but whose cadences he began to trust.

One night, after the children had drifted away and the fire had fallen to embers, Atea's mother set down her weaving and looked at him directly for the first time.

"You are not like the others," she said, in Tahitian. Her voice was calm, but it carried weight.

Nicholas, uncertain, met her eyes. "How do you mean?"

She considered. "You do not try to take. You try to understand. That is different. But understanding is not always enough."

He nodded slowly. "I know."

Atea, seated beside him, said nothing—but her hand found his beneath the woven mat.

One evening they sat at the edge of the lagoon as dusk fell, the light stretched long over the water. Nicholas had been silent a while, his hands resting on his knees, his eyes fixed on the last ripple of the departing canoe.

"You think too much when the light goes," Atea said. Not a rebuke, merely an observation.

"Do I?" he asked, though he already knew she was right.

She nodded. "Your body is here. Your work, your voice, your eyes. But something in you looks past this place—backward, or forward, I don't know. You are between two places. That is a hard place to stand."

He looked at her. "And where do you stand?"

"Here," she said, simply. "Always here. That is what makes it easier for me." She paused. "But I would not wish to change places with you."

He did not answer. But he felt the truth of her words, like the steady pull of the tide beneath the surface.

By early December the chart was nearly complete. Every passage, every curve of reef and inlet, had been fixed and inked. Nicholas laid the final strokes across the southern headland with a care that bordered on reverence, his hand steady, his notes precise.

That night, after the village had quieted, he sat beside Atea beneath the trees. Her head rested lightly against his shoulder, the scent of her hair mingling with the breeze from the lagoon. No words passed between them for some time. There was no need.

He thought, idly, of England. Of Devon. Of Exeter and its damp stone halls. The memory came gently, like a childhood song, familiar, faint, already softened by time.

"I shall finish the chart," he murmured at last.

Atea made no reply, but her fingers closed around his, warm and sure. And in that moment, he knew—without doubt, without dread—that if no ship ever came, if no orders ever followed, he would not mind.

Not here. Not with her.

The next morning broke silver-grey and still, the lagoon as smooth as paper. Nicholas awoke early and checked the drying ink. There were only notations to complete, small corrections to latitude. The larger work was done.

Two days later, the sun was high overhead when Markham returned from a supply errand inland. He ducked into the low doorway of their dwelling, dust on his boots and satisfaction in his bearing.

"It's a remarkable achievement, sir," he said, surveying the finished charts spread out on the woven floor mat. "The Admiralty will be most impressed when we return."

"Markham," he said after a long moment, "I believe it would be wise for one of us to return to Tahiti."

The quartermaster looked up, his weathered face betraying nothing. "Sir?"

"There is always the possibility that another European vessel might call there," Nicholas continued. "If so, it would be prudent to have a representative of His Majesty's Navy present to secure passage. Or relay word."

Markham nodded slowly. "A sensible precaution, sir. And who do you propose should undertake this duty?"

Nicholas drew a breath. "I think it should be you. I..." He hesitated. "I should remain here to complete some additional observations. Tidal movements, longer-range reef soundings—material that might enhance the Admiralty's understanding of the region."

If Markham saw through this thin justification, he gave no sign. "Very well, sir. When should I depart?"

"Chief Puni has informed me that a trading canoe will sail for Tahiti in three days. He has offered to secure passage for you."

Three days later, by their reckoning the 9th of December 1777, Nicholas stood on the beach as the large sailing canoe was made ready.

"Sir," said Markham quietly, brushing a bit of sand from his sleeve, "with all due respect, I've a few more miles under my keel than you."

He turned to look out across the lagoon. The water was flat as blown glass, its colours shifting from turquoise to deep indigo where the reef gave way to sea. Beyond it, the island rose green and gold beneath the early sun, its peaks wreathed in a gauze of mist like something half-remembered from a dream. Birds moved through the palm crowns in sudden bursts, and from downwind came the scent of fruit and woodsmoke.

Markham let out a breath, quiet and slow. "You'll finish the work. That much I'm sure of. But there's more to reckon than just charts and bearings. A place like this—" he gestured with his chin, almost absently—"it has a way of making a man think. Not of duty, or advancement, or the next ship on the list. Just... what a life might be, if one were to choose it."

He turned back to Nicholas, eyes clear beneath his lined brow. "Most of us never get the chance. But you might. And if you did—well, I wouldn't call it a failure to take it."

He held Nicholas's gaze a moment longer, then nodded once and stepped aboard.

Neither man voiced what both understood—that years might pass before another European vessel called at these islands. Not until

HMS Bounty arrived a decade later would Tahiti see another ship of any nation, though neither could know it then.

As the canoe caught the wind and moved away from shore, Nicholas raised his hand in farewell. Markham returned the gesture without drama, then turned his gaze forward, toward Tahiti and whatever fate awaited him there.

Nicholas stood watching until the vessel had vanished through the reef passage. Then he turned inland, toward the village path and the grove of breadfruit trees, where Atea waited—her expression a mixture of sympathy for his friend's departure and quiet joy that Nicholas remained.

"You have sent him to wait for a ship that may never come," Atea said softly as they walked along the shore.

By the new year of 1778, their life had settled into rhythm on one of the smaller *motu* near the western reef—a quiet crescent of palm and coral sand, where the breeze was constant and the sea never far. The main village lay distant across the lagoon, its smoke visible but its noise absent.

There had been no formal decision. No marked beginning. One night he had remained after supper, the stars high and the tide low, and in the morning, he had helped carry the fishing net down to the shore. After that, he did not return to the hut he had shared with Markham.

They built a shelter of woven palm thatch and driftwood, simple but dry, and set their hearth in the lee of a fallen tree. Atea arranged their space with quiet competence, placing each item with a sense of belonging that Nicholas admired but did not disturb. His charts were kept in a sealed bamboo tube beside her basket of taro.

And it was there, one quiet evening, as the light turned golden on the reef, that he felt—not for the first time, but more clearly than ever—that something had shifted within. Not with a storm, but with stillness. The light was falling long across the lagoon, golden and low. On the *motu*, the reef sound was a steady hush, like breath at the edge of sleep. Nicholas sat cross-legged beside a flat board propped on stones, another detail chart half-finished before him, its lines crisp where the ink had taken cleanly to the tapa cloth.

Atea was rinsing taro root at the shallows, her back to him, her hair twisted into a loose knot that had begun to fall in the breeze. Beside her, a small cooking fire smoked gently, and a pot hung from a greenwood hook, bubbling faintly.

"You're using too much of the brown ink," she said, without turning.

"It darkens unevenly," Nicholas replied. "I'm trying to even the wash."

"You're fighting the cloth," she said. "Let it dry the way it wants to."

He said nothing, but set the pen aside and leaned back on his hands, watching her. The curve of her neck, the loosened braid falling across her shoulder, the smudge of ash on her wrist—none of it theatrical, none of it arranged. It was how she moved when she thought no one was looking.

She glanced over, sensing his gaze. "The pot is nearly done," she said. "You should eat."

He stood, brushed the sand from his palms, and crossed the short space between them. The island was small enough to walk across in a minute. The reef caught the tide not twenty paces from their hut. Beyond it, only the open Pacific—vast, blue, and empty.

He looked around—at the fire, the woven palm mat on which they slept, the coils of cordage she'd re-coiled half a dozen times, the little carved hook she used to stir the pot, darkened now from a hundred meals.

None of it was his. And yet none of it felt foreign anymore.

"You know," he said softly, "I don't think I've wished to be anywhere else. Not once."

Atea looked up, her expression unreadable in the half-light.

"Then don't," she said. "Not while the sea stays quiet."

He didn't answer.

But he stayed.

A year later, January 1779 arrived in the Society Islands as it always did, with little change in the perpetual warmth and brilliant light of the tropical sun. The most noticeable difference was the increased humidity and the brief, violent downpours that marked what passed for summer in these southern latitudes. More than fifteen months had passed since *Resolution* had departed and for Thomas Markham, standing on the eastern headland of Matavai Bay, those months had wrought changes he would not have believed possible even a year before.

His sturdy frame had grown leaner, more sinewy, though no less powerful for the transformation. His skin, already weathered by years at sea, had deepened to a dark mahogany, and the faded blue lines of tatau that marked his forearms rendered him nearly indistinguishable from the island men among whom he had made his place. Having adopted the local custom of removing facial hair—the Tahitians considering beards uncivilized, he now plucked his whiskers with a shell tool, as native men had taught him. The linen of his last remaining shirt had long since yielded to the climate, replaced by a simple pareu at his waist and a short cape of tapa cloth draped over one shoulder, the mark of a man formally adopted into a chief's household.

Markham's sharp eyes scanned the western horizon, where a fleck of sail had appeared from the direction of Bora Bora, its claw shaped sail marking it as a native craft. He had taken to this daily vigil some months earlier, not solely from any hope of European contact, but from the sailor's ingrained habit of reading the sea and its moods.

As the vessel drew closer, it resolved itself into a double-hulled voyaging canoe, large and well-handled. Voyagers from the leeward islands were rare at this season, when sudden squalls made crossing perilous. Markham's interest sharpened. He settled into a watchful stance, feet braced against the incline, content to wait.

Nearly an hour passed before the canoe entered the bay proper. Its crew paddled now with slow strength, the sail lowered in the traditional gesture of respect. Even at a distance, Markham's eye, honed by decades at sea, caught something familiar in the tall figure standing at the bow.

Mr. Cruwys.

A complex current moved through him: pleasure at the sight of his young officer, concern at the unexpectedness of his arrival, and beneath it all, a quiet recognition that such a journey likely heralded change.

He descended the slope with deliberate ease, the path long familiar. By the time he reached the shore, the canoe had grounded gently on the sand. Its occupants moved with practiced efficiency, saying little. Nicholas stepped ashore.

His skin had darkened, his hair grown long and bound in the island way, his face smooth and bare in the Tahitian fashion. He wore tapa and cord, not uniform. But the change was more than outward.

Markham saw it in the way he stood—in the stillness of his frame, the weight he carried not as burden but as something already absorbed. The bright, unformed midshipman of fifteen months before was gone. In his place was a man marked by both joy and sorrow, by a life lived fully beyond the strictures of rank and rule.

"Markham," said Nicholas, his voice steady but rough-edged, as though English sat less comfortably in his mouth than it once had. "It's good to see you."

"And you, sir," Markham replied, stepping forward to clasp the offered hand. The reflexive deference of a seasoned seaman to his officer remained, even after all this time. "Though I confess your arrival is... not what I expected."

A shadow crossed Nicholas's face. "My circumstances have changed. I'd speak with you—privately—after I've paid respects to Tu."

Markham nodded, noting the fluency with which Nicholas used the Tahitian honorific. "Of course, sir. I've a *fare* nearby. It's modest, but quiet enough for conversation."

"Good," Nicholas said. "I'll join you shortly. I need to walk a while first."

He turned without further word and set off along the shore.

Like Bora Bora, Tahiti was still beautiful. That was the worst of it.

The frangipani still bloomed in white clusters. The palms still moved lightly on the trade winds. Children still played in the shallows, their laughter unbroken by grief.

But Nicholas no longer saw it as he once had. He passed the same canoes, the same hearth-smoke curling into morning air, and felt as though he were looking through smoked glass, present, but not reached. The world had not changed. He had.

Two hours later, Nicholas sat cross-legged on the woven mat floor of Markham's *fare*, the modest dwelling bearing the marks of its occupant's seafaring life: impeccable tidiness, a coiled line in the corner, and two carefully preserved navigational instruments hanging from the central post. A simple meal of breadfruit, roasted fish, and coconut had been provided by Markham's Tahitian household. He too had been formally adopted during his stay, as many visitors were.

"She died a fortnight ago," Nicholas said without preamble, his gaze fixed on the middle distance. "Atea. From an infection after a reef injury. A rogue swell caught her over the coral."

Markham absorbed this without speaking at first. He heard the effort behind Nicholas's voice—controlled, even, but ragged at the edge, as if each word had to be carried past a barrier. At last he said, quietly, "I'm truly sorry, sir. I'd gathered from the trading canoes that you had taken her as your wife."

His weathered features softened with her memory. Atea's beauty had been striking, even here where grace seemed to grow as abundantly as palms. But it was more than that. She had carried an inborn dignity, a quiet intelligence that lived in her eyes and in the measured way she moved through her world. He remembered the early survey days in the outriggers, charting the reef passages, how she corrected their misunderstandings without condescension, her knowledge always precise, never offered to display. He had noticed how Nicholas watched her hands as she showed the patterns in the swell that marked hidden shoals, the young officer's expression betraying not mere admiration, but something deeper. Markham had seen it forming and recognized it for what it was.

"She was exceptional," he said at last. "I saw it in those weeks we worked together. She had a presence you don't often meet."

Nicholas nodded once, sharply. "We were married in their custom last March." He paused, then: "She was…" The word hung there, unfinished. "Extraordinary, Markham. She taught me to see these islands as she saw them—not as coordinates on a chart, but as a world entire."

His voice faltered. He waited a beat, mastering it. "The healers said she was recovering. But then—"

He didn't finish. He didn't need to. Markham understood. Here or in England, wounds could betray their bearers long after the danger seemed past.

Nicholas rose and moved to the open doorway, his back to the room, shoulders held rigid with the effort of stillness. Outside, sunlight dappled the village path. Somewhere nearby, children laughed.

"When the pain came and the wound wouldn't close, she was calm," he said. "Certain it would pass as nature intended. The old women brought herbs, sang over her. She welcomed them. I did nothing but hold her hand."

He fell silent.

Markham remained seated, understanding that this telling was not a conversation. It was a reckoning.

"Her voice grew faint. The light left her eyes." Nicholas's hand drifted to his chest. "She touched my face and spoke of our next life. Said we would meet again beneath different stars."

The stillness that followed was not empty. It was dense with the weight of all that had been lost—not just a woman, but a world. A place. A future.

Nicholas turned again.

"They honored me with the mourning rites," he said. "We fasted for seven days. Kept vigil. The tattooist marked my shoulder with the sign of her family. To bind me to her spirit in the next life."

He paused, his voice quieter now.

"They buried her in the sacred grove above the western reef. Her favorite place. They say her spirit watches over the sailors who pass there, guides them home."

Markham nodded. Not in agreement, but in respect. Truth was not the point.

"They offered to keep me, treat me as kin. I couldn't stay." His voice sharpened slightly, not from anger but from clarity. "Every tree, every reef we walked together, everything speaks of her. And I cannot bear their voices."

He drew breath.

"When I first came to Bora Bora, I saw it as Captain Cook taught me: a coastline to be measured, charted, described. She showed me its soul. Its sacred ground. I see too much now to be blind again. But not enough to belong here without her."

The admission cost him. He did not lower his eyes, but something in him dropped.

"What are your intentions, sir?" Markham asked, falling naturally back into the formality of quartermaster to officer.

Nicholas's gaze sharpened, focusing on him with sudden clarity. "I mean to find passage back to England—or at least to a European port. The survey work is complete. More than complete. I have charts and journals that would make Cook himself proud, knowledge of currents and reef passages no other European navigator has yet recorded. This must not be lost just because we are, for now, cut off."

As Nicholas spoke of voyages west and trading networks, Markham observed the transformation. The grief was not gone, only channeled, like a flood redirected into irrigation canals. It was how men endured such losses: not by outlasting them, but by turning sorrow toward purpose.

"A worthy goal, sir," said Markham. "But as you know, no European vessel has called here since *Resolution* departed. And unless the Admiralty has altered its patterns, we cannot expect another for some years yet."

"I am aware," said Nicholas, his tone sharpening with something of his old command. "That's why I mean to go to them, rather than wait to be found. The trading networks reach far into the Pacific. To Fiji, to Samoa, perhaps even farther. European ships, East Indiamen and others, must pass through those waters. If we can reach them, our chances improve."

Markham considered this. It was true that trading vessels crossed those routes, though few came so far east. "You propose to cross nearly four hundred leagues of open ocean in a canoe? I'd wager even the Tahitians would call it madness."

Nicholas gave a faint smile. "Not in those words. But they admitted such voyages are rare now—not these seventy years past, they say. Yet their ancestors did it often. Atea told me the old traditions: deliberate expeditions of discovery, navigating by stars and the shape of the sea."

"And have you secured a vessel? A crew?" asked Markham.

"Not yet. But Tu has agreed to consider it. He respects Cook's memory, and he understands that as an officer of the Navy, I'm bound, if I can, to return, especially now." Nicholas paused. "I had hoped that you might accompany me, Markham. Your skills as a quartermaster would be invaluable. Few men can read the sea and stars better than you. I will not order you, given the nature of the voyage and the length of time we have already spent here."

Markham was silent for a long moment, weighing the proposal. He had found an unexpected peace in these islands, a belonging that had eluded him throughout his years of naval service. The family that had taken him in treated him as one of their own; he had learned their ways, their language, even taken a Tahitian wife the previous spring—a widow some years younger than himself, with a quiet calmness that reminded him of his long-dead English wife. He had not expected, after so many years at sea, to find a life where his days were not counted in bells and watches, where he was simply a man, not a quartermaster. Yet even here, amid all that was freely given, the pull of duty had never entirely loosened its grip. He had sworn himself to the King's service, and though the Admiralty surely believed them lost, that oath still held weight.

Nicholas's voice had been steady, free of presumption. *I will not order you.* That was the difference, and Markham felt it keenly. There was no demand in Nicholas's words, only an acknowledgment of shared experience and the freedom to choose. That freedom mattered.

"When do you propose to depart, sir?" he asked finally.

"As soon as a suitable vessel can be prepared. Two weeks, perhaps three." Nicholas studied him with quiet understanding. "Does this mean you will join me?"

Markham exhaled slowly. "It means I will consider it carefully, Mr. Cruwys," he replied, the formality a mark of both respect and gratitude. "A voyage like this is not lightly undertaken, as I am sure you understand."

Nicholas nodded, offering nothing further. Markham appreciated that as well. They sat in silence for a time, each man lost in his own thoughts as the afternoon light slanted across the woven mat floor, casting patterns from the open walls. Outside, the sea's murmur threaded through the sound of village life, women calling across courtyards, the gentle tapping of tapa beaters on wood.

Nicholas said at last, "If we make the voyage and somehow reach England, it will have been nearly three years since *Resolution* last saw us. The Navy has likely presumed us lost."

Markham gave a slow nod. "It wouldn't be the first time men turned up after the Admiralty had inked them into the margins. But if Captain Cook still lives, and if he's made it as far as Batavia or home, I'd wager he hasn't forgotten us."

Nicholas nodded, though he could not know that at that very moment, far to the north in the Sandwich Islands, events were unfolding that would forever alter the course of Captain Cook's final voyage.

He ran a hand through his hair, a gesture that for a moment recalled the eager young midshipman Markham had once known.

"You should rest, sir," Markham said gently, noting the deep fatigue drawn across the younger man's features. "You've travelled far—and grief makes its own demands. My home is yours for as long as you need it."

Nicholas accepted the offer with a grateful nod. "Thank you, Markham. I am indeed weary, though sleep has been an elusive companion these past two weeks."

Later, as darkness fell over Matavai Bay, he lay on the sleeping mat Markham had provided, but true rest would not come. Behind closed eyes, he saw Atea as she had been in life—laughing as she guided their canoe through a difficult reef passage, her eyes bright with mischief; showing him the patient rhythm of spearfishing in the shallows; lying beside him in the cool hush of night, her breath soft against his skin. The memories were precious, and unbearable.

All of it swept away by a single wound, and the quiet betrayal of time.

She had not seemed in danger at first. The healers said the cut was clean. She moved carefully but without complaint. For days, the swelling eased, the fever held off. They all believed she was recovering.

And then, suddenly—she was not.

What remained was duty, and the knowledge he had gathered. It could not fill the hollow her absence had left, but it was something to steer by. A fixed point when all other landmarks had vanished beneath the waves.

CHAPTER SIX

The pahi canoe ran sleek through the long Pacific swell, her twin hulls gliding with an ease no European vessel could match. She was swift—light as a bird upon the water—her woven lashings as strong as iron yet supple enough to move with the waves. Nicholas had long since ceased to question the seaworthiness of these vessels. That much, at least, had been proven.

And this pahi was larger even than others he had seen, and though sound clearly older, a true ocean voyaging canoe with a small shelter and two masts. Tu had sent for her from one of the other islands, and they had departed Tahiti amongst much ceremony, for no voyage such as this had been made for many, many years.

The first days passed easily, the southeast trades steady in the rigging, the claw shaped pandanus sails drawing clean. The canoe scudded westward beneath a wide and empty sky. By night, the stars emerged in their familiar order—*Matariʻi* bright above the mast, marking their course. The Tahitian crew, eight men chosen by Tu for their strength and experience, worked with quiet discipline. They carried no compass, no quadrant. Their sense of direction came from the shape of the swells, the shift of the wind, the flight of birds, the color of the water beneath them.

Nicholas sat beside Tua, the navigator and now a friend, his gaze following the older man's hands, trying to absorb rather than analyze.

"You see?" Tua said, tapping the gunwale with a calloused finger. His eyes stayed fixed on the horizon. "The wind pulls the water. The water shapes the waves. We listen. Some things we remember. Some we guess."

Nicholas did not pretend to understand. But he listened.

Markham, though ever skeptical, had begun to observe with a kind of grudging respect. His decision to come had been made quietly, but Nicholas had seen the gravity in it—the choice of a man stepping out of safety, out of ease, without illusion.

"Strangest damn way of navigating I ever saw, Mr. Cruwys," he muttered one evening, as the canoe held its line under a darkening sky. "But I'll not say it doesn't work."

Nicholas suspected that Tua navigated less by certainty than by instinct—correcting course by feel, by small corrections invisible to the untrained eye. It was not the unbroken tradition Atea had spoken of, nor the science Cook might recognize. But it was enough.

On the fifth night, the sky shifted. It began with stillness. The wind, so steady until then, faltered—then vanished. The swell slackened. The clouds, soft and high in the afternoon, thickened into a smothering quilt that dulled the stars to a faint and listless glow.

Nicholas woke to the first violent gust, the canoe lurching hard as the wind tore at the sail. Markham, already awake, had braced himself against the gunwale, his eyes flicking between the sky and the sea.

"Something's coming, sir," he said grimly.

Then the squall was upon them.

The wind struck like a broadside, slamming into the canoe with such force that Nicholas had to seize the nearest line or be pitched bodily into the sea. The crew scrambled to reef the sails—their movements swift, unpanicked—but the wind came too fast. Rain sheeted down in a blinding, deafening torrent.

A wave, black and immense, rose out of the night and broke clean over them. For a moment, Nicholas was underwater, his grip on the lashings the only thing between him and the abyss. Salt stung his eyes, filled his mouth; the cold stunned him. Then he broke the surface, gasping, spitting brine, vision clearing just enough to see Markham still aboard, soaked but alive, his fingers white on the hull.

The crew fought the sea like men under fire—bailing, hauling, lashing down what could be saved. Tua shouted orders in clipped, urgent syllables. Nicholas could scarcely hear them above the wind's shriek, but the men moved as one, unhesitating.

It was three hours before the storm blew itself out, leaving them adrift on a slate-grey sea. The canoe had held. One sail was torn in two places, the rigging strained, their provisions battered and soaked.

Nicholas sat, drenched and shaking, breath coming hard, arms numb with effort.

Markham exhaled, flexing his fingers as though confirming they still obeyed. "Well, Mr. Cruwys," he said, voice hoarse, "I'll give it this—it's a damn sight drier below decks on a frigate."

Nicholas laughed, short, breathless. He was cold and battered. And yet, looking around—at Tua calmly inspecting the lines, at the others already setting about repairs—he knew they had endured.

For twelve more days they pressed westward. Supplies ran low; fresh water was rationed with care. The crew fished when they could, but the hunger gnawed steadily. The sky stayed merciful, the wind reliable, but even so, the wear began to show.

Then, just after dawn on the eighteenth morning since their departure, a voice rang out from the prow.

"*Manu!*"

A bird—high, fast, moving with purpose. Land was near.

And then they saw it: a distant green hump on the horizon. A murmur of relief passed through the crew like a breeze after stifling heat.

Twelve hours later, as the day's light began to fade, with the green heights of *Savai'i* towering before them—six thousand feet above the sea, vast and certain against the sky, they rounded the nearest headland. Nicholas stared.

A ship.

Not a Royal Navy ship, nor a Spanish merchantman, nor one of the Dutch East India Company's lumbering Indiamen. A brigantine—sleek, low in the water, her sails furled, her hull painted dark. A flag fluttered lazily from her stern, its colors indistinct in the dying light.

Markham stiffened beside him. "Portuguese," he muttered. "Didn't expect to see one of those out here."

Nicholas, scanning her lines, felt a flicker of hope. England and Portugal had been allies for centuries. If there was any foreign flag they might safely approach, it was this one.

"We go to her," Nicholas said.

Markham gave him a glance. "You're certain of that, sir?"

Nicholas nodded. "She's a trader. And we've nothing to lose."

Markham exhaled through his nose, then rolled his shoulders, as if shedding misgivings. "Aye, sir. Let's see what this rogue's about."

The brigantine rocked gently in the harbor swell as the *pahi* paddled alongside, greeted by welcoming gestures from the crew. It had been eighteen months since Nicholas had last stood on *Resolution's* deck, and the broad sweep of a ship's planked decks—the feel of her motion underfoot—was at once familiar and foreign, like the memory of a language he no longer spoke fluently. The air smelled of tar and salt, with a trace of tobacco and something citrus—dried fruit, perhaps, stored below against scurvy. Markham followed a pace behind, slower, more cautious, his eyes sweeping the deck: the crew, the rigging, the disposition of weapons. He was a man who trusted instinct over optimism, and instinct told him to keep his guard.

The Portuguese captain regarded them with what looked like quiet amusement. He stood with the ease of long command—relaxed, but never careless. There was a way he held himself, weight evenly distributed, that suggested a man who had learned never to turn his back too readily.

As Nicholas stepped forward, the captain's eyes moved over him, his sun-darkened skin, the tapa cloth, the shark tooth pendant at his throat. Then to Markham: broader, older, his arms marked with tatau, his posture unmistakably that of a sailor turned watchman. The captain's gaze lingered a beat longer, then he gave a slight nod, as if confirming a private guess.

"And what do I call you?" the captain asked in accented English, his tone easy but edged—like a man who weighed every word and seldom gave one away. "You have the look of a man who does not belong here, *senhor*."

Nicholas met his gaze steadily, considering. The captain of the *Santa Rita* was of medium height but broad through the shoulders, his dark hair tied carelessly at the nape, his coat unbuttoned in the tropical heat. A pistol hung at one hip, a sword at the other. A man, Nicholas suspected, who belonged to no country but his own ambitions. Perhaps thirty-five or forty, though the lines in his face told of hard years and harder choices. His dark eyes gleamed with intelligence, and the worn hilt at his side suggested a man of trade—or smuggling. Or piracy, depending on the day.

"Nicholas Cruwys," he said, inclining his head slightly. "Midshipman in His Majesty's Navy. This is Thomas Markham, my quartermaster." He paused, then added, mild but pointed, "And you have the look of a man who belongs nowhere."

The captain laughed, tipping his head. "Ah, but *you* are right, my friend. I go where the wind takes me. And today, it has taken me here."

He looked Nicholas over again, slower this time. "Midshipman. Quartermaster. Yet you arrive in a canoe. I think you have not come from England recently."

Nicholas did not rise to it. "We had a ship. *Resolution.* We were separated from her nearly eighteen months ago, in the Society Islands."

"*Resolution*?" the captain repeated, his brows lifting. "Captain Cook's ship?"

"The same."

The captain was silent a moment, regarding them anew. Then he nodded to one of his men, a wiry fellow with gold hoops in his ears and a knife at his belt, who vanished below without a word.

He turned back to Nicholas.

"I imagine you have a story worth hearing."

Nicholas gave a slight nod, understanding that no offer of aid would come before their value had been weighed. He did not rush, nor embellish; life in the islands had taught him that patience was often the stronger hand.

"We were part of Captain Cook's expedition," he said. "Surveying the islands of the South Pacific. We were sent on an extended mission to chart the reefs west of Tahiti. A storm took us before we could return. *Resolution* sailed on, believing us lost."

He let that rest in the air.

"Since then, we've lived among the islanders. Learned their ways. But our duty remains: to return to the world we left behind."

The captain listened without comment, his fingers tapping idly on the hilt of his sword. At length he said, "And so you mean to sail west. Hoping to find passage home."

"That is our goal."

The captain tilted his head. "And yet, *senhor*, you have made no request of me."

Nicholas smiled, just slightly. "Not yet."

The captain laughed—a sharp, genuine laugh, not unkind. "I like a man who does not beg before the answer is given." He gestured broadly to his ship. "I am bound for Macau and the Pearl River before year's end. I have business in these waters first. If you wish to sail with me, you are welcome—provided, of course, that when we reach Macau, you pay fair passage."

Nicholas met his gaze without blinking. "And if we cannot?"

The captain's smile did not falter, but his hand paused on the hilt of his sword.

"I do not deal in debts, *senhor*. Only agreements. If you do not pay, then you will find your own way from whatever port I leave you in."

Nicholas inclined his head. It was a fair offer, from a man like this. "Then we have an understanding."

"Good." The captain extended his hand. "I am Duarte Silva."

Nicholas took it, noting the rough calluses—hands that had known the sword, and the rope as well.

The morning air was thick with the scent of salt and damp earth, the tide pulling gently at the shore where the pahi voyaging canoe lay drawn up on the Samoan beach, awaiting her departure for Tahiti. The beach, a narrow curve of pale sand beneath the towering green slopes of *Savai'I*, was quiet, save for the rhythmic hush of the waves and the occasional cry of a seabird overhead. The last embers of their night's fire smouldered low, tendrils of smoke curling into the still air, marking the place where they had spent their final hours feasting and laughing among the people who had carried them this far.

Tua stood apart, arms crossed over his chest, watching as Nicholas and Markham made their final preparations. There had been no talk of turning back, no second-guessing. Their path had been fixed the moment Nicholas stepped aboard the *Santa Rita*. And yet, standing now beside the canoe that had borne them across over a thousand miles of open ocean, he felt the weight of what they were leaving behind.

The farewell was brief, as all such partings were among Tua's people. There were no speeches, no lingering embraces—only quiet words, the clasp of a hand, a nod that carried more than any farewell ever could.

"You have learned much," Tua said, his deep voice steady. "But you will never learn all."

Nicholas met his gaze and understood. He had been given a glimpse into another world, a different way of knowing the sea—but it was not his to keep. He was bound for another.

Markham, never one for sentiment, gripped Tua's hand in a firm shake. "I won't insult you by saying I'll be back," he said. "But I won't forget."

Tua gave him a faint smile—a rare thing, and all the more meaningful for it. With that, there was nothing more to say.

The canoe was pushed into the surf, her twin hulls rising and falling in the shallows as her crew leapt aboard with the ease of men born to water. Tua was the last to step in, his silhouette stark against the morning sun as he raised a hand—not in farewell, but in acknowledgment.

Nicholas and Markham watched as the *pahi's* sails were hoisted, caught the wind, and carried her out into the open blue. She moved as she always had—light, effortless, a part of the sea itself.

They turned toward the ship's boat waiting in the shallows, manned by four of Silva's crew. The Portuguese sailors watched without comment, their eyes curious, unreadable. The wood of the oars creaked softly in their locks as Nicholas and Markham waded out and climbed aboard. With a few clean strokes, the boat pulled away from the shore, carrying them back toward the *Santa Rita*—toward a world of ledgers, of iron and gunpowder, of shifting alliances and uncertain returns.

Later, on the quarterdeck, Nicholas looked out to sea, his gaze lingering on the tiny dwindling shape of the canoe against the sky. Then it was gone. He turned his eyes forward, to the ship that waited, and to the life that called him back.

The *Santa Rita* moved as only an independent trading ship could—beholden to no crown, bound to no colony, answering only to wind and market. She slipped along the edges of empire, where Dutch merchants, Spanish governors, and Chinese traders spoke in coin, not allegiance. For Nicholas Cruwys, it was to be an education unlike anything the Royal Navy had ever provided.

Though nominally a passenger, Nicholas had volunteered to stand regular watch—not from obligation, but to stave off the creeping inertia of idleness. Captain Silva gave him a long, speculative look, then nodded once and said, "*Muito bem.* The sea is full of volunteers—most drift back to their hammocks by the second night."

But he assigned Nicholas to the starboard watch without further protest.

The long hours aloft or pacing the deck offered unexpected opportunities to learn the subtleties of Silva's world. Portuguese phrases, once heard as incomprehensible commands, gradually took shape—words forming patterns, patterns forming speech. "Your ear is good," Silva remarked one evening, leaning against the taffrail with a cigar in hand, its tip glowing faintly against the dark. "Most Englishmen butcher our language beyond repair."

"The islands taught me to listen," Nicholas replied in Portuguese, the words settling more easily with each passing day. "When your life depends on understanding, you learn quickly."

Silva smiled. "So you do."

In their sixth week aboard, south of Mindanao, the *Santa Rita* had encountered a Sulu *prahu,* sleek and fast, prowling for soft targets. It veered off the moment the brigantine's gunports opened, but the encounter had prompted Silva to reappraise his passengers—with interest, and caution.

"Your Royal Navy teaches you the sword, I presume," said Silva the following morning, his eyes narrowing against the glare as Nicholas stepped barefoot onto the deck, coatless in the rising heat.

"It does," Nicholas replied, adjusting his grip on the wooden practice blade Silva handed him. "My skills are adequate, I believe. I was fortunate enough to take the prize in arms at the Academy."

Silva raised an eyebrow—not in disbelief, but in fresh appraisal. "Ah. So not merely 'adequate,' then. English modesty, or misdirection?"

"Modesty," Nicholas said, not quite smiling. "But I've no illusions. The *salle* and the deck are different ground."

"That, at least, is true." Silva's grin was quick and sharp. "The Navy teaches you to fence like a gentleman. I will teach you to fight like a man who expects no quarter."

What followed was a lesson in what Silva called *verdadeira esgrima*—true swordsmanship. He moved with the easy precision of someone who had fought more times than he could recall. His style was born not in academies but on wharves and decks, in boarding actions and ambuscades down narrow alleys ashore. There were no formal guards, no pauses for points. Only shifts of weight, slashing arcs, sudden feints—moves meant not to impress but to kill.

Nicholas matched him stroke for stroke, parrying with instinct, his footwork light, his ripostes sharp and economical. The rhythm of the bout quickened. Silva's eyes lit with something between approval and curiosity.

"Ah," he said, stepping back after a particularly nimble exchange. "You've been taught well. And not just in theory."

"The cutlass is not a subtle blade," Nicholas said, his breathing steady. "But I was taught to respect it."

"And to use it," Silva replied, tapping the side of his own practice blade lightly against Nicholas's shoulder. "Good. Then we'll not start at the beginning. We'll start where things become interesting."

Each morning, they met amidships, Silva clearing the deck of onlookers with a curt word before beginning. With wooden facsimiles of different fighting blades, they engaged in bouts that left Nicholas bruised, humbled—but sharper with each passing day.

"Faster," Silva would snap, striking with serpentine speed at Nicholas's exposed side. "In the time you just took to think, your entrails would be cooling on the planks."

Where the sword tested Nicholas's reflexes, the pistol demanded steadiness. Silva was a master of the flintlock—able to strike a swinging lantern at twenty paces, a feat that seemed to defy the weapon's infamous inaccuracy. His firearms were meticulously kept: barrels oiled, flints fresh, powder stored in sealed copper to guard against sea damp.

"The pistol is not a gentleman's weapon," Silva told him one morning, as they stood at the stern rail firing at floating scraps cast over by the boatswain. "It's not for honor. It's for effect. Aim for the center of the man."

By the third week of these lessons, Nicholas could feel the change in his body: his stance more grounded, his movements more instinctive. The Navy had given him discipline. Silva's teaching gave him something else—a feral edge, a way of seeing that measured every shift in light, every twitch of motion aboard ship.

Markham, coiling line nearby, watched one of their sessions and offered a dry appraisal. "At this rate, sir, you'll be a proper corsair by the time we reach Macau."

Nicholas wiped sweat from his brow, breathing hard. "Let's hope it doesn't come to that."

Over the next several months, the *Santa Rita* ranged across the southwest Pacific, exposing Nicholas to sights and experiences he could never have imagined in his Devonshire youth. Silva kept him close during his dealings, and Nicholas came to observe not only the intricacies of barter and negotiation, but the broader codes of the layered social worlds of foreign ports, and of men's needs.

Nicholas learned that a gentleman must choose his pleasures with the same care as his wine or his words. While the common sailors flocked to louder brothels, thick with risk and rough promise, Silva, ever the quiet tutor, steered him toward those establishments that catered to a more discerning clientele—places where the linen was clean, discretion expected, and companionship offered with a degree of grace and mutual regard, not vulgarity. It was not prudery, Silva said once, but practice. The business of being a man lay in knowing what one could enjoy without becoming enslaved by it.

In those quiet, lamplit rooms, some no more than perfumed silences, a murmured name, a passing warmth, Nicholas felt no shame, no internal division. What he had shared with Atea had never been possessive, never shaped by the jealousies of European romance. He knew, with a conviction born of their time together, that she would not have disapproved. In her world, love and desire were not enemies. The body was not a battleground for the soul.

And yet, as the months passed, Nicholas found the edges of her memory softening. Nearly a year gone, and her voice—once so distinct—had grown elusive, her face less immediate, as if seen through rippling water. He did not blame the women whose touch brought momentary ease, nor himself for seeking it. But the fading of Atea's image unsettled him more than any dalliance ever could. It was not guilt he felt, but sorrow—that something once so vivid could recede, not through neglect, but by the quiet workings of time.

She had belonged to a world apart, and he knew now he would never return to it. The grief was no longer raw, but it had deepened into something quieter, a private keel beneath the surface of his days, steady, unseen, and unforgotten.

They traded heavily in the Spice Islands, bartering nutmeg in the Banda archipelago, where Silva's reputation earned them welcome among men who would slit a stranger's throat for so much as an extra weight in cloves. The scent of spices hung heavy on the wind, cinnamon and mace mingling with the salt air, the holds of the *Santa Rita* gradually filling with carefully packed barrels and crates. The prices fetched in Macau would be four times what Silva had paid, and Nicholas began to understand the violent mathematics of the spice trade that had driven European powers to claim these islands, no matter the cost in blood.

In the markets of the Spice Islands, where Dutch authority extended only as far as the range of their cannons, Nicholas witnessed deals struck with grave solemnity, ritual exchanges of gifts followed by hard-nosed haggling in a patois of Malay, Portuguese, and Dutch. Silva taught him the significance of certain gestures, the meaning behind the seating arrangements, the subtle insults conveyed in the offering of specific beverages. It was diplomacy on the knife's edge, where one misstep could transform a profitable exchange into a deadly confrontation.

They moved on to the Malay coast, where they met Arab merchants with dhows heavy with silk, and even further to French-controlled Pondicherry, where rum and muskets changed hands in dark alleys. In these bustling ports, Nicholas became acquainted with the varied facets of port life, including the understanding that the choices one made, even in leisure, reflected upon one's character and standing. Silva's dealings were conducted with the studied neutrality of a man who recognized no flag but profit, and Nicholas observed with mounting fascination how the Portuguese captain navigated not just the treacherous channels between islands, but the equally dangerous waters of international trade beyond the auspices of European patrols.

"Neutrality is power, Nicholas," Silva said one evening, as they sat in his cabin sharing a bottle of Madeira—aged by the round voyage to India and back, its caramelized sweetness prized by those who knew. "The Portuguese empire may wane, but Portuguese traders endure, because we can speak to all sides. Remember that, if ever you command your own ship."

It was three days after they had left the Banda archipelago, the *Santa Rita* making good time under a fresh southeast wind, when the lookout's cry broke the routine of the morning watch.

"Sail! Three sails to windward!"

Nicholas was at the rail in an instant, glass extended. The ships had emerged as if conjured—rising from behind a small islet that until moments ago had masked their approach. Even at this distance, he could tell they were no traders. Their low, rakish silhouettes and the way they cut through the water with predatory urgency left little doubt.

"Praus," Silva said beside him, his voice cool despite the imminent danger. "Malay pirates. Fast, and well-placed. They've been waiting for us."

He turned to his first mate, issuing a rapid stream of orders that sent men racing to battle stations. Gun crews sprang to their posts. The master gunner was already shouting for tompions to be pulled, powder brought up from below.

Markham appeared at Nicholas's side, his weathered face set in the same grim line Nicholas had seen when storm clouds built on the horizon.

"Looks like you'll be making use of those new skills, sir," he said, testing the edge of the heavy boarding axe Silva had handed him from the ship's armory.

Nicholas nodded, feeling not panic, but a steady clarity take hold. His hand moved to the curved hanger at his hip—a sailor's blade, plain but sharp-edged, honed to slice clean through rope or bone. It lacked the ornate basket hilt of a naval officer's dress sword, but it had a weight that felt earned.

Silva had passed it to him a few weeks before with a dry remark: "This is no gentleman's ornament. It's a fighting blade. It's ended more men than any gilded court sword."

Now, Nicholas drew it without hesitation. He glanced down at the blade in his hand, at the careful geometry of the edge, the clean curve meant for nothing but violence. He felt no trembling, no racing pulse. Only a curious stillness.

He had been in danger before—storms, sickness, the cold mathematics of lost bearings—but this was different. This was men against men. And some, before the sun set, would likely be dead.

Was he afraid?

He didn't think so. But he wasn't sure what fear was supposed to feel like anymore. Whatever was coming, it no longer felt abstract. It felt close. Real.

He gripped the hanger a little tighter.

"We'll see," he said, "if I've learned anything useful."

Silva strode the deck with assured confidence that steadied his crew, barking instructions as the gun crews worked with practiced efficiency. The brigantine's eight six-pounder cannon, four to a side, were cleared for action, their black muzzles protruding from the opened ports. Small arms were passed out: muskets, pistols, and cutlasses for the crew to repel boarders, if it came to that.

"They'll try to come alongside and board us," Silva said, handing Nicholas a loaded pistol to pair with his sword. "Their craft are too light to mount heavy guns, but they carry forty, maybe fifty men each, armed and eager. If they get aboard in numbers, we're finished."

The three praus were closing fast, their triangular sails full-bellied with wind. They moved in a practiced formation, fanning out to approach from different angles. Each was sixty feet long, narrow-waisted, with high, carved prows shaped like fantastical beasts—symbols meant to frighten as much as inspire.

"They're trying to head us off," Nicholas observed, watching their approach. "Catch us in a pincer."

Silva nodded approvingly. "You see it. Yes, they want to force us to choose which one to evade, leaving us vulnerable to the others." He turned to the helmsman. "Steady as she goes. Let them come. We show no fear"

The distance closed with alarming speed. At five hundred yards, Silva ordered the starboard guns run out. The gun captain waited, allowing the lead prau to close further, holding fire until Silva's command would ensure maximum effect.

"Ready!" Silva called, his eyes fixed on the narrowing gap.

At two hundred yards, the prau's deck came into view—crowded with men brandishing weapons that caught the sun in hard flashes. Their war cries rose over the water, shrill and guttural, meant to break nerves before blades ever crossed.

"Fire!"

The deck shuddered as the four guns roared in near-unison, coughing smoke and flame. Nicholas watched the iron shot tear through the air—two balls struck just below the waterline, the others smashed into the hull higher up. Wood exploded in splinters. Screams rose where war cries had been. The prau staggered in the water, listing slightly as seawater poured through its side—but it kept coming.

"They're still coming," Nicholas said, moving to the starboard rail, pistol in one hand, hanger in the other.

"They're committed now," Silva replied, watching the gun crews to reload. "Pride and desperation, always a dangerous mix."

From amidships, the first mate shouted and pointed, another prau was sweeping wide to flank them from the opposite side.

Silva cursed under his breath. He saw it at once: the trap was closing. Two minutes, maybe less, and they'd be caught between the praus with half their guns empty.

"Mr. Cruwys, take charge of the swivel guns on the foc'sle," Silva ordered. "Focus on the second vessel."

Nicholas sprinted forward. Two small swivel guns were mounted along the rail, each manned by a pair of sailors. The pieces were already loaded, bags of musket balls packed to tear through flesh at close range. He took a quick bearing on the approaching prau, adjusted the angle of both guns, and waited.

As the vessel came within range, Nicholas shouted, "Fire!"

The swivels barked, unleashing their deadly scatter. The pirate deck erupted—men pitched overboard, others dropped where they stood. But the prau kept coming, fresh attackers surging forward to replace the fallen.

Aft, the first vessel had closed the gap. Grappling hooks arced through the smoke and bit into the *Santa Rita's* rails and rigging. As crewmen rushed to cut the lines, the third prau emerged from the haze, sweeping toward the brigantine's stern like a knife aimed at her spine.

Silva bellowed orders, redirecting men to the aft rail. The starboard battery spoke again, the reloaded guns roaring in unison. The third prau took the full blast amidships. Her hull cracked, folded inward. Men leapt over the sides as she began to sink.

But the moment of triumph vanished in a heartbeat.

With a splintering crash, the first prau slammed into the *Santa Rita's* starboard quarter. The shock sent men sprawling. Before they could rise, the pirates were upon them, swarming over the rails, kris daggers flashing.

Nicholas tightened his grip on the hanger, its slightly curved blade catching the sunlight with a predatory gleam. Designed for the slash, the weapon's weight was perfectly balanced for the quick, brutal cuts Silva had drilled into him. As his fingers closed around the worn sharkskin grip, the lessons of the past weeks crystallized into instinct.

The first attacker came at him with a roar, swinging a heavy parang in a wide, deadly arc. Months ago, Nicholas might have retreated or attempted a formal parry. Instead, he stepped into the swing— shoulder low, weight forward—and drove the hanger up beneath the man's ribs in a sharp, rising thrust.

The impact jolted through his arm. The blade met resistance, then punched deep. Hot blood spattered his wrist and forearm. The pirate gave a strangled grunt, less rage than surprise, and Nicholas saw his face contort, mouth working soundlessly, eyes already losing focus. A length of glistening red slipped from the gash as the man collapsed, dragging the blade partway down with him.

Nicholas yanked it free with a wet, tearing sound. The steel came back slick and warm in his grip. For a heartbeat, that sound seemed louder than the battle around him.

Then it was gone—swallowed in the din.

The deck was a chaos of individual struggles. Blades rang, pistols cracked, and men shouted and staggered across blood-slicked boards. Nicholas moved without thought now. The hanger rose and fell, his stance balanced, his steps precise. He fought with a cold clarity that felt both alien and inevitable, every cut Silva had taught him, every counter, now deployed without hesitation.

Markham was nearby, his powerful frame turning with brutal economy as he swung his boarding axe. The weapon rose and fell with grim certainty, clearing a wide arc around him.

"To the quarterdeck, sir!" he shouted, catching Nicholas's eye through the smoke and fury. "They're pressing for the aft rail."

Nicholas nodded and began fighting his way aft, parrying a thrust from a scarred pirate whose face was a lattice of ritual tattoos. He cut the man down with a swift stroke to the throat, then ducked as a spear whistled past his ear. Three more pirates barred his path to the quarterdeck, but before he could close, Silva appeared behind them, pistols drawn.

"Down!" the captain barked.

Nicholas dropped to one knee just as Silva fired both barrels. Two pirates fell in a tangle of limbs. Nicholas surged forward to meet the third, their blades colliding with a sharp, ringing clash.

This one was different—a leader, perhaps. His movements were controlled, precise. He parried Nicholas's first attack and launched a rapid sequence of cuts that forced him back a pace. They circled, probing, steel flashing as each sought an opening.

Across the deck, the tide was shifting. The second prau, raked again by the swivel guns, was retreating, and the crew of the *Santa Rita* was pressing the remaining boarders toward the rails. But the fight was far from won.

Nicholas's opponent feinted high, then cut low—a classic setup, meant to draw the guard. But Silva had taught him to watch the hips, not the blade. Nicholas pivoted, letting the slash pass to his left, and countered with the diagonal riposte Silva had drilled into him a hundred times.

The blade sliced across the pirate's chest—not deep, but enough to stagger. Nicholas pressed, relentless. *When you have the advantage, finish it,* Silva had said. *Mercy in battle is an indulgence that costs lives.*

The man recovered faster than expected. As Nicholas moved to close, he drew a small throwing knife from his belt and snapped it toward Nicholas's face.

Nicholas jerked aside—but not fast enough. The blade traced a burning line across his cheek before clattering to the deck. The moment's hesitation was all the pirate needed. He lunged, kris flashing toward Nicholas's midsection.

Nicholas twisted. The blade missed his organs but bit deep below the ribs. Pain erupted—hot, immediate. He staggered but stayed upright, swinging in a desperate backhand that caught his attacker across the throat.

The pirate dropped, blood pulsing from the wound in rhythmic, fading surges.

Nicholas stood swaying, one hand pressed to his side, warm blood seeping between his fingers. Around him, the battle blurred. The clash of steel, the cries of men, the shouts of command, all faded to a distant roar behind the rushing in his ears.

He was dimly aware of Markham's voice, the quartermaster fighting toward him.

Through a haze of pain, Nicholas saw Silva leading a final charge that broke the attackers and drove the surviving pirates back to their crippled vessel. The prau pulled away, its deck crowded with the wounded, leaving their dead behind. The *Santa Rita's* crew cheered, but Nicholas heard it as though underwater—distant, warped, slipping away.

He tried to take a step. His knees gave way. The deck surged up to meet him, the world tilting into darkness. The last thing he saw was Markham's face, tight with concern, and Silva's, expressionless, already gauging whether he would live.

Pain woke him.

It lanced up from his side in a hot, tearing wave—deep, ragged, alive with every breath. Something cold and damp pressed against the wound. The creak and sway of the ship only worsened it, each motion sending a jolt through the meat below his ribs. His face burned too, a sharp, stinging ache across one cheek.

He opened his eyes to a world too bright, too sharp. He tried to speak, but managed only a dry, rasping sound.

A face loomed over him, weathered, bearded, with eyes the color of iron. The ship's surgeon, a man Nicholas had seen but rarely spoken with. His hands were surprisingly gentle as they probed the wound, though each touch sent fresh waves of pain surging through his side.

"He's awake," the surgeon called to someone beyond Nicholas's field of view. "Fever hasn't taken hold—yet. The night will tell."

Footsteps approached: the soft, deliberate tread of Silva's Spanish leather boots. The captain's face appeared above him, studying Nicholas with the same cool scrutiny he might give a damaged sail or a barrel gone sour.

"The blade went deep," Silva said, speaking to the surgeon rather than to Nicholas. "Will he live?"

"If infection stays clear. I've cleaned it, packed it with herbs and honey. The rest is God's concern."

Silva nodded, then leaned closer. "You hear that? No dying on my ship, *Inglés*. It's bad luck. And I've invested too much in your education."

Nicholas tried to nod, but even that sent a jolt of pain through his ribs. Silva seemed to read it all the same. His expression softened by a fraction.

"Rest now. The ship is safe, the pirates gone." He stood. "I need my cabin back within the week, so heal fast."

With that, he was gone, and darkness closed in once more.

Time lost its meaning after that. Nicholas drifted in and out of consciousness, caught in a liminal space between waking and dream. Sometimes he felt hands tending his wound, voices murmuring urgently above him. Other times, there was only darkness, and the steady throb of pain in his side.

Fever came and went, carrying strange visions in its wake: Atea walking beside him on an English beach; Cook and Silva deep in conversation at the captain's table; his father standing at the *Santa Rita's* rail, watching him with that same unreadable gaze.

Faces came and went at his bedside—Markham's quiet concern, the surgeon's focused scrutiny, and, now and then, Silva himself, checking on his investment.

Once, in the deepest hours of fever, he saw his mother. She sat beside him as she had in childhood, a cool hand resting on his brow. He tried to speak—to tell her all he had seen—but no sound came. His lips formed the words, but the world gave him no voice.

The fever broke on the third night.

He woke drenched in sweat, the pain in his side dulled from searing to bearable. His mouth was dry, his limbs heavy with weakness, but his mind was his own again.

He lay still, taking quiet inventory of his body.

Moonlight filtered through the stern windows of Silva's cabin, casting pale, restless patterns across the deck as the ship rolled gently in the swell. Nicholas became aware, dimly, of a figure seated in the shadows—Markham, head drooping in exhausted sleep, his vigil kept despite the weight of his own fatigue.

"Water," Nicholas rasped.

Markham jerked awake at once, alert in an instant, as years of night watches had trained him. He rose, poured water from a pitcher, and knelt beside the cot, lifting Nicholas's head with care.

"Easy, sir," he murmured, steadying the cup. "Small sips. Too much, and it won't stay down."

Nicholas obeyed, the coolness spreading through him like a reprieve. When he had drunk what he could, Markham eased him back, his movements practiced, almost tender.

"How long?" Nicholas asked, his voice rough but clearer.

"Three days since the attack," said Markham, the relief audible. "The surgeon feared you wouldn't see the second night. Fever ran high, you were talking the whole time. Tahiti, Cook, places I've never heard of."

Nicholas closed his eyes, absorbing it. Three days lost to delirium. He had never been wounded before. Never known the helplessness of being wholly in another man's hands. It unsettled him more than he cared to admit.

"And the ship?"

"Damaged in the quarter from the boarding collision, but sound enough," Markham said. "We lost four. Seven wounded besides you." His face darkened. "The pirates fared worse. One sunk. One limped off, half her crew down. The third broke off and never closed."

Nicholas nodded, and winced, the motion tugged sharply at his side. "And Silva?"

"The captain is well. Gave up his cabin for you—not something I expected of the man. He's been looking in on you regular, though he does his best to make it seem accidental." Markham's mouth twitched in the ghost of a smile. "I believe you've impressed him, sir. Told the surgeon to use his own Madeira for the tincture. 'Good wine makes good blood,' he said."

That drew a faint smile from Nicholas. "Silva counts every *real* in his ledger. If he's pouring good Madeira into me, he must expect a return."

"Help me sit," he said, shifting.

Pain burst white in his right side. Markham's hand came firm to his shoulder.

"Not yet, sir. The surgeon was plain, you're to lie still till the wound begins to close. It's near your liver. A wrong move could start the bleeding again."

His tone, though respectful, was final. For a moment he was no longer the subordinate but the man who had seen such wounds too often to flinch from plain counsel.

"I've seen men survive the blade, only to die three days later from pride and movement."

Nicholas let the breath out slowly. "Very well. But I'll speak with Silva when he's next free."

"He'll be glad to find you in your right senses, sir. Keeps asking after your 'English constitution,' as he puts it."

As if conjured by the mention of his name, Silva appeared in the doorway, his silhouette edged by lantern-light from the passage beyond. He paused, regarding Nicholas in silence before stepping fully into the cabin.

"Welcome back to the living," he said, his tone dry as bone. "You chose a most inopportune moment to take your rest, Mr. Cruwys." He shook his head, "I must tell you," Silva said, "I expected somewhat better from a man I have personally instructed in swordplay. Your form was correct, until the final moment. There, you pressed too eagerly."

"The lesson," Nicholas rasped, motioning faintly toward his bandaged side, "remains with me."

"As it should. Lessons written in blood—those are not soon erased."

He leaned forward, his expression sharpening. The usual amusement faded; what remained was thoughtful, grave.

"You acquitted yourself with great address. That captain, he was not a mere pirate. No. He had training. Discipline. He knew the forms of combat practiced in his country—fast, precise, meant to kill. And many men—good men—have died by his hand."

Silva inclined his head in that subtle, deliberate way Nicholas had come to recognise. "Your posture was good. Your responses were correct. But there is one lesson more: even the most well-conducted engagement may still draw its price. The blood-toll—it does not wait, and it does not ask permission."

"The ship?" Nicholas asked.

"We have made repairs sufficient for our purpose." Silva's voice held no concern. "Indeed, the attack has simplified our route. There was a certain Chinese official in Mindanao who had begun to take an unwholesome interest in our cargo. Now, we know, and we bypass that port altogether and make directly for Macau."

His eyes gleamed with quiet satisfaction.

"Sometimes misfortune reshapes itself into opportunity, if one is flexible enough to see it."

Nicholas nodded. Of course. For Silva, even an ambush at sea was a matter for the ledger, costs weighed, losses assessed, a new course charted.

"Your goods remain untouched," Silva went on, "When you are stronger, we shall review your accounts. The latest rumours from Canton are favourable. Certain luxuries grow scarce with the unrest further west. This means good prices—if one has the goods, and the nerve to sell them."

Nicholas felt an odd surge of gratitude for the conversation. Silva did not speak to him as an invalid to be humoured, but as a fellow merchant temporarily delayed in his affairs. It was, in its way, a mark of regard.

"Thank you," Nicholas said. "For the use of your cabin, and for your instruction."

Silva waved the words aside with a flick of his fingers. "You may consider it an investment in your continuing education. The lesson of the *kris* is a sharp one. No man's skill is proof against every wound. The true measure is this: whether he heals, learns, and returns to the fray wiser than he was."

Over the next three weeks, Nicholas endured the slow, ungentle work of recovery. The wound in his right abdomen closed by degrees, though it remained sore and pulled sharply when he turned too quickly.

Each day brought a quiet progression: sitting upright unaided, pacing the cabin with care, finally standing on the quarterdeck again to feel the wind on his face. Markham remained at his side throughout, steady, uncomplaining, enforcing the surgeon's orders with the calm authority of one who had seen too many men undo their own healing.

And in the stillness of those long hours, Nicholas found himself dwelling not only on the fight, but on its proximity—the brute intimacy of it. Blade meeting flesh. The wet shock of impact. The final exhalation of a man struck through.

He had killed two men. Killed them cleanly, his mind and reflexes trained honed like that edge of the sword itself. Wounded two others he could recall in the chaotic intensity of the hand-to-hand fighting, though in the press of bodies on the blood-slicked deck, there may have been more. Those men had faces, perhaps families waiting in villages upon these islands, lives now severed by his hand as cleanly as the edge of his blade had severed flesh.

There had been no warning, no overt deliberation, only the narrowing of time, the rising blade catching the sunlight, the decision made before thought had time to intervene. He had moved swiftly, as necessity demanded, and felt nothing in the moment but the economy of the act: parry, thrust, withdraw, slash.

It was only afterward, alone in the cot with the ship creaking gently about him, that he registered the strangeness of it—that such a thing could pass without some great shudder of the soul.

Perhaps that would come later. Or perhaps it would not come at all.

He did not know whether to be disturbed by that.

The wound would heal; that much was clear. But it would leave its mark, something had closed behind him, and could not be re-entered. Was it the last form of innocence?

They were two days out from Surabaya, the Java Sea lying broad and heavy under a pale sky, when Silva appeared at the doorway of the chartroom. Nicholas had taken the small space over by quiet consent, spreading his instruments and papers on the sloped writing desk just abaft the mainmast companion. He was working now by the angle of the light, transcribing reef notations onto fresh chart-paper with a fine brass divider.

At his elbow lay the bamboo tube he had fashioned in Tahiti—sealed with pitch, wrapped in sailcloth, the ends bound with waxed twine. It contained the tapa cloth originals of his surveys, drawn in the lagoons and headlands of Bora Bora months ago, now carried with near-religious care.

Silva tapped once on the frame. "Mr. Cruwys—might I see your charts?"

Nicholas looked up. "Certainly, sir."

He cleared a corner of the desk and carefully unrolled one of the fair copies—neatly rendered in black and crimson ink on linen-backed stock. Beside it he placed the bamboo tube, then opened a smaller folio containing a second set of transcriptions, near-identical to the first, but rolled tighter and less annotated. The fine tapas cloth versions remained untouched—too delicate now for frequent use.

Silva examined the sheets in silence. He tilted one to the light, checked a bearing against the compass drawn in the corner, and tapped a reef passage lightly with one finger.

"These are very fine," he said. "Measured, consistent. I've seen masters with fewer soundings and less clarity."

"Thank you, Captain."

Silva gave a slight nod, then turned and returned a moment later carrying two cylindrical tubes—shorter than the bamboo one, but clearly of professional make: brass, lined with tin, each sealed with a turn-key cap and bearing a small stamped mark in Dutch script near the rim.

"I had these made in Surabaya," he said, setting them down with care. "They'll take a full roll. You'll find them tight enough to keep ink dry in a monsoon."

Nicholas reached out and took one of the tubes in hand. It was weighty, cleanly soldered, and cool to the touch. "They're remarkable. Thank you."

"Divide the contents," Silva said. "One copy in each. Store them apart—one forward, one aft. Redundancy is not extravagance. If the worst happens, you may only save one. Better one than none."

Nicholas gave a faint smile. "You've a low opinion of fate."

"I've a long acquaintance with it," Silva replied mildly. He paused, then added, "The sea does not preserve talent, my friend. Only preparation."

He glanced down again at the lines of reef and bearing. "Preserve these. If nothing else survives of us, they may yet speak."

By the time they entered the South China Sea, Nicholas had resumed light duties. His side still warned him against sudden motion, and he moved with care. Silva, watching from the shade of the quarterdeck awning, gave a faint nod of approval and said nothing.

"You will carry that scar the rest of your days," he said, his voice calm, almost contemplative. "But scars are a sailor's biography, written on the body. They tell the story of where we've been, and what we've survived."

Nicholas nodded. His hand moved unconsciously to his side, where the kris blade had gone in. "I'm beginning to understand," he said, "that the journey changes us, whether we will it or not."

"Indeed," Silva agreed, his weathered face thoughtful in the fading light. "The sea strips away pretense. It reveals the true timber beneath the paint. Some men break under its weight. Others"— he paused, glancing at Nicholas with a rare, appraising look—"others are tempered by it, like steel drawn from the fire."

Nicholas did not reply at once. But he held the older man's gaze, and the silence between them had the shape of understanding.

"Speaking of change," Silva said, producing a small ledger from within his coat, "your goods have come through the voyage entirely unhurt. The porcelain remains intact, and the textiles have taken no water." He handed the book to Nicholas. "While you were recovering, I took the liberty to update your accounts. The rumours from Macau are favourable, certain luxuries grow scarce, which means better prices for those who arrive with goods to sell."

Nicholas accepted the ledger and scanned its pages. Silva's figures were, as always, exact to the last farthing. The tidy columns represented more than potential profit—they were a thread to the future. If—when—he returned to England, he would need more than honourable service. A naval officer without ship or commission could expect few open doors, unless he brought capital of his own.

"I owe you for this, too," Nicholas said, lifting the book slightly. "Not only for the advance, which I believe I've now repaid—but for the instruction. The Navy teaches navigation and gunnery, yes. But not how a man survives by his wits in foreign ports."

Silva smiled, but only faintly. "Then let us say we are even. I consider this part of your education, Nicholas. In my view, the sailor who understands trade is never entirely at the mercy of events. Ships may founder, commissions be lost, but the skill to make profit—this is a thing that does not depend on flags or fortune."

CHAPTER SEVEN

Just seven days into the new year of 1780, Nicholas stood on deck watching the shore slip by as they approached Macau. The wide estuary of the Pearl River was lined with numerous islands along its western shore, and teemed with Chinese junks, their curious battened sails stretched taut on bamboo yards, their hulls painted in vivid hues and adorned with stylised eyes. Most were coastal traders, single-masted craft with high, ornate poop decks. Fishing sampans crowded the waterways.

Nicholas's eye was drawn to a larger vessel abandoned along the shore of one of the islands not far from the mainland, its hull half-buried in mud. It was high-sterned, broad-beamed, and long out of service, its paint flaking, its rigging long since stripped. One mast stood askew, the others collapsed like snapped spars, the whole listing slightly in the tide. It was unlike anything he had seen in the working trade, neither European nor of the familiar South China Sea type. He asked Silva about it, but the captain only gave a brief shrug. "A relic," he said. "From another time. China once sent ships across oceans. Now she waits, and others sail to her."

Macau came into view at last from the haze off the larboard bow, a sliver of Europe pressed against the immensity of China. Founded by the Portuguese in the sixteenth century, it had endured through a careful combination of diplomacy and bribery, securing a foothold in Chinese waters at a time when all other Europeans were barred from the Middle Kingdom. It stood as a testament to the tenacity of

Western ambition in the face of Oriental power: tolerated, but never embraced.

Through his glass the city was a curious hybrid. Jesuit churches stood beside Chinese temples, cobbled lanes twisted into alleys crowded with spice-sellers, goldsmiths, and Cantonese hawkers. The European quarter centred on the Praia Grande, a sweeping bay lined with elegant whitewashed houses and shuttered arcades. Beyond it sprawled the Chinese district, dense and inward-turning: a labyrinth of alleys and workshops where craftsmen laboured over silks, lacquerware, porcelain, and carved ivory destined for the West. The air was thick with the mingled scent of incense, oil smoke, and the dust of a thousand industries.

There were fewer European ships here than Nicholas had seen in Batavia or the Malacca Strait. A Dutch Indiaman lay anchored off the Praia Grande; a Spanish brig out of Manila swung at her moorings further up the harbour. Portuguese traders clustered close to the mole, their hulls broad and low, painted in the older style.

But no British ships.

Markham had expected at least one East Indiaman at anchor, or perhaps a Royal Navy sloop on station, or a some other British merchant ship resupplying before the turn of the monsoon. Yet as *Santa Rita* rounded the final headland and the full sweep of Macau's harbour opened before them, the Union Jack was conspicuously absent.

"Unusual, sir," Markham murmured at Nicholas's side, his brow drawn in quiet concern. "Macau always has British ships. Something's amiss."

Silva, standing just aft, caught the remark. He turned, a faint smile touching his mouth though not his eyes. "Perhaps your countrymen are otherwise engaged," he said, his tone mild but edged. "One of my men spoke with that bumboat alongside just now. News has come—your king is at war."

Nicholas stiffened. "War?"

Cook's expedition had departed England in a time of mounting tension with the American colonies, but not open conflict. They had sailed from a nation at peace. Now, like all long voyages, theirs had become a passage not only through distance, but through time. They had left one world and returned to find another.

Silva nodded, drawing a small tobacco pouch from his coat and filling his pipe with the careful economy of a man delivering unpleasant truths. "Your American colonies have risen in full revolt. France has joined them. Spain follows. It is no longer rebellion, it is war between empires."

Nicholas said nothing for a moment. This was not some distant colonial quarrel, it was a global contest. If Britain now stood against both France and Spain, there was little wonder her ships were absent from the South China Sea, for they would not likely sail without convoy.

"The East India Company still keeps its factory in Canton," Silva went on, striking a light for his pipe, "but their ships come less often now. The Cohong merchants grow uneasy. Too many debts unpaid."

Nicholas had heard of the Cohong, the official guild of Chinese merchants, appointed by the Emperor and entrusted with all trade with the West. They were gatekeepers to the riches of China, and their favour was not easily regained once lost.

"How current is this news?" he asked, his mind turning to charts, distances, the long drift of information across the globe.

Silva shrugged. "Six months, perhaps a little less. News does not fly to the East, but when your Britain and France quarrel, every port takes notice."

It was a Dutch trader at a tea warehouse the following day who filled in the details, first of the war, and then, more devastatingly, of Captain Cook and the expedition.

The private dining room at the rear of the Dutch factory offered a modest refuge from the January damp that crept through Macau's narrow lanes. A charcoal brazier lent the air a faint metallic tang; the shutters were drawn against the evening haze. Nicholas warmed his hands around a porcelain cup of tea, watching as Willem van Keppel, factor for the Dutch East India Company, unfolded a letter whose creases suggested a long and various journey.

"So—you wish to know of the wars, Captain?" Van Keppel's English was precise, his consonants cleanly struck. A Dutchman seasoned by decades in the tropics, his ruddy face betrayed little despite the reversals now pressing upon his nation. "I fear my knowledge is as dated as last year's almanac, though still fresher than your own, I dare say. I have wintered here while you were threading coral passages and waiting on monsoon tides."

He took a measured sip of genever from a squat, thick-bottomed glass.

"We know with certainty that our Republic remains officially at peace with Britain—though one would not guess it from their conduct at sea. They stop our ships at will, seize cargoes bound for neutral ports, and threaten St. Eustatius with blockade. Word from Batavia speaks of mounting British interest in the Coromandel coast—Negapatam in particular. Nothing confirmed, but the merchants have grown wary." A shadow passed over his features. "The warehouses there are full, they say."

"And the American rebellion?" Nicholas asked, his tone deliberately neutral.

Van Keppel offered a thin smile. "Still ongoing. The last reliable intelligence reached us in August, also via Batavia. General Clinton had withdrawn from South Carolina; there was heavy fighting in Virginia, though the particulars grow misty the farther east one travels. Yorktown was mentioned—some French success, I think—but I confess the names of these American places blur together for me."

He refilled his glass, the clear spirit catching the lamplight in a slow glimmer.

"The French and Spanish remain committed to the rebel cause, which does your government no favours. The division of British strength between three theatres is a circumstance devoutly welcomed in The Hague—though of course one cannot say so aloud."

He glanced toward the brazier, as if the red coals might overhear.

"In India," he continued, "the news is somewhat clearer. Hyder Ali grows more assertive by the month, encouraged—so it's said—by French whispers in Madras and beyond. Your Company's forces are stretched thin. Coote is expected to return, but has not yet taken the field. The Marathas appear to be drawing toward an accommodation with the British, though nothing is signed. It may complicate matters for everyone else."

Nicholas sipped his tea in silence.

"And hereabouts?" he said after a pause.

"The Tây Sơn rebellion continues in Annam," Van Keppel replied. "The Chinese Emperor is preoccupied in the west, dealing with unrest among the Muslim tribes. None of it touches us directly, though the Tây Sơn situation has troubled the rice trade to some degree."

Nicholas asked, "Annam?"

"What the French priests refer to as Cochinchina, and I've heard certain geographers call Vietnam," Van Keppel said. He tapped the letter on the table.

"This arrived from my cousin in Batavia three weeks ago. The British have increased their naval presence in the Straits of Malacca—two of our merchantmen were stopped and searched last month. They claimed to be hunting contraband, but in truth they mean to throttle our commerce and remind us who rules the sea."

He folded the letter with precise fingers, pressing each crease flat with the edge of his hand.

"We are caught between giants, *Mynheer*: the Chinese, who barely tolerate us; the British, who would see us ruined; the Portuguese, who cling to this rocky outpost; and the Spanish, who sit watchful in Manila. And all of us wait upon news already stale by the time it finds us."

He raised his glass once more, his smile dry.

"This is why I trade in tea and porcelain rather than in politics. With the former, at least, I may examine the wares before I hazard my purse."

Van Keppel poured another measure of genever—for himself, none offered—and sat back, regarding Nicholas with the quiet calculation of a man accustomed to weighing strangers by what they chose to say, and what they left unspoken.

He said no more. The silence that followed was not unfriendly, but nor did it beckon confidence. It was the sort of silence in which ships are bought and sold.

Nicholas set down his cup.

"Have you heard any news," he asked, "of *Resolution* and *Discovery*?"

Van Keppel raised his brows a fraction. "The ships?"

"Yes."

"I have," he said. "Though not recently. They were here—briefly—in November. Took on water and some provisions. Put out again within the fortnight. *Resolution* was foul below the waterline, I think, but they did not remain for careening."

Nicholas's expression did not change, but something in his bearing stilled.

"Did they say where they were bound?"

"The Cape, then England. They had been to Kamchatka, I was told. And before that—" He paused. "The Sandwich Islands. Do you know them?"

Nicholas looked up. "Yes."

Van Keppel nodded once, as if that answered something he had not asked.

"I assume you have heard nothing?"

"Only fragments," Nicholas said. "Nothing I trust."

"Then I will give you what I know," Van Keppel replied, setting down his glass. "Captain Cook is dead."

There was no sound in the room but the soft hiss of the brazier and the creak of one shutter in its frame.

Nicholas's jaw tightened, but he said only, "How?"

"Killed ashore. There was some quarrel, something stolen. He went to take one of their chiefs as a hostage, a thing he had done before, and not without success. But this time it went wrong. He was struck down in the surf. The body taken."

He spoke plainly, without embellishment.

Markham shifted beside him. "Was it quick?" he asked.

Van Keppel glanced his way. "I cannot say. The reports differ. Some say he was stabbed. Some say he was beaten. Some that only part of him was returned. Hands missing. Ritual, perhaps."

Nicholas's fingers rested on the edge of the table. Not clenched, but rigid.

"And the ship?" he asked.

"She endured. *Discovery* too. Clerke took command, but he was ill, dying, they said. He pressed north to the ice. Died in Kamchatka. Gore finished the voyage. They passed through here under his command. That much is certain."

Van Keppel refilled his glass with care. "A hard loss," he said, not unkindly. "Not only for England."

Nicholas inclined his head. He did not trust his voice.

Over the following days, Nicholas pieced together the full account, scraps of news gathered from traders, pilots, and European merchants. It verified what Van Keppel had said. Cook had returned to the Sandwich Islands in early 1779, after charting the North American coast and probing the Bering Strait in search of the fabled passage that had eluded every navigator before him. But something had gone wrong. A boat had been stolen; Cook had attempted to seize the island's king as leverage, a miscalculation that had cost him his life.

"Missed them," Markham muttered, arms folded, the disappointment plain in the slump of his shoulders. "By how long?"

"Just under a month," Nicholas replied. His voice was flat, but there was bitterness beneath it, a cold current running deep.

Markham let out a long breath. "Hell of a thing, sir."

Nicholas nodded. The irony was not lost on him. They had crossed half the Pacific—survived storms, thirst, hunger, and thatched their own sails with island-grown fibre. They had come in a vessel no Englishman would have trusted out of sight of land. And now, after all that, they had missed their ship by a handful of weeks.

Cook was dead. And the last link to that world, the men who had shared it with him, was gone.

If *Resolution* made it home, what would be said of Nicholas Cruwys? That he had vanished into the Pacific? That he had died nameless, island-lost, in some forgotten bay?

He stood a long moment, watching the ships shift at anchor, the tide whispering against the piers. The boy who had sailed from Portsmouth was gone, washed away, perhaps, in that first storm off Bora Bora. In his place stood someone else: a man thoroughly bred to sea, who could chart a course across half the world by sun and stars; who could speak Portuguese in a trade-room; who had killed in battle, felt the weight of a blade as it ended another's life, and once felt a blade nearly end his own. And more than all of that, he had known deep and full love—for a year, on a distant island, until it was lost to the sea and to fate.

The Pacific had remade him, just as it had taken Cook in the end.

He turned from the water and looked back toward the city. Macau bustled as ever, where trade knew no mourning, and men of all nations bought and sold the world for coin. The past had slipped its moorings.

What remained was the voyage still ahead.

The morning mist clung low over the waters of the Pearl River delta as the British East Indiaman *Vansittart* dropped anchor in the Macao roadstead. At more than a thousand tons, she towered above the smaller trading vessels that clustered nearby, her three tall masts and freshly painted black hull—with its crisp yellow strake—marking her unmistakably as one of John Company's finest. Built at the Perry yard in Blackwall in 1777, she had already completed two successful voyages to the East and was counted among the most dependable ships in the Company's fleet, now plying the lucrative China trade under the command of Captain James Burney, a seasoned officer with fifteen years at sea.

Nicholas stood on the Praia Grande, watching as the ship's boats were lowered into the still, silty water. A ripple of feeling passed through him—part anticipation, part relief. After a week in Macao—

a week of restless waiting and increasingly uncertain calculations—the sight of *Vansittart* seemed nothing short of providential.

"A fine vessel," Silva observed beside him, his gaze measuring the ship with a mariner's practiced eye. "Well able to look after herself compared to most, which is perhaps why she is here. She will reach Calcutta in six weeks, if the weather remains kind."

Nicholas nodded. "If the captain will have us."

The sun, pale at first, began to burn through the mist as they turned back toward Silva's compound. Nicholas had spent the past week in a frenzy of trade, liquidating what goods remained—textiles, porcelain, spices—into silver dollars at rates that would have horrified him only months before. But desperation had a way of redrawing the boundaries of prudence.

In Silva's study, Nicholas counted out the coins. Eighty Spanish dollars, equivalent to near £18, a fair sum for their passage from Samoa to Macau.

"I cannot accept this," Silva said, pushing the money gently back across the table.

"I insist," Nicholas replied. "You've given us passage, food, shelter. It's only right."

Silva's weathered face broke into an unexpectedly warm smile. "Keep your coins, Nicholas. You will need them, for Calcutta, for the next thing."

Nicholas began to protest, but Silva raised a hand.

"Please. Consider it payment—for the most diverting months I have known in years. Adventure, intrigue—your assistance with the pirates. You English have a talent for disrupting the natural order."

"I'm not sure whether to thank you or apologize," Nicholas said with a wry smile.

"Neither is necessary between friends," Silva said. He rose and crossed to an ornate cabinet, which he unlocked with a small brass key. "However, I should like you to accept something before you depart—in place of the other I provided."

From within he withdrew a leather-wrapped bundle and laid it on the table. As he unfolded the wrap, Nicholas saw the gleam of steel and brass: an *espadim* of extraordinary quality, its elegant proportions marking it at once as something far removed from common naval issue.

"Portuguese workmanship at its finest," Silva said, drawing the blade partway from its scabbard. "Toledo steel. Forged in '74 by Matias Herrero, master of the Toledo Guild. I commissioned it specifically for shipboard use. Note the balance—straight-bladed, shorter than a cavalry sabre but longer than the usual *espadim*, with a reinforced spine for parrying."

He drew the blade fully. Its polished surface caught the light with a blue-silver gleam that spoke of meticulous tempering.

"The hilt is Portuguese—by João Ferreira of Lisbon, made to my exact specifications. More substantial at the knuckle-guard than is typical, with reinforced quillons. The grip is ray skin, bound with silver wire. It will not slip, whether wet with salt water—or with blood."

He balanced the sword on two fingers. "The fulcrum lies precisely one-third from the guard, as I requested. It permits excellent control in the cramped quarters of a ship's deck—or the alleys of certain port cities—yet retains enough presence at the tip for a decisive cut." He tapped the flat of the blade with a fingernail, drawing a clear, singing note. "This will turn aside a boarding-axe without failing. It will pass cleanly between ribs, or sever a small hawser in a single stroke."

Then he turned the hilt toward Nicholas.

"The pommel is weighted with lead to perfect the balance. The blade thickens near the guard for strength, then tapers to preserve quickness. This is not merely a sword, my friend, it is a tool made to solve a particular kind of fight.

It has served me well. In circumstances I hope you will not see. But a gentleman returning to the Company's waters should carry a gentleman's defence."

Before Nicholas could reply, Silva reached beneath the table and placed a mahogany case before him. Inside, on red velvet, lay a matched pair of dueling pistols, barrels octagonal, steel finely blued.

"Henry Nock," Silva said. "Finest pistols in Europe. Balanced like a sword. I have hit a playing card struck at twenty paces."

"Silva, I can't—"

"You can. You will." Silva's voice held no heat, only certainty. "India is not Canton. But neither is it London. A gentleman must be properly armed."

Nicholas lifted one of the pistols. It rested in his hand like a living thing—light, exact, assured.

"Thank you," he said quietly. "I will treasure them."

"Then see that you live to do so," Silva replied, dry as ever.

Two days later, Nicholas stood before a mirror in the shop of Ah Wong, Macao's foremost tailor to European gentlemen. The man fussed around him with meticulous care, making final adjustments to a midshipman's uniform, not quite regulation, but close enough to pass casual inspection.

"The blue coat is finest light English wool," Ah Wong said proudly. "White lapels and cuffs, as per Royal Navy standard. Brass buttons in proper arrangement: eight to the lapels, three at each cuff."

Nicholas regarded his reflection. The dark blue coat with white facings transformed him. Where a lieutenant's uniform bore gold lace and sharper lines, the midshipman's dress retained a certain modesty, the mark of a young gentleman officer still making his way. The white waistcoat and breeches stood crisp against the blue; the black silk stock was neatly wound at his throat. His cotton stockings disappeared into square-toed black shoes with plain brass buckles, not the silver-mounted dress of formal parade, but entirely proper for service afloat.

With his sun-darkened complexion, the faint scar that traced his left cheekbone, and the Toledo steel at his hip, he looked every inch the young officer who had seen distant stations. The simplicity of the uniform suited him. He had never cared for ornament, even before his years among the islanders had taught him that substance counted more than style.

Markham, who had accompanied him to the fitting, surveyed the ensemble with a craftsman's approval. "The very image of a gentleman adventurer, sir. It lacks only a proper hat."

Ah Wong, attentive to the cue, produced a cocked hat of the bicorn pattern, fitted with the correct cockade. Nicholas placed it on his head and inclined it slightly—a finishing gesture.

With the naval attire complete, their attention turned to civilian dress. Nicholas selected several garments suitable to a gentleman of modest fortune: two plain but well-cut frock coats one bottle green, the other navy blue; buff-coloured breeches; a few linen shirts of fine weave, and several neckcloths in white and muted silk. Nothing showy, but respectable: the sort of wardrobe a naval officer might wear while on leave or travelling between appointments.

Markham's choices were, as ever, practical: a coat of slate-coloured wool, a canvas waistcoat, plain breeches, and shoes built for endurance rather than style. He dressed now as he always had—like a man ready to haul a chest up a companionway or stand his watch in a squall.

"We must be ready for all circumstances," Nicholas said as the tailor entered their choices in his ledger. "The uniform will serve when required, but in some ports, civilian clothes may be the wiser course."

The following morning found them in a hired sampan, approaching the towering hull of the *Vansittart*. Up close, the ship was even more impressive. Her black-painted hull stretched 130 feet from stem to stern, rising twenty-five feet above the waterline to the main deck, and another fifteen to the towering poop. Gunports lined her flanks, revealing the gleam of iron cannon behind open lids. At her prow, a carved figurehead—perhaps Britannia herself—gazed resolutely ahead, while the Red Ensign fluttered at the stern, proclaiming her allegiance to the British Crown.

A bosun, his silver call hanging on a lanyard around his neck, answered their hail with a perfunctory "Boat ahoy!" and, upon learning their business, told them to come aboard.

The deck stretched before them, holystoned to a pale gleam, brass fittings polished to mirror brightness. The *Vansittart* might sail under a merchant flag, but she carried herself as one might expect of a naval vessel. The resemblance to a frigate was deliberate. Company ships of this class were heavily armed and governed with a discipline that echoed His Majesty's service—from the cut of the officers' coats to the roll of the drum at divisions. For a moment, Nicholas felt a flicker of familiarity. After so many months adrift in irregular company, there was something oddly reassuring in the trim precision of it all.

They were met by a young officer who introduced himself as Mr. Lamb, third mate.

"Captain Burney is expecting you, Mr. Cruwys," Lamb said, giving Nicholas's midshipman's uniform a glance of mild curiosity. "This way, if you please."

The great cabin of the *Vansittart* occupied the full width of the stern, its broad windows offering a panoramic view of Macao's crowded anchorage. Captain James Burney rose as they entered, a man of thirty-five or thereabouts, lean-faced, with intelligent eyes and the weathered complexion of one long accustomed to sun and salt.

"Mr. Cruwys," he said, offering a hand. "I received your note. Unusual to seek passage without going through the Company's agents, but not without precedent."

Nicholas returned the handshake, then straightened slightly. "Captain Burney, I must be frank with you. The situation I described in my letter was incomplete."

Burney's expression did not shift, but his eyes sharpened. He gestured to a chair.

"Then please, sit both of you. I imagine this will take some explaining."

Over the next hour, Nicholas laid out the course of his extraordinary journey. He spoke plainly, without embellishment. He described his service aboard *Resolution* under Captain Cook, his role as a midshipman during the third voyage of discovery, and the assignment to survey Bora Bora's reefs and harbours that had separated him and Quartermaster Markham from the expedition.

He recounted the storm that had driven them off station, the long absence of their ship, and their eventual integration among the islanders. Then the journey eastward to Samoa in a *pahi* canoe outfitted with native rigging, and finally their nearly secured safe arrival in Macao aboard a Portuguese merchant vessel.

"We learned that *Resolution* had departed only some three weeks ago," Nicholas said at last. "Our sole aim now is to return to England. I carry survey work for the Admiralty and hope to resume my career in the Navy."

Burney had listened in silence throughout, his face impassive but attentive. Now he rose and walked to the stern windows, his hands clasped lightly behind his back as he looked out over the morning haze.

"An extraordinary story, Mr. Cruwys," he said after a long pause. "And yet, entirely plausible to anyone who knew Captain Cook."

Nicholas was surprised, but said nothing, waiting as Burney gathered his thoughts.

"I served as second lieutenant aboard *Resolution* during Cook's second voyage," the captain said at last. "Those years shaped my understanding of what it means to be a proper seaman—and a true navigator. Cook was unlike any commander I have known before or since. His precision with charts, his care for his men, his determination in the face of the unknown—these made him more than a captain. They made him a discoverer."

Burney's gaze remained fixed on the harbour. His voice, though measured, carried an unmistakable depth of feeling.

"His method of command was singular. While others ruled through fear or rigid observance of the Articles, Cook led by example, and by expectation. He demanded excellence because he lived it himself, in every aspect of the service, from celestial navigation to the prevention of scurvy. His men followed him across the world's edge not because they were ordered to, but because they trusted him."

He turned back to Nicholas. "When word came of his death in the Sandwich Islands, it struck hard. Not just the loss of a commander, but of England's finest navigator. His legacy lives on in those who served with him, who learned his ways and kept to them. Any midshipman who sailed under Cook, and carries forward that knowledge, deserves every consideration."

Burney inclined his head. "I will grant you and your quartermaster passage to Calcutta, Mr. Cruwys. This ship will return to Macao thereafter, but from there I imagine you'll have no difficulty finding a Company vessel bound for England."

"Thank you, Captain," Nicholas said quietly. Relief came not as a flood, but as a tide gently turning.

"I can pay for our passage, of course."

"Three hundred Spanish dollars for yourself, one hundred for your man, standard Company rates in this part of the world," Burney said. "It comes to just under £30, all told. I believe you may recover the cost in Calcutta through the proper channels. If not, the Navy may yet see you repaid. Men with experience in distant waters are always needed, especially those trained under Cook."

He paused. "If it suits you, I shall refer to you as a merchant officer, let us say Mr. Nicholson, returning to India. It will avoid unnecessary questions, and certain political curiosities best left unexamined."

Nicholas nodded. "That would be very welcome."

"Very good." Burney turned to his desk. "Mr. Lamb will show you to your quarters. You'll share a cabin with my fourth officer, Mr. Saunders. Your man can berth with the petty officers. Dinner for the officers and passengers is served at four bells in the afternoon watch."

The cabin assigned to Nicholas lay to starboard on the gun deck, small, but tidy and well-kept. It held two narrow berths, a table, and lockers stowed beneath the bedding. His cabin-mate, Mr. Saunders, was a quiet, scholarly young man who received Nicholas with evident relief. He had feared, he admitted, another indigo agent or tea clerk, prone to complaint and ignorant of ships. To find a fellow mariner—and one of Cook's—was more than he'd hoped.

Nicholas spent the remainder of the day exploring the *Vansittart*, marvelling at her construction and equipment. She carried a crew of one hundred, including officers, and mounted twenty nine-pounder cannon on her gun deck, with smaller six-pounders positioned on the forecastle and quarterdeck. Though she was a merchantman by commission, she was fitted to fight if pressed. Yet for a ship so heavily armed, the complement struck him as modest. Barely a hundred hands to manage sail and gunnery alike. But this was not the Navy, and the Company prized economy nearly as much as order. Still, the rigging was tight, and the crew, a mix of British sailors and lascars from the Malabar Coast, worked with an ease that bespoke seasoned habits and Burney's firm but measured hand.

At dinner, served in the great cabin, Nicholas was introduced to the other officers: First Lieutenant Harrison, a square-built man with the gravity of long service; Second Lieutenant Phillips, a reserved and bookish figure who served as navigator and was said to calculate lunar distances in his sleep; the surgeon, Dr. Campbell, a lean and taciturn Scot; and Mr. Forsyth, the purser, whose quick, appraising eyes took stock of every man's plate and posture with silent efficiency.

Among the passengers were two tea merchants returning to Calcutta, a Company clerk bearing sealed dispatches, and a missionary with his pale, tight-lipped wife, bound for Bengal. Nicholas played his part as a merchant officer seeking return passage to England via India, fielding inquiries about the China trade with practiced brevity. He spoke easily but revealed little. Captain Burney, for his part, made no allusion to their earlier conversation, introducing him simply as "Mr. Nicholson, lately of the merchant service."

As the meal concluded, Burney raised his glass.

"Gentlemen and Mrs. Wilson, your health. We sail with the morning tide upriver to Canton. I expect to spend a week there at most, then, God willing, we shall round the Sunda Strait and reach Calcutta within seven weeks of leaving this coast, assuming the northeast monsoon holds steady."

Nicholas lifted his glass with the others, a quiet sense of relief stirring in his chest. After months of uncertainty and hazard, he was once again bound for familiar waters. India lay ahead, its shape and meaning still unknown, but the deck beneath his feet felt steady, solid, almost like salvation.

Later that evening, as Nicholas stood at the rail watching the lights of Macao shimmer across the tide, Markham joined him without a word. The breeze had freshened slightly; canvas rustled aloft, and the swell slapped gently along the hull.

"We're fortunate, sir," Markham said at last, his tone quiet, practical. "A fine ship. Steady hands. No fuss."

Nicholas nodded. "After the season we've had, I'll not quarrel with sound timbers and a competent captain."

He rested a hand on the hilt of Silva's sword, the brass warm from his coat. "When we reach Calcutta, we'll be halfway home."

Markham glanced sidelong. "And after that—England, sir?"

"Yes," said Nicholas, without looking away. "After all this time."

The lights of Macao glittered on the water, their reflections trembling with each slow rise of the swell. Though the *Vansittart* had yet to weigh anchor, the city already seemed to drift behind him, like a place half remembered. The air was laced with spice, smoke, and the faint sweetness of foreign gardens. In the dark, a bell tolled from some mission tower ashore, distant and uncertain, as if struck by memory rather than hand.

CHAPTER EIGHT

The *Vansittart* slipped into the opaque, silt-heavy waters of the Hooghly on the morning of March 21, 1780, her topsails reduced, her courses set, and her pace governed by the river's indifference. On the quarterdeck stood Captain Burney, issuing orders with crisp economy as towboats nosed alongside. Local boatmen, lean and bare-limbed, strained at long sweeps to guide her through the shifting, deceptive channel, each bank a potential trap of sand and tide.

The passage from Macau had taken longer than expected, nearly seven weeks. In the Bay of Bengal adverse winds had delayed them; near the delta, the need for unrelenting vigilance, where the river changed its bed like a restless sleeper, had slowed their advance to a crawl. Now, as the sun burned through the morning mist, the land revealed itself: a realm of low green banks, groves of palm and tamarind, and the distant shimmer of whitewashed temples and domes.

Nicholas found himself recalling their departure from China. The journey upriver to Canton had been a revelation, the East Indiaman making stately progress against the Pearl River's current, her great bulk dwarfing the local craft that scattered before her. For sixty miles they had threaded through a landscape that seemed plucked from a silk painting: terraced rice fields climbing impossibly steep hillsides, limestone karsts rising from morning mists like the spires of some fantastical cathedral, ancestral shrines perched on promontories where incense smoke curled skyward. At each bend in the river, new wonders revealed themselves, punctuated by the intrusive formality of customs barriers where Chinese officials in their quilted winter robes and formal hats boarded to examine papers with barely concealed disdain.

Canton itself had been both imposing and restrictive—the *Vansittart* taking her place among the forest of trading vessels anchored off the Thirteen Factories, that narrow strip of land where all Western commerce with China was confined. The ship had ridden at anchor while sampans swarmed about her hull like water beetles, ferrying merchants, compradors, and endless crates of porcelain and tea. Captain Burney had remained aboard throughout their week-long stay. Instead, a constant procession of Hong merchants had come aboard to negotiate, their elaborate courtesies barely masking shrewd business acumen, while the ship's officers took turns supervising the loading of cargo under the watchful eyes of the Hoppo's customs men. Now, as the green-gold delta of Bengal opened before them, Nicholas wondered how the ordered rigidity of Canton would compare to the chaotic vitality of Calcutta, where East and West had achieved a different, if no less complex, accommodation.

Nicholas stood watching this new world of India emerge with the slow certainty of tide. India came not with spectacle but with accumulation, with layers of sound, scent, and colour that pressed themselves gently but inexorably upon the senses.

The Hooghly, lifeblood of Bengal, teemed with life. Country boats with high, curling prows and patched tanbark sails ferried goods between thatched river villages. Massive barges rode low in the water under the weight of rice, jute, and cotton bound downriver toward the sea. Sleek budgerows, the covered boats of native grandees and European agents alike, glided past in silence, their rowers working in quiet synchrony. And above them all, loomed the East Indiaman.

The air grew thicker as they pressed farther inland, laden with humidity, and rank with the mingled scents of mud, smoke, spice, and something sweetly pungent Nicholas could not place. Tropical growth crowded the banks in unruly profusion: dense thickets of bamboo, towering palms with fronded heads, and flowering trees whose shapes and colours defied any name he knew. In occasional clearings, glimpses of village life emerged: whitewashed temples with curved, improbable roofs; thatched huts clustered beneath banyan trees whose roots descended like ropes from their massive limbs; women in bright saris kneeling at the water's edge, slapping wet cloth against stone in rhythmic motions that might have been ritual or simply practice honed by generations.

Captain Burney had told him of this approach. "The Hooghly," he'd said, somewhere off Cape Negrais, "is among the most dangerous rivers known to navigation. Shifting sands, treacherous currents, and squalls that rise without notice. She's taken more ships than all the pirates between here and Borneo. We'll take on a pilot at the mouth, a native who knows every shoal and turn. Even then, daylight only."

Now, watching the Indian pilot stand calm beside the helmsman, Nicholas understood the caution. The man wore a plain white dhoti and a loose kurta, his bearing unshowy but assured. He gestured lightly with one hand, murmuring instructions in accented but precise English, guiding the ship into the deepest thread of the channel, where the current ran swift and dark but sure.

By late afternoon, the scattered river hamlets gave way to more substantial habitations: low, colonnaded bungalows set back from the water among groves of tamarind and mango, their whitewashed walls gleaming through the greenery. Then came godowns and stone quays, cranes and bundled coir, men swarming over bales and barrels. The air thickened again, not with scent now, but with commerce. Rounding a broad elbow of the river, the city emerged at last: Calcutta, sprawled along the eastern bank, heat-hazed and immense, its skyline a confusion of domes, flagpoles, and tiled roofs beneath the fading light.

The city had the improbable grace of a composite—part England, part empire, and wholly its own. At its centre loomed Fort William, the vast star-shaped bastion that served as the military heart of the East India Company's Bengal Presidency. Its white stone walls and bristling cannon proclaimed British power in no uncertain terms. Yet as the *Vansittart* advanced up the Hooghly, Nicholas noted a curious detail: the fort's heaviest guns did not face the river, but inland, trained not on foreign fleets but on the city and the land beyond, as though the greater danger lay not in maritime assault but in the restless territories the Company now claimed to govern.

Beyond its glacis stretched the European quarter, laid out after the catastrophe of 1756 and rebuilt in the wake of Clive's reconquest. Here the architecture was shaped by the demands of Bengal's pitiless heat and monsoon fury. Verandas stretched wide beneath the weight of their own shade; ceilings soared high to draw off rising heat; louvred shutters and deep eaves sought every vagrant breeze as though air itself were rationed.

Farther inland, the Company's Calcutta gave way to the living tumult of the native *Kolikata*: a maze of brick and thatch, of bamboo scaffolds and stone shrines, of Hindu temples dense with carved deities and Muslim mosques with slender minarets rising clean above the press. The air thickened with incense and smoke and the metallic scent of sweat; the alleys teemed with cries and colour.

The *Vansittart* made her final approach as the sun dipped westward, casting a mellow, golden light across the Hooghly. At anchor in the broad stream, awaiting their turn to dock, lay a dozen East Indiamen and several Royal Navy vessels. Their presence, uncommon in such numbers, hinted at the widening scope of war with France and her allies.

Most prominent among them was *HMS Burford*, a seventy-gun ship of the line, flying the flag of a Rear-Admiral of the Blue. The sight stirred Nicholas with something close to longing. He had learned from Burney that this was Rear Admiral Edward Hughes, lately arrived to assume command of the East Indies Station, a fighting officer with a reputation for firmness in action and a just hand. If any man could assist in his return to England and the King's service, it would be the admiral.

The *Vansittart* dropped anchor and furled her sails neatly to the piping of orders. Small boats soon clustered round, native lighters and Company runners, and Burney descended the companionway to confer with his ship's agent, a thick sheaf of papers under one arm.

It was near an hour before he reappeared, coat unbuttoned against the heat. Finding Nicholas near the break of the poop, he nodded toward the shore where dusk had begun to settle over the low, spreading city.

"I've secured a room for you at Wilson's Hotel. Best accommodations in Calcutta, though that's damning it with faint praise. This place is no friend to the English constitution, heat's the least of it. You'll do well to take care not to overdo."

Nicholas nodded. "I'm grateful for your assistance, Captain. The voyage from Macau has been most comfortable."

Burney offered a faint smile and glanced toward the *Burford*, her hull now darkening in the evening light. "I shall furnish you with a letter of introduction. Admiral Hughes is known to favour men of merit, whatever their circumstances."

The following morning, Nicholas rose before dawn, determined to present himself to the admiral before the worst of the heat set in. He had spent two hours or more the previous night attending to his appearance, ensuring that his midshipman's uniform—though not strictly regulation—was immaculate. The blue coat with its white facings had been carefully brushed; the brass buttons polished until they shone like coin. His breeches and stockings were spotless, and his black shoes gleamed with fresh blacking.

Markham had assisted with these preparations, his seaman's hands deft with needle and thread where small repairs were needed, his eye for naval turn-out steady and sure. Neither man spoke of what the morning meant, yet both understood it without saying: this was Nicholas's first step back toward the life that had been so abruptly derailed thirty one months ago—over two and half years—and half a world away.

"You look proper naval again, sir," Markham said at last, stepping back to survey the result. "Though if you'll pardon me, there's something different about you now. Can't quite name it, but you don't carry yourself quite like that young gentleman who sailed with Captain Cook."

Nicholas nodded, understanding precisely what Markham meant. The face that looked back at him from the small mirror in his quarters was leaner, harder, the eyes more watchful.

"Let us hope the admiral sees it as improvement rather than corruption," he said dryly.

They left Wilson's Hotel as the first light broke over the city, the air marginally cooler before the full force of the Indian sun asserted itself. The streets of the European quarter were already stirring, palanquins carrying officials and merchants to their duties, native servants hurrying on morning errands, the occasional British soldier making his way back to barracks after a night of excess.

At the waterfront, Nicholas hired a budgerow to carry them out to the *Burford*. The boat—low, broad, and canopied amidships—moved cleanly through the press of harbour craft, its six rowers pulling with quiet synchrony. As the warship drew nearer, Nicholas felt a layered surge: pride at returning to a vessel of the Royal Navy, apprehension at how he might be received, and beneath both, a settled steadiness. Whatever lay ahead, he had come through worse.

The *Burford* rose above them, a seventy-gun ship of the line in full dignity, larger by far even than an Indiaman like *Vansittart*. Her hull was freshly painted in black with a broad ochre strake along the gunports, her lines sharp, her brightwork muted by tropical sun but cleanly kept. Gunports stood open to admit the morning air, revealing the black muzzles within. A blue flag of a Rear-Admiral flew square at her mizzenmast; the White Ensign hung limp at her stern. On the quarterdeck, officers in blue and white moved with the measured assurance of a crew long accustomed to their station—a ship at anchor, but not at rest.

As their budgerow came alongside, Nicholas called up to the officer of the watch. "Request permission to come aboard to report to the admiral, sir!"

There was a brief pause. Then a head appeared at the entry port. "Who goes there?"

"Nicholas Cruwys, midshipman, Royal Navy, formerly of *HMS Resolution* under Captain James Cook."

The name produced a visible reaction. After a short exchange with someone out of sight, the officer called down, "Permission granted. Come aboard, Mr. Cruwys."

Nicholas ascended the accommodation ladder with practiced ease, despite his years away from the service. At the entry port he removed his hat and saluted the quarterdeck, the timeless gesture of respect observed by every naval officer, regardless of rank or station.

A lieutenant stepped forward. "I am Lieutenant Denham, Flag Lieutenant to Admiral Hughes," he said, returning the salute. His uniform was immaculate: a dark blue coat with white lapels and cuffs, fastened with polished brass buttons. White breeches and stockings completed his attire, and his black shoes gleamed despite the humid air. Though his face bore the weathering of years at sea, his appearance reflected the fastidious standards expected aboard a flagship. "I understand you wish to see the admiral."

"If he will receive me, yes sir," Nicholas replied, handing over Captain Burney's letter of introduction. "I have information regarding Captain Cook's expedition that may be of interest to the Admiralty."

Denham's eyebrows rose slightly. "Captain Cook? We received word some months ago of his death in the Sandwich Islands. A great loss to the service."

"Indeed, sir. I was separated from the expedition before that tragic event. I've been attempting to return to England since."

Denham regarded him with renewed interest, his gaze taking in the midshipman's uniform, well-maintained, but marked by subtle deviations from the current regulation cut. "Wait here, Mr. Cruwys. I shall inform the admiral of your arrival."

As Denham disappeared below, Nicholas took the opportunity to study the *Burford*. She was a ship of the line of the older pattern, built in the 1750s but still formidable. Her decks were immaculate, her brasswork gleaming. Her discipline was unmistakable: everything stowed, lines flaked, blocks squared. This was the standard of a flagship, efficiency not merely enforced, but habitual.

The crew moved about with quiet purpose, casting the occasional glance toward the stranger in a uniform just a touch out of time.

Markham, standing a respectful pace behind, leaned in to murmur, "She's a well-found vessel, sir. Older than some, but properly handled. Look at the run of her rigging, clean, balanced. And not a frayed line in sight."

Before Nicholas could respond, a young lieutenant, no older than himself—nineteen or twenty at most—stepped lightly across the deck. He gave a quick, companionable smile.

"My name is Morgan," he said. "It appears you've quite a story to tell."

"Aye, sir," Nicholas replied. "Though may I ask first—what is the latest news of the war?"

Morgan's smile faded as another officer, slightly older and more formal in bearing, joined them. "Soames," he offered, with a curt nod. "A sorry business, all told. What began as colonial unrest has swept outward to encompass half the globe. The Americans remain stubborn. Washington survived that brutal winter at Valley Forge in '78, and worse still, they've secured the French."

"France signed formal treaty terms with the rebels last year," Morgan added. "Admiral d'Estaing brought a fleet into American waters. The Spaniards followed suit, declared war last June, eager as ever to reclaim Gibraltar."

"His Majesty now faces enemies on all sides," Soames said grimly. "France, Spain, the American Congress, and whispers of Dutch sympathy besides."

Morgan lowered his voice slightly, glancing toward a knot of officers by the mainmast. "North's ministry has shifted strategy—Philadelphia abandoned, the fighting now centred on the southern colonies. Savannah fell at year's end; Charles Town was under siege, last we heard."

Nicholas's eyes narrowed. "And the naval situation?"

"Precarious," said Morgan. "Our squadrons are stretched to the limit, fighting in the Channel, the Caribbean, the Indian Ocean. Sir Edward keeps this station at constant readiness. Suffren is rumoured to be in these waters with a French squadron, and the Company Council's in a state. They fear too much has been drawn westward to protect too little here."

He gestured toward the anchored merchantmen in the harbour. "Trade continues, but under strain. Insurance rates have doubled. Piracy thrives in the lulls. What began as rebellion is now a contest for empire, Cruwys. And this," he added, casting a look toward the eastern bank, "is its most distant frontier."

He adjusted his hat. "Welcome back to His Majesty's service, my friend. You've returned at a most interesting juncture."

Lieutenant Denham reappeared on deck. "The admiral will see you now, Mr. Cruwys. Your man may wait here."

Nicholas followed him below, aft through the companionway to the admiral's quarters in the stern. A marine sentry stood rigid at the doorway, musket grounded, gaze fixed ahead.

Denham knocked once. A voice within answered, "Enter."

The great cabin of *HMS Burford* was spacious by naval standards, a handsome room, its curved stern windows admitting the full light of morning. The space had been fitted for both duty and comfort. A broad table occupied the centre, strewn with charts, logs, and folded correspondence. One bulkhead held shelves of books: navigation, Admiralty orders, a scattering of history and philosophy. A smaller desk near the far beam bore the tidy clutter of private correspondence: sealing wax, penknife, and the neat loops of a half-finished letter.

Rear Admiral Edward Hughes rose from behind the chart table as they entered. He was a compact man, somewhere in his early sixties, his face deeply lined by sun, salt, and command. His white hair was tied back in a formal queue; his undress blue coat bore the broad gold lace of his rank at the cuffs, the buttons dulled slightly with use but clean. Despite the hour and the oppressive heat, he looked perfectly composed. His gaze settled on Nicholas, steady, alert, and coolly appraising.

"So, you are the ghost from Cook's expedition," the admiral said, without preamble. "I have read Captain Burney's letter, as has my flag captain, Captain Stewart." He inclined his head toward a short, square-built man in the undress uniform of a senior post captain, standing a few paces off with arms folded behind his back.

"Your claim is extraordinary, Mr. Cruwys—or should I say, Mr. Nicholson, as you presented yourself to the East India Company?"

Nicholas stood at attention, his hat tucked under his arm, the polished brass chart tube held in his left hand.

"I am Nicholas Cruwys, sir, midshipman, *HMS Resolution*. The alias was adopted with Captain Burney's suggestion and approval—intended as a precaution, to allow me to make my report to the proper authorities before rumours or speculation from other passengers could outrun me."

Hughes gave a small, noncommittal nod, one that acknowledged the explanation without necessarily granting it credence.

"You claim to have been separated from Captain Cook's expedition in 1777, to have survived among the natives of the Society Islands, and subsequently to have found your way here by a succession of native craft and merchant vessels. Do you possess any proof of this singular journey?"

"I do, sir," Nicholas replied steadily. He stepped forward half a pace and laid one of Silva's brass tubular chart cases carefully on the edge of the admiral's table.

"I have detailed charts of Bora Bora and other islands in the Society group, drafted under Captain Cook's instructions and completed aboard a Portuguese merchantman en route to Macau. These are fair copies; the originals remain with my other effects ashore, stored in a second watertight case. I have also kept a journal throughout—my observations, movements, and encounters. And I am confident that my knowledge of the expedition's personnel and objectives would withstand any comparison by those who served with Captain Cook."

Hughes's expression remained neutral, but his eyes had sharpened with interest. "Lieutenant Denham, please have my steward bring refreshments. Mr. Cruwys, Captain Stewart and I have much to discuss."

As Denham withdrew, Hughes gestured to a chair. "Be seated, Mr. Cruwys. The formalities have been observed; now we may speak more comfortably. Tell me, how came you to be separated from *Resolution*?"

For the next hour, Nicholas gave a measured account of his experience, beginning with his assignment to survey Bora Bora, continuing through the storm that had driven them far off course, their survival among the islanders, and the long, piecemeal journey westward that had brought him, in time, to Calcutta. He was thorough but not prolix, knowing that the more improbable elements of his story required no embellishment. Of his marriage and his time with Atea, he said nothing.

Hughes listened with steady attention, interjecting only to pose occasional incisive questions—revealing a seasoned understanding of the Pacific's geography, currents, and the practical realities of navigation. He showed particular interest in Nicholas's observations of islander seamanship, and in Captain Silva's assessments of the shifting balance of power in the East Indies.

"Your journey has been extraordinary," Hughes said at last. "Few men would have endured as much, and fewer still would have preserved a sense of duty throughout. The charts you mentioned—please present them."

Nicholas leaned forward and took up the brass tube he had placed on the table. He unscrewed the cap with care and withdrew a sheaf of neatly rolled charts, fair copies of his original surveys, transcribed aboard *Santa Rita* under Captain Silva's instruction, using Dutch chart paper of fine weight, linen-backed for strength.

"These and a second set were copied from the originals I made on tapa cloth at Bora Bora, sir" he said. "The originals as I mentioned remain ashore with my effects, in a second watertight case. These are more legible."

He unrolled one on the admiral's table, a rendering of the reef-bound approaches to the island's northern lagoon. The work was clean and restrained: reef lines traced in crisp ink, soundings marked in fathoms, current arrows drawn with delicate precision, and bearings set with a master's hand. The influence of Cook's method was clear, but the draughtsmanship was Nicholas's own—careful, economical, exact.

Hughes and Stewart studied the charts with a professional eye, noting the accuracy of the meridian lines and the care given to scale and orientation.

"These are exceptionally well executed," Stewart said at length. "They bear the stamp of Captain Cook's method, his insistence on thoroughness and exactitude. The Admiralty will value them highly."

Admiral Hughes regarded Nicholas for a moment in silence. "And what are your intentions now, Mr. Cruwys? Is it your purpose to seek a passage home?"

"I conceived it my duty first to present myself to the senior naval authority in these waters, sir, and to deliver into your hands these charts, along with the observations contained in my journal. That obligation fulfilled, I would hope—always supposing the service has not forgotten me—to resume my place within it."

Hughes gave a slow nod. "Quite correct. And now you have done so. The Navy always has need of officers of initiative and resource, especially in times such as these."

He paused, weighing something. "Return to your lodgings, Mr. Cruwys. I must examine your materials in greater detail and consider the matter further before making any decision. You shall hear from me shortly regarding any further arrangement. In the meantime, I expect you to prepare a formal report, detailing your movements and observations from the last point of contact with Captain Cook to the present."

Nicholas recognized the dismissal, rose and bowed slightly. "Aye, sir. Thank you for your attention, Admiral. I shall await your instructions."

"Very good." Hughes turned to his desk with deliberate finality. "Lieutenant Denham will see you ashore."

After Nicholas had gone, Hughes turned to Captain Stewart. "Well, Stewart, what do you make of our castaway?"

"His story is extraordinary, sir," Stewart replied carefully, stepping forward once more to the chart table. "Almost too much so. And yet—his familiarity with *Resolution's* company, his grasp of Cook's methods—these are not details a pretender would conjure lightly."

Hughes nodded. "And the charts? Your assessment?"

"They bear Cook's hand by way of another. The reef passages, the soundings, the current notations—all executed with remarkable care. Either he is who he claims, or he has had access to materials drawn directly from the expedition."

"Just so," Hughes murmured, his eyes fixed on the rendered shoreline of Bora Bora beneath its fine network of inked bearings. "He carries himself with a kind of self-possession uncommon in one of his years. Not arrogance, something quieter. Settled."

"The Pacific alters men, sir," Stewart observed, his weathered face thoughtful. "I've seen it before, in traders and deserters alike. The ones who remain long enough—who live by the tides, rather than merely observing them—return changed in ways that England can neither comprehend nor fully welcome home."

He paused, gathering his thoughts.

"Nearly two and half years ago. He'd have been, what, seventeen when separated from *Resolution*? Scarcely more than a boy. And now he speaks as one who has lived, not simply passed through. His understanding of the islanders struck me as... personal, bone-deep. Not merely the careful observations of a King's officer. He has learned to see the world through their eyes, not merely record their customs for the amusement of gentlemen in London who collect such accounts like rare specimens."

Stewart's fingers traced a faint line on the chart between them, as if marking an invisible boundary.

"The Admiralty expects men to visit these waters and remain unchanged—to catalog, to measure, to claim. But the Pacific demands more. It asks for immersion. The islanders know this. They've watched us come and go for decades now. They recognize the difference between those who merely visit their world and those who have allowed it to inhabit them."

Hughes set down his glass and leaned back in his chair. "Have Jennings make discreet inquiries with the Company clerks. There may be muster rolls or fragments of the *Resolution's* original list from when she passed through these waters. And ask Denham to submit a formal assessment of the charts, I want his independent view on their quality."

"And in the meantime, sir?"

"In the meantime," Hughes said, reaching for a fresh sheet of foolscap, "we shall observe how our Mr. Cruwys comports himself in Calcutta. Richard Atkinson's dinner tomorrow should prove... instructive. A man reveals much when he believes he is merely making conversation."

Nicholas emerged from the cabins into the sunlight, where Markham stood waiting, his concern only half-concealed.

"Well, sir? How did the admiral receive you?"

"With appropriate caution," Nicholas replied as they made their way to the accommodation ladder. "He wishes to examine the charts in more detail before coming to any decision."

As their hired budgerow pulled away from *Burford's* towering hull, Nicholas looked back at the ship, a silhouette of order and purpose against the hazy river. He felt a mingled sense of hope and uncertainty. The first step had been taken; the path beyond it remained obscure.

Wilson's Hotel occupied a substantial compound on Esplanade Row, overlooking the maidan, the great open green that separated Fort William from the European residential quarter. The building was typical of the colonial style in Bengal: two storeys of whitewashed masonry with deep verandas supported by classical columns, set within a walled garden where liveried servants moved discreetly among potted ferns and flowering shrubs.

Nicholas's room lay on the upper floor, a spacious chamber with high ceilings, polished teak floors, and tall shuttered windows that opened onto a shaded balcony. A punka—a great cloth fan suspended from the ceiling—was drawn by rope through a hole in the wall, worked by a servant outside in slow, practiced rhythm, keeping a steady breeze moving through the stifling air.

The furnishings were spare but elegant: a four-poster bed draped with mosquito netting, a writing desk of local hardwood, two cane chairs, and a wardrobe of dark mahogany that glowed faintly in the light. It was not luxury, but it was comfort, of the sort that came dear, in such a place.

After the cramped confines of shipboard life, the room seemed almost extravagantly large. Nicholas stood at the window, gazing out over the city stretched hazily to the horizon. Calcutta, under the late morning sun, shimmered like a mirage, dust hung in golden sheets along the roads, the air alive with voices in a dozen tongues, the scent of spice, woodsmoke, and flowering trees drifting on a sluggish breeze.

"Will there be anything else, sir?" Markham asked quietly.

Nicholas turned. "No—not at present. But there is something I've meant to speak to you about."

The quartermaster straightened slightly, his expression unreadable. "Sir?"

Nicholas crossed the room and opened his sea chest. From it he drew a small leather pouch and placed it on the table. "Since we left Samoa, you've maintained the fiction of being my servant. It's served our purposes well enough. But we both know it isn't the truth."

He untied the pouch and counted out several Spanish dollars, their worn silver faces catching the light, the currency of the East, accepted from Batavia to Canton. "There's no reason to continue the pretence here. Take these. You've earned some liberty."

Markham blinked, startled. "Sir, I—"

"I insist," Nicholas said. "You've stood by me in circumstances few men would have faced, let alone endured. If not for your steadiness, I doubt I'd have lived to see Samoa, let alone Calcutta."

He pressed the coins into Markham's weathered hand. "Call it overdue pay. Go. Walk the streets like a free man. We'll speak again tomorrow."

A rare smile touched the quartermaster's face. "Thank you, sir. Truth be told, it's been a long while since I had shore leave with coin in my pocket."

"Just mind yourself in the bazaars," Nicholas cautioned, "Captain Burney warned that European sailors occasionally stumble into customs they don't understand."

Markham just smiled "No fear on that account, sir," he replied, "I've visited ports from the Coromandel Coast to Canton. I know how to mind my step."

Through the tall windows, Nicholas could see the busy street below, a constant flow of palanquins, ox-carts, and the occasional European carriage navigating the broad avenues of the White Town district.

"I simply meant—" Nicholas began, then stopped himself, feeling a touch of embarrassment at his presumption. Though he outranked Markham, the older man's experience in Asian ports clearly exceeded his own.

"I understand perfectly, sir," Markham replied with no hint of offense, dabbing his forehead with a handkerchief. "And your caution is well-placed. Calcutta may appear civilized where we sit now, but venture beyond the European quarter, and even old hands can find themselves in difficulty. The Company has built itself a little England here, but step outside these walls, and we're still very much in Bengal."

After Markham departed, Nicholas found himself alone for the first time in months. The silence was unnerving after the constant sounds of shipboard life, the creak of timbers, the slap of water against the hull, the steady press of men moving in confined space. Now there was only stillness, broken faintly by the rhythmic tug of the punka overhead and the distant murmur of life beyond the garden wall.

He seated himself at the desk, intending to begin notes for the formal report, consulting his journal for dates and particulars. But the heat pressed in like a weight, thick and unmoving, and his focus slipped. Sweat beaded at his brow and ran down the back of his neck, despite the lazy sway of air stirred by the fan.

With a sigh, he laid down his pen and stretched out on the bed. The linen was warm but dry, the netting above barely stirring. Within minutes, the weariness of the past weeks caught him up, and he drifted into a sleep deeper than he had known since first leaving *Santa Rita*—a sleep untouched by the groan of cordage or the shouted changes of watch.

He woke to soft knocking at the door. The light had shifted; the hard gold of afternoon had deepened into the amber haze of early evening. A servant stood outside, barefoot on the polished teak, bearing a silver tray with a sealed note upon it.

"For sahib," the man said, bowing slightly as he presented the letter.

Nicholas broke the seal at once. It bore the admiral's mark, and he expected a summons. But the note within was brief, and signed not by Hughes, but by Lieutenant Denham.

> *Mr. Cruwys,*
>
> *Admiral Hughes has directed me to inform you that your passage money from Macau has been reimbursed as a courtesy to an officer of His Majesty's Navy. The enclosed draft on the Company bank may be presented at their offices on Council House Street.*
>
> *Furthermore, several officers of the squadron, along with officials of the East India Company, dine tomorrow evening at the home of Mr. Richard Atkinson, a senior Company director. Admiral Hughes suggests your attendance would be welcomed, as the gentlemen have expressed interest in your remarkable journey.*
>
> *A carriage shall call for you at seven.*
>
> *Your obedient servant,*
> *Lt. M. Denham*
> *HMS Burford*

Enclosed with the note was a bank draft for four hundred Spanish dollars—the precise sum Nicholas had paid for passage from Macao for himself and Markham aboard the *Vansittart*. It was drawn on the Calcutta branch of Alexander & Company, payable at sight—a detail that spoke volumes about the admiral's connections in the merchant community.

It was no small amount; four hundred Spanish dollars would represent nearly half a lieutenant's annual pay. In Bengal, where Company rupees were the common currency, Spanish dollars retained their value as international specie, trusted from Manila to Muscat for their reliable silver content.

Nicholas stared at the paper with quiet astonishment. In naval affairs, such prompt reimbursement was unheard of. Officers routinely waited years to recoup legitimate outlays, often forced to petition the Admiralty through a labyrinth of clerks and paymasters, each application disappearing into the vast bureaucracy of Whitehall. That this sum had been settled within a day—without so much as a receipt requested—strongly suggested that, despite the admiral's cautious manner during their interview, certain decisions had already been made regarding his status.

The dinner was no less significant. A private invitation to dine among senior Company men and naval officers was remarkable in itself, more so given his humble rank. An invitation from a captain, let alone an admiral, was never a request. And in Bengal, the East India Company represented authority in its most concentrated form. It controlled trade, revenue, law, and land. Its senior officials governed provinces, commanded regiments, and sent reports to London only after decisions had already been enacted.

To be introduced into such a circle, under these circumstances, was no ordinary favour. For an officer whose career had been interrupted by accident, war, and a wandering course across half the globe, it might prove invaluable.

Nicholas rang for a servant and requested a bath. If he was to dine among the elite of Calcutta, he would not appear as a castaway, nor merely as a passenger, but as an officer in His Majesty's Navy.

The following morning, he made his way to Messrs. Palmer & Company, Tailors and Habitmakers, on Clive Street. The establishment occupied the ground floor of a respectable building near the Company's offices, its entrance marked by a modest brass plaque rather than the painted signs or bolts of dyed cloth favoured by the native bazaars.

Inside, the air was cool and dim after the glare of the street. The floorboards were polished teak, and glass-fronted cabinets displayed bolts of fine cloth, brass buttons, and other accoutrements of a gentleman's wardrobe. A ceiling fan turned languidly overhead, its cord vanishing behind a partition where a Bengali servant worked the pull with mechanical regularity.

A thin, precise Englishman approached from behind a counter of bolts of cloth, his perfectly tailored coat showing not a wrinkle despite the heat. He assessed Nicholas with the practiced eye of a man who had fitted generations of officers and officials for both service and society.

"Good day, sir. Palmer at your service. How may I assist you?" His accent held the clipped precision of London, unmarred by years in the East.

"I require a naval uniform," Nicholas replied. "A midshipman's uniform. My previous one has not survived the tropics unscathed."

Palmer's expression did not shift. If the request surprised him, he gave no sign. He had no doubt heard stranger tales of colonial adventure, and the habit of hearing without reacting had surely contributed to his success among the discreet gentlemen of the Company's service.

"Certainly, sir," he said, reaching for a measuring tape that hung around his neck like a talisman of his trade. "Naval officers are always welcome at Palmer & Sons. We outfit many of the King's officers who pass through Calcutta."

Nicholas hesitated. It was a delicate point. At nearly twenty, he had already outgrown the typical age for a midshipman, at least for those with sufficient talent or, more crucially, the right connections. By now, such young men would have passed their examination and been made lieutenant. His own interrupted service rendered the matter ambiguous.

"I'm afraid the situation is somewhat... unusual," Nicholas said, choosing his words carefully. "I have been away from the service for some time."

Palmer nodded, his face a study in professional neutrality. "Sir, in Calcutta, unusual circumstances are our daily bread. I have fitted

Company men returning from captivity, officers thought lost at sea, and gentlemen whose exact rank required... discretion." He gestured toward a raised platform before a trio of mirrors. "If you would step this way, we can begin measurements."

For the next hour, he submitted to the precise and silent theatre of tailoring. Palmer and his Bengali assistants moved with practiced efficiency, consulting pattern books, selecting materials, and discussing the finer points of regulation regarding naval dress.

"The uniform has undergone modest revision since '74," Palmer noted as he chalked out the shoulder on a length of fine blue wool. "The cut is trimmer, the lapels a shade broader. Nothing radical, but enough to be remarked upon by those with an eye for detail."

By the time Nicholas departed, he had ordered not only three regulation midshipman's uniforms, but also two sets of civilian clothing: frock coats in bottle green and navy blue, waistcoats of sober pattern, fine linen shirts of a quality he had not worn since leaving England, and the various small necessities that marked a gentleman properly turned out in Calcutta society. Though he had acquired similar items in Macau, the materials here were finer, the cut more current, and the impression more unmistakably one of re-entry—less survival, more return.

"One uniform shall be ready by this afternoon, sir, as you requested," Palmer assured him. "The others, along with the civilian attire, will require three days. Might I suggest the blue coat and buff waistcoat for evening functions? The combination is particularly favoured by naval gentlemen when not in uniform."

Outside, the full force of the Indian sun struck like a physical blow after the relative cool of the shop. Nicholas paused to adjust the broad-brimmed hat he had purchased, a local adaptation that no fashionable Londoner would have recognised, but which had become common among European residents of Bengal.

The streets bustled with activity. Palanquins bore Company officials and merchants to their appointments, carried by teams of four bearers who moved at a swift trot despite the heat. European ladies passed now and then in covered carriages, glimpsed through muslin curtains drawn to protect delicate English complexions from the tropical sun. British soldiers of the Company's European regiments stood guard before government buildings, their red coats modified with lighter fabrics, faces flushed beneath their tricorn hats.

Everywhere, the contrasts of empire were on display: the recently completed Writers' Building with its distinctive arcaded verandah, where Company clerks labored over ledgers and correspondence; scaffolding surrounding the new St. John's Church, still rising to rival parish churches in England; Bengali servants in white cotton moving silently through European compounds; the occasional elephant bearing a native nawab or zamindar through streets designed for horse-drawn carriages; the mingling of languages, religions, and manners in the markets, where trade went on regardless of who claimed authority. The ambitious construction sites scattered throughout the European quarter spoke of the Governor-General's determination to transform what had been, just decades earlier, a collection of warehouses and modest dwellings into a capital worthy of British ambitions in the East.

Nicholas spent the remainder of the morning and early afternoon exploring this expanding European quarter. He visited a stationer who sold English almanacs and gazettes, months out of date but eagerly purchased nonetheless, alongside pamphlets on Company affairs and a few treatises on Hindu customs penned by Company chaplains. He walked along the riverfront, watching the endless movement of country boats, Arab dhows, and Company vessels that tied Calcutta to the world beyond.

What struck him most was the peculiar bubble in which the British lived, a carefully sustained illusion of English life, transplanted to the banks of the Hooghly, preserved by ritual and distance. It reminded him, curiously, of life aboard ship: a self-contained world governed by its own rules, afloat amid something vastly larger and not entirely knowable.

Later he collected the uniform, and as evening approached, returned to Wilson's Hotel to prepare for dinner at the Atkinson residence. He bathed and shaved, grateful for the simple luxury of fresh water, unmeasured and abundant after years of shipboard rationing. He dressed with care in his newly pressed midshipman's coat, his hair tied back in a formal queue.

In the mirror, he saw a man who might pass casual inspection as a midshipman—just. But any close observer would see the truth: the weathered cast of his face, the deep tan that would never quite fade, the fine lines at the corners of his eyes from years of squinting against ocean glare, and the pale scar that traced one cheek like a line drawn by memory.

The carriage arrived precisely at seven, a well-sprung barouche bearing the East India Company's coat of arms upon the door, drawn by a matched pair of chestnut horses. The driver, a turbaned Bengali, offered a respectful nod as a liveried footman stepped forward to open the door.

Calcutta wore a different aspect in the evening. Lanterns glowed from the verandas of European houses, casting golden pools across trimmed lawns. The fierce heat of the day had given way to a more bearable warmth, and a light breeze carried the scent of night-blooming jasmine. As they moved away from the commercial centre toward the residential districts where senior Company officials kept their compounds, the streets widened, the buildings grew more stately, and the gardens more expansive.

The Atkinson residence occupied a corner lot. A grand, two-storey mansion ringed by well-tended grounds, its façade illuminated by lanterns along a curving drive. Servants in white livery stood ready to assist arriving guests, while others moved deftly through the crowd with trays of wine and iced water. Through the tall windows, Nicholas glimpsed a company already assembled, perhaps thirty or forty, dressed in formal evening attire, circulating through the bright rooms in the practiced choreography of colonial society.

As he stepped down from the carriage, a voice called his name.

He turned to see Lieutenant Denham approaching, resplendent in dress uniform, a glass of wine already in hand and a glint of amusement in his expression.

"Ah, Mr. Cruwys! Excellent timing. Come, let me make introductions. There's considerable curiosity about you, I assure you. One doesn't often encounter a gentleman presumed lost with Captain Cook, suddenly reappearing in Calcutta."

Nicholas followed Denham into the house, passing through a wide entrance hall where turbaned servants moved with silent efficiency, collecting hats and gloves from the arriving guests. Beyond lay the main reception room, spacious and handsomely appointed, with high ceilings from which hung crystal chandeliers brought at enormous expense from Europe. The furniture was a curious blend: English pieces in the latest London fashion stood alongside carved screens and inlaid tables of unmistakably Indian workmanship. Tall windows stood open to admit the evening air, their curtains stirring in the faint breeze.

The company was predominantly male. Company officials wore rich coats of bottle green, claret, or dark brown, with silk waistcoats in shades of buff, cream, or pale blue. Naval officers in blue and white mingled with Bengal Army men in scarlet coats trimmed with gold, the whole effect one of varied but deliberate splendour. The handful of women present were chiefly the wives of senior officials, attired in the latest European fashions despite the heat, their faces flushed with warmth and social exertion.

"Mr. Richard Atkinson," Denham murmured, guiding Nicholas toward a portly gentleman holding court near the centre of the room. "Senior Director of the Company's Bengal operations. His reach extends from the Governor-General's council to London itself. Be respectful, but not obsequious—he prefers men who hold their own."

Atkinson turned as they approached: a man in his fifties with the florid complexion of an Englishman long resident in the tropics and unreconciled to its demands. His waistcoat strained slightly over a prosperous belly, and diamond pins glittered in the folds of an elaborate neckcloth.

"Ah—Lieutenant Denham! And this must be our mysterious castaway." He extended a broad, ring-laden hand. "Richard Atkinson, at your service. We've been most intrigued by the reports of your arrival, Mr. Cruwys. Admiral Hughes mentioned your extraordinary journey."

Nicholas took the proffered hand, noting the measuring look in Atkinson's eyes beneath the genial tone. "The admiral is generous in his interest, sir. I'm grateful for the invitation this evening."

"Not at all, not at all. Any gentleman associated with Captain Cook's expeditions is welcome in this house. A great loss—to the service, and to the empire. I had the privilege of meeting him when he called at Madras during the second voyage. A most impressive man."

The conversation soon widened as others gathered, drawn by the novelty of Nicholas's presence. A naval captain who had served in the Pacific questioned him closely about the Society Islands. A Company merchant inquired about the prospects for trade in those distant waters. A gentleman from the Asiatic Society—a scholarly circle devoted to Oriental studies—expressed keen interest in Nicholas's observations of Polynesian languages and customs.

Nicholas navigated the questions with measured precision, offering sufficient detail to satisfy curiosity, but never indulging in excessive elaboration. He maintained the deliberate balance between candour and restraint that governed such colonial assemblies, a conversational discipline shaped as much by omission as by speech. Throughout, he was acutely aware of being assessed, not solely for the information he could supply, but for his manner, his bearing, and his potential value to the intertwined interests of the Navy and the Company in these far-flung waters.

As the evening progressed, the gathering shifted from the reception rooms to a long dining table laid along the veranda. Punkas swung slowly overhead, stirred by servants beyond the shuttered windows, offering some relief from the lingering heat. Crystal and silver gleamed under the glow of dozens of candles, and liveried attendants moved silently among the guests, serving a meal that blended European technique with Indian ingredients: roasted meats in tamarind glaze, spiced lentil purées, mango chutney beside cold tongue and dressed greens.

Nicholas found himself seated beside a striking woman in her early thirties, Lady Helena Montague, as she introduced herself, wife of Sir William Montague, a judge of the Supreme Court then on circuit in Patna. Unlike many European women in India, whose complexions had suffered under the climate, Lady Helena's beauty seemed only enhanced by the tropical setting. She wore a gown of pale blue silk taffeta, cut in the latest London fashion, its fitted bodice tapering to a narrow waist before flowing into voluminous skirts supported by discreet panniers. The neckline—lower than would have been deemed proper in England, but entirely acceptable under the more relaxed standards of colonial society—revealed a generous décolletage, which Nicholas found himself making a deliberate effort not to observe.

The gown's elbow-length sleeves ended in cascades of delicate lace, echoed in the fichu that draped loosely across her shoulders, offering the suggestion of modesty without its substance. Her light brown hair was dressed high in the English style, threaded with small pearls and a scattering of local blossoms—an artful blend of metropole and colony that framed her face while leaving her neck elegantly exposed. Around her throat gleamed a single strand of pearls that, despite Nicholas's best efforts at restraint, drew the eye to the rise and fall of her breath. Her blue eyes held a lively intelligence, and her knowing smile suggested that she regarded colonial society as both theatre and fieldwork, and was entirely aware of the effect she had, especially upon men who had long been deprived of feminine company.

"So, Mr. Cruwys," she said, once the first course had been served, "you must find Calcutta quite a change after your years in the Pacific. Tell me—how do our humble efforts at civilization compare to the natural paradise of Tahiti, that one so often reads about in Captain Cook's accounts?"

There was a subtle challenge in her tone: a test, not merely of experience, but of sensibility. Nicholas considered his response before speaking.

"They are different worlds, Lady Montague, each with its own kind of beauty, and its own complexities. The islands possess a natural splendour that defies simple description, but they are not the idyll some writers suggest. Their societies are rich and ordered in their own right, and not without their tensions."

He gestured lightly toward the garden beyond the veranda, where fireflies drifted through flowering shrubs, their flickering light echoing the stars above.

"Calcutta," he continued, "has a beauty of its own, perhaps more constructed than natural, but no less real for that."

She smiled, seemingly pleased with his answer. "A diplomatic response, Mr. Cruwys. Many gentlemen who have passed time among 'noble savages,' as the *philosophes* would style them, return either in raptures of romanticism or in frank disdain. You seem to have kept to a more temperate course."

"I have tried to observe rather than to judge, my lady. It's a habit Captain Cook instilled in his officers."

"A valuable habit indeed, and one too rare among our countrymen in these parts." She took a sip of wine, studying him over the rim of her glass. "And what of the women of the islands, Mr. Cruwys? The accounts we receive suggest they are remarkably... hospitable to European visitors."

Nicholas felt a flush rise to his cheeks. The question touched on ground he had avoided since leaving Bora Bora—his bond with Atea, her death. The grief, though no longer sharp, remained unhealed, a quiet ache beneath the surface.

"The Polynesian peoples observe different customs in the relations between men and women," he said at last, his tone deliberate. "Their openness is often misread by European observers, who see license where there exists, in fact, a distinct moral framework, with its own boundaries and expectations."

Lady Helena's eyes sparkled with interest. "You are being delicately vague, Mr. Cruwys. Did you perhaps form... attachments during your time among them?"

The question caught him off guard. No Englishwoman of her rank would have asked such a thing in London—certainly not of a gentleman newly introduced. But Calcutta, he was learning, had its own codes: a looser propriety shaped by heat, distance, and the peculiar intimacy of a colonial society clinging to itself amidst the vastness of India.

"I came to respect their culture, and their people," he said evenly, his tone gentle but final.

"Ah—discretion." She smiled again, this time with a touch of mischief. "A quality I admire, though it deprives me of livelier conversation. My husband—though I fear he has no firsthand knowledge—claims the Navy breeds either perfect gentlemen or perfect rogues, with little ground between. You, I suspect, fall into the former camp."

The remainder of dinner passed pleasantly, the conversation turning to less personal topics: recent news from Europe, the artistic merits of current publications, and the peculiarities of Bengali customs as interpreted by the British. Nicholas found Lady Helena an engaging companion, her wit and intelligence a welcome contrast to the technical discussions of navigation and warfare that had long defined his conversational world. Mindful of his social duties, he made an effort to also address the lady seated to his left—a middle-aged woman more intent on her food and wine than the conventions of polite exchange.

As the evening drew to a close, guests began to depart in a rustle of silk and murmured farewells, carriages waiting in a line of soft lanternlight. Nicholas, drawn into a final discussion with several Company men about the precise locations of certain Pacific islands, lingered longer than intended. When at last he made his farewells, he discovered the organized transportation had already gone.

"No matter," said Lady Helena, appearing at his side in the entrance hall. "My carriage can convey you to your hotel. Sir William's absence allows me the rare freedom of departing when I please, rather than according to his inclinations."

Outside, her carriage waited, a handsome vehicle, discreetly marked with the Montague coat of arms on the door. As they settled into its plush interior, Nicholas became acutely aware of her presence—the scent of jasmine that clung to her gown, the rustle of silk as she adjusted her skirts, the elegant tilt of her head as she regarded him in the dim glow of the carriage lamp.

"You made quite an impression this evening, Mr. Cruwys," she said as the carriage set into motion. "Richard Atkinson seldom invites naval officers to his table unless they command at least a frigate. He must see some potential advantage in your acquaintance."

"I'm not certain what advantage I could offer," Nicholas replied, with quiet honesty. "I have no command, no official standing, not even confirmation that I remain on the Navy's books."

"You are known to be from a respected family," she said, her tone slightly more measured. "But more importantly, you possess knowledge, Mr. Cruwys, knowledge of places and peoples that interest both the Company and the Crown. And in Calcutta, information is a currency as valuable as silver or gold."

She leaned forward slightly, her face catching the shifting light of the carriage lamp. "Besides, you underestimate your own appeal. A gentleman who has survived what you have, who has seen what most men cannot even imagine... such a man exerts a certain fascination for those of us bound by the narrow confines of colonial society."

Her gaze was direct. The meaning beneath her words would have been unmistakable in any drawing room. Here, in the close warmth of a moving carriage, it carried the force of quiet invitation.

Nicholas felt a tangle of sensations—desire, certainly, for Helena was beautiful and confident and close. He had not lived like a monk since leaving Bora Bora. There had been brief arrangements, quietly managed in ports where discretion was understood. But those had been physical, occasional, and without consequence—comfort offered and taken, but never fully shared.

This was different.

Helena was no fleeting companion, no figure in a foreign room. She was clever, influential, well placed—and entirely in command of herself. To accept her invitation would be to cross not a moral line, but a social threshold, with unknown consequences.

And beneath the flicker of desire, another feeling stirred. Not guilt, but memory. Atea was no longer a raw wound, but she remained with him nonetheless: not jealous, not possessive, simply present. Her voice, her gaze, her gentleness. She belonged to a part of his life that had not followed him here, yet had shaped the man he had become.

"Lady Montague—" he began.

"Helena, please. I think we've moved beyond such formalities, don't you?" She shifted slightly, so that her silk skirts brushed his knee. "We are far from England, Mr. Cruwys, and farther still from the expectations we were raised to observe. That distance can be a kind of liberty."

Her hand came to rest lightly on his forearm—deliberate, but without pressure.

Nicholas was acutely aware of her nearness—the scent of her perfume of lemon and cloves, the smooth precision of her voice, the implied control in her every gesture. He had crossed distant seas, endured hunger, violence, and loss. But this was another kind of test: one that offered warmth and risk in equal measure.

"Helena," he said quietly, testing the intimacy of her name. "I'm honoured by your... interest. But I must be honest. I'm not in a position to—"

"To offer any permanent attachment? Lord, no. That is very far from my intention." A smile played at the corners of her mouth, a smile of layered, deliberate complexity. "Permit me to speak with perfect candour. Sir William has passed his half-century, and his attentions are directed elsewhere. He concludes his circuit in a fortnight's time. Until then, I find myself in possession of a freedom seldom granted the wives of Englishmen in these parts."

She shifted slightly, the silk of her gown whispering in the close air. "I merely suggest we afford one another such society as might render the intervening weeks more tolerable, indeed, more agreeable."

The carriage slowed as it approached Wilson's Hotel.

Nicholas studied her more closely now. Beneath the polished beauty and confident address, he saw a woman who had built her poise carefully—who had constructed her armour against the peculiar exile of colonial life. Too bound by propriety to engage deeply with India itself, yet too far from England to sustain the social network that had once defined her world.

"You didn't come to India willingly, did you?" he asked, the words escaping before he quite intended them.

Helena's expression shifted, surprise briefly eclipsing seduction. "How perceptive. No. I did not. William's appointment came three years ago—a significant step for his career. One that could not be declined." She looked away, her profile clean and austere in the shifting light. "My preferences were not consulted."

Nicholas recognised something in her tone, an echo of what he had come to know in the Pacific: the dislocation, the inward realignments demanded of those transplanted far from their own world. Helena's exile was wrapped in silk and shaded by punkas, but it was no less real for its outward luxury.

"In some ways," he said quietly, "you've travelled as far from home as I have, though by a different route."

She turned back to him, her eyes widened slightly, not in flirtation, but in surprise. "That is... a most unusual observation from a gentleman. Most see only the privileges of my position, not its confines."

For a moment, the practiced social poise faded. In its place stood a woman of sharp intelligence, searching not for conquest but for recognition. The space between them shifted—no less charged, but altered. Two castaways, acknowledging one another across the breadth of different solitudes.

"Would you care to come inside?" Nicholas asked at last. "I'd like to hear about the London you left behind."

Her smile returned, gentler now, less rehearsed. "I thought you'd never ask."

Later, in the darkness of his room, with Helena asleep beside him, Nicholas lay awake, watching moonlight shift through the shutters. Their encounter had not unfolded as he had expected. What began as physical consolation had deepened—slowly, unexpectedly—into something more complex: an exchange of confidences, of stories, of the particular solitude known only to those who live between worlds.

Helena had spoken of her life in England—her education, uncommon for a woman of her station; her hopes for intellectual companionship in marriage; and her quiet disillusionment with colonial society, where conversation seldom strayed beyond gossip or complaints about the help. Nicholas, for his part, had spoken of Polynesian culture, of the respect afforded to women in many of the islands, of the balance he had observed in domestic life. He did not speak of Atea. That chapter remained sealed, a memory too personal for casual recollection.

The physical release had been potent—a rupture in the long silence that had settled over him since Atea's death. He had not lived untouched in the years since, but this had been different. As he lay now, listening to Helena's steady breathing beside him, he felt not emptiness but something nearer to recognition. There had been connection—not only of bodies, but of solitude, of two lives unmoored from their original course. For a moment, they had reached one another honestly, not in longing or possession, but in understanding. It was not love, but it was something rare: a shared acknowledgment of exile, and the brief comfort of being seen.

He rose quietly and crossed to the window, gazing out across Calcutta's sleeping streets. Their understanding, whatever it was, would end with Sir William's return. But he sensed, in Helena, not merely a lover but an ally: someone who, like himself, inhabited that uncertain space between belonging and departure.

He turned back toward the bed. Her dark hair lay spread across the pillow, her face relaxed in sleep, free for the moment of its social armour. The deeper matters—Atea's memory, the shape of grief, the uncharted road ahead—remained untouched and unspoken. But for now, there was this: a reprieve, however brief, from isolation.

Outside, a night bird called, its voice strange and solitary in the Indian dark. Nicholas listened, thinking of all the birds he had known: the parrots of Tahiti, shrieking in the palms; the albatrosses above the southern oceans; the gulls wheeling over Devon's grey harbours. Each belonged to its own world, its own air.

And he, like them, was still aloft, still searching for the sky that would bear his weight without effort, and the place where he might come to rest.

Three days after the dinner at Atkinson's residence, and two days after he had delivered his written report to the ship, Nicholas received another summons to the *Burford*. This time, when he arrived on deck, Lieutenant Denham greeted him with a more formal manner than previously, a subtle shift that Nicholas immediately noted but could not interpret.

"The admiral wishes to see you immediately, Mr. Cruwys," Denham said, leading him below without further explanation.

In the great cabin, Nicholas found not only Admiral Hughes but also Captain Stewart and a clerk, seated with writing materials already arranged at a side table. The atmosphere was markedly changed: the charts had been cleared away, and the long table bore only a single leather folder stamped with the Admiralty seal.

"Mr. Cruwys," Hughes began, "I have reviewed your materials thoroughly and consulted with my officers regarding your situation."

Nicholas stood at attention, uncertain of what was to come. "Yes, sir."

"Your case presents certain... irregularities," Hughes continued, regarding him from across the table. "Under normal circumstances, a midshipman separated from his ship would report to the nearest naval authority at the first opportunity. Nearly two and a half years have passed since you left *Resolution*."

"I understand, sir," Nicholas replied, feeling a cold weight settle in his stomach. "The circumstances—"

Hughes held up a hand. "I am well aware of the circumstances, Mr. Cruwys. Captain Stewart and I have discussed them at length." He fixed Nicholas with a level gaze. "The question before us is one of proper recognition of service. You were, in effect, continuing your duties as assigned by Captain Cook—surveying the islands, gathering navigational data, maintaining records. That these duties were performed under extraordinary conditions does not diminish their value to the service."

Nicholas remained silent, hardly daring to hope.

Hughes opened the folder and withdrew a document inscribed with the flowing script of his clerk. "In my view," he continued, studying the paper with a practiced eye, "your time at the Royal Naval Academy at Portsmouth and aboard *Resolution* under Captain Cook, combined with your subsequent seamanship in returning to British jurisdiction, effectively exceeds the six years required for consideration as lieutenant."

He placed the document on the desk between them.

"You have served at sea nearly continuously, if not conventionally. Two years as a cadet-midshipman at Portsmouth, nearly eighteen months aboard *Resolution* under Captain Cook, and then the extraordinary circumstances of your return journey—which, while unorthodox, demonstrates precisely the initiative and resourcefulness we seek in our officers."

Hughes tapped a finger against a particular paragraph. "The Board's requirements specify 'practical experience in seamanship, navigation, and the management of men.' Your log entries and Captain Stewart's depositions confirm you have demonstrated practical knowledge of celestial navigation, leadership under adverse conditions, and tactical judgment when confronted by hostile forces. These are not theoretical exercises, Mr. Cruwys, but real tests, met under circumstances few officers twice your age have encountered."

He reached for another document in the folder. "Captain Stewart has further informed me that your charts and calculations show a degree of proficiency well beyond what is typically expected of a midshipman. Indeed, he suggests your work rivals that of Masters Mates with considerably more formal training."

The admiral leaned back, his chair creaking softly, and gazed down at the folder. "The Naval Board typically concerns itself with the quantity of service, Mr. Cruwys. In your case, I believe we must consider its quality as well."

The admiral looked up. "Tell me, Mr. Cruwys—did you ever sit for your lieutenant's examination during your time aboard *Resolution*?"

"No, sir. I had not yet reached the required age or service time. And once we left the Cape, there was no opportunity."

Hughes nodded. "And you are now—what, twenty?"

"Nearly. In five weeks, sir."

The admiral exchanged a glance with Captain Stewart, who gave a subtle nod.

"War creates necessities, Mr. Cruwys," Hughes said, his tone now more conversational. "We find ourselves stretched thin across these waters, and with the French and Spanish increasing their presence daily, the Navy has need of capable officers. Technically, you remain part of *Resolution's* complement—never discharged, never reassigned. Your absence was involuntary and due entirely to the exigencies of service."

He lifted a third document from the folder. "I have therefore decided to issue you an acting commission as lieutenant, effective immediately, pending confirmation by the Admiralty upon your return to England. In addition—"

He paused and laid the commission aside.

"—I will direct Captains Hartley, Fenwick, and Hardcastle to sit a board for your examination when the squadron next makes Bombay. If you satisfy them, your commission shall be forwarded to the Admiralty as confirmed."

Nicholas felt a surge of emotion that threatened to unseat his careful composure.

"Sir, I—"

"Captain Stewart will administer the oath," Hughes interrupted.

Captain Stewart stepped forward, holding out a Bible. "Place your hand upon the book, Mr. Cruwys."

Nicholas did as instructed, his fingers steady despite the churn of thought.

"I, Nicholas Cruwys," Stewart prompted, "do solemnly swear to be faithful and bear true allegiance to His Majesty King George the Third..."

As Nicholas repeated the words, he felt their full weight, not merely the formality, but what they represented. This was not simply a promotion. It was restoration. Recognition. A path forward from the long uncertainty that had shadowed him since the *Resolution* sailed on without him.

When the oath was concluded, Hughes handed him the commission.

"Congratulations, Lieutenant Cruwys," he said. Then, with a flicker of dry amusement, "I imagine Mr. Palmer will be delighted to see you again so soon. You may be the only officer in this station to require two different sets of uniforms in a single week."

Nicholas smiled at the rare levity. "I shall endeavour to maintain a more consistent rank going forward, sir."

"See that you do," Hughes replied, his tone back to iron. "The King's cloth doesn't grow on trees, even in Bengal."

Lieutenant Denham stepped forward and presented another document, the columns of figures precisely rendered in a clerk's meticulous hand. "Your accounts have been adjusted to reflect your promotion. Admiral Hughes has ordered back pay for the entire period of your absence—calculated at midshipman's rate of £2 3s per month until today, and lieutenant's pay of £4 4s per month henceforth."

Nicholas accepted the paper with unconcealed surprise. The sum was considerable—nearly £73, representing back wages for his time since leaving *Resolution*. The Admiralty rarely paid officers for periods of absence, even when officially sanctioned. For time spent outside naval service, such payment was virtually unprecedented. The document bore the countersignature of the station's Purser, making it immediately negotiable at the Company's treasury office.

His eyes moved down the neat columns, noting the deductions for slop chest charges that had been automatically applied and then struck through with a note in the margin: "Waived by order of Admiral Hughes." Even the customary sixpence in the pound typically withheld for the Greenwich Hospital fund had been included in the total.

It was roughly equal to what he had managed to save during his time with Silva, carefully accumulated in Spanish dollars and Portuguese escudos. Combined with those funds, and the reimbursement for the passage aboard *Vansittart,* he was by no means wealthy, but with care, he would have no immediate financial concerns. A junior lieutenant could live modestly but respectably on his pay, particularly in the East Indies where opportunities for prize money were more abundant than on the Channel Squadron.

He folded the document carefully, aware that in the naval hierarchy, such financial independence, modest though it was, represented a significant advantage. Many junior officers lived perpetually in debt to pursers and local merchants, their meager pay insufficient for the expenses required to maintain their position.

"This is... most unexpected, sir. I am grateful for the Admiral's consideration."

"Furthermore," Hughes added, "your man Markham has been entered on the squadron's books as a quartermaster, with appropriate back pay. His skill and experience merit no less. We've also authorized his advancement to master's mate, should he wish to remain in the service."

"He will be most grateful, sir—as am I," Nicholas replied, genuinely moved by this unexpected generosity.

Hughes drew yet another paper from the folder. "Now, to more immediate matters. *HMS Lynx*, a sloop of sixteen guns, arrived four days ago with dispatches. She is short a fourth lieutenant and will depart for England within the week, calling at Bombay, Gibraltar, and then home with dispatches of our own."

He handed Nicholas the paper—formal orders assigning him to *Lynx* under Captain Henry Walsh. "You will report aboard tomorrow at eight bells in the forenoon watch. The voyage should provide ample opportunity to reacquaint yourself with the routines of His Majesty's service."

He paused, his expression shifting—still formal, but more pointed. "I might add, Lieutenant, that a certain caution ashore will serve you well. Calcutta offers many... distractions for young officers. The hospitality of particular Company households can prove especially hazardous to one's career."

Nicholas felt the heat rise to his face and wondered just how much the admiral knew.

Hughes continued, his tone deliberately casual. "Sir William Montague is due to return within the week. A formidable jurist, with considerable influence at Government House. Not a man whose displeasure one would wish to provoke, particularly at the outset of a promising career."

"I understand perfectly, sir," Nicholas replied, keeping his expression carefully neutral.

"I thought you might," Hughes said, the corners of his mouth twitching. "Naval service offers many perils, Lieutenant Cruwys, but those at sea are often more straightforward than those ashore. The former may cost a man his life. The latter, his reputation—and his future."

"As for your charts and your report on the Society Islands," Hughes continued, shifting tone with practiced ease, "I shall be forwarding copies to the Admiralty. However, you will deliver the original documents in person. My orders to Captain Walsh reflect this. The information you've gathered is of considerable value to the service. You have made a significant contribution, regardless of the circumstances under which it was compiled."

Nicholas understood this for what it was—not merely a courtesy, but a confirmation: that his work would be properly attributed, his observations acknowledged. For all the admiral's emphasis on wartime necessity and shortages of officers, this order—to carry the charts himself to the Admiralty—was the clearest endorsement he could receive.

"I am honoured, sir," he said quietly.

"Very good. That will be all, Lieutenant Cruwys," Hughes said, returning to the full formality of command. "I suggest you make your preparations expeditiously. *Lynx* is a fine vessel, but her accommodations are limited. You would be wise to travel light."

"Aye, sir."

After Nicholas followed Denham from the cabin, Admiral Hughes turned again to his flag captain.

"An impressive young man, Stewart. Cook chose his protégés well," Hughes said, studying the charts still spread before him. "There's something in his bearing—a self-sufficiency one rarely sees, even in officers ten years his senior."

"Aye, sir," Stewart replied. "And if half of what he says about that Portuguese trader Silva is true, he's had an education few naval officers could claim."

Hughes nodded, returning the papers to their folder. "Silva's reputation is well known in these waters—trader, smuggler, and privateer by turns, depending on which offers the greater profit. Yet that rogue seems to have taught our young lieutenant lessons worth learning."

"Valuable ones, no doubt," Stewart said with a wry smile, "though perhaps not all suitable for His Majesty's service."

"Indeed." Hughes stepped to the stern windows and looked out toward the harbour, where Lady Montague's distinctive carriage had again been seen departing Wilson's Hotel that very morning. "Cruwys may have survived savages and storms, but he remains perilously naive to the dangers of civilization. Calcutta's drawing rooms can be more treacherous than any coral reef."

"Shall I speak with Captain Walsh, sir? Ensure our new lieutenant is kept gainfully occupied aboard until they weigh, and perhaps even in Bombay?"

"An excellent suggestion, Stewart. Walsh is discreet, and understands the value of a promising officer. See to it he's informed of Cruwys's... particular circumstances. The Navy has invested no small effort in his return. I should prefer he arrive in England with his prospects—and his neck—intact."

CHAPTER NINE

The morning wind off the Malabar Coast came fresh from the southwest, filling *HMS Lynx*'s sails and driving her northward at a brisk seven knots. Nicholas stood at the weather rail, feeling the familiar rhythm beneath his feet. The sloop heeled gently under the wind's pressure, her copper-sheathed hull slicing cleanly through the rolling swells, leaving a foaming wake that stretched straight to the horizon.

Three weeks had passed since their departure from Calcutta. After clearing the treacherous mouth of the Hooghly, they had stood southward, rounded the wild coasts of Ceylon, and turned northwest along the western shore of India. Now they were making for Bombay—the great port and dockyard that served as the principal base for British naval operations in the western Indian Ocean.

Lynx was a ship of character. Built at Deptford in 1771, she was classed as a ship-sloop of sixteen guns: fourteen six-pounders on her main deck and two three-pounders on the quarterdeck. Though small by the standards of even a frigate, let alone a line of battle ship, she embodied the qualities most prized in her class—speed, agility, and the ability to operate where heavier vessels dared not. Her lines were finer than most ships of her rate, with a sharp entry at the bow and a clean run aft that made her exceptionally swift. Her coppered bottom—a relatively recent innovation—kept her free of marine growth and preserved her sailing qualities in warm waters.

Measuring 100 feet on the gun deck and 28 feet at the beam, she made efficient use of her modest dimensions. Her three masts—fore, main, and mizzen—carried the full rig of a ship. The flush main deck held her battery, with the captain's cabin and officers' quarters aft, the crew's berths forward, and the galley amidships. The quarterdeck above ran from the mainmast to the taffrail, providing space for the officer of the watch and the helmsman at the double wheel. Below, the hold carried all the necessary stores of naval life—water casks, salted provisions, powder and shot, spare cordage and canvas—each carefully stowed and vigilantly overseen by the gunner, boatswain, and purser.

What *Lynx* lacked in size, she made up for in sailing qualities, and her present commander knew precisely how to exploit them.

Captain Henry Walsh stood now on the quarterdeck, his compact frame radiating authority. At five feet six inches, he was shorter than most of his officers, a fact that seemed only to intensify the force of his presence. He was an experienced officer, and—at eight and twenty, he held the rank of Master and Commander, the title of "Captain" being a courtesy afforded any officer in command of one of His Majesty's vessels. His face already bore the fine lines of responsibility and command. What Walsh lacked in stature, he made up in voice: it could carry from the quarterdeck to the forecastle without strain.

Nicholas had quickly come to understand Walsh's ways: he demanded excellence, tolerated no laxity, yet tempered rigour with a shrewd sense of practical seamanship that reminded Nicholas, more than once, of Cook. There were no acres of gleaming brass aboard— just the trim around the binnacle.

And for all his occasional severity, Walsh was undeniably skilled. His seamanship was beyond question, and his navigation methodical and exact. In the three weeks since clearing Calcutta, Nicholas had seen ample evidence of why Walsh, despite a sometimes acerbic temperament, had risen to command and held the respect—if not always the affection—of his officers.

Yet it was in gunnery that Walsh's true passion revealed itself. He held an unshakable belief in the decisive power of accurate fire. Three times a week, regardless of weather or sea-room, he ordered gun drills: crews timed, performance measured, precision demanded. When powder and shot could be spared, targets were towed astern, and extra grog awarded to the gun crews whose rounds landed closest to the mark.

As a result, *Lynx*'s gunners could load and fire with remarkable speed.

Nicholas, as fourth lieutenant, had been given charge of the starboard battery—seven six-pounders and their respective crews. Each morning, he inspected the guns: ensuring they were properly secured, that the touch-holes were clear, the gun tackles correctly rove and rigged. During action stations, he would command that battery directly—relaying firing orders from the quarterdeck, and ensuring their execution with efficiency and control.

Walsh's emphasis on gunnery made these duties far from ceremonial. Nicholas spent hours with his men, drilling them in the sequence of loading, running out, aiming, and firing. Under his supervision they practiced dry runs—rammers and sponges in precise coordination—adjusted elevation with handspikes, and trained to maintain their rhythm even if casualties struck mid-action. His time with Silva had given him valuable insight into the practical realities of shipboard gunnery, but he was careful to uphold the Royal Navy's established routines, the language and sequence the men knew and trusted.

The crews responded well to his leadership. During the most recent exercise, his starboard battery had achieved the fastest loading time aboard—a fact that earned a rare nod of approval from Walsh himself. The commander had watched him closely during the drill, his expression unreadable, but his interest unmistakable: the eye of a sailor measuring another by the only standards that mattered, calm, control, and command under pressure.

Life aboard the sloop required adjustment. Though Nicholas had spent years at sea, the routines of a Navy vessel were more rigid than those of Silva's trading brigantine, or the fluid, communal logic of Polynesian voyaging canoes. Even compared to *Resolution*, *Lynx* ran tighter—perhaps a consequence of war, or of Walsh's particular command style. With a company of 125 men confined in close quarters, every movement was choreographed by necessity and tradition, the ship a floating society whose survival depended on both precision and unspoken accord.

For Nicholas, the most immediate change was his integration into the gunroom. As fourth and most junior lieutenant, he occupied the smallest of the officers' cabins: a space scarcely six feet by four, fitted with a narrow cot, a small sea chest, and a folding writing desk. Yet even this cramped compartment was a luxury compared to the communal berths he had known as a midshipman. More than that, it marked his formal entry into the company of commissioned officers, with all the privileges, expectations, and invisible boundaries that entailed.

Lynx's gunroom itself was a compact space at the stern, just forward of the captain's cabin. A polished mahogany table stood at its centre, surrounded by bench seating built into the bulkheads, with the cabins opening off on either side. A small skylight admitted angled shafts of daylight; at night, brass lamps swayed gently from the deckhead, casting a warm, uneven light. Here the ship's officers took their meals, held their briefings, and passed what little leisure their duties allowed.

Nicholas's first dinner in the gunroom had been an education in the unspoken codes of a man-of-war's interior life. As on all His Majesty's ships, regardless of size, the captain dined alone in his cabin—preserving the necessary remove between commander and subordinates. Perhaps once a week, Walsh would invite a select few to dine with him, an honour both coveted and faintly dreaded, given his exacting standards and penetrating eye. Less frequently still, the gunroom would return the gesture, extending a formal invitation of its own.

The gunroom belonged to the commissioned officers: the four lieutenants, the marine officer, and the sailing master—who, though holding a warrant rather than a commission, was by courtesy and long tradition treated as a gentleman. The surgeon, Mr. Crawford—a portly, red-faced man possessed of an inexhaustible supply of improbable tales—and the purser, Mr. Findlay, whose pinched features matched precisely the expectations of his post, joined the table by invitation rather than by right.

Midshipmen, as officers-in-training but not yet commissioned, dined separately under the eye of the senior midshipman. They were occasionally invited to the gunroom, either as a mark of approval or for some particular instruction, but such appearances were exceptions, not habits.

Lieutenant Hargrove, as senior, presided at the gunroom table. The sailing master, Mr. Ainsley, held a position of honour near him, a gesture of respect for his twenty years' service and his essential role in the ship's navigation. Opposite sat Lieutenant Sinclair, the marine officer: a spare, formal Scot whose manner left little to speculation.

Nicholas, as the most junior lieutenant, took his place at the foot of the table beside Second Lieutenant Chester—a somewhat graceless frowning, round-faced officer of perhaps eight-and-twenty, and Third Lieutenant Harrington, a reserved man not more than two years older than Nicholas with clear aristocratic connections and the manner to match.

The atmosphere combined formality with the camaraderie born of shared confinement and mutual dependence. Conversation ranged over matters nautical and practical; sea stories circulated freely, as did the port and wine, drawn from the officers' private stores and maintained in a locker abaft the bulkhead. Brandy made occasional appearances, its consumption governed less by regulation than by custom and the discipline expected of King's officers, men obliged to be alert at all hours, and fit to command.

Even in these relaxed moments, certain topics remained off-limits. Politics, religion, and criticism of superiors were studiously avoided, as was any speculation regarding the captain. These were not matters for the wardroom. Such restraint was not merely etiquette—it was survival, both social and professional.

It was during one of the rare dinners in the captain's cabin, to which Nicholas had been invited along with Lieutenant Hargrove, Master Ainsley and Dr. Crawford, that Walsh had first questioned him about his experiences in the Pacific.

"So, Mr. Cruwys," Walsh had said, fixing him with a level stare as he sipped his wine, "Admiral Hughes speaks highly of your charts. You were with Cook, I understand?"

"Yes, sir. Aboard *Resolution*, during the third voyage—until I was separated from the expedition in late 1777."

This had prompted a sequence of pointed questions, Walsh's inquiry as precise and deliberate as his seamanship. Crawford expressed particular interest in the medicinal practices of the Polynesian peoples, while Ainsley asked after their methods of navigation. Even the normally reticent Hargrove had stirred when Nicholas described the construction and handling of double-hulled voyaging canoes.

"Remarkable vessels," Ainsley had remarked. "I've heard accounts of their speed and seaworthiness, though I confess I've found them difficult to credit."

"They are remarkable, sir," Nicholas had replied. "I travelled more than a thousand miles in such a craft—from Bora Bora to Samoa. In certain conditions, they can outpace even a fast vessel like *Lynx*, though in heavy weather I imagine she would still have the heels of them."

Walsh had looked thoughtful at that. "Interesting indeed. Though to carry weight of cargo or artillery—God forbid—a hull with depth is still needed."

The conversation had then turned to more familiar naval concerns: the French squadron reported off Mauritius; the difficulty of maintaining copper sheathing in tropical waters; the variable quality of provisions across the East Indies. Nicholas contributed as appropriate—never overstepping, but offering what knowledge he had—careful to demonstrate both competence and the deference expected of a junior officer among his seniors.

As the days passed, he had gradually found his place within the gunroom hierarchy. His practical experience in the Pacific and his time aboard Silva's ship gave him insights that even veteran officers found valuable, while his formal training under Cook provided a foundation of professional knowledge that earned respect.

As the junior lieutenant, Nicholas bore responsibility for supervising *Lynx*'s four midshipmen, a smaller complement than that to be found on a frigate or ship of the line, but typical for a vessel of her class. Mr. Farley, the senior at seventeen, showed promise: a quick mind for mathematics, though prone to impatience. Mr. Latham, sixteen and the son of a naval captain, displayed natural authority but an irksome awareness of his pedigree. Mr. Colby, at fifteen, was the quietest—pale, slight, but possessed of a quiet tenacity when tested. And finally Mr. Willis, the youngest at barely fourteen, still round-cheeked and occasionally homesick, yet eager to please and swift to learn.

Nicholas found that his time under Captain Cook had furnished him with methods to train these young gentlemen in the arts of navigation and seamanship, while his years among the Pacific islanders had instilled a patience that served him well when dealing with their youthful errors and occasional high spirits.

"Mr. Cruwys," Walsh called, his eyes finding Nicholas at the rail, "you've the noon sight to take, I believe."

"Aye, sir," Nicholas replied, touching his hat in acknowledgment.

"See that it's accurate to the minute. I'll not have my officers producing slipshod calculations."

The captain's tone held its usual edge, but Nicholas had begun to distinguish the subtle gradations in Walsh's manner. This was routine, not rebuke.

He made his way aft to collect his octant, purchased in Calcutta, nodding to First Lieutenant Hargrove as he passed. Hargrove—a lean, saturnine man, older than the captain by some years—had served under Walsh for nearly two years. He had developed the impassive expression of an officer who had long since learned to weather his captain's moods without visible reaction. He returned Nicholas's nod with the slightest inclination, then resumed his scrutiny of the binnacle, confirming their course with the care that marked every officer aboard *Lynx*.

The tropical sun stood high overhead, nearing its zenith. Nicholas adjusted the instrument, bringing the solar disc down to the horizon, measuring the angle with practiced motions of the index arm. About him, the ship held her course, the pulse of naval routine steady: men at their stations, the helmsman intent on the compass, lookouts peering from the tops, the wind drawing clean through the rigging.

In a few hours, they would sight the approaches to Bombay—that great outpost of British power in the East. But for now, there was only the ship, the sea, and the immutable mathematics of celestial navigation.

Lieutenant Harrington appeared beside him, his sextant in hand—an expensive instrument still rare with most officers. "Fine day for a sight," he observed dryly. "The captain will expect our calculations to match to the minute, of course."

"Of course," Nicholas replied, with a faint smile.

Harrington's austere features relaxed into a rare expression of amusement. "Still, there are worse commanders to serve under. He may be demanding, but he's damnably effective."

Nicholas nodded as he completed his observation, noting the precise time on the deck watch. He would now retreat to the relative quiet of his cabin to work the figures—longitude by reckoning of time, course and distance from his last lunar distance calculation two nights before, latitude by new meridian altitude. Without one of Harrison's precious chronometers aboard—devices still so rare that only a handful of naval vessels carried them—determining longitude remained a laborious process, requiring careful observation of the moon's position relative to fixed stars, only of course when visibility allowed, followed by complex mathematics and reference to the tables in the Nautical Almanac.

It was a procedure he had performed hundreds of times under Cook's exacting tutelage. The great explorer had been among the first to test chronometer number K1, a copy of Harrison's H4, during his second voyage. Nicholas had watched in awe as Cook had shown the midshipmen the three newer chronometers by John Arnold that were on board for the third voyage, though *Resolution* had still relied primarily on lunar calculations as a check against the experimental timekeeper's accuracy even on the third voyage, when Cook had also carried three of John Arnold's newer chronometers. That meticulous approach to navigation—the patient observations, the careful calculations, the cross-checking of results—was a skill that bound him to Cook, to the service, to the world he had once feared lost beyond recall. Even now, years later, he could hear the explorer's precise instructions as clearly as if the man himself stood at his shoulder, watching with that careful, assessing gaze that had shaped a generation of naval officers.

The gunroom was empty when he returned with his completed work. He laid the neatly written sheet upon the table, ready for comparison with the figures of Harrington and the master. He knew his position would be sound—not from arrogance, but from the long hours of practice under Cook's exacting eye. The thought brought a sharp pang of grief for his former captain, now forever lost to the sea he had mapped with such devotion and precision.

Nicholas was about to return to the deck when the door to the captain's cabin opened and Walsh emerged, a bundle of papers in hand, and saw him through the open door to the gunroom.

"Ah, Mr. Cruwys. Your calculations?"

"Yes, sir. Just completed."

Walsh scanned the sheet with narrowed eyes, comparing the figures to his own. After a moment, he gave a grudging nod. "Satisfactory. Your training under Cook is evident."

Coming from Walsh, this was effusive praise.

"Thank you, sir."

Walsh fixed him with a penetrating look. "Admiral Hughes spoke particularly of your time among the Pacific islanders. He suggested it might prove useful to the service, should operations shift in that direction."

"I learned a great deal during my time there, sir," Nicholas replied carefully, uncertain where this was leading.

"No doubt." Walsh set the papers aside. "When we reach Bombay, you will prepare a report—detailed, mind you—on the harbours, approaches, and defensive capacities of the principal islands you visited. Strategic assessments, Mr. Cruwys. Not pretty sketches of palm trees and native girls."

Nicholas felt a flicker of discomfort at the tone. "Of course, sir. Though I would note that many of these islands lack formal defenses in the European sense. Their strategies—if you can call them that—are... different."

"Different or not, they must be understood if we're to maintain British interests in the Pacific. The French and Spanish are already active in those waters." Walsh's tone left no room for debate. "You'll deliver the report before we leave Bombay. We remain only long enough to reprovision and deliver dispatches."

"Aye, sir. I'll begin at once."

Walsh nodded, already turning away. "You have the first dog watch, I believe?"

"Yes, sir."

"Carry on, then."

As the captain disappeared towards the companionway, Nicholas stood a moment longer, the weight of the request settling on him. From a naval standpoint, it made perfect sense: his knowledge of the Pacific islands represented rare and valuable intelligence. But reducing those islands—their people, their homes, their complex societies—to a catalogue of strategic assets gave him pause.

He thought of Bora Bora, of Atea, of the men and women who had taken him in when he was lost. They had asked nothing of him but respect. Now he was to assess their usefulness for war.

He was a British officer, sworn to King and country. Yet his experience had given him other loyalties, quieter but no less real. How should he frame his report? What to emphasize, what to omit? Harbours, reefs, and anchorages were one thing. But what of the people, their customs, their strengths, their vulnerabilities?

It was not a matter of betrayal or loyalty, but of responsibility. To his service, to the islanders, to his own conscience.

These thoughts followed him as he returned to the deck to prepare for his watch. The tropical sun beat down from a cloudless sky. As fourth lieutenant, his duties were clear and defined.

But the conflict within him remained: the quiet knowledge that he was no longer quite the midshipman who had sailed with Cook, nor entirely the naval officer his uniform proclaimed.

As the afternoon faded into evening, Commander Walsh stood alone on the windward side of the quarterdeck, his thoughts turning to his newest lieutenant. Cruwys had proved a surprising addition to *Lynx*'s complement—not at all what Walsh had expected when Admiral Hughes informed him he would be receiving a young officer absent from the service nearly three years.

Walsh had anticipated someone half-broken by his experiences, perhaps too long among "savages" to return easily to discipline, or worse, a youth infected with the dangerous romantic notions of "noble island life" that had begun to circulate in fashionable circles after the publication of Cook's journals. Instead, he had found a capable, even-tempered officer who combined formal training with practical knowledge honed under extreme conditions.

What impressed Walsh most was Cruwys's adaptability. He had stepped back into the rhythm and hierarchy of a King's ship with little friction, bringing with him certain methods and habits picked up elsewhere. His navigation retained Cook's exactitude, yet bore traces of other influences—notations on currents and local conditions that hinted at islander techniques and the seasoned pragmatism of that Portuguese trader, Silva. Walsh, who held that a true seaman's skill could not be taught but only revealed, had been quietly pleased with what he saw. A man either had a feel for a ship, or he didn't—and Cruwys did.

More importantly, the young lieutenant showed a steady hand with men. The starboard gun crews worked willingly under his direction, responding to quiet competence rather than threats or sharp correction. He treated the sailors with respect but held the proper distance, neither condescending nor too familiar. Walsh valued that rare equilibrium; it spoke not only to character but to a deeper understanding of command.

Whether Cruwys would continue to prove himself remained to be seen. The voyage home would offer no shortage of trials—especially off the Cape and near Gibraltar, where French or Spanish forces might be encountered. But Walsh had developed an eye for potential during his own rapid rise through the ranks, and in Nicholas Cruwys, he sensed the makings of something more than a merely competent lieutenant.

A shout from aloft interrupted his reflections. "Deck there! Land ho!" The lookout's voice carried clearly down from the masthead. "Land bearing three points off the starboard bow!"

Walsh raised his glass toward the quarter. "Mr. Harrington," he called to the officer of the watch, "take a glass to the masthead."

"Aye, sir." Lieutenant Harrington slung a telescope over his shoulder and began to climb swiftly up the shrouds. A few minutes later, his voice rang down from the top.

"On deck there—Bombay, sir, without doubt. The high ground behind the harbour's just visible."

Walsh gave a curt nod of satisfaction. When Harrington returned to the deck, Walsh said, "Very good. We'll take in the t'gallants before sunset and stand off and on until morning. I'll not risk those harbour shoals in the dark."

"Aye, sir."

As Harrington moved off to relay the orders, Walsh remained at the rail, studying the smudge of land rising from the sea. Bombay—gateway to India's western shore and home to one of the finest natural harbours in the East. After three weeks at sea, *Lynx* would soon be in port, delivering her dispatches and taking on stores for the long voyage westward to Gibraltar.

The morning sun crowned the island of Bombay with golden light as *HMS Lynx* made her final approach to the harbour. Unlike their arrival in Calcutta—where the ship had been forced to navigate the treacherous currents and shifting sandbanks of the Hooghly—Bombay offered a deep, protected anchorage, accessible directly from the open sea. Walsh stood on the quarterdeck, personally conning the ship through the channel, his orders crisp and precise as *Lynx* threaded her way between the rocky shoals guarding the harbour mouth.

Nicholas, having just completed the morning watch, remained on deck to observe their entry. Bombay presented a striking contrast to

Calcutta. Where the Bengal capital sprawled low across riverine plains, Bombay rose more dramatically from the sea, its central ridge forming a natural spine from which the settlement spread toward the shores. A faint haze softened the city's outlines, but Nicholas could already distinguish the features that marked it as one of Britain's principal strongholds in the East.

To the south stood the grey ramparts of Bombay Fort, the seat of British military and administrative power. Its angular geometry and European façades stood in sharp contrast to the organic spread of the native town beyond. Church spires rose beside Hindu temple towers and the minarets of mosques, a visual testament to the layered complexity of the trading port. The waterfront teemed with motion even at this early hour: fishing boats setting out under oar and sail, cargo dhows with their high bows and lateen rigs maneuvering in the anchorage, lighters and bumboats plying between shore and the deeper-drafted vessels at moorings.

"A handsome prospect, is it not, Mr. Cruwys?" Walsh remarked, stepping to the rail beside him once the ship had safely cleared the narrows. "Quite different from Calcutta."

"Indeed, sir," Nicholas replied. "The harbour seems better suited to naval operations."

Walsh nodded at the observation. "Precisely why the Admiralty maintains Bombay as our principal naval base in the East Indies. Calcutta may be the seat of the Company's power, but Bombay offers what sailors value most—a deep, sheltered harbour with good holding ground, accessible in all seasons. The monsoon strikes here, to be sure, but not with the destructive force it brings to the open coast or the river ports."

As *Lynx* neared her assigned anchorage, Nicholas studied the vessels about the harbour with professional interest. Several East Indiamen rode at anchor, their high sides and bluff bows marking them plainly as traders. Closer to the fort lay a two-decker fourth rate—*HMS Salisbury*, fifty guns, with a frigate riding farther out. Their presence underscored Britain's naval commitment to its eastern dominions.

Smaller craft moved ceaselessly between ship and shore: officers' barges, Company boats, native craft heavy with goods and provisions. It was a floating mirror of the wider world, hierarchical, polyglot, constantly in motion. The harbour, even at this early hour, was a living map of empire.

The guns of Bombay Castle, at the heart of the fort, commanded the harbour's approaches. Unlike Calcutta, where a trading factory had expanded into a city by stages, Bombay had been shaped from the start with both commerce and defence in mind. The Portuguese had recognized its strategic worth long before ceding it to the British as part of Catherine of Braganza's dowry upon her marriage to Charles II. Under Company rule, it had become a formidable bastion guarding the western flank of British power in the Indian Ocean.

"Stand by to let go the anchor," Walsh ordered, as *Lynx* turned into the wind and lost way. "Let go."

The anchor plunged, and the cable ran out with a thunderous rumble through the hawsehole. The ship settled, bow facing the harbour mouth.

Scarcely had *Lynx* come to rest when the harbour began to converge upon her. A boat flying the Company's flag approached from the direction of the fort—clearly bearing officials come to receive the dispatches from Bengal. Around them circled native bumboats, laden with fresh produce, chickens in wicker cages, and earthenware jars of water, holding off at a respectful distance as they awaited permission to come alongside and trade with the crew.

Nicholas observed all this with the practiced eye of a naval officer assessing a new port, but also with the broader perspective of a man who had seen many harbours across the globe. Bombay differed from Calcutta not merely in physical geography, but in its character. Where Calcutta felt distinctly Bengali beneath its European overlay, Bombay was something else entirely—a true trading entrepôt, where cultures had blended and overlapped across generations.

This was evident even from the deck. The docks swarmed with figures in remarkable variety of dress and manner: Parsi merchants in their high-crowned caps and long coats; Hindu traders marked on the brow with caste signs; Muslim sailors in loose trousers and sleeveless vests; Jewish merchants whose ancestors had sought refuge in India centuries before; Chinese and Malay seamen whose junks and dhows knit India to the farther East. Europeans were present, but not dominant—moving through a commercial world in which they were participants, not unquestioned masters.

"A proper Babel, is it not?" observed Dr. Crawford, who had joined Nicholas at the rail. "I've always found Bombay the most intriguing of our eastern holdings. Calcutta may be grander, Madras more purely English in its habits—but Bombay, ah—Bombay has a soul of its own."

"It seems so," Nicholas replied. "Have you served here before?"

"Three separate commissions," the surgeon said, smiling. "I was here when the word reached us of Clive's victory at Plassey. That dates me, doesn't it? The city has changed—grown, certainly—but its essence remains the same. Commerce rules here, Mr. Cruwys. Even the Company's governors know that Bombay's prosperity lies in allowing its many communities to manage their own affairs with as little interference as possible."

As they spoke, a signal broke out on *Salisbury*, instructing *Lynx*'s captain to repair on board.

Soon the captain was descending into his gig, the boat's crew pulling smartly toward the anchored fourth-rate. Nicholas watched as Walsh was piped aboard *Salisbury* with the ceremony due his rank, then vanished below to the captain's quarters. Nearly an hour passed before the gig returned, Walsh climbing back aboard *Lynx* with a thoughtful expression.

As the ship settled into the routine of arrival, Nicholas anticipated receiving orders to supervise shore liberty for the starboard watch, as was customary for junior lieutenants. He was therefore surprised when Walsh summoned him to his cabin shortly after returning from *Salisbury*.

"Mr. Cruwys, a change of plans," Walsh said, his tone conversational but allowing no argument. "You will not be supervising shore liberty today. I require your presence for a more useful duty."

"Governor Hornby has requested that at least three officers attend a reception at Government House at six bells this evening. Full dress uniform." Walsh's expression was unreadable, but there was the faintest suggestion of satisfaction in his voice. "Admiral Hughes' flag captain conveyed certain… reservations about your going ashore in Bombay, given recent incidents in Calcutta. Nonetheless, I have made my own assessment of your judgment, Mr. Cruwys, and consider such caution unnecessary in this instance."

Nicholas felt a mixture of surprise and gratitude. That the captain was aware of his entanglement with Lady Montague was clear; that he had chosen to disregard the implied warning was not something Nicholas had expected.

"Aye, sir. Thank you, sir."

Walsh waved off the thanks. "It's not a matter of trust, but practical necessity. You're familiar with Company protocols from your time in Calcutta, and you conduct yourself well among officials. Lieutenant Chester can supervise liberty. Lieutenant Harrington will accompany us—his family ties to several Company directors may prove advantageous. That is all."

After Nicholas departed, Walsh's eyes briefly flickered toward the quarterdeck where through his skylight he could hear Lieutenant Chester berating a young midshipman over some trivial matter. He frowned. While Chester was adequate at maintaining discipline aboard ship, his questionable judgment during the last squall and inability to properly assess the sail trim generally made him as unreliable at sea as his complete lack of social graces and tendency toward petulance made him unsuitable for delicate negotiations that required anything resembling tact or diplomacy. It made Walsh thoughtful indeed, for if anything should happen to Lieutenant Hargrove, he could not see Chester as first lieutenant of his beloved *Lynx*.

An hour later, Nicholas was in his cabin. He had the gunroom steward bring basins of fresh water—one hot, one cold—for a proper sponge down and shave. He combed and dressed his hair, cleaned his teeth, and drew on his best uniform coat, its white lapels bright, the buttons polished to a mirror gleam. His waistcoat, white breeches, and silk stockings were pristine, carefully folded and preserved in his sea chest along with his best shoes. For his sidearm, he buckled on the sword Silva had given him in Macao: a beautiful and deadly piece with a sharkskin grip, silver mountings, and a blade light enough for precision but strong enough to command respect. It would serve well as the dress sword required for formal occasions. And he felt better with a real weapon at his side in any case.

As he dressed, Nicholas reflected on Walsh's decision to include him in the party to Government House. It was not merely a vote of confidence; it was an opportunity to observe the true machinery of power in British India—Company administration, where decisions were made behind closed doors and polished teak tables.

He stepped into the gunroom adjusting his neckcloth just as Harrington entered, already in full dress uniform, every element precise.

"Almost ready, Cruwys? The captain's having the gig prepared. Apparently we're to be received with full ceremony at the Apollo Bunder."

He paused, watching Nicholas adjust his sword belt. "Fine weapon. I've seen you wear it before, but never had the chance to ask. Not standard pattern, I think?"

"A gift," Nicholas replied, drawing the blade partway from its scabbard. Even in the low light of the gunroom, it flashed bright. "From a Portuguese trader I sailed with after leaving the Society Islands."

Harrington stepped closer, clearly intrigued. "Toledo steel, unless I'm very much mistaken. Light cavalry pattern, but with a very slight curve more common in Iberian blades."

At a nod from Nicholas he took the sword with care and turned it in his hand, carefully examining the grip and edge.

"The balance is excellent. I've studied fencing since I was a boy," he said, "with my father's armourer. This—this is exceptional work. Subtle in the hand."

A spark passed between them—something between a challenge and an invitation.

"We should practice sometime," Harrington went on. "A blade like this deserves to be understood. I'd be curious to see how you handle it, given your... unconventional education."

Nicholas smiled, recognizing both the professional interest and the offer of camaraderie. "I learned a few things from that trader—unorthodox, perhaps. Not quite the method they taught at Portsmouth."

"All the better," Harrington said. "Shall we ask the captain's permission? I promise to keep it professional. And entertaining."

Nicholas nodded, and Harrington continued, "You must tell me more about your travels sometime. My grandfather served on the Board of the Company—left quite a collection of Pacific artifacts in the London house. He would have found your experiences fascinating."

His tone was earnest, not merely polite, and Nicholas felt the faint but unmistakable shift that marked the beginning of something more than formal acquaintance.

Before Nicholas could respond, the high, piercing notes of the bosun's call rang out across the deck, the traditional signal for the captain's departure. Officers gathered smartly on the quarterdeck as custom required, side boys took their stations at the entry port, and the boatswain's mate stood ready with his silver pipe.

Lynx's gig was alongside, and moments later, Walsh stepped out of his cabin in full dress uniform. He surveyed Harrington and Nicholas with a raised eyebrow.

"Gentlemen," he said, voice dry, "so good of you to attend. Let us be about our duty."

They descended into the waiting gig and shoved off, the oars rising and falling in crisp rhythm as the boat turned toward shore.

The sun was beginning to dip, casting long amber shadows over the city as they approached the landing. Their destination was the Apollo Bunder—Bombay's ceremonial landing place, used for formal arrivals and departures. Situated near the Fort and the Company's principal offices, it was one of the oldest and most dignified approaches to the city, its broad stone steps bearing the weight of governors, admirals, and Company grandees for more than a century.

As they came ashore, they saw an elaborate Company coach standing ready, a troop of native cavalry drawn up nearby as escort, a striking display of colonial pageantry. Eighteen horsemen of the Bombay Presidency Horse rode matched bays, their pagri turbans of white with red tips a vivid contrast to their dark blue jackets with scarlet facings—the distinctive uniform of the Bombay forces that differentiated them from their Bengal and Madras counterparts. Each man bore a curved tulwar at his side and a carbine slung across his back.

The troopers were primarily Marathas and Konkani Muslims, recruited from the western coastal regions where horsemanship had long been prized among the warrior castes. Several wore the distinctive mustaches of veteran cavalrymen, their bearing reflecting years of service to the Company.

They were led by a European lieutenant, who gave a greeting and a salute to Captain Walsh as they neared. The officer's gold epaulettes caught the morning sun, his white breeches and polished boots immaculate despite Bombay's dust and heat.

The coach rolled through the streets of Bombay as evening softened the city's outlines. Their escort moved with practiced ease, their formation a mobile wall of discipline and colour.

Nicholas, seated across from Walsh and Harrington, watched as the layered complexity of the place revealed itself. Wealthy Indian merchants passed by with quiet self-possession: a Gujarati in a gold-threaded silk kurta, borne in an ornate palanquin; a Parsi in a black coat and high-crowned hat riding in a sedan chair. Street children crouched nearby, their thin limbs a jarring contrast to the surrounding opulence.

A nobleman's palanquin, inlaid with mother-of-pearl, passed a cluster of labourers picking through refuse. A massive elephant stood at a street corner, its mahout brushing its flanks with methodical care. The air shimmered with scent—wood smoke, spices, salt, jasmine, and the riper odours of a crowded city nearing the end of its day.

Street vendors offered wares of exquisite delicacy: muslin so fine it could be drawn through a ring, silk brocades in colours that dazzled the eye, carpets that had taken months to weave. Voices rose in

Marathi, Gujarati, Portuguese, and English—a polyglot marketplace, vibrant and immediate.

They passed through Hornby Vellard, the reclaimed causeway that had turned Bombay from a scatter of marshy islands into a single, contiguous city. Here, architectural contrasts grew even sharper—Portuguese villas with wide verandahs beside British compounds and Marathi townhouses. Narrow lanes crowded with wooden balconies cast alternating bands of shadow and light.

Nicholas took it all in with a practised eye. He had seen poverty before—in Portsmouth, and elsewhere—but never quite this combination of extremes. In Bombay, the contrasts were not merely stark; they were dynamic, layered, constantly in motion. A nobleman's palanquin, a polyglot merchant at trade, and a starving child could all inhabit the same street—and in that strange coexistence, there was a vitality unlike anything he had yet encountered.

Harrington leaned close, his voice low but not conspiratorial. Captain Walsh, absorbed in studying the passing streets, seemed content to allow the junior officers their conversation. "Quite a spectacle, isn't it? One might almost believe we've stumbled into some impossible paradise, were it not for the poverty," He paused, glancing at Nicholas. "Though I suppose you know something of true paradises, don't you?"

An image bloomed in Nicholas's mind—not just a memory, but a vision of pure, unspoiled beauty. Bora Bora as it truly was: a landscape so perfect it seemed conjured from the dreams of gods. The lagoon a crystalline blue so pure it hurt to look at, colors so vibrant they seemed to pulse with life. Atea standing on a pristine white beach that curved like a perfect smile, her dark hair lifted by a wind that carried the scent of frangipani and sea salt. Their simple grass hut—not a place of poverty, but a perfect harmony with the landscape, its walls open to reveal a world of breathtaking beauty. Breadfruit trees laden with fruit, the central slopes and peak rising in impossible green perfection, the sea a living, breathing entity that seemed to whisper ancient secrets. It was a paradise that existed beyond the comprehension of European imagination. A world where beauty was not something to be possessed, but something to be lived, breathed, inhabited. Where every moment was a perfect balance of abundance and simplicity, where human life existed in sublime connection with the natural world.

The memory was so vivid, so achingly beautiful, that for a moment the colours of Bombay—its stone, its dust, its wealth—seemed grey and inert by comparison. Nicholas felt an ache rise in him—not only for Atea, but for the entire way of being he had once known, and that he now understood to be far more rare, and more precious, than any civilization could comprehend, and one now gone beyond recall.

The Indian escort remained impassive, their eyes constantly scanning the crowd—a moving barrier of discipline and readiness. One among them, slightly older than the rest, met Nicholas's gaze for a moment. A long scar ran from temple to jaw, a quiet testament to years of service in hard places.

As they neared Government House, the city's tumult gave way to manicured gardens and paved approaches. The great residence rose ahead, a monument to order and ambition: whitewashed walls, arcaded verandahs, and perfectly trimmed hedges laid out with geometric precision. The grounds, bathed in the amber light of newly lit lamps, spoke of prosperity and planning. Servants—both Indian and European—moved with quiet competence, setting final touches in place for the reception.

The coach slowed before the main entrance. The escort fanned out in practiced formation, their discipline unobtrusive but unmistakable. Sepoys of the Governor's bodyguard stood at rigid attention, their red coats with yellow facings and white crossbelts replicating the uniform of their European counterparts, though adapted with looser cuts and lighter materials for the coastal Bombay climate. Unlike the Bengal establishment, where the Governor-General's guard displayed elaborate ceremonial dress, the Bombay guard maintained a more practical military bearing suited to the Presidency's frontier position, where threats from Maratha forces and Mysore remained constant concerns.

Harrington leaned slightly toward Nicholas. "Ready, Cruwys? In places like this, every word, every gesture carries weight."

Nicholas nodded, a faint smile on his lips. After the islands of the Pacific, the trade ports of the East, and even his short time in Calcutta, he understood precisely what Harrington meant. Bombay was a world of sharp contrasts and shifting ground—where cultures met, collided, and sometimes blended into something entirely new.

The reception at Government House began as the last light faded from the Bombay sky, candles and oil lamps casting a warm glow across the immaculately tended gardens. Servants moved silently with silver candelabras, their flames forming pools of shifting light across polished surfaces and among the gathered guests.

Governor William Hornby embodied the East India Company's authority. In his late sixties, he carried himself with the gravitas of a man who had administered empire for decades. Though slightly below average height and grown corpulent with years of tropical service, he moved with a surprising agility that belied his bulk.

His face bore the signs of long years in the East—ruddy, weathered, deeply lined. His complexion was tanned and faintly mottled from the sun, yet his eyes—clear, pale blue—remained sharply observant. The tropical heat had not stooped his back nor softened his bearing; he stood square-shouldered, straight-backed, every inch the Company's representative.

His greeting to the officers was direct, his manner brisk.

"Captain Walsh," he said, extending his hand. "Your arrival is well timed. Admiral Hughes speaks highly of your command."

Walsh acknowledged the compliment with a crisp nod. "You're too kind, Governor. *Lynx* is a capable vessel."

When Nicholas was presented, Hornby's gaze sharpened with genuine interest.

"Mr. Cruwys. Your experiences under Captain Cook have occasioned considerable discussion in official circles."

"I trust my observations have been of some use, sir," Nicholas replied, careful in tone.

Hornby gave a single nod and turned to greet another guest, leaving Nicholas to navigate the complex, half-visible structures of Company society.

The hall was a vibrant tableau of colonial society, a carefully choreographed display of power, wealth, and hierarchy. Naval officers in crisp blue uniforms clustered near the edges of the room, their conversation a low murmur punctuated by the occasional burst of laughter. East India Company merchants in rich waistcoats stood in measured groups, exchanging trade gossip and political speculation. Local Indian nobles in traditional dress moved with quiet dignity, their presence a reminder of the complex social fabric underlying authority in British India.

Nicholas found himself near a group of naval officers from various ships, listening more than speaking, a glass of punch in hand. Captain James Hartley of *HMS Salisbury* held the floor—a senior post-captain, weathered by decades at sea, whose reputation commanded immediate respect. Now in his early fifties, his face bore the sun-darkened complexion of a man long accustomed to all climates. His career had been distinguished, if not meteoric—earned not by patronage, but by steady competence. He had served in the Seven Years' War, much of it in the Indian Ocean and Bay of Bengal, watching the Company's maritime reach expand. A scar along his left jaw, acquired during a boarding action off Sumatra in '62, marked him as a man who had earned his rank with steel as well as seamanship.

"So there we were," Hartley was saying, his voice pitched with the carry of long habit, "off the Malabar coast near Calicut. Three Arab pirates—fast xebecs with lateen rigs—thought they'd found an easy prize."

A ripple of amusement passed through the gup.

The tale unfolded with the ease of long practice. Hartley's hands moved as he spoke, unconsciously sketching manoeuvres in the air, his gaze distant with recollection. Unlike the embellishers one often encountered in officers' messes, Hartley's storytelling was known for its precision—almost clinical in its detail, all the more compelling for its restraint.

Nicholas listened with quiet attention. He recognised in Hartley the understanding that every engagement, every encounter at sea, was both a tactical exercise and a study in human behaviour. The other young officers hung on every word. To them, Hartley was more than a storyteller—he was a living connection to a generation of seamen who had watched Britain rise to naval supremacy, a supremacy now once again under challenge from France and Spain.

The room hummed with silks and low voices, the gentle clink of crystal, the soft music of conversation. Servants moved among the guests with polished ease, offering silver trays laden with small delicacies—delicate porcelain cups of spiced tea, glasses of chilled punch, and confections that spoke to the subtle art of colonial hospitality.

It was in the midst of this carefully managed social tide that Miss Caroline Carlisle appeared, moving with fluid confidence. She was striking in a way that altered the room's rhythm—her pale complexion meticulously preserved from the Indian sun, her fair golden hair styled with elegant precision. Her gown, pale blue silk, clung and floated by turns, catching the chandeliers' light as she passed. Conversations slowed. Wives and sweethearts—both present and presumed—watched her with polite tension. Several offered greetings; more pursed their lips in subtle vexation, envy thinly veiled by manners.

She was the daughter of a senior Company official and a wealthy merchant well known in Bombay society—but familiarity had not dulled her effect. Her presence still commanded attention.

Nicholas noticed her at the edge of the naval circle and made a deliberate effort not to stare. Young, he thought—perhaps twenty-two—but as she came closer, he revised that. Likely near his own age, in fact. Her waist was slim beneath the silk, her figure lightly curved, but it was not softness alone that caught his eye. There was strength beneath the grace—something in the way she moved, in the erect set of her shoulders, that spoke of discipline. Not the affectation of posture school, but the bearing of someone accustomed to riding, walking, living actively in her own body. The gown's modest bodice revealed the upper swell of a full, high bust, framed without display. A heavy gold necklace held a single emerald, catching fire in the candlelight.

She moved through the crowd with calm assurance, exchanging pleasantries with several officers she clearly knew. As she reached the group of naval officers and nodded familiarly to Captain Hartley, he said, "Gentlemen, may I have the pleasure of presenting Miss Caroline Carlisle, daughter of Mr. Carlisle, a Director of the Company."

Nicholas and the others bowed. And then as she turned to face him, there were her eyes: green—not merely unusual, but arrestingly deep and bright. Clear, intelligent, and intensely present. He felt them on him even before she spoke, as if she were taking measure and offering none of her own.

"Lieutenant Cruwys, is it not?" she said, her gaze settling on him with unexpected directness, her eyes sparkling with curiosity, "I've heard the most extraordinary accounts of your travels. They say you've seen corners of the world few Englishmen have ever reached."

When she spoke, her voice was low and well-modulated—carrying that particular cadence he had come to recognise in women of standing: studied casualness, backed by practiced control. And it was then he understood. She was not merely beautiful. She was *particular*. Self-possessed. Not delicate, but defined. She changed the quality of the room, not by demanding attention, but by giving none of it away unearned.

Nicholas, who had spent years among people who valued quiet strength above ornament, found himself—for the first time in some while—uncertain what to say.

She had positioned herself with graceful precision at the correct social distance, her fan moving in slow, practiced arcs, her posture turned just so to catch the light. Nicholas, though still young and by no means accustomed to women of her standing, was keenly aware of the importance of propriety—particularly with Captain Walsh observing discreetly from the far side of the group.

"My experiences have been unusual, certainly, Miss Carlisle," he replied, keeping his tone pleasant but measured. "Though I expect many officers could say the same."

"I doubt that very much, Mr. Cruwys," she said, a smile lighting her features. "Few officers have lived among the islanders of the South Seas, or sailed in their astonishing craft. My father speaks often of

Captain Cook's journals. He holds them in great admiration. To meet someone who served with him—it is quite out of the ordinary."

Nicholas felt himself warming to the sincerity in her tone. "Captain Cook was a remarkable man. His precision in navigation and cartography changed how we understand the Pacific, and how we think about exploration more broadly."

"And after all that," she said, tilting her head slightly, "how do you find Bombay society? I imagine it must seem terribly... conventional by comparison."

"On the contrary," Nicholas said, surprised by his own ease. "India's complexity fascinates me—the interplay of cultures, the layers of history, the ancient traditions alongside European systems. The islands I knew were beautiful, but often self-contained. Bombay, by contrast, stands at a true crossroads of civilization."

Her eyes brightened, clearly pleased by his reply. "How refreshing to speak with an officer who observes, Mr. Cruwys, rather than merely catalogues. Most gentlemen I encounter see only what they expect to find."

Before he could respond, a subtle shifting in the crowd brought another presence to her side—a gentleman of medium height and portly build, his fine coat strained slightly across a rounded middle, dark hair thinning and grey at the temples, and eyes sharp with practiced assessment.

"Father," Caroline said, turning slightly, "may I present Lieutenant Nicholas Cruwys of *HMS Lynx*. Lieutenant Cruwys served with Captain Cook and has the most fascinating experiences to share."

She turned back to Nicholas, her voice composed. "Lieutenant, this is my father, Mr. Edward Carlisle—Senior Director of the Company's Western India Trading Division, and principal of Carlisle Trading."

Mr. Carlisle extended his hand—a firm grip, appraising. "Ah, the young officer mentioned in Admiral Hughes's dispatches. Your journey from the Society Islands to Calcutta has caused no small stir in Company circles, Lieutenant."

"Sir," Nicholas replied, bowing slightly, aware he was being measured by one of the most influential men in Bombay. And by the other officers in the group, including Hartley and Walsh.

"I understand you've prepared detailed charts of several islands previously unmapped by European navigators," Carlisle continued. "Such knowledge could prove valuable to Company interests. The Pacific trade routes grow increasingly vital as our traditional channels face disruption from the present hostilities."

"My first duty, sir, is to deliver those observations to the Admiralty," Nicholas answered, his tone courteous but firm. "But I would be happy to speak more generally on the navigational challenges in those waters."

Carlisle's eyes narrowed briefly, then he smiled, the expression tinged with real appreciation. "Well answered, Lieutenant. Loyalty to one's service is always admirable." He cast a sidelong glance at his daughter, whose interest was not lost on him. "Perhaps you'll join us for dinner before your ship departs? Caroline maintains a small salon for civilised conversation. I suspect your experiences would provide a welcome respite from the usual colonial speculations."

"I should be honoured, sir, subject to my captain's permission for shore leave," Nicholas replied, acutely aware of what such an invitation signified. The Carlisles clearly occupied the uppermost echelon of Bombay society.

"Excellent. Tomorrow evening, then. Seven o'clock." Carlisle inclined his head and turned as another Company official approached, drawing him into conversation.

Caroline remained, her fan still moving in slow, deliberate arcs. "My father rarely extends such invitations to officers below the rank of commander," she said quietly. "You've made quite an impression."

"I'm not sure I've done anything to deserve it," Nicholas said honestly.

Her laugh was soft, almost musical. "Oh, but you have, Lieutenant Cruwys. You've intrigued us both, which is no small feat in Bombay. Novelty is common. Substance is rare."

She hesitated, then continued, more softly: "I should like very much to hear more about your time among the islanders. They say you learned their language, their way of thinking. What was that like?"

Something in her tone—genuine, searching—cut through his caution. She was not merely curious. She wanted to understand.

"It changes you," he said simply. "To see the world through entirely different eyes—to realise that what you've always taken as universal truth is only one way of seeing."

Caroline studied him with those extraordinary green eyes. "How fascinating. And rather dangerous to conventional thinking, I would imagine."

"Indeed," Nicholas replied, a faint smile touching his lips.

"Then we shall have much to discuss tomorrow evening," she said, her voice warm with anticipation. "Until then, Lieutenant Cruwys."

She offered a graceful inclination of the head, and with a final glance—lingering just long enough to register interest without impropriety—she moved off to rejoin a group of Company wives.

Harrington, who had watched the exchange in silence, regarded Nicholas with a look of amused disbelief. "Good Lord, Cruwys," he murmured, voice pitched low. "I've never seen Edward Carlisle show that kind of interest in a junior officer. The man effectively controls half the trade of the western Indian Ocean. And his daughter…" He gave a slow, appreciative whistle. "She's refused proposals from two Company directors and a baronet. You've made an impression."

"I merely answered their questions," Nicholas replied, uncomfortable with Harrington's tone.

"And that," Harrington said dryly, "may be precisely what did it. Honesty is a rare coin in Company circles."

He paused, his expression shifting from amusement to calculation. "Still—you should tread carefully. The Carlisles don't just entertain; they maneuver. Caroline isn't some colonial debutante looking for a name to attach hers to. She's her father's confidante—and, by quiet reputation, his most effective agent in certain matters best not discussed in large rooms."

Before Nicholas could reply, a voice cut in from just behind them.

"Gentlemen."

They stiffened instinctively. Captain Walsh's tone was crisp, but unreadable.

"I trust your attention remains on the matter at hand," he said, not raising his voice, yet somehow filling the space. "The Governor has invited us to remain at Government House for the night. Official hospitality," he added, with the barest inflection at the corner of his mouth. "There will be a conference at breakfast."

Nicholas cleared his throat. "Sir—I've received an invitation to dine with Mr. Carlisle and his daughter tomorrow evening. With your permission, of course."

Walsh's gaze narrowed slightly, reading more than the words, then eased. "Ah. The Company Director. Useful connections, Mr. Cruwys. Yes—you have my permission. But return to the ship by midnight. We sail with the morning tide."

"Thank you, sir," Nicholas said, conscious of Harrington's suppressed grin beside him.

Nicholas's guest room was a testament to the careful hospitality of Government House. Broad windows with wooden shutters stood open to the night, allowing the tropical air to drift through the space. A four-poster bed occupied one side of the room, its white muslin netting gathered like a veil around the posts. A writing desk of polished mahogany stood near the window, a brass lamp casting a steady circle of light across its surface.

It was near midnight when he had finally changed out of his formal coat and—after the rare luxury of a true bath—into a loose set of linen sleeping clothes laid out by a servant. The evening had cooled, and the high-ceilinged room held the breath of night air. His journal lay open before him, the page filling with reflections: Governor Hornby's reception, the unexpected invitation from the Carlisles, and the flickering interplay between his present and the memory of the Pacific.

The room smelled faintly of jasmine from the gardens, mingled with the scent of clean linens and the faint mineral tang of old wood. A ceramic pitcher of water stood near at hand, cool in the moist air.

His thoughts returned to Caroline Carlisle: the intelligence behind her questions, the unfeigned curiosity beneath her social ease. The way her eyes studied, rather than merely admired. There was depth there—and direction. Harrington's warning about the complexity of her family seemed well founded, but it had not lessened her intrigue.

As the building settled into quiet, Nicholas considered the strange course that had brought him here: from midshipman to castaway, from islander to lieutenant of a King's ship, and now to the attentions of one of the most influential families in British India. The path ahead was uncertain, but almost for the first time since Bora Bora, he felt not mere duty, but anticipation.

He closed the journal, blew out the lamp, and lay back beneath the muslin netting. The linen sheets were cool, the bed a kind of floating world unto itself. Tomorrow would bring the Governor's conference, and dinner with the Carlisles, each charged with possibility. But for now, in the hush of the tropical night, Nicholas allowed himself a memory of Atea: not in grief, but in acknowledgment.

That part of him would always belong to the Pacific. But another part, he sensed, had begun to shift.

The next morning, they were summoned to breakfast in the Governor's dining room. The atmosphere was different from the previous evening's reception, more formal, with a sense of purpose that hung in the air.

The dining room was spacious, with large windows overlooking the extensive manicured gardens. A long mahogany table was set with a gleaming service of delicate china, polished cutlery, and crystal glasses that caught the morning light. Servants moved silently, bringing dishes of fresh tropical fruits, freshly baked rolls, cold meats, strong tea, and thankfully, coffee.

Initial conversation was light and social. Servants circulated, refilling tea and coffee, removing empty plates. The naval officers exchanged pleasantries about their recent voyages, the local climate, and the intricacies of naval life in the Indian Ocean. As the meal progressed and plates were cleared, Governor Hornby signaled to the servants. With practiced efficiency, they withdrew, leaving the naval officers alone with the Governor.

Hartley broke the silence. "Sir, I presume this meeting concerns more than a morning repast?"

A slight smile crossed Hornby's face. "Indeed, Captain. What I'm about to discuss requires the utmost discretion."

Hartley leaned forward, his weathered hands now resting on the now-clear tablecloth. "Regarding the need for convoy, I expect?"

"Precisely," Hornby began, "*Lynx* brought urgent dispatches from Admiral Hughes concerning a growing threat from French maritime operations, confirming what we had already suspected. Intelligence suggests a coordinated effort of privateers operating from Mauritius, potentially supported by naval vessels from the French Indian Ocean squadron."

He paused, scanning the assembled faces before continuing.

"Gentlemen," he said, his voice firm, "as you are aware, there are six of our best East Indiamen here in port, loaded and ready for passage home: *Fortitude, Earl of Hertford, Bengal Queen, Ocean, Lord Clive,* and *Bombay Merchan*t. As you may also know, the Company's annual revenue is approximately £4 million. These six ships carry a total cargo valued at more than £750,000—comprised of tea, cotton and silk textiles, spices, indigo and other dyes, saltpeter, bullion, botanical and zoological specimens, exotic woods, and various luxury goods from across the Indian subcontinent and surrounding trading regions. This represents about twenty percent of the Company's total annual revenue. The potential loss of such a cargo, and indeed of the ships themselves, would be a substantial economic blow to the Company and, by extension, to the country's interests, especially at this juncture in the war. Furthermore, it is not just the monetary considerations at stake, but the safety of our passengers."

The looked down, consulting a small stack of notes at his elbow.

"*The Fortitude's* passenger accommodations are fully occupied by the Earl of Pemberton, Lord Ashton, His Majesty's Special Envoy to the Governor-General's Council in Bengal, and his party, now returning to England.

The Bengal Queen will carry several notable individuals. Sir William Mackenzie, a senior Company administrator being recalled to London following a critical five-year posting, will be aboard with his wife and two young children. Accompanying them is Dr. James Harlow, a noted botanist who has spent the past several years collecting specimens throughout India—his collection carefully preserved in custom-built traveling cases.

Aboard *Lord Clive*, we have a group of missionaries bound for home, including the Reverend Thomas Bridgewater, who has spent fifteen years establishing missions in western India and now returns to report to his sponsoring society in London.

Finally, gentlemen, *Ocean*—the largest of the fleet, and under our senior captain—will carry a young noblewoman, Lady Julia Carrington, travelling to join her husband, a senior military officer stationed at Gibraltar. Her personal maid and a military escort will accompany her."

The Governor paused briefly, then added, "In addition, Mr. Carlisle, a leading merchant of the City and a Director of the Company, will also be returning aboard *Ocean*, together with his daughter, Miss Caroline Carlisle, and their household servants, following three years in India."

His gaze lifted momentarily and seemed to settle, if only for a breath, on Nicholas—who remained still.

He stepped closer to the table and tapped a finger on the sea-lanes threading the western ocean.

"Admiral Hughes and I are agreed: though tensions with the Dutch are rising, the convoy will make for Cape Town to take on supplies, weather permitting, or unless damage or dire necessity forbids it. In that event, or in case of separation en route, the most serviceable port of rendezvous will be Portuguese Angola, at Luanda. It remains neutral, and offers adequate means for refit if required."

He looked up, his tone hardening.

"As you are aware, the Indiamen—though stout—are not built for speed. For them, the passage may take five, even six months. Which is why it is imperative they depart without delay, while—unusually for this late in the season, the northeast monsoon still holds in our favour. Should we wait further, we risk the full setting-in of the southwest monsoon. At that point, our ships may find themselves becalmed, or worse—beating against adverse winds to reach the southeast trades. The passage would be lengthened, and the danger compounded."

He let the words hang a moment in the stillness of the room, then continued.

"Accordingly, we will commit all available naval ships to the convoy's protection. *Salisbury* will serve as the senior ship, with the escort squadron under Captain Hartley—now Commodore Hartley's—authority. *Thetis*, 32, Captain Richard Fenwick, will accompany her, as will *Lynx*."

He paused again.

"That *Lynx* is reassigned from her independent duties as dispatch vessel should indicate the seriousness with which we regard the matter."

He looked round the table. "I do you no dishonour, gentlemen, when I say I wish we had more ships. But—" he gave a small shrug "—we must make do with what the service provides."

Captain Hartley leaned forward. "What specific intelligence do we have about the French, Governor? Numbers of vessels? Typical sailing patterns?"

Hornby spread a chart of the Indian Ocean across the table, his finger tracing the strategic position of Île de France—Mauritius.

"Our latest reports indicate a flotilla of at least six privateers, capable of striking swiftly and vanishing again into the trade routes. They've been particularly active in the region between Madagascar and the African coast."

"Armament?" Hartley pressed.

"Most are lightly armed but exceptionally fast, and carry large crews," Hornby replied. "Typically they mount between eight and fourteen guns, with crews ranging from seventy to one hundred men. Our sources suggest they are led by a particularly aggressive captain—Jean-Baptiste Troude—who has had considerable success raiding our shipping lanes."

Hartley gave a grim nod. "And naval support?"

"Two frigates have been observed operating from Port Louis," Hornby said. "Thirty-six and thirty-two guns, both recently commissioned—within the last three years."

The officers exchanged glances but said nothing. Hornby continued.

"Your orders are to escort the convoy to England. Gibraltar remains under siege by the Spanish and is not secure. Your primary charge is protection. As you are now fully briefed, these ships carry not only goods of considerable value, but passengers of importance—and, I may add, intelligence as well.

"You are to engage and drive off any privateers or French naval vessels encountered, but the safety of the convoy is to be your first consideration at all times. I need not remind you of the gravity of this charge, given that we are, for a time, stripping this station of all naval strength—diverting even *Lynx* from her priority of carrying dispatches home with all possible speed."

The Governor cleared his throat and leaned forward, hands clasped on the table.

"There is one further matter, gentlemen," he said. "The war deepens. The French continue to threaten our Caribbean holdings, building on Admiral d'Estaing's seizure of Saint Vincent and Grenada last year. Our situation in the American colonies remains unclear, with mixed reports from the field.

"Here in India, our seizure of the French port of Mahé last year has provoked Hyder Ali of Mysore, who regarded it as under his protection. Conflict with him may be imminent.

"Meanwhile, I am relieved to report that Admiral Sir George Rodney succeeded, in January, in breaking through to resupply the garrison at Gibraltar, which appears to be holding—at least for now. But other nations may yet enter the war against us."

He let that settle, then added:

"In anticipation of precisely such a development—and in view of growing Dutch hostility and the possible closure of the Cape—I took the liberty, with Admiral Hughes's concurrence, of dispatching a courier overland to Egypt three weeks ago."

"The courier carried a formal request to the Admiralty," the Governor said, "urging that additional naval escort be dispatched with all possible speed to intercept and reinforce your convoy. He departed by fast packet from Bombay to Basra, then overland by caravan through Aleppo and Cairo, and on to Alexandria, where the Company maintains a cutter to bear dispatches westward across the Mediterranean."

He tapped the table lightly with one finger.

"The dispatch included the convoy's likely composition, estimated departure, projected route, and the anticipated strength of your escort. It warned of confirmed French privateer activity out of Mauritius, with naval support, and noted the possibility of French or Dutch cruisers operating near the Cape."

Hornby leaned in slightly. "Were rendezvous points included?"

The Governor nodded. "They were. The Admiralty was urged to dispatch a squadron to meet the convoy at one or more designated points in the South Atlantic. The first is Luanda. The second is farther west, off Ascension Island. The third, nearer home, in the waters approaching the Canaries. If no escort appears at any of these stations within the timeframes set, the convoy is to proceed under your command, Commodore Hartley, with vigilance and discipline, to England."

He sat back in his chair, his tone measured but edged with gravity.

"I assure you, gentlemen, every effort has been made to ensure your safety. If the courier made good time, and if the Admiralty acts with proper urgency, you may yet be met at sea once you round the Cape."

He looked from face to face, and finished quietly.

"We are counting now on foresight and seamanship. And perhaps a little good fortune."

There was a brief pause.

Commodore Hartley looked to the two other warship commanders seated beside him.

"As the Governor has already said," he began, leaning slightly over the chart, "we depart with the last breath of the northeast monsoon." His finger traced a deliberate arc across the Indian Ocean. "These final weeks may still offer a window of predictable winds—a gift not to be squandered. Southeast of Ceylon, we'll likely encounter variable winds and confused currents before the full onset of the southwest monsoon. We must make the southeast trades before that moment."

He paused, the tip of his finger now resting clear of the Indian coast, gauging invisible distances with the seasoned eye of a man long accustomed to crossing them.

"With these Indiamen—heavy-laden for all their worth—we may expect a passage of six to nine weeks to the Cape, assuming fair weather and no mishap."

His hand moved northward along the African coast.

"As the Governor has made clear, should we suffer damage, become separated, or require fresh water or stores, the only planned diversion is Portuguese Angola, at Luanda—a neutral anchorage, and friendly to our cause. Beyond that, we must rely on what the sea and our own preparation can provide. We shall ride the Benguela Current northward along Africa's shoulder."

He looked directly at each officer in turn, his voice firm now.

"A fortnight's grace—no more—before the monsoon turns. We must be decisive."

He swept a final glance across the table.

"My written orders will be distributed before the evening gun. They will include the rendezvous points already communicated to the Admiralty. We sail with tomorrow morning's ebb. I'll not have any captain claim ignorance of his station."

The afternoon found Nicholas in his cabin aboard *Lynx*, preparing for the evening ahead. He laid out his uniform with deliberate care: the blue coat with its white facings brushed smooth, brass buttons polished bright, breeches and stockings immaculate. The Portuguese sword hung ready by its belt.

He dressed with the same economy he brought to a gunnery problem—but the silence carried a certain weight.

The examination to confirm his acting promotion would not take place.

He had hoped, and not idly: Admiral Hughes himself had spoken of the board to be assembled in Bombay—Captains Hartley, Fenwick, and Hardcastle, and Nicholas had prepared accordingly. His logs were in order, his charts corrected, his gunnery notes neat and exact. He had reviewed sail evolutions until they came to him by reflex; the signal books, the regulations, even the subtler points of the Articles.

Now, with the convoy's early departure and the captains preparing their ships, the matter was deferred, and in any case with Hardcastle's frigate on patrol there were only two and not the requisite three post captains available.

It was no more than the service allowed. There was some hope the examination might occur later, perhaps at the Cape or Luanda if the convoy met with other naval ships, or indeed the possible reenforcing squadron, or in England. But naval time was a slippery thing; promises ashore often foundered at sea. For the moment, he remained an acting lieutenant: rated, but not yet secured.

Yet not everything had been stripped away. Captain Walsh had taken the trouble to confirm that Nicholas would keep his invitation to dine with the Carlisles. That had mattered—more than he might admit. And though the evening offered no promises, it did offer her.

Caroline.

He had not meant to be drawn in, had not, indeed, realized that he was. But something in her—measured, attentive, never once trying to please—had stayed with him. There had been no girlish flutter, no posed civility. Just a kind of clarity, as though she had spent too long among Company men and had chosen to read the world with care. He wanted to see her again. It was as simple as that.

He made his way to the quarterdeck, where Lieutenant Harrington stood the watch. The light was softening now, gold along the waterline, the harbour crowded but still.

"Ah, Mr. Cruwys," Harrington called with his usual good humor, "dressed to impress the Bombay elite, I see. A far cry from your Pacific adventures, I'd wager."

"Indeed, sir," Nicholas acknowledged with a slight smile. "I require a boat to the landing, if you can spare one."

Harrington's eyes gleamed with amusement. "Dining with the inestimable Mr. Carlisle and his fair daughter, I recall. A significant step up from the gunroom's fare." He turned toward a boatswain's mate. "Have the cutter manned to take Mr. Cruwys ashore, and be ready to collect him by half-past eleven. We wouldn't want him to run afoul of the Captain's curfew."

"Thank you," Nicholas said. "I appreciate the accommodation."

"Think nothing of it, Mr. Cruwys," Harrington replied, lowering his voice. "Though I expect a full account tomorrow. The Carlisles move in rarefied circles, even by Company standards. Such connections could prove valuable to an ambitious officer."

As the boat's crew assembled, Nicholas made his way down to the entry port. The cutter rode smoothly across the harbour, the men pulling with practiced ease. At the stone landing steps, the Carlisles' carriage was already waiting—an elegant barouche with polished wood panels bearing the discreet emblem of Carlisle Trading, drawn by four matched chestnuts whose grooming bespoke meticulous care. A liveried servant stood by the door, with two more on the box.

Flanking the carriage rode four sowars of the Bombay Native Cavalry in their distinctive dark blue jackets with scarlet facings—the traditional colors of the Bombay Presidency forces. Each horseman wore a white pagri turban with a touch of regimental blue at the crown, and carried a tulwar at his side and a carbine secured to his saddle. The men sat their mounts with the easy confidence of experienced cavalry, their presence a mark of Mr. Carlisle's influence within the Company. In Bombay, where Maratha raiders still occasionally ventured close to Company territories, such armed escorts were as much practical necessity as status symbol for prominent merchants and officials traveling beyond the settled areas.

The officer in charge, a native daffadar with an impressively waxed mustache and three service chevrons on his sleeve, sat straighter in his saddle as Nicholas stepped off the boar, giving a crisp salute that spoke of years under British drill.

The boat's crew exchanged glances of impressed approval. Nicholas smiled faintly to himself, knowing the tale would be throughout the ship within minutes of the boat's return.

"Fine carriage, sir," said Jenkins, the coxswain, nodding toward the crest. "The Company's grandest, by the look of it."

"Aye, indeed," Nicholas replied, stepping up into the carriage with a nod of thanks to the servant.

The carriage moved off through Bombay's European quarter, past the high façades of East India House and the residences of senior Company officials, before turning—somewhat to Nicholas's surprise—toward a district where wealthy Indian merchants and minor princes maintained their homes. Two of the sepoys rode ahead, and two behind. The escort moved with smooth precision, their presence a mark both of Carlisle's standing and of prudent caution in a city where wealth could invite unwelcome attention.

At length they passed through a set of ornate gates, guarded by more liveried servants, and entered a curving drive lined with flowering trees, their blossoms releasing a heady fragrance into the evening air. The sepoys peeled away at the gate as the carriage continued toward the main house.

The building that came into view was not the European-style mansion Nicholas had expected, but a striking fusion of Mughal and Western design. The central structure rose two stories, its cream-coloured walls inlaid with red sandstone tracery. Wide verandas wrapped the upper and lower floors, supported by slender columns of polished stone. The windows were tall and arched, many fitted with delicate screens to allow the air to circulate while providing shade and privacy. Lanterns hung from the veranda ceilings, their golden light just beginning to bloom as dusk settled over the gardens.

At the base of a broad staircase, the carriage drew to a halt. A servant in a crisp white uniform trimmed with gold stepped forward to open the door.

"Lieutenant Cruwys," he said, bowing slightly. His English was formal and precise, shaped by a faint but polished Indian accent. "Mr. Carlisle awaits you, sahib. Please—this way."

Nicholas was led through an entrance hall that took his breath with its quiet splendour. The floor was paved in marble, laid in a geometric pattern of black and white, while the high ceiling bore intricate plasterwork picked out in gold and deep blue. Niches along the walls held bronze figures and delicate porcelain from China, each subtly lit by oil lamps set in silver holders. The effect was one of cultivated opulence, wealth displayed with discernment rather than ostentation.

The servant guided him into a broad salon where overhead punkahs fans were being pulled in silent rhythm by unseen hands or feet, lending a soft and steady breeze to the evening air. The furnishings offered a graceful fusion of East and West: English chairs and settees upholstered in silk brocade; low tables inlaid with mother-of-pearl; Persian carpets of exquisite weave spread across sections of the marble floor.

Caroline rose to greet him from a settee near the long windows, her movements composed and unhurried. She wore a gown of pale green silk that caught the lamplight with every shift of her form—cut in the European style, but unmistakably of Indian fabric, fine as breath. A single strand of pearls lay at her throat, their soft gleam rising and falling with each step.

"Lieutenant Cruwys," she said, her voice low and perfectly modulated, with a smile that conveyed warmth without excess. "How very good of you to accept our invitation. I trust the carriage was adequate to the occasion?"

"Most comfortable, Miss Carlisle," Nicholas replied, offering a formal bow. "Though I confess I did not expect such remarkable surroundings. The house is... exceptional."

"It belongs to the Raja of Baroda," came Mr. Carlisle's voice as he entered from a side door, one hand tucked neatly behind his back.

"He maintains it for his visits to Bombay, but permits its use by certain Company officials when absent. One of many mutually agreeable understandings that give shape to business in India."

The merchant was dressed for the evening in a coat of excellent English cut, though Nicholas noted the adaptations to the tropical air: a lighter cloth, a looser fit, a waistcoat of ivory silk embroidered with gold thread in a motif that echoed the house's own ornament.

"Lieutenant," Carlisle continued, extending a firm hand, "welcome. I trust Captain Walsh raised no objection to your joining us?"

"None at all, sir," Nicholas replied, returning the handshake. "Though I must be back aboard by midnight. As you know, the convoy sails with the morning tide."

Carlisle nodded. "The *Ocean* is fully provisioned, and we are packed to the bulkheads. Yet I admit to a certain melancholy. Three years in India is not lightly set aside. I believe this will be my last voyage from these shores. England calls us home at last."

As they settled into their chairs, a servant appeared bearing a silver tray set with crystal glasses filled with a pale golden liquid.

"Nimbu pani," Caroline explained, accepting one with a slight lift of the wrist. "Lime water, with a touch of sugar and salt. Far more refreshing than wine in this climate, though we shall have European wines with dinner, for those who prefer them."

Nicholas took a glass and sipped. The drink was indeed perfectly suited to the evening: tart, faintly sweet, and bracing. Through the open doors, he could see the gardens lit by lanterns strung from branches and along the stone paths. Fountains played into tiled pools, the quiet splash of water lending a calm, steady rhythm to the setting.

"I understand you were present at this morning's convoy conference," said Carlisle, his tone casual, though his gaze was intent. "Any developments likely to affect our voyage to England?"

Nicholas weighed his answer. He was under no specific injunction, but discretion was a habit, not a rule.

"Nothing of concern to your own journey, sir," he said. "The usual matters, French privateers, cruisers out of Mauritius. But the convoy will sail under escort. *Lynx* is joined by *Salisbury* and *Thetis*. A respectable force, and well commanded."

"Indeed," said Carlisle, dabbing at his lips with a napkin of fine lawn. "Those ships and their freight represent a rather substantial interest for the Crown. I believe the Company estimates returns of—what—close to a quarter-million sterling from this convoy alone."

He paused, studying Nicholas with the quiet appraisal of a man accustomed to weighing both cargo and character.

"And I admit to a more immediate interest. My own ventures aboard *Ocean* amount to some £23,000 at invoice. Not to speak," he added, his tone shifting, "of the rather greater value of my daughter's safety."

"Father," Caroline said gently, with just the faintest smile. "Must we speak of invoices over nimbu pani? I doubt Lieutenant Cruwys came ashore to hear of Company dividends."

Carlisle gave a short, rueful chuckle, his manner softening at once.

"Quite right, my dear. Old habits. One does not simply forget thirty years in trade. Your mother used to say much the same—that I could never keep my ledgers from the table."

There was a pause at that, brief, but felt. Nicholas caught it in the shift of breath, in the slight tightening of Caroline's expression. The mention of Mrs. Carlisle had brushed something still near the surface.

Caroline reached across and touched her father's hand lightly. "Five years," she said. "And she remains our conscience in more ways than one."

Silence followed—a brief, well-bred silence, neither strained nor theatrical. Nicholas, out of habit more than thought, straightened in his chair. In the service, grief was seldom spoken of; here it was acknowledged with grace, and borne without display.

Caroline's gaze had turned inward for a moment, her features composed, not distant but held in reserve, as if she carried her sorrow in a vessel too fine to spill. Nicholas watched, uncertain whether to speak or remain still. The manners of such households—

this fluency of feeling and form—moved according to laws he had not been taught.

She turned then to Nicholas, her tone poised, but with a note of mischief just beneath.

"My mother," she said, "was the true diplomat of this household. She had a gift for smoothing Father's more... direct approach to both business and conversation."

Watching her he understood that despite his years in the Pacific and his exposure to a variety of cultures, European women of quality remained distinctly beyond his reckoning. Their manner—at once graceful, assured, and exact, seemed to operate by codes only half visible to an outsider. The education, the polish, the soft fluency of tone: it was a kind of cultivated opacity.

He told himself he was beginning to understand such women, or at least to admire the precision with which they eluded understanding.

As the dinner continued, Caroline spoke of acquaintances in Bombay society, mentioning with particular warmth the social circle organised by Lady Montgomery, the Governor's wife.

"Her gatherings have been something of a refuge," she said. "She's created a salon where conversation occasionally rises above colonial scandal and shipping schedules."

Carlisle nodded. "My daughter has made herself welcome among the senior Company families. Lady Montgomery has been especially kind in introducing her to the proper circles, particularly in my absences."

"In a place where European women are so few," Caroline added, "such connections become something more than ornamental."

Her tone struck the perfect balance between polite obligation and genuine gratitude, so deftly poised that Nicholas was not sure which predominated.

The conversation turned then to Nicholas's own path from midshipman under Cook to his present station aboard *Lynx*. Caroline's questions were perceptive, showing a grasp of the scale and nature of his experiences that caught him off guard.

"You've lived a life few Englishmen can imagine, Lieutenant," she said, studying him with those keen, steady deep green eyes. "I should think it changes how one sees the world."

There was something in her manner—a composed curiosity, perhaps—that Nicholas found increasingly intriguing. The social forms she navigated so fluently seemed to contain the outline of something deeper. He could sense the intelligence there, but could not quite fix its angle or depth, rather like trying to take a sounding in a fast current.

From there the conversation widened, touching on Nicholas's impressions of trade in the East Indies and Pacific, Carlisle's reflections drawn from decades in commerce, and Caroline's steady stream of thoughtful questions, revealing a mind more attuned to the wider world than most of her station, or any station.

As twilight deepened into evening, a senior servant appeared in the doorway. "Dinner is served, sahib," he announced with a formal bow.

The dining room carried forward the house's theme of elegant fusion between East and West. A long table of polished mahogany dominated the centre, laid with English silver and crystal alongside fine porcelain from China. The chairs were European in design but fitted with cushions of richly embroidered silk. Tall windows stood open to the garden, while ceiling fans turned in steady rhythm, keeping the air cool and alive with movement.

The meal itself was a kind of culinary diplomacy as well: familiar English fare offered alongside subtle introductions to Indian flavour. The first course was a clear soup scented with ginger and lemongrass; then a lightly curried fish in a sauce just bold enough to intrigue, not offend. The main course presented a choice, roast lamb with mint sauce in the traditional English manner, or chicken prepared with aromatic spices. Both were accompanied by potatoes and perfectly seasoned rice. Throughout, the servants moved in silence, replacing plates, replenishing glasses, and anticipating needs before they were spoken.

"Our chef is Bengali," Carlisle said, as Nicholas complimented a particularly well-balanced dish. "He trained under an Italian in

Calcutta, and spent three years in England with the former Governor. His palate, like his résumé, is exceptionally well-travelled."

As the meal progressed, Nicholas found himself watching the interplay between father and daughter with growing interest. There was real affection there—quiet, assured—but something more layered than mere familial closeness. Caroline did not simply attend her father's conversation; she shaped it. She asked questions that clarified, redirected, or deepened the discussion, and when trade in the Mediterranean was raised, she offered an observation about political developments in Naples that might affect shipping routes.

The comment was brief, but exact. Not the kind of remark learned at a drawing-room table.

Nicholas found himself revising his earlier impression. Caroline was not merely her father's social companion or polished daughter of the house; she had the bearing of someone long accustomed to the practical currents of power. Not overbearing, never showy, but engaged, alert, and evidently used to being heard.

"You seem remarkably well-informed about European politics, Miss Carlisle," Nicholas observed during a lull in the conversation.

"Caroline manages our correspondence with factors in Rome, Naples, and Marseilles," her father replied, with unfeigned pride. "She reads Italian and French as easily as English, and has an enviable memory for detail. Frankly, Lieutenant, she's proven more valuable to Carlisle Trading than many clerks with twenty years at a desk."

"Father overstates things," Caroline said, with the faintest smile, but her expression showed she did not mind the praise. "I merely take an interest. When one sees how events in Naples affect shipping in Smyrna, or a treaty in Vienna reshapes the price of saltpetre in Madras—well, trade begins to look less like chance and more like chess."

After dinner they withdrew to a drawing room where Indian and European musical instruments stood side by side in quiet display. Beyond the tall windows, a wide terrace looked out onto the moonlit garden. The scent of jasmine hung thick on the air.

"Now, Lieutenant," said Caroline, turning toward him with composed curiosity, "I believe you promised to speak more about the navigation techniques of the Pacific islanders. My father finds the subject endlessly absorbing, and I confess I'm no less intrigued."

For the better part of an hour, Nicholas described the astonishing methods by which Polynesian navigators crossed thousands of miles of open ocean without chart or compass—reading the stars, the swells, the colour of the water, even the flight of seabirds. Both Carlisles listened with real attentiveness, their questions thoughtful and precise, their interest clearly more than polite performance.

As the evening drew on, Mr. Carlisle excused himself briefly, leaving Caroline and Nicholas alone on the terrace. Below them, the garden lay quiet, the fountains splashing softly, a night bird calling somewhere in the shadows.

"I've enjoyed this evening immensely," Caroline said, her voice softer now, shaded with something unspoken. "It's rare to speak with someone who has seen the world with his own eyes, and hasn't simply read about it in dispatches."

Nicholas turned to her. "I've enjoyed it as well," he said, more frankly than he'd intended. "Your home—or your temporary one—is extraordinary. And your hospitality has been... generous beyond expectation."

She hesitated just a moment. Then: "Will you write to me?"

The question was quiet, but direct.

"If you are able," she added, before he could reply.

Nicholas was still forming his answer when they heard the soft tread of her father's return. Caroline stepped back, the distance between them subtly reasserted.

"Lieutenant," said Carlisle, re-entering the room, "it's nearly time for your return, I think. I've had the carriage brought round."

"Thank you, sir," Nicholas said. "You've been most generous."

"Not at all," Carlisle replied, extending his hand with warmth. "A pleasure to spend our last evening in India in such agreeable company. I've no doubt we'll see more of each other on the voyage—when the weather allows, the officers and passengers often contrive to visit."

The mantel clock struck eleven. Nicholas took his leave, conscious of the time and the distance back to *Lynx*. The carriage awaited at the foot of the steps, its lanterns glowing amber in the soft dark. The escort, he noticed, had grown. Now eight sepoys stood ready, their blue and scarlet jackets vivid beneath the torchlight. A prudent addition, no doubt, given the hour.

"Until our next meeting, Lieutenant," said Caroline, standing beside her father at the entrance.

"I look forward to it, Miss Carlisle," Nicholas replied, bowing to them both before stepping into the carriage.

As the vehicle pulled away down the lantern-lit drive, the sepoys once again arrayed in quiet formation around it, Nicholas found himself turning over the evening in his mind. The Carlisles belonged to a world far removed from the motion of the sea or the directness of Pacific harbours—a world governed by influence, cultivated ties, and conversations that mattered long after they ended. It was not a world he fully understood, but he had begun to see its contours.

And Caroline—she was not merely accomplished or well-placed, though she was clearly both. There was something in her manner that resisted summary. Intelligence, grace, restraint—he had encountered each of these before, but never in one person, and never quite like this. She was not remarkable by comparison; she was simply remarkable.

The carriage turned into the darker streets leading back toward the harbour. Bombay had quieted now, the city shuttered and sleeping: a flicker of lamplight on wet stone, a lone bullock cart creaking off into the alleys, the faint hush of the tide along the quay.

As they approached the landing, Nicholas saw *Lynx's* cutter already waiting, the crew seated at their oars, still and ready beneath the swinging lantern.

Farther out, the darker shapes of *Salisbury* and *Thetis* loomed in the outer roads—larger ships, heavier guns, the proper teeth of the escort. Beyond them, he could make out the six East Indiamen, their hulls broad and still under the stars, each heavy with cargo, passengers, and the promise of a voyage home.

CHAPTER TEN

The second week of May 1780 found the convoy sailing south-southwest, ten days out from Bombay, bound for the Cape. The six East Indiamen: *Fortitude, Earl of Hertford, Bengal Queen, Ocean, Lord Clive, and Bombay Merchant,* held formation in a carefully maintained column, their broad hulls riding low under the weight of cargo and company treasure.

HMS Salisbury and *HMS Thetis* sailed two miles to windward of the convoy, *Thetis* a cable's length ahead of her senior. From that position, they could bear down swiftly in the event of attack while preserving the tactical advantage of the weather gage. *HMS Lynx* ranged six miles ahead on a long lead, her crew alert for sails or signals. The hulls of the convoy lay beyond sight from her deck, but *Salisbury* was well within signaling distance.

The northeast monsoon still held, steady and dry—driving the fleet across the open waters of the central Indian Ocean. Nicholas stood his watch on the quarterdeck of *Lynx,* eyes shifting from canvas to horizon, then down to the long roll of the sea. The wind was even, but there was something else: a subtle cross-chop in the swell, a longer rhythm beneath the surface pattern. The light had taken on a crystalline quality, the air drier than it had been at noon. Something was changing.

"Mr. Harrington," he said, as the third lieutenant approached for his own watch, "I believe we may see a shift in the weather before morning. The sea has a particular character tonight."

Harrington gave him a measuring glance, then turned to study the water himself.

"The glass shows nothing unusual," he said after a moment. "And the sky holds steady. But—what precisely are you seeing?"

Nicholas kept his voice steady. "The primary swell has lengthened since midday, and there's a faint secondary set from the west, just enough to disturb the earlier rhythm. It's subtle, but I've seen similar conditions in the Pacific, particularly around the Society Islands. There, a swell change often preceded a wind shift by half a day or so. The islanders were masters at reading it."

To his quiet satisfaction, Harrington did not dismiss this out of hand. Instead, he watched the water a moment longer.

"I've heard similar claims from the Lascars," he said at last. "They speak of reading the sea's skin as we read a chart. Most of us lack the eye for it."

He nodded toward the horizon. "Show me what you're observing."

For several minutes, Nicholas pointed out the signs: the increased interval between swells, the faint interference line from the west, the changed texture where some wavelets now broke irregularly across the surface. Harrington listened with close attention, his questions few but sharp—probing and specific, revealing the habits of a practical and open mind.

"Most instructive, Mr. Cruwys," he said finally. There was a trace of amusement in his voice, but it was not unkind. "We shall note your prediction and see come morning whether these Pacific instincts hold true in the Indian Ocean."

The following dawn proved Nicholas correct. The wind had shifted in the night, backing two points to the west and freshening steadily. When Nicholas came on deck, he found Harrington already there, hands clasped behind his back, studying the sail set and the state of the sea with a familiar, steady gaze.

"Your sea-reading holds up, Mr. Cruwys," he said, without preamble. "A useful talent, particularly in waters where the weather declines to consult the glass before turning contrary."

Nicholas inclined his head. "Thank you, sir. I'll try not to let it go to my head."

Harrington gave a brief smile, one that flickered more in the eyes than at the mouth. "Just see that your log reflects proper doctrine. The Admiralty prefers its forecasts to arrive after the fact. Fewer embarrassments."

Nicholas allowed himself a dry smile. "I believe the correct entry is: *'Weather observed to change in accordance with expectations.'*"

"Exactly," Harrington said. "A form of naval modesty—prediction without presumption."

They stood companionably a while, the wind pressing steadily from the northwest now, ruffling the sea in long blue furrows.

Two days later, with no other ships sighted, Nicholas's thoughts drifted—as thoughts will in long quiet watches—from the present moment to a memory not long past. The recollection rose unbidden, like a tide. He found himself returned to the morning of departure from Bombay.

He had stood on deck with a telescope in hand, watching as a native boat, broad-beamed and shaded by a canopy aft—came alongside *Ocean*. By local standards, it was a substantial craft, nearly forty feet in length, with a patched lateen sail and the look of something well maintained. But next to the towering hull of the East Indiaman, it was dwarfed entirely.

An elaborate boarding ladder had been lowered: rope sides, wooden steps, the sort reserved for passengers of distinction. From beneath the canopy, Mr. Carlisle appeared first, well dressed, his coat of dark blue broadcloth and a cream-and-gold waistcoat catching the morning light. He stepped carefully toward the ladder, hat secured, each movement deliberate. Sailors stood by to assist. Behind him, the baggage had already begun to rise: bandboxes, trunks, and cases secured to lines from the main yardarm and hoisted up in practiced succession, swinging against the hull in a controlled rhythm.,

Caroline came next.

Even from this distance, her movement was unmistakable: poised, composed, neither hurried nor hesitant. She wore a pale blue traveling dress that seemed to hold the morning's own light, the cut unmistakably London, but its grace entirely her own. She began the climb, a servant just behind her, one hand raised lightly to steady the skirt against the breeze.

Nicholas had watched, the glass steady in his hands, but his thoughts anything but. There had been no second meeting, no final word between them before sailing. Yet he was surprised, more than he liked to admit, by how often she had occupied his mind since.

Both Helena Montague in Calcutta and Caroline had shown real interest in his experience, both intellectually curious, unafraid to speak plainly. That frankness had never troubled him. Years in the Pacific had accustomed him to a different kind of reserve, where the body was less guarded, the intentions less disguised. He had not been unsettled to recognize in either woman a self-possession that spoke of experience. Nor had he been naïve about their interest. But Caroline was different.

It was not conversation alone, nor even beauty, though he would not deny either. It was the manner in which she had listened. Her questions neither idle nor ornamental, but searching in their quiet way. She had asked not what he had seen, but how it had changed him. She had looked at him with something like wonder, not for the strangeness of his stories, but for the shape of the man they had made.

That moment lingered. More than Helena's elegance, or Atea's stillness, the kind of stillness that made silence feel whole. Atea had never needed words to convey what she felt, nor to understand what he carried. She had belonged to her world in a way that asked for nothing and explained nothing, and in that there had been peace.

It both intrigued and unsettled him that Caroline—so different, so clearly of another world—could reach some buried part of him that he had believed long since settled. He had not thought himself susceptible to such attachments. Not since Atea. And yet, the thought of Caroline's eyes—steady, intelligent, and unread—rose with the memory of that morning and refused to be dismissed.

As quickly as the memory had surfaced, Nicholas felt it retreat, overlaid by the press and rhythm of the sea. The *Lynx's* quarterdeck came back into focus, the taut lines, the scent of canvas and salt, the familiar creak of timber under sail. Lieutenant Harrington stood a few paces off, hands clasped behind his back, watching the horizon, but not unaware of Nicholas's brief abstraction.

"A restless mind makes for a poor lookout, Lieutenant Cruwys," he remarked, tone mild but laced with amusement.

Nicholas turned, expression composed. "The sea offers many distractions, Mr. Harrington."

Harrington's glance lingered a half-second longer than usual—curious, perhaps, or quietly assessing—but he said nothing more.

Later that afternoon, with Captain Walsh's assent and the weather steady, they met again on the main deck. Stripped to shirts and breeches, they stood clear of the rigging amidships, with their personal blades in hand.

"You mentioned your Portuguese friend's unconventional methods," Harrington said, loosening his shoulders as he adopted a relaxed first guard. He nodded toward Nicholas's weapon. "I'm curious to see how that blade behaves in the hands of someone who knows its character."

Nicholas smiled slightly, lowering the point with casual precision. "As am I, sir."

The first few exchanges surprised everyone.

Nicholas moved with a fluidity that belonged neither to the fencing halls of English gentlemen nor to the stripped-down practicality of naval training. His sword seemed an extension of his own reach, responding to Harrington's attacks with a precision that drew murmurs from the watching hands.

Harrington was no novice. Years of formal instruction, combined with natural athleticism, made him a formidable opponent. His weapon—a regulation officer's sword with a straight blade, brass guard, and wire-wrapped grip—was clearly of superior make; the damascened steel caught the sun in pale whorls.

What had begun as a friendly bout quickly took on the edge of a genuine contest.

Back and forth they went—parry, thrust, disengage, recover—neither giving quarter, neither pressing beyond the lines of discipline, yet both testing the other's reserves with increasing seriousness. The crew watched, rapt. It was no mere drill, but a kind of dance—more art than exercise, more contest than performance. Their blades rang against each other with a rhythm that had its own strange harmony.

At last, they broke apart, both breathing hard, swords still raised but points dipped. A glance passed between them—brief, level, and marked with something new.

"Remarkable," Harrington said, a genuine smile breaking through his usual restraint. "You're full of surprises, Mr. Cruwys."

Nicholas gave a slight bow, not the stiff formalism of quarterdeck ceremony, but something quieter: acknowledgement, and perhaps thanks.

Captain Walsh, who had been observing the entire exchange from the rail with his customary mix of professional detachment and dry humour, stepped forward at a leisurely pace.

"Gentlemen," he said, just loud enough for the crew to hear, "I trust your maritime talents still extend somewhat beyond decorative swordplay?"

A soft ripple of laughter ran through the deck, quickly muffled, but unmistakable.

The moment was broken by the lookout's voice, sharp, steady, and pitched with that peculiar clarity particular to men accustomed to being heard across open water.

"Sail ho! Southwest by south!"

Walsh was in motion at once, raising his telescope with the easy precision of a man who had spent more years looking through such instruments than not. He scanned the horizon, eyes narrowing as he sorted sky from sea. At his elbow, the signal midshipman stood poised, flags in hand.

A flurry of colours broke at the masthead—*Lynx* signaling *Salisbury*, reporting the sighting, its bearing and uncertain character. Commodore Hartley's reply came within minutes, crisp and unmistakable to any experienced officer:

Investigate and report.

Walsh's orders came quick and clean. "Set the topgallants. Hands to stations. Come to the wind."

Lynx responded at once. Her crew sprang to their posts, canvas shook loose with a snap, and the sloop leaned into her course, accelerating out of formation. Her fine hull sliced through the sea with purposeful ease, no longer held to the convoy's pace.

"Discretion before valour, gentlemen," Walsh remarked evenly, his gaze fixed ahead. "We observe. We do not engage."

Within the hour, more sails appeared, first faint and wavering, then resolving into hulls from the masthead. At Walsh's nod, Nicholas climbed to the upper main top, glass in hand. He steadied himself against the shrouds, watching the approaching formation.

He slid down a backstay to the deck to report. "Two frigates leading, sir—no colours yet. Astern of them, five smaller vessels: one ship, possibly a corvette, two brigs, and two schooners. They're in loose order, but moving together. Privateers, most likely."

"Interesting," Walsh murmured after a moment, the single word carrying more weight than a paragraph might. "Not a chance gathering, I think."

Nicholas understood. These were no opportunists, not an accidental alignment of predators, but a coordinated enemy force. It was exactly what they had been told to expect. And if *Lynx* had found them, it was certain the enemy had marked the convoy as well.

"A concerted effort," Walsh said to Lieutenant Hargrove. "Royal French men-of-war working with their privateers."

He paused, watching the sails lift against the pale morning.

"They know what they're about."

Lynx came about, beating back toward the convoy. The wind had freshened, and she met it with sharp, deliberate tacks, each one bringing her closer to *Salisbury*.

Nicholas, supervising the signal midshipman and his party nearby, listened carefully as he directed the preparation of flags for the upcoming communication. The young midshipman selected the appropriate flags with nimble fingers, laying them out in sequence for rapid hoisting.

As they approached within signal distance with *Salisbury*, Walsh ordered a detailed report sent to the Commodore. Nicholas oversaw the process as the flags rose and fell in complex patterns, the silent conversation between ships carrying information that could mean the difference between safety and disaster: two French frigates—one a sleek 36-gun vessel with a recently coppered bottom visible when she heeled, the other a slightly smaller 32-gun ship with distinctive white bands along her hull—accompanied by a heavy armed corvette of 22 guns, two brigs of 16 and 14 guns each with the low, predatory lines of privateer-built vessels, and two swift schooners, smaller but dangerous at close quarters with probably large crews.

Salisbury's acknowledgment came quickly, followed by fresh orders: the convoy tightened formation, the merchant vessels drawing closer together for mutual protection.

By mid-afternoon, Nicholas could see the changes in the convoy's disposition through his glass. The six East Indiamen had closed ranks, sailing in two columns of three ships each. *Ocean* was second in the windward column. *Salisbury* and *Thetis* had moved to positions closer astern of the convoy but still just to windward, from where they could run down to interpose themselves between the merchants as any attack developed. Even as he watched, their gun ports opened as they cleared for action.

More signals broke out from *Salisbury* with their number, and without waiting and reading them directly, Walsh ordered, "Back to our station, Mr. Harrington," Walsh ordered. "We'll maintain observation through the night. I want lanterns ready should we need to signal after dark."

"Aye, sir," Harrington replied, already moving to relay the orders.

As *Lynx* resumed her position as the convoy's eyes, Walsh called his officers to his cabin for a brief conference.

"Gentlemen," he began, his voice level but with an underlying tension that communicated the gravity of their situation, "we are facing a true naval squadron. The frigates alone plus that heavy corvette match *Salisbury* and *Thetis* if well-handled, especially given *Salisbury's* age and slower speed notwithstanding her twenty-four-pounders. She's nearly forty years old, and perhaps none too strong in her timbers after over ten years of tropical service."

He paused, looking out at the French vessels visible on the horizon. "So, we are outnumbered, though not yet outmaneuvered."

The ship's master, Mr. Ainsley, cleared his throat. "The wind is holding from the northeast, sir. If it maintains, we'll have the weather gauge come morning."

Walsh nodded. "A small advantage, but one we shall exploit if necessary." His gaze swept over each officer in turn. "Our advantage lies in discipline and coordination. The East Indiamen carry guns, though their crews are not trained to naval standards and their rate of fire will be painfully slow compared to a warship. Their smaller merchant crews will struggle to serve even half their guns effectively. We must be prepared to meet any eventuality to secure the safety of the convoy."

As twilight approached, tension aboard *Lynx* grew palpable. Walsh ordered the drum to beat to quarters, and the ship settled down in in readiness to her vigil, maintaining her position relative to both the convoy and the French squadron, even as the gap between the two forces narrowed.

Night fell with the sudden completeness unique to tropical latitudes, one moment the sky ablaze with sunset colors, with the French ships to leeward and the convoy to windward all now just hull up on their respective horizons, the next plunged into darkness relieved only by stars and the eerie phosphorescence of tropical waters. The bow wave glowed with an ethereal blue luminescence as *Lynx* maintained her vigilant patrol.

Two hours later a cry of "Deck there, ship two points off the starboard bow!"

Nicholas raised his glass, straining to see through the gathering darkness. For a moment, he saw nothing, then, a flickering light, quickly extinguished. A lantern, perhaps, or a signal light briefly exposed.

"Signal to *Salisbury*," Walsh said evenly. "Enemy appears to be manoeuvring under cover of darkness."

A blue light hissed to life at the break of the quarterdeck, flooding the sails above in spectral glow. Its glare reached far across the water, too bright for comfort. Moments later, an answering flare burst into view from *Salisbury's* deck, brief, brilliant, and unmistakable.

The crew stood ready, every man at his station. But no guns fired. The dark held. The sea, disturbed only by the ship's wake, seemed to wait with them. Every ear strained for the scrape of a hull, every eye searched the void beyond the reach of the flare's dying glow.

The crew stood to arms, each man at his station, weapons primed. But the attack did not come. The night stretched on, thick with anticipation. Every eye strained into the dark, every ear attuned to the faintest shift in wind or water.

Dawn broke with tropical suddenness, the eastern sky flaring from indigo to gold in a matter of minutes as the sun breached the horizon. In the new light, the 36-gun frigate remained visible to the southwest, accompanied by the corvette, the smaller brig, and two schooners—all holding their distance. But the 32-gun frigate and the larger brig had vanished.

Walsh's expression tightened. "They've divided their force. Signal *Salisbury*: enemy force divided, smaller frigate and one brig not in sight."

"Could they have withdrawn, sir?" asked Lieutenant Chester.

"No," said Walsh flatly. "They've circled to approach from another quarter. Mr. Ainsley, double the lookouts aloft."

The day dragged with agonising slowness. The convoy held its southwest course under heightened vigilance, the visible French ships now running a few miles to leeward, keeping pace but not closing, close enough that even the merchant captains could make them out. *Lynx* was ordered astern of the windward column, her crew alert but steady.

Noon came and went beneath a punishing sun, the heat pressing down like ballast. Still no sign of the missing vessels.

Then, at three bells in the afternoon watch, signal flags rose smartly on *Salisbury's* mainmast. Nicholas raised his glass and read the message aloud with practiced precision.

"*Salisbury* signals: enemy vessels sighted to the northeast, sir. The 32-gun frigate and the larger brig, approaching from windward."

Walsh gave a grim nod. "Their masts give them the vantage. The French swung round under cover of darkness and are closing from windward with the weather gauge and speed in their favour."

Almost at once came another hail from the masthead. "Deck there, southwestern enemy ships making sail, turning hard on the wind!"

The French intent was immediately clear: a converging assault from two directions, intended to divide the British escort and press the convoy from both flanks. Commodore Hartley's response was swift. *Thetis* was ordered to intercept the frigate and brig to the northeast, while *Salisbury* herself passed through the convoy to cover the leeward column, placing herself between the merchantmen and the 36-gun frigate to the southwest. *Lynx* was instructed to remain on station, ready to reinforce where needed.

From his post, Nicholas had a clear view of *Ocean*. Her starboard gunports stood open, revealing eight guns on her gundeck and five on her quarterdeck and foc'sle—twenty-six in all both sides—a respectable battery by merchant standards, made up of a mix of nine and six-pounders. Yet he knew well that few East Indiamen could bring their full weight to bear. Even with a stout crew, most lacked the trained hands to serve more than half their pieces with efficiency, even one side.

He could make out a knot of red coats on her quarterdeck, the Company troops, no doubt, mentioned in the Governor's briefing as accompanying Lady Carington. Their uniforms stood out, a flash of regulation amidst the rougher order of a merchantman's crew. Below decks, the passengers would have withdrawn to the hold, seeking what shelter there was. Caroline would be among them, frightened no doubt, but composed, he felt certain.

The battle developed swiftly, the convoy and the main French force closing one another at a combined speed of more than ten knots. *Thetis* wore round and stood boldly to the northeast to intercept the windward enemy, her captain clearly resolved to engage the 32-gun frigate and her consort brig before they could threaten the merchant ships.

But the French had planned well. As the larger ships exchanged their first ranging shots—*Thetis* with the 32-gun frigate, *Salisbury* with the 36-gun and the corvette following astern—the three remaining French vessels hauled to port, altering course to the northwest. Their intent was plain: to slip past the now-engaged British warships and strike at the convoy directly, where it was least defended.

"The smaller brig and the schooners are making for the gap," Walsh observed, his voice tight with controlled urgency. "They mean to cut out two of the windward Indiamen—likely the *Bengal Queen* and the *Ocean*."

Indeed, the three French vessels were bearing down on the windward column, their course angled directly toward the exposed merchantmen. Several of the Indiamen were already firing, their civilian crews doing what they could, but the shots fell short or went wide. The lack of training showed. Where a Navy gun crew might manage three rounds in five minutes, or even better in crack gunnery ships like *Lynx*, these crews struggled to fire once in that span, their numbers too few for the labour of loading, running out, and laying the guns with any speed or precision.

"Up two points to starboard, Mr. Ainsley, and set the main course," Walsh ordered. "We'll cut them off before they close with the convoy."

Lynx came up smartly with the wind moving from aft forward to her starboard beam, her bow slicing clean through the water as she altered course to intercept. The two schooners, seeing the sloop of war bearing down, altered course slightly, ranging out to either side, attempting to split her attention. But the brig held steady, making straight for *Ocean*, the largest and most richly laden of the Indiamen in the windward column.

"Mr. Cruwys, your battery will take the schooner to starboard. Mr. Harrington, the one to larboard."

Nicholas acknowledged with a crisp, "Aye, sir," his mind already working the ranges and angles. The starboard schooner was closing fast at four hundred yards, perhaps a shade less. Her black hull rode low, and her great spread of fore-and-aft canvas marked her out as a hunter: fast, lean, and meant for pursuit.

"Stand ready," Nicholas called to his gun crews. "Fire as you bear—aim for her hull."

The first exchange came swiftly. *Lynx's* starboard battery spoke out in sequence, each gun thundering as its captain found his mark. The schooner replied at once, her lighter pieces spitting defiance. Shot splashed around *Lynx* in erratic succession; one struck home with a solid thump, splinters flying as the hull shuddered.

To port, Harrington's battery engaged the second schooner with similar ferocity. But the greater danger lay ahead: the brig was pulling past her consorts, steering directly for *Ocean*. Both *Ocean* and *Bengal Queen* had opened fire, but their shots with a few exceptions were wide or fell short. The privateer's answering fire raked *Bengal Queen's* bow cruelly, her rigging lurching under the blow, splinters leaping from her forward bulwarks. She began to sag out of line to leeward, trailing smoke and confusion.

From windward, banks of powder smoke drifted low as *Thetis* engaged both the 32-gun frigate and her brig consort. Beyond the leeward column came a continuous roar, broadside after broadside from the heaviest ships. *Salisbury's* deeper guns spoke clearly, the ponderous boom of her twenty-four-pounders rising above the sharper crash of the French fire.

"The brig will reach *Ocean* before we can intercept," Walsh said grimly.

Nicholas felt a cold knot tighten in his belly at the thought of Caroline Carlisle aboard a vessel about to be boarded by privateers. But there was no time for sentiment. The schooner off their starboard quarter had altered course, wearing to port, perhaps to run parallel with *Lynx*, or to open the range and join the rush on *Ocean*.

"Helm, two points to starboard, luff us up and cross her stern," Walsh ordered. Then, to Nicholas: "Mr. Cruwys, prepare to fire."

The manoeuvre was perfectly judged and caught the schooner unprepared in the middle of her turn, *Lynx* turning up wind with a speed that belied her size. As the enemy vessel presented her vulnerable stern, Nicholas gave the order, and his battery fired as one. The raking broadside tore into her with brutal precision. Though *Lynx* carried a modest weight of metal, the effect was devastating: the schooner's rudder was shattered, leaving her crippled, and other shots punched through her lower deck.

One of these must have struck a powder charge—perhaps by shattering a lantern. It wasn't her magazine, but a gout of flame burst from her stern windows, followed by dense smoke and the unmistakable sound of men screaming.

"Well struck!" Walsh called. "She's crippled. Now for the other."

Lynx fell off the wind as she turned back to larboard to engage the second schooner. But already the situation off *Ocean's* starboard side had reached a crisis. The French brig had closed to within fifty yards of the Indiaman on a near reciprocal course, her deck bristling with men ready to board. *Ocean's* guns were still firing, and now Nicholas could make out passengers as well as crew on her deck, some bearing muskets and pistols, mustered at the rail to defend their ship.

The second schooner, seeing her consort ablaze and out of action, bore away in retreat. But *Lynx* was well within range, and Harrington's battery fired with cool precision, hulling her repeatedly and with two shots hitting home at deck level. The schooner's main gaff came down with a crash, her deck engulfed in canvas. A chance shot had carried away the halyard.

The privateer replied, but her fire was wild, shot passing high or splashing harmlessly into the sea.

"She's crippled for the moment," Walsh said, "now for the brig."

But they were too late to prevent the boarding. Even as *Lynx* came about, the French brig crashed alongside *Ocean's* starboard side, grappling irons flying across the narrowing gap to bind the two hulls together. French boarders swarmed over the rail, met at once by the determined resistance of *Ocean's* crew and the handful of Company soldiers posted aboard.

"We'll board from the other side and support her defence," Walsh ordered, his voice clipped with urgency. "Lieutenant Hargrove and Mr. Cruwys—you'll lead the forward party, take the starboard gun crews and the marines. I shall go aft with Mr. Harrington, Mr. Chester, and all others save the warrant officers and ship's boys. Mr. Ainsley, you'll remain in charge of *Lynx*. Bring us alongside."

The master nodded. "Aye, sir, though I'd rather be going over!" He took the helm himself and conned the sloop in with steady hands, bringing *Lynx* neatly from astern up *Ocean's* unengaged larboard side.

Hargrove and Nicholas moved forward to the break of the forecastle. Around them gathered their party: marines with fixed bayonets, seamen armed with cutlasses, boarding pikes, and axes, all bearing the tight-lipped look of men about to cross into close action.

As the two ships bumped gently, grapnels soared across the narrow span and bit home. Walsh raised his voice.

"Boarding parties—away!"

"Forward, men!" Hargrove called, and led the charge with a shout, cheering as they leapt for *Ocean's* foremast chainplates. Nicholas followed, vaulting across the narrowing gap. He caught a shroud, swung up, and planted his boots on the channel rail below. His sword came free in a single motion, its familiar weight a comfort. At his belt hung the pair of elegant pistols also gifted by Silva.

The scene on *Ocean's* deck was chaos. French boarders had already taken the starboard side, fighting their way inward against the desperate resistance of the merchant crew. The enemy held the centre of the upper deck. Amid the melee, the small detachment of Company infantry—red-coated and tightly formed—had drawn up a line across the waist at the break of the quarterdeck. Their volleys were crisp and well-aimed, cutting down attackers as they advanced. But they were few, and the French pressed forward with the discipline of seasoned men.

A cheer went up as Nicholas and Hargrove's party struck from forward from behind the attackers, steel flashing as they charged into the fight. Caught between two forces, the French faltered, some wheeling to face this fresh threat, others still driving toward the quarterdeck.

The combat was immediate and brutal. Nicholas caught the thrust of a boarding pike on his blade, swept it aside, and answered with a cut that opened the man's forearm to the bone. Another assailant came on with a boarding axe, the heavy iron whistling toward his head. Nicholas slipped inside the arc and drove his blade into the man's chest, a clean thrust, precisely as Silva had taught him.

All around him the deck had become a slaughter-ground. The sharp crack of musket fire mingled with the clash of steel and the raw, wordless grunts and yells of close combat. Blood slicked the planking underfoot, making every step uncertain. Men fought in knots and pairs, the smoke drifting low, the air thick with sweat, burnt powder, and desperation.

Lieutenant Hargrove fought with the steady precision of a veteran, his movements economical and sure. Nicholas fought beside him, the two officers complementing each other's efforts without need for words. Amid the madness, it struck Nicholas that he had never fully appreciated the First Lieutenant, perhaps because Hargrove's quiet competence had always stood in Walsh's more commanding shadow.

They drove forward together, forcing a wedge into the heart of the French boarding party. From astern came renewed cheering as Captain Walsh led the after boarding party swarming aboard via the mizzen shrouds, reinforcing the defenders at the quarterdeck rail. The tide of battle began to shift. The French, pressed from fore and aft, were yielding ground, fighting hard, but beginning to buckle.

In a brief lull, Nicholas scanned the scene and caught sight of a knot of passengers ahead of the quarterdeck, men who had armed themselves and joined the defence. At their centre stood a slightly portly older gentleman in a powder-stained coat, wielding a worn smallsword with surprising skill. Even in the chaos, Nicholas recognised him at once.

Mr. Carlisle.

The older man was plainly winded, his breath coming hard, his face mottled with the flush of exertion. And even as Nicholas watched, he saw a French sailor step forward, raising his cutlass high for the killing stroke.

Nicholas reacted without thought. In one motion he switched the sword into his left hand and his right dropped down closed around the grip of one of his pistols. He drew it smoothly, cocking the hammer in a single practiced motion. Smoke hung low across the deck, thick with the acrid sting of powder.

Sixty feet. A long shot.

He shifted with the roll of the ship, left foot forward, weight steady. No hesitation. The barrel came level. His eye aligned to the sight, fixed on the Frenchman's head—little else was visible. Breathe in. Exhale. The flint snapped down on the frizzen, a burst of sparks, then the pan flashed.

A heartbeat later, the main charge fired.

The pistol kicked hard in his hand, but Nicholas had braced for it. He held position for half a second longer, even as the smoke leapt up around him. Through it, he saw the Frenchman jerk backward, his head half torn away in a spray of blood and bone, then collapse at Carlisle's feet.

The older man turned, blinking, then raised his sword in salute before retreating toward the safety of the Company line.

From the quarterdeck, Walsh had seen it all. His eyes met Nicholas's—something between approval and appraisal in the look.

"Good shooting, Mr. Cruwys," he called, his voice steady above the din. "Now keep the other close. We're not done yet."

A sudden cry of alarm drew Nicholas's attention. Lieutenant Hargrove had engaged the French boarding party's leader—a tall officer in a blue coat with gold epaulettes—in a fierce and measured duel. As Nicholas turned, he saw Hargrove lunge, his blade striking true into the Frenchman's shoulder.

But even as the officer staggered back, a shot rang out from the brig's rigging. A musket ball struck Hargrove full in the chest. He stood a moment, frozen in place, a look of mild surprise on his face, then crumpled to the deck.

Nicholas was at his side in an instant, but one glance told him the truth. The wound was mortal. Hargrove's eyes were already glazing, blood bubbling at his lips as he tried to speak. Nicholas leaned close and caught the last, urgent whisper:

"Finish it, Cruwys. Drive them back."

With a cold surge of fury, Nicholas rose to his feet. "To me!" he cried to the nearest men. "For the First Lieutenant—drive them back!"

The sailors answered with a roar, their assault renewed with sudden vengeance. Nicholas led them forward, cutting through the wavering French line. Already shaken under British pressure, the enemy began to break. The French commander aboard the brig, seeing his men faltering on both flanks, shouted the order to retreat. The boarders fell back, hacking away grappling lines as they went, desperate to disengage.

From aft came a shout: "After them! Mr. Harrington—take that brig!"

But there was no answer. Harrington, too, had gone down.

Nicholas heard and did not hesitate. Rallying what men he could, he led them in pursuit. They leapt across to the brig, falling upon the retreating French with grim determination. For several minutes, battle raged anew upon the enemy's deck. But the fight had gone out of them. Bloodied, leaderless, and demoralised, the French began to falter.

Their captain, coat torn and blood streaking his brow, stepped forward amid the wreckage of his quarterdeck. Smoke drifted in heavy swirls; the last shots died away into silence.

"Monsieur, je me rends."

Nicholas, chest heaving from exertion, straightened. His gaze locked with the Frenchman's—cool, steady. He summoned the French drilled into him by a tutor long ago—halting, perhaps, but sufficient.

"Votre épée, monsieur."

With grave formality, the French captain extended his sword, hilt-first. Nicholas received it with a nod, then handed it to a nearby Company soldier.

"Dites à vos hommes de poser leurs armes."

The Frenchman hesitated for a breath, then turned and gave the order. Muskets, pistols, and cutlasses clattered onto the blood-slick planks.

A cheer went up—then another. It swelled and echoed as one of the British sailors reached the halyard and hauled down the French colours. The great white Bourbon flag came fluttering down amid the smoke and cries of victory.

Back on *Ocean's* quarterdeck, Captain Walsh turned with a broad smile. "Very well done indeed, Mr. Cruwys!" he said, then swung away, voice rising as he resumed command and gave fresh orders.

Nicholas, still catching his breath, turned to take in the broader scene.

To windward, *Thetis* was engaged at close quarters with the 32-gun French frigate. The two ships lay nearly abeam, exchanging furious broadsides at point-blank range. Though the British frigate was somewhat the smaller of the two, her captain had handled her with masterful boldness, outmanoeuvring both adversaries. The accompanying French brig had drifted well down to leeward, low in the bows, pumps sending fountains of water over the side—clearly no longer a factor.

Salisbury, for her part, was giving a good account of herself. Though slower and heavier, she had brought her broadside to bear upon the 36-gun French frigate close on her port quarter, while the corvette hung farther off her port bow. Her twenty-four-pounders on the lower deck thundered into the French frigate with heavy effect, while the twelve- and six-pounders above raked the smaller ship. But the enemy replied in kind, firing full broadsides into *Salisbury's* rigging. Nicholas could hear the unmistakable, ghastly howl of chain shot overhead, a banshee's shriek followed by the savage tearing crash as canvas, cordage, and spars were rent apart. Damaged rigging streamed down her side in thick bundles, and both her fore-topmast and mizzen had come down under the battering.

As Nicholas watched, a sudden cheer rose from *Thetis*. The 32-gun French frigate had struck her colours, surrendering after a punishing exchange that had left both ships mauled. *Thetis* had prevailed, but at heavy cost: her rigging was reduced to shreds, her hull holed in several places, smoke drifted from amidships where a fire still smouldered, and thin rivulets of blood ran from her scuppers.

A fresh burst of signal flags climbed the halyards aboard the 36-gun French frigate. She and the corvette, though holed and scarred, still had their masts and yards. Both ships bore away, angling downwind to avoid being raked. They made full sail, drawing clear of the labouring *Salisbury*, and fired a few parting rounds, more defiance than design.

Up to windward, the larger French brig also set more sail and began to break off, though still down by the bows with water shooting from her pumps over the side, and the second schooner, which had re-rove her mainsail halyard, followed her out of the fight.

As the last scattered shots died away and cheering continued from the five East Indiamen, who, save for their gunnery, had been largely spectators, the true cost of the action began to show.

Though the convoy had been spared the brunt of the engagement, the toll aboard the naval vessels—and *Ocean*—was severe. The decks of *Thetis* and *Salisbury*, and *Lynx* to a lesser degree, bore the scars of close action and sustained fire, and many of their crews had fallen. *Ocean*, having borne the weight of the boarding assault, had also suffered heavy casualties. From where Nicholas stood, the aftermath was unmistakable: the cries of the wounded still rose from *Ocean's* blood-slick deck, echoed faintly from *Lynx* alongside. The other ships lay silent by comparison, too distant to hear.

Lieutenant Hargrove lay still upon the deck, his body now covered with a British ensign in a mark of honour. Across both ships, men moved with quiet efficiency: tending the injured, gathering the dead, righting what could be made fast. Lieutenant Harrington, though pale and bloodied, had regained consciousness and now moved with effort, a wan smile on his face as he passed from group to group.

Nicholas remained on *Ocean's* quarterdeck, overseeing the transfer of the most grievously wounded French prisoners. The acrid reek of powder still hung in the air, and beneath it, the deeper smell of blood and salt and scorched wood. Spars lay splintered, sails hung in tatters, and the rails bore the fresh scars of close-quarters fighting. The work of recovery had begun, and it was grim.

Captain Hamilton of *Ocean* emerged from below. In the immediate aftermath of the victory, he had seen to the passengers. Though usually a genial man, he now carried himself with the grave composure of a senior Company officer. His coat was torn, his cravat stained with smoke, but he came with a measured step toward Captain Walsh, who was conferring with Harrington nearby.

"Captain Walsh," Hamilton said, offering a formal bow, "I cannot adequately express my gratitude for your timely intervention. Without *Lynx*, my ship would surely have been taken."

Walsh returned the salute with quiet formality. "We did no more than our duty, Captain. Your crew—and your passengers—fought stoutly."

"Indeed they did," Hamilton agreed. Then his gaze shifted, scanning the deck until it settled on Nicholas. "In fact, two of my passengers have expressed a wish to speak with one of your officers. If you can spare Lieutenant Cruwys for a few minutes, Mr. Carlisle desires to thank, in person, the officer who saved his life during the engagement."

Walsh looked at Nicholas, his expression blank other than a twitch, possibly of amusement or annoyance, at the corner of his mouth. Then he turned back to Hamilton. "Very well. Mr. Cruwys, you may attend to this courtesy. Mr. Harrington has the prisoners well in hand."

"Aye, sir," Nicholas replied, suddenly aware of his own condition, his coat torn and stained, his face smudged with powder, the edge of dried blood still visible along one sleeve.

Captain Hamilton led him aft to his cabin, a space that bore witness to the particular luxuries afforded to commanders of the East India Company's largest ships. The design of *Ocean* was such that no guns were fought from the great cabin, and so, despite the violence amidships, the room had escaped untouched, and unlike in the Navy, its contents had not been struck below. Thick carpets covered the deck, and polished furniture gleamed in the lamplight. Landscapes in gilt frames hung beside mirrors, and a pair of silver lamps reflected softly in the glass. On a small table stood a decanter of Madeira and several cut-glass tumblers, evidently brought out in the aftermath.

Mr. Carlisle rose as they entered, now in a fresh coat and cleaner linen, though his colour had not fully returned. His expression, when he saw Nicholas, brightened with unfeigned warmth.

Beside him stood Caroline.

Her bearing was composed—elegant, as ever—but shaded now by a new gravity, the kind shaped not by tragedy but by the quiet pressure of recent hours. She wore a dark grey gown of unadorned but excellent cut, her hair drawn back without ornament, the arrangement plain yet exacting. In the cabin's muted light, the fair tone of it—more a golden ash—only served to heighten the clarity of her eyes: a lucid, improbable green, like sea-glass turned in the hand. In the charged stillness between them, Nicholas was struck, absurdly, and with no little force, by the memory of a Venetian portrait he had once seen: something in the line of the shoulders, the precision of gaze, the silence behind it. Not empty, but poised, like the pause before a note is struck on a well-tuned string.

When she looked at him, her expression changed, reserve melting into something warmer, tinged unmistakably with concern, as her eyes took in the blood, the powder, and the fatigue drawn in lines across his face.

"Lieutenant Cruwys," Captain Hamilton announced, "I believe you are already acquainted with Mr. Edward Carlisle—Senior Director of the Company's Western India Trading Division, and principal of Carlisle Trading—and his daughter, Miss Caroline Carlisle."

"Mr. Carlisle. Miss Carlisle." Nicholas bowed formally. "I'm relieved to find you both unharmed."

"Lieutenant," Mr. Carlisle said, stepping forward and grasping Nicholas's hand with surprising warmth, "once again I find myself in your debt. First your company graced our final evening in India, now I owe you my very life." He glanced toward his daughter. "I cannot say how deeply I appreciate the manner in which you so efficiently dispatched the fellow who meant to strike me down."

Nicholas returned the handshake with due firmness. "I'm glad I was close enough to be of service, sir. Though I must say, your own defence was commendable. Few gentlemen of—if you'll forgive me—your years and station would acquit themselves so ably with a blade."

Carlisle chuckled. "The advantages of a misspent youth, Lieutenant. My father insisted on proper instruction with the smallsword. Skills thoroughly learnt, it seems, do not entirely desert a man, though I admit I hadn't expected to test them quite so vigorously at this stage.

Still, without your intervention, the outcome would have been… less favourable."

"Father insisted upon remaining on deck," Caroline said. Her voice was quiet, perfectly balanced, each word considered, pride clearly present, but laced with restrained concern. "He declined the purser's advice that the Senior Director would do more good below."

"The ship and my cargo are one and the same, my dear," her father replied. "And I could hardly hide when there was work to be done."

Caroline stepped forward slightly. Her gaze, steady and unmistakably direct, took Nicholas in. What might have seemed forward in a London drawing room felt entirely natural here.

"You're wounded, Lieutenant," she said, indicating the rent in his sleeve where blood had darkened the cloth.

"A scratch only, Miss Carlisle," Nicholas replied. In truth, he had scarcely noticed it amid the chaos.

"Even so," she said gently, "it should be cleaned." She moved to a cabinet and returned with a small box of medical supplies. "If you'll allow me, I have some experience."

Nicholas glanced toward Mr. Carlisle, who gave the faintest of nods.

Nicholas removed his bloodstained coat, and Caroline set to the task with quiet assurance, first rolling the sleeve of his shirt above the wound. Her hands moved with a confidence born not of theory but of practice. A subtle trace of jasmine clung to her, light, but distinct. Though composed, Nicholas could not help but be keenly aware of her nearness—not only the gesture, but the care it conveyed.

"There," she said at last, pinning the dressing in place with practiced delicacy. "That should prevent infection until your ship's surgeon can see to it properly."

"Your skill does you great credit, Miss Carlisle," Nicholas said. Their eyes met—briefly, but unmistakably. "Thank you."

Mr. Carlisle, observing the exchange, gave no comment, but his expression had taken on a more thoughtful cast. He gestured toward the table.

"Captain Hamilton has kindly provided a decanter. Will you join us in a glass, Lieutenant? After such violence, a small civility seems not merely welcome, but necessary."

As they settled into the cabin's armchairs, Nicholas became aware of Caroline studying him with a measured gaze. There was concern in her fine features, certainly, but also something cooler, more analytical. It was not merely gratitude for her father's rescue, but an assessment that seemed to weigh deeper matters. She maintained perfect composure in the presence of her father and Captain Hamilton, but Nicholas sensed layers of thought behind those calm green eyes, thoughts he could not quite interpret.

"Well, Lieutenant," Mr. Carlisle said, handing Nicholas a glass of Madeira, "you've shown today that your talents extend well beyond navigation and polite conversation. That shot was remarkable, particularly given the circumstances."

"Fortune favoured the attempt, sir," Nicholas replied, accepting the glass. "I'm only grateful it succeeded."

"Fortune, perhaps," Carlisle said, raising his own glass in salute, "but skill most certainly. Few men could make such a shot from a moving deck, through powder smoke, with a life hanging in the balance."

He paused, then continued in a tone of frank admiration. "And fewer still would lead a boarding party to seize the enemy vessel. I saw you from the quarterdeck, once our own was secured. The way you rallied your men, the manner in which you leapt to the brig, most impressive. You fight like a man born to command."

Caroline's fingers tightened slightly around her glass at that last phrase, her composure slipping for the briefest instant. It was not distress at the violence, Nicholas would have expected no such delicacy, but something subtler. A flicker of recognition, perhaps, at what that quality might mean for her father's view of the man before him. The expression passed quickly, but not before Nicholas caught it—a moment of calculation behind the mask.

And then, as Mr. Carlisle spoke on, Nicholas felt the weight of Caroline's gaze. It was steady, appraising, too calm to be infatuation, too thoughtful to be mere curiosity. It reminded him, oddly, of the way senior officers observed promising midshipmen: noting posture, timing, temperament. It was not the gaze of a young woman overcome by heroics; it was something more deliberate, and in its way, more arresting.

When she realised he had noticed, the colour in her cheeks deepened, very slightly, but she did not look away. Instead, she took a measured sip of Madeira, and in the motion her neckline shifted just enough to reveal the elegant curve of her throat and the rise and fall of her breath. It was not flirtation. Yet there was, unmistakably, a current between them: an awareness heightened by danger shared and survival earned.

Mr. Carlisle, for all his commercial pragmatism, was not blind to the glance that passed between his daughter and the young officer. His gaze shifted from one to the other with the same thoughtful appraisal he might apply to a complex negotiation. There was no disapproval in his expression, merely observation. A faint adjustment in his posture suggested he had come to some provisional conclusion, not a decision, but a recognition of potential.

He cleared his throat softly—a courteous reminder of his presence.

"As I was saying, Lieutenant," he continued, his tone neutral once more, "your conduct today has only confirmed my initial impression: you are an officer of uncommon ability and character. When we reach London, I should be pleased to offer you introductions to certain associates who value such qualities. Lord Sandwich at the Admiralty is an acquaintance of longstanding through Company matters. He might take an interest in your experience, particularly your time in the Pacific."

Nicholas felt a brief stillness at the mention of the First Lord. Behind Carlisle's unassuming tone lay an offer of extraordinary consequence: few lieutenants without family or fortune could hope to draw such notice by ordinary means. He inclined his head, understanding the mixture of opportunity and obligation that had just been extended.

"That is most generous, sir," he said with quiet care. "I'm grateful for the consideration."

"It is the least I can do," Carlisle replied, "for the man who spared me a premature departure from this world."

Captain Hamilton, who had stood discreetly near the door, cleared his throat. "Forgive the interruption, Mr. Carlisle, but Lieutenant Cruwys's ship appears to be preparing to get under way, along with her prize."

"Of course, of course," Carlisle nodded, setting down his glass. "Naval matters must take precedence. We have detained the lieutenant quite long enough."

As Nicholas rose to take his leave, Caroline stepped forward with quiet poise.

"Lieutenant, might I have a private word before you depart? A message for Captain Walsh regarding the ladies among the passengers, which I would prefer to convey through you."

Mr. Carlisle and Captain Hamilton exchanged a brief glance. Then Carlisle inclined his head. "Of course, my dear. Captain Hamilton, perhaps you would be good enough to show me the extent of the damage to the foc'sle? I have some concern for her structural integrity on the remainder of our passage."

The two older men withdrew, the cabin door left conspicuously ajar, as propriety required. Caroline moved a step closer, her voice lowering just enough to ensure their privacy without violating the conventions that still held sway, even here.

"You neglected to mention at dinner that you were such a formidable fighter," she said, the ghost of a smile touching her lips. Her tone held a trace of mischief, tempered by the weight of the day.

"There was no occasion to speak of such things in polite company," Nicholas replied softly. "And I believe our conversation took a more agreeable turn."

A hint of colour touched her cheeks, but her gaze did not waver. "Indeed it did. I find myself… deeply thankful that fate has brought us together again, though I might have wished for less perilous circumstances." Her eyes flicked briefly to his bandaged arm. Then, with a glance toward the open door, she added, low and deliberate:

"I believe, after today, you may call me Caroline, at least when we are not in company."

It was bold. Improper, by London standards. But they were far from London now, and death had passed close enough to make such niceties feel faintly absurd.

"You must take care of that wound, Nicholas," she said, speaking his name with calm assurance. "Promise me you'll have it properly examined."

Her concern, simply expressed, touched him more than he expected. "I promise... Caroline."

She glanced once more toward the door—no one yet returned—then, in one swift and graceful motion, she stepped forward and kissed him on the cheek. It was the lightest touch, gone almost before he registered it. Yet it left a warmth that had nothing to do with the tropical air.

"For saving my father," she murmured, drawing back. Her eyes held both boldness and something more fragile, shyness, perhaps, but not uncertainty. "I could not bear to lose him, as we lost Mother."

Then, with the sound of footsteps nearing, she gathered herself and adopted a more formal tone.

"Please inform Captain Walsh that the ladies among *Ocean's* passengers are deeply grateful for *Lynx's* timely assistance, and that we shall remember the conduct of her officers and men when we come to speak of these events in London."

Her voice dipped once more, just for him. "And know, Nicholas, that I shall look forward to our next meeting. Father has already spoken of inviting Captain Walsh and his officers to dine, once the ships are made fit again."

Before he could reply, she stepped back, precisely measured, precisely proper, just as Hamilton and Mr. Carlisle reappeared. Nicholas bowed with composure to all present, his expression unreadable, and took his leave.

Back aboard *Lynx*, Nicholas found Captain Walsh on the quarterdeck. The older man's expression was as composed as ever, but the faint lift of one eyebrow suggested curiosity—or amusement—at his lieutenant's return.

"I trust Mr. Carlisle expressed his gratitude in appropriate form?" Walsh asked, his tone even, though his eyes held a knowing glint, and he glanced the now bandaged arm.

"Most generously, sir," Nicholas replied, keeping his own manner scrupulously professional. "He offered introductions in London that may prove of some value when we return."

"Indeed?" Walsh nodded, the glint sharpening. He studied Nicholas a moment longer with that appraising gaze of his, quiet, exact, and never hurried. "And Miss Carlisle? Did she entrust you with any particular message?"

Nicholas met his captain's eye without wavering. "Only the particular thanks of the ladies aboard *Ocean*, sir—for our timely intervention."

"I see," Walsh murmured. A trace of dry humour flickered at the corners of his mouth. "Well then, Mr. Cruwys, now that the courtesies have been observed, let us return to business. The convoy has escaped, but only just. Our losses are not inconsiderable, though they could have been far worse."

He paused, scanning the horizon with a captain's practised eye. "We've a prize to secure, damage to assess, and the convoy must be fit to sail again within three days if we're to reach the Cape before the season turns. I shall expect your report on the captured brig by eight bells."

"Aye, sir," Nicholas replied, quietly grateful for the return to solid duty.

Walsh turned slightly, then added, almost as an afterthought, "We shall maintain our vigilance. The convoy has acquitted itself well, and so have you, Mr. Cruwys. Third Lieutenant: a post of significant responsibility, especially in our present undermanned state. But one, I believe, you've earned."

Nicholas inclined his head with respectful gravity. "Thank you, sir. I shall do my best to be worthy of your trust."

As Walsh turned away, Nicholas's gaze drifted toward *Ocean*. The battle was done, for now. Yet his thoughts moved between worlds: the new duties he had taken on as third lieutenant, and the memory of Caroline Carlisle, poised, self-possessed, yet capable of unexpected boldness.

The day had altered many things—his rank, his station, and perhaps his future. Yet much remained unchanged: the boundless sea stretching beyond the masts, the hard uncertainty of the voyage still ahead, and the intricate weave of duty, ambition, and desire that formed the fabric of a naval officer's life.

Later that evening, Captain Walsh sat in his cabin with Lieutenant Harrington, reviewing the day's events over a glass of port. The small oil lamp suspended from the deck beams above swayed gently with the ship's motion, casting shifting shadows across the captain's features.

"I've spoken with the Commodore," Walsh said, setting down his glass. "He's agreed to transfer Lieutenant Chester to *Thetis* as second lieutenant. She's down two officers and needs reinforcement."

Harrington gave a single nod. "A sensible arrangement, sir."

Walsh did not elaborate, nor was it necessary. Among officers, such matters were understood without explanation. Chester had not disgraced himself, but neither had he shown the steadiness required in the wake of Hargrove's death. *Lynx* needed a capable second in command, and Harrington would now stand as first lieutenant.

"Lieutenant Cruwys handled himself remarkably well during the action," Walsh observed.

Harrington, who had regained consciousness in time to witness Nicholas's actions firsthand, nodded in agreement. "He rallied the men without hesitation after Hargrove fell, sir. No panic, no theatrics—just clear orders given with confidence. The men responded as if they'd been under his command for years rather than minutes."

Walsh's keen eyes studied his new first lieutenant. "You sound almost impressed, Mr. Harrington. Rather a departure, I believe, from your initial assessment when he first came aboard at Calcutta."

"I acknowledge my judgment has evolved, sir," Harrington replied. "I was skeptical of an officer who had spent years outside proper naval service, particularly one who'd lived among islanders and served aboard a Portuguese trader. I expected his habits would have decayed."

He paused. "I was mistaken."

"Indeed?" Walsh prompted, a hint of amusement in his eyes. He had known Harrington long enough to recognise when his carefully maintained certainties were being revised.

"Cruwys brings perspectives we lack, sir," Harrington continued, surprising himself with the clarity of his conviction. "His time in the Pacific. even his service with that foreign captain, has taught him adaptability. He isn't bound by habit, and he isn't afraid to act."

Walsh nodded slowly. "Cook chose his officers carefully. Cruwys must have shown promise even as a new midshipman to be taken on for the voyage. Then to survive being cast away and return to the service by merit alone, these aren't the achievements of an ordinary officer."

"No, sir. They are not," Harrington agreed. "He maintains proper naval discipline without the rigidity that often comes with it. His men respect him without fearing him, a balance many never find."

Walsh studied his first lieutenant with interest. Harrington came from true naval aristocracy: generations of service, connections throughout the Admiralty, the assurance of eventual promotion to post-captain and indeed flag rank through family influence as much as merit. That such a man would speak with genuine respect of a lieutenant whose background, though he sprang from an ancient and respected family such as the *Cruwyses*, was clearly far from London and society, represented a notable endorsement.

"You believe he should have the prize command, then?" Walsh asked, his tone neutral.

Harrington hesitated only briefly. "I do, sir. Cruwys has earned the chance. While he lacks experience in certain formalities, he learns quickly. And with the convoy, he'll be under both our eyes and the Commodore's."

Walsh's expression revealed nothing. "Interesting. Many lieutenants in your position would be angling for the prize themselves. It's traditionally the prerogative of the senior lieutenant."

"I serve best where I am, sir," Harrington replied with pragmatic ease. "*Lynx* needs an experienced first lieutenant who knows her crew and capabilities. Besides," he added with a rare, ironic smile, "I believe the dignity of my family's naval tradition will survive."

Walsh chuckled at this candid acknowledgment of social realities, stated with such economy. "Very well, Mr. Harrington. I shall recommend to the Commodore that Lieutenant Cruwys be appointed prize master of the brig. He surprised you, didn't he?"

"He did, sir," Harrington admitted. "It's a useful reminder: ability sometimes forces recognition despite every obstacle. The Navy is not always as meritocratic as we pretend, but now and then, merit breaks through."

"A philosophical observation, Mr. Harrington?" Walsh said lightly. "Perhaps Mr. Cruwys's unconventional thinking is proving contagious."

His tone was dry, but his eyes held approval.

"I'm pleased to see it. An officer who cannot recognise merit in unexpected quarters will never command men to their fullest."

Dawn two days later revealed the fruits of feverish labour across the convoy. The French 32-gun frigate—now christened *HMS Audacious* by her captors—rode low in the water beside *Thetis*. Both vessels bore the unmistakable scars of their brutal engagement. *Thetis* carried jury masts where her foretopmast and mizzen had come down, the shortened spars a poor match for her otherwise graceful lines. *Audacious* was in worse condition: her mainmast was gone entirely and had been replaced by a makeshift rig cobbled together from her spare spars.

Despite their wounds, the frigates retained enough sail to keep pace with the convoy, though they would struggle if the wind turned foul or freshened beyond a moderate breeze. Commodore Hartley had transferred a substantial portion of *Salisbury's* crew to form *Audacious'* prize crew, given *Thetis's* heavy casualties. Command of the prize had gone to *Thetis*'s first lieutenant, a promotion to commander all but assured, should she reach port.

By contrast, *Lynx* and her prize—the 14-gun brig that had attempted to take *Ocean*—showed little outward sign of their clash. The brig's rigging had been re-reeved, and her damaged bulwarks mended from the damage of coming fast alongside. She was a handsome vessel: sleek, well-proportioned, clearly built for speed rather than burden. Unlike many privateers, which began life as merchantmen hastily armed for war, this brig had been designed for fighting. Her lines bore the mark of a skilled French naval architect, sharp at the entry, fine on the run, with a marked tumblehome. Walsh proposed she be renamed *HMS Growler*, and Commodore Hartley had concurred.

Salisbury had fared reasonably well, considering the ferocity of her engagement with the 36-gun French frigate and the corvette that had accompanied her. Her rigging had been largely restored, though her scarred hull and the spliced timbers of her yards bore silent witness to the punishment she had taken. Nearly two feet of water had poured in before a breach at the waterline was stopped—first with hammocks and sailcloth, then by the carpenter himself, who went below with tools and oakum and had yet to reappear.

The six East Indiamen rode quietly nearby. Their high sides and bluff bows gave them the stolid appearance of patient draft horses among blooded racers. Only *Bengal Queen* and *Ocean* had suffered serious damage, and even that was modest compared to the havoc wrought upon the Navy ships. Yet some twenty men from *Ocean*'s crew had died in her defence, a grim reminder that even a brief engagement, when it came to boarding, could exact a brutal toll.

"Mr. Cruwys."

Nicholas turned to see Lieutenant Harrington approaching. His uniform was freshly brushed, his step composed. His expression betrayed nothing, but there was no mistaking the quiet weight of his new office. He was now first lieutenant of *Lynx*.

"Captain Walsh requests our presence in his cabin."

Nicholas nodded. "Do you know the purpose of the meeting?"

Harrington's mouth quirked in a half-smile. Already sounding more the first lieutenant, he replied, "I believe it concerns the disposition of our prizes, among other matters. But it is not my place to speculate on the captain's intentions." The corners of his eyes betrayed a flicker of amusement at his newly assumed gravity.

Together they descended to Walsh's cabin, where they found the captain seated at his table alongside the master, Mr. Ainsley, charts and papers spread in orderly array.

"Gentlemen," Walsh said without preamble as they entered. "Be seated. We have matters to address before the convoy gets under way."

The two lieutenants took their places around the table, where glasses of Madeira awaited them—the dark amber liquid catching the morning light through the stern windows. It was a quiet signal that the conference, while serious, would proceed without undue stiffness.

"First," Walsh began, "let us consider the state of our squadron. As discussed last night during the captains' conference aboard *Salisbury*, *Thetis* and *Audacious* are fit to maintain convoy speed in fair conditions—no more. Their jury rigs are sound enough, but limited. *Salisbury* has fared better, though her injuries are not slight."

He paused, letting his gaze pass slowly over each of them, eyes sharp with habitual scrutiny.

"Commodore Hartley has established a modified formation to reflect these constraints, which I shall now relay."

Walsh turned to a paper on the table, the new formation inked in a practiced hand that Nicholas recognised as that of *Salisbury's* master.

"The East Indiamen will maintain their double column. *Thetis* will fall in astern of the windward line, *Audacious* astern of the leeward. Both will be well positioned to defend, but likely unable to maneuver should fresh threats arise."

His finger traced the formation as he spoke, tapping each silhouette with methodical precision. "*Salisbury* will take station to windward, four cables off the convoy's beam. *Growler* will sail in company with her. *Lynx* will resume her duties as scout, ranging ahead."

"This brings us to the matter of our prize."

He looked up.

"Under ordinary circumstances, Mr. Harrington, as my senior surviving lieutenant after the transfer of Lieutenant Chester, you would assume command of *Growler* as prize master," Walsh said, his tone matter-of-fact. "But these are not ordinary times. With Hargrove lost, and Chester transferred to *Thetis*, I require an experienced first lieutenant aboard *Lynx*. You alone have the familiarity with her company to carry that weight."

Harrington nodded. "I understand completely, sir."

"Good. I thought you would." Walsh turned to Nicholas. "Mr. Cruwys—you will take command of *Growler* as her prize master."

The words settled with weight. Nicholas felt the surge—surprise, pride, the sharp bite of responsibility—but kept his expression contained.

"Thank you, sir. I am honoured by your confidence."

Walsh returned the nod, not warm, not cold, simply measured. "Your conduct during the engagement displayed both initiative and judgment. The capture of the brig was due in large part to your actions. It is fitting you should carry her on this next leg."

Walsh slid a sealed packet across the table, the red wax bearing the impression of his signet ring.

"These are your orders. As I said, you will sail in company with *Salisbury*, on the windward station. Commodore Hartley will issue tactical direction should we encounter enemy forces, but otherwise, the brig is yours to command."

He took a measured sip of Madeira before continuing.

"You will be provided with a prize crew of forty men, roughly half her proper complement. Sixteen will come from *Lynx*, including two gun captains, the carpenter's mate, and Midshipman Foley. The remainder will be drawn from *Salisbury*, including Master's Mate Williams, a gunner's mate, and several trained seamen."

He paused to ensure Nicholas had taken this in.

"Mr. Williams will serve as your second-in-command. Mr. Foley, as acting lieutenant."

Nicholas noted the composition carefully, aware that the quality of his crew would shape the success or failure of his temporary command.

"Understood, sir."

"The French sailing master—Monsieur Leclerc—will remain aboard as your prisoner. He has given his parole and will assist in handling the vessel; he knows her character better than any of us. I'm told he is a professional seaman and harbours no particular animus toward the English. Treat him with appropriate courtesy, but remember, he remains a prisoner of war and may be recalled to his allegiance under certain conditions."

"Aye, sir."

"Very good." Walsh stood, his compact figure silhouetted against the windows. "Transfer your effects to *Growler* immediately. The convoy will get under way at one bell of the forenoon watch."

As they left the cabin, Nicholas felt a moment's pause—not hesitation, exactly, but the quiet recognition of change. His first command, even if only as prize master of a captured enemy brig, marked a turning point.

Harrington fell into step beside him as they made their way up to the quarterdeck.

"Congratulations are in order, Nicholas," he said, his tone genuine despite what must, logically, have been disappointment. "*Growler*'s a fine little ship. You've earned the opportunity."

"Thank you," Nicholas replied. "Though I admit, I expected you would take the command, as is customary."

Harrington shrugged, his aristocratic features composed in their usual half-amused expression.

"Walsh made the right decision. The convoy depends on *Lynx* being handled properly. With Hargrove and Chester gone, I'm the logical choice to serve as first lieutenant."

He glanced at Nicholas.

"Besides, I'll have other opportunities. Your conduct during the battle—the rally after Hargrove fell, the boarding, the French captain's surrender—those are the sorts of moments that shape a career."

They paused at the rail, looking out over the calm sea where *Growler* lay hove-to, her sleek lines a striking contrast to the bulkier East Indiamen.

"She's a beauty," Harrington observed. "French-built for war, not a converted merchantman. Designed for speed and pursuit from the keel up."

Nicholas nodded, studying the vessel with a critical eye.

"She's coppered below the waterline, too. Unusual for a privateer."

"Indeed. You've been given a ship of quality, Nicholas. Make the most of it." Harrington's smile deepened with genuine warmth.

"I shall endeavor to do credit to *Lynx* and her officers," he replied. "And I expect you'll have your command long before I receive mine."

An hour later, Nicholas stood on the quarterdeck of *HMS Growler*, surveying his new command. The brig's main deck stretched clean and uncluttered before him, her fourteen guns—seven to a side. His new crew moved with the purposeful confusion of men still finding their stations aboard an unfamiliar ship.

Sixteen of them had come from *Lynx*—men he knew and trusted. The rest were drawn from *Salisbury*, and brought with them the steadiness of a veteran crew. Master's Mate Williams, a weathered seaman in his late thirties, would serve as his first officer and principal advisor in matters of seamanship and navigation.

Monsieur Leclerc, the French sailing master, stood nearby, watching the preparations with the professional eye of a man long used to ships and the sea. He appeared to be in his mid-forties, grey hair tied back in the French style, his eyes squinting against the light as if still gauging the horizon for weather. Nicholas had spoken with him briefly and found him cooperative, knowledgeable, and understandably reserved

At precisely one bell in the forenoon watch, the convoy began to stir. The sound of bosun's pipes and shouted orders drifted across the water. Topsails, then courses, and finally topgallants were loosed to catch the breath of the northeast monsoon. One by one, the ships gathered way, their bows lifting gently as they pushed through the long, easy swell.

Growler took the wind with a satisfying crack as her canvas filled, the sails drawing taut against the yards in orderly sequence. The brig heeled slightly, surged ahead, and was underway.

"Bring her two points to starboard," Nicholas ordered. "We'll take station two cables astern of *Salisbury*."

"Aye, sir," came the reply from the helmsman, a *Salisbury* man named Pullman, with the quiet assurance of long habit.

Growler responded with a liveliness that spoke to her design. She heeled slightly as she caught the wind, then settled, cutting cleanly through the water, her bow wave curling back from the cutwater.

"She handles well, monsieur," remarked Leclerc, observing from nearby in accented but serviceable English. "Very responsive to the helm when she is properly trimmed."

Nicholas inclined his head, acknowledging the Frenchman's expertise. "What else can you tell me of her sailing qualities, Monsieur Leclerc?"

Leclerc considered a moment, his weathered face intent. "She points higher than most square-rigged ships, within nearly five points of the wind in favourable conditions. She is quick in stays, and carries her way well through the wind's eye. In light or moderate air, she will outrun most frigates, though of course she cannot stand against their guns." A flicker of pride touched his expression. "She was built at Cherbourg in 1778. The design is by Monsieur Sané."

Nicholas recognised the name. Pierre Sané was among the finest of French naval architects, known for ships that married speed with combat capability.

As *Growler* took up her assigned station to windward of the convoy, Nicholas watched the formation taking shape. At its heart, the six East Indiamen continued in two parallel columns of three, their heavy hulls ploughing steadily through the sea with *Ocean* still second in the windward line, her freshly patched bulwarks plainly visible even at this distance. Astern of the convoy, *Thetis* and *Audacious* maintained their assigned positions at the rear of each column. Though their jury rigs limited their handling, they appeared capable of keeping pace with the merchant vessels in the current favorable conditions. A jet of water still showed *Audacious* working her pumps intermittently.

Far ahead, *Lynx* resumed her scouting role, her sleek form diminishing with distance as she ranged ahead to give early warning of any threat. Nicholas felt a brief pang at leaving the ship that had been his home since Calcutta, but it passed quickly. What remained was the clear weight of present responsibility. He was now in command, however temporary the appointment might prove.

"Signal from *Salisbury*, sir," called Midshipman Farley, who had been assigned as his junior officer. "They're acknowledging our position and ordering us to maintain station."

"Very good, Mr. Farley. Acknowledge the signal."

As the flags rose and fell in their silent exchange, Nicholas felt the rhythm of command begin to settle in his body. The coming weeks would test him in ways he could not yet predict, but he felt equal to the task. From midshipman to castaway, from lieutenant to prize master—each step had shaped him for this.

The responsibility sat well. *Growler* answered the helm with precision, and the convoy sailed in careful formation ahead, each ship where it ought to be. It was a pattern imposed on the sea, fragile perhaps, but for now, it held.

The following morning, Nicholas entered his cabin—*his* cabin—with a faint sense of unreality after having been on deck since before sunrise. Other than a few hours of sleep during the middle watch, it was the first moment he had had to himself since taking command. Settling the watches, keeping *Growler* to her station, and—he admitted it—the unfamiliar weight of sole responsibility for a ship, had kept him constantly on deck. Now with the brig sailing easily before the northeast monsoon, the captain's privilege of solitude at last presented itself.

The stern compartment of HMS *Growler* was unexpectedly generous in its proportions, and untouched by the battle. Unlike the cramped quarters he had occupied as a lieutenant aboard *Lynx*, this cabin spanned the full breadth of the brig, nearly fourteen feet at its widest, with a curved stern pierced by five large windows that admitted a flood of morning light as the sun rose astern.

Bookcases had been built into the forward bulkhead, filled with navigational texts, charts, and several volumes of French literature, which Nicholas made a mental note to examine in due course. A set of charts lay neatly stowed in a purpose-built locker, and several small paintings of French harbours adorned the walls.

The large locker beneath the bench under the stern windows yielded a more tangible discovery. Here, the French captain had stowed his private stores: nearly two dozen bottles of Bordeaux and Loire wine, each cushioned in its own padded niche; a small keg of cognac; jars of preserved fruit; a half-wheel of cheese wrapped in muslin; a cured ham in a canvas sack; and a wooden box containing a two dozen lemons, still firm and fragrant. Such comforts, carried by officers of every navy to leaven the monotony of shipboard fare, represented a quiet luxury—especially aboard a vessel of war.

It was clear the French captain had been a man of means. The double cot was slung to starboard, neatly made with linen far finer than anything issued by the purser. A substantial desk stood bolted to the forward bulkhead, its surface inlaid with green leather bordered in gilded tooling. Along the larboard side stood a dining table with four chairs.

Nicholas ran his hand over the smooth desk, feeling the slight give of the leather beneath his fingers. The drawers revealed a number of personal items that spoke to the habits of a fastidious man: a silver-mounted writing set, complete with inkwells, sanders, and a selection of quills; several sheets of high-quality paper bearing the watermark of a Parisian stationer.

He sat. Still absorbing the transformation that had occurred—from fourth lieutenant to captain in the space of a single action. He knew the command was temporary, likely to be relinquished upon their arrival in England, if not at the Cape. Yet in this moment, the reality could not be denied. Within these wooden walls, he was captain.

Master after God. Responsible for his ship and her people, answerable to none but Commodore Hartley, and to him only in matters of station and fleet order.

His reverie was interrupted by a knock at the door.

"Enter," he called, straightening instinctively.

Master's Mate Williams appeared, touching his forehead in salute. "Beg pardon, sir. The watch is changing, and I thought you might wish to know we've made good ninety-two miles since noon yesterday. Still holding perfect station with *Salisbury*."

"Thank you, Mr. Williams. The brig handles well."

Williams nodded and withdrew. A moment later, another knock, this time from the purser's steward, carrying a covered tray.

"Your breakfast, sir," the man said, setting it on the table and retreating with quiet efficiency. "As requested—coffee, not tea."

Nicholas offered a brief nod of thanks and uncovered the tray. The smell of strong coffee rose at once, rich and bitter, and suddenly he realised just how hungry he was. The tray held a generous portion: ship's biscuit, a thick slice of preserved ham, a wedge of hard cheese, and, unexpectedly—one of the French captain's lemons, quartered and arranged beside a small dish of coarse salt. The coffee had been poured into a tin mug set on a blue-and-white saucer, clearly taken from the private stores. A small civility, but not unnoticed.

The ham was salt-heavy, the biscuit hard, but hunger made both welcome. He finished all of it, sipped the coffee slowly, and let the moment settle. It was the first meal he had taken alone in months. The solitude was not uncomfortable, it was simply unfamiliar.

Afterwards, still sipping his coffee, Nicholas resumed his quiet exploration of the cabin.

On the bulkhead above the desk, he discovered a small cabinet he had missed earlier. Inside were the ship's medical stores: a modest assortment of tinctures, bandages, and instruments. There was also a leather case containing navigational tools: a finely made French sextant, dividers, parallel rules, and a pencil set for chart work.

The sensation of having his own space aboard a ship was almost disorienting. As a midshipman, he had slung his hammock with a dozen others in a space barely large enough for half that number. As a lieutenant aboard *Lynx*, his cabin had been little more than a narrow cot and a sea chest. Even aboard Silva's ship he had only a small cabin.

Nicholas changed into a fresh shirt and was surprised as he noticed that the French captain's washbasin was of fine porcelain rather than the usual tin. Such small luxuries, he reflected as he shaved carefully at the small mirror mounted on the bulkhead, were among the compensations of command, at least among the French.

Here, though modest by the standards of a larger ship, was a place where he had room to move, and to think. To feel the ship as something now his: no longer merely a post, but a charge. Not just a part of the machine, but its responsible centre.

Tomorrow would bring its own demands. But for now, in this moment, he could savour the rarest of naval privileges: solitude at sea. A captain in His Majesty's Navy, if only for a time, with a fine French prize beneath his feet and a course set fair to round the Cape of Good Hope.

For three weeks, the convoy sailed steadily southwest, blessed with fair winds and clear skies. The northeasterly monsoon held longer than was usual for the season, propelling them across the Indian Ocean at a steady seven knots for days at a stretch. *Growler* proved herself a fine sailor—too fine at times, often having to reduce canvas to avoid outpacing *Salisbury*. Nicholas found himself growing increasingly attached to his temporary command, admiring her responsiveness and trim under sail.

He spent more time on deck than an experienced captain might have done, often remaining long after his presence was strictly required. But Williams had proved himself thoroughly competent, and Nicholas grew to trust the brig in his hands. The older man had served nearly twenty years afloat, including a spell aboard a privateer during the Seven Years' War. His instinctive sense of wind and weather, and his quiet command over the crew, reassured Nicholas that *Growler* remained in good hands even when he withdrew below.

Midshipman Foley, too, had begun to show steady promise. Though young, he stood his watches attentively, often paired with Leclerc, who remained under parole and had settled into his unofficial role with quiet precision. Between the two of them, Nicholas found that the brig's movements were well observed and competently relayed, even in his absence.

Sometimes Nicholas would stand at the windward rail, watching the light shift across the sea or observing the convoy's alignment with quiet satisfaction. At other times he would speak with Williams or Leclerc on matters of navigation, helm, and trim—drawing on their experience with the hungry interest of an officer determined to master every part of his profession.

The crew—initially a patched company of men from two different ships—had begun to knit together under shared discipline. The daily routines of naval life, watches, drills, meals, inspections—offered a framework that bound them more quickly than familiarity. Nicholas had continued Walsh's practice of regular gun drills, timing the crews as they rehearsed the precise choreography of loading, running out, and simulating fire, with occasional live practice by section. By the end of a fortnight, they had shaved nearly fifteen seconds off their time, an improvement Nicholas recorded in the log with quiet pride.

"They're coming along nicely, sir," Williams remarked one morning as they watched the forenoon watch holystoning the deck with the deliberate rhythm of seasoned hands. "Pulling together like they've been shipmates for years, not weeks."

Nicholas nodded. "They're good men, by and large. Hard workers. Though I still find Simmons bears watching."

Simmons, a maintopman from *Salisbury*, had shown a tendency to idle when unobserved—a fault Nicholas had addressed through the bosun's mate, without recourse to formal discipline.

"Aye, sir. But even he's finding his legs. Nothing like the smell of prize money to sharpen a man's sense of duty. Word is *Growler* and *Audacious* will fetch handsomely once we make England. Every man in the squadron to take his share, as is proper."

Nicholas had already encountered the less pleasant aspects of command. Twice in the first fortnight, he had been obliged to stop the grog of men caught fighting during the dog watches, a modest punishment by naval standards, but one that sent a clear signal: discipline would be maintained.

The men accepted it with the resignation of sailors long accustomed to naval justice, and order was restored without further incident.

A more serious matter arose in the third week, when Dawson—one of the *Salisbury* contingent, with a record of past offences—was caught stealing a silver tobacco box from the carpenter's mate. The evidence was clear: the box was found hidden in Dawson's kit. It was not a matter that could be overlooked. Theft aboard ship was regarded with particular severity, given the closeness of life at sea and the limited possessions each man could claim as his own.

Nicholas had wrestled with the decision, acutely aware of the weight of his first serious disciplinary action as captain. That morning, he had ordered the crew mustered to witness punishment: eighteen lashes with the cat-o'-nine-tails, administered by the bosun's mate while the offender was seized at the grating. The sentence was moderate by naval measure—many captains would have ordered two or three dozen for the same offence—but Nicholas found no satisfaction in it. Only necessity.

"I've heard of captains who enjoy this part of command," he said to Williams later that day, as they stood together watching the hands change watch. "I cannot understand it. To order a man flogged—even when it's deserved—is a grim necessity, not a source of pride."

Williams had nodded, his manner grave. "That's because you've a conscience, sir. The men see that. They saw you didn't flinch, but they also saw you took no pleasure in it. That's the mark of a proper officer, if you don't mind my saying so."

Monsieur Leclerc had proven a valuable addition to the ship's company, despite his status as a prisoner. Beyond his knowledge of *Growler*'s handling, he demonstrated an exceptional grasp of celestial navigation—particularly the lunar distance method for determining longitude, refined in recent decades by both English and French astronomers. His willingness to share his expertise, and to compare notes with what Nicholas had learned from Cook, had earned him a measure of respect. Nicholas had taken to inviting him to dine in the cabin several evenings each week, finding his conversation engaging and his insights into French naval practice quietly illuminating.

"She was built for the Caribbean station, originally," Leclerc explained one evening, over a supper drawn from the former captain's private stores. "But with the war, they sent her to Mauritius instead. Lighter hull than your English brigs—faster off the wind, but more lively in quartering seas."

Nicholas nodded. He had already noted how the brig responded with particular sensitivity to shifts in wind direction. Though they had so far met only squalls rather than true weather, those encounters had confirmed both *Growler*'s speed and her more active motion compared to the steadier, slower merchantmen.

"It is the compromise, yes?" Leclerc continued, sipping from his glass. "You cannot have both perfect speed and perfect steadiness in a vessel this size. But she will outrun what she cannot outfight, which is the point."

Two days later a boat came across from *Salisbury* bearing written instructions for *Lynx* as the two ships lay hove to. *Growler* was ordered to bear away and deliver them to *Lynx* some three miles ahead of the van. Nicholas welcomed the opportunity to stretch the brig's legs, freed from the constraint of matching speed with slower vessels.

"Make more sail, Mr. Williams," he ordered, his voice carrying easily across the quarterdeck without strain. "Let's see what she can do with a fair wind. I believe we may set the topgallants."

Williams touched his hat, betraying only the quiet satisfaction of a sailing master with a fine vessel under him. "Aye, sir. We might carry royals, if the wind holds steady."

"Very good, Mr. Williams," Nicholas replied, raising his glass ahead. The sails of *Lynx* stood out sharp against the horizon, her hull just visible above the white-capped swell when both ships rose together. She was now held closer than before the French engagement—no more than a league or so ahead, her topsails gleaming in the morning sun.

The crew sprang to their work with confidence, setting additional canvas and trimming sail to perfection. *Growler* responded beautifully, her speed building steadily until she was making nearly nine knots, slicing through the water with an ease that drew appreciative nods from even the most seasoned hands.

Nicholas glanced back toward the convoy, now diminishing by the minute, and felt a quiet surge of pride in his temporary command. The wind, fresh from the northeast off the port quarter, was perfect for the brig's best point of sailing. He allowed himself the brief pleasure of simply feeling her motion. The living pulse of a well-found ship under competent hands.

They reached *Lynx* in just over an hour, heaving to at a cable's length and preparing to lower a boat. To Nicholas's surprise, Captain Walsh signaled that he would come aboard *Growler* rather than receive the dispatches by boat.

As Walsh climbed to the deck, receiving the honours due his rank and saluting the quarterdeck, Nicholas noted the captain's appraising glance, quietly taking in every detail of the brig's condition.

"A fine morning for a sail, Mr. Cruwys," Walsh observed, returning the salute. "Your ship looks well."

"Thank you, sir. She handles admirably."

Walsh nodded, a flicker of professional approval crossing his features. "Let us step below. I have some matters to discuss."

In the cabin that Nicholas now called his own, Walsh took a seat with the easy assurance of an officer long accustomed to command. Nicholas ordered his steward to bring coffee, and they spoke at first of general matters—the progress of the convoy, the weather ahead, the state of the hands—before Walsh turned, as Nicholas knew he must, to more particular concerns.

"I observe you've continued my practice of regular gun drills," Walsh said, his tone neutral, though his eyes held a flicker of amusement. "We saw you blazing away the other afternoon."

"Yes, sir," Nicholas replied. "I've found it maintains both their skill and their spirits."

"Indeed. The Commodore mentioned it in our last communication. It seems he's noticed your enthusiasm." A smile tugged at the corner of Walsh's mouth. "He remarked that he had half a mind to order you to desist, lest your frequent practice serve as a beacon to any enemy in the vicinity."

Nicholas felt a flush rise. "I hadn't considered that aspect, sir. I'll reduce the frequency of drills at once."

Walsh raised a hand. "The Commodore was not entirely serious, Mr. Cruwys. In fact, he followed the remark by saying he wished more of his captains shared your attention to gunnery. He considers it a mark of professional seriousness." Walsh's smile deepened slightly. "I took the liberty of pointing out that you were simply continuing my own emphasis on the subject."

Nicholas recognised it for what it was, Walsh taking partial credit, while also offering genuine approval. It was a graceful manoeuvre, and one that spoke to the delicate politics of command.

"I learned from your example, sir," Nicholas said carefully.

"Good. It's pleasing to see the habit carried forward," Walsh replied with a satisfied nod. "A touch extravagant with the powder, perhaps, but valuable for training the men's ears to the true sound of battle. Continue as you have, but with a little more time between exercises."

"Aye, sir. Thank you."

Walsh sipped his coffee, studying Nicholas over the rim of the cup. "You seem to have settled into command with remarkable ease, for so junior an officer."

There was a brief pause, then Walsh's tone shifted, still informal, but carrying greater weight.

"There has been some discussion regarding the disposition of *Growler* after we reach England. The Commodore believes she would serve well as a dispatch vessel, given her sailing qualities and the present shortage of small warships in home waters. In any case, the Admiralty will almost certainly purchase her into the Service rather than sell her off."

This was not unusual. Many captured vessels, especially those of good design or particular utility, were bought into the Navy and commissioned under new captains.

"Such being the case," Walsh continued, "she would require a permanent commander for the voyage home, even past the Cape. And as you've already demonstrated your ability to handle her effectively, I have suggested to the Commodore that you might be confirmed in command for the return to England."

Nicholas felt his pulse quicken. To be entrusted with command of a prize warship all the way home from the Indian Ocean was no minor matter. It would mean not only additional time in independent command, but increased visibility to the Admiralty. In wartime, such opportunities were rare, and for a young officer, they could make a career.

"At twenty, it is early," Walsh added, "but not without precedent. I've known men to receive their commander's rank at your age, though most had the benefit of family connections, or were the nephews of First Lords."

The implication was clear. Nicholas had no such backing. But merit—combined with fortune—might still open the same door.

"That would be... a considerable honour, sir," he said, keeping his composure despite the thrill behind the words. "Well beyond anything I had expected."

"Indeed," Walsh said. "Opportunities like this don't come often. The Commodore seems impressed by your conduct, both during the action, and since. Command of *Growler* for the voyage home wouldn't guarantee promotion. But it would certainly strengthen your case."

Nicholas inclined his head. "I'm grateful for your confidence, sir. And for bringing this to my attention."

Walsh nodded, apparently satisfied with the reply. He rose, signaling the close of the meeting.

"Nothing is decided yet. Much depends on the state of the vessels when we reach Cape Town. But continue as you have been, Mr. Cruwys, and you may find your temporary command lasts longer than you anticipated."

As Walsh departed to return to *Lynx*, Nicholas accompanied him to the deck, where the bosun's mate piped the side and due honours were rendered. He remained at the rail as Walsh descended into his boat and pulled away, then turned aft and re-entered his cabin, his mind grappling with this unexpected intelligence.

The prospect of commanding *Growler* all the way to England, and even the distant possibility of a step in rank, brought a sensation he could scarcely define. He had entered the naval service with modest expectations, his family's connections being respectable enough in Devon and the West Country but carrying little weight with the Admiralty. His years separated from the service in the Pacific islands had seemed to dash any hope of advancement along conventional channels. Yet now, through a series of extraordinary circumstances, he found himself potentially on the cusp of preferment that would normally be years in the future, if it came at all.

He was perfectly aware that many worthy officers never rose above lieutenant, their abilities notwithstanding, and in times of peace lieutenants were sometimes beached on half-pay for decades, while midshipmen with gleaming credentials might pass their examination with distinction yet never receive their commission. The Navy was a capricious service, where merit alone was rarely sufficient; it required also interest, circumstance, and the singular luck of being in precisely the right place when opportunity presented itself.

Growler's bell struck four, the clear bronze notes marking the change of watch and summoning Nicholas back to his immediate responsibilities. There would be time enough for castles in Spain. For now, he had a ship to command, and the surest path to advancement lay in the perfect execution of his present duties.

The convoy's steady progress continued uninterrupted for three more days, with no sign of enemy activity. *Lynx* ranged ahead, hull up from *Salisbury*'s masthead lookouts, and usually from *Growler*'s as well. The East Indiamen maintained their formation with remarkable consistency, their civilian masters proving themselves competent seamen despite the naval officers' tendency to regard merchant captains with thinly veiled condescension.

As they approached the southern limit of the monsoon's influence, approximately eight hundred miles north of the Cape, Nicholas began to notice subtle changes in the weather pattern. The steady northeasterly that had propelled them so reliably began to fluctuate, veering unpredictably before settling back into its established pattern. Cloud formations changed, with the high, thin streaks giving way to more substantial cumulus that built throughout the day before dissipating in the evening.

"The monsoon will fail us soon," Leclerc observed one morning as they took the dawn observation together. "Perhaps three days, perhaps five. Then we will have the variables until we reach the westerlies."

Nicholas had been expecting this transition. The great wind systems of the Indian Ocean were well-documented in the naval charts, with the monsoon giving way to a belt of variable winds before the strong westerlies that circled the Cape could be reached. This intermediate zone, known to mariners as the variables, could prove challenging, with periods of calm interspersed with unpredictable squalls and shifting breezes that required constant attention to sail trim.

"We should prepare the crew for more frequent sail changes," Nicholas replied. "And perhaps practice reefing the topsails. It's been so long since needed I fear they'll have grown slow."

Leclerc nodded approvingly. "A wise precaution. In the variables, sometimes you must reef all sails in minutes when a squall approaches, then shake them out again just as quickly when it passes."

Four days later, Leclerc's prediction proved accurate. The convoy awoke to an unfamiliar stillness: the sails hung limp, and the sea had lost its wind-driven texture, transformed into a glassy expanse broken only by the long, gentle heave of oceanic swell. The monsoon had failed at last, leaving them becalmed in the variables, some three hundred miles from the Cape.

By noon, the heat had become oppressive. The sun blazed down from a cloudless sky, turning the deck planking hot to the touch and forcing the men to seek what shade they could. Work slowed to a crawl aboard every vessel, limited to essential duties performed at a pace meant to conserve effort.

From his place on the quarterdeck, Nicholas could see the convoy arrayed across the still sea, the sails of the East Indiamen hanging as lifeless as washing on a windless day. *Salisbury* had signaled to maintain station, which required little effort without wind. The ships drifted with the current, maintaining their positions more through inertia than seamanship.

Late in the afternoon, a boat was observed putting out from *Ocean*. It rowed toward *Salisbury* with deliberate strokes, the oarsmen keeping a steady rhythm despite the heat. An hour later, signal flags climbed the halyards aboard *Salisbury* and were repeated throughout the convoy.

"Message from *Salisbury*, sir," reported Midshipman Foley, lowering his glass. "Captain Harrington of the *Ocean* requests the pleasure of all captains' company for dinner at six bells in the evening watch, weather permitting. A boat will be sent."

Nicholas nodded. Such invitations were a familiar part of convoy life during periods of calm—occasions for the exchange of information and the maintenance of those personal connections that helped bind a scattered fleet into a functioning whole. That it came from the senior East Indiaman, rather than the Commodore, indicated a civilian gathering rather than a formal naval council—one likely to include the Company's prominent passengers.

"Signal our acknowledgment, Mr. Foley."

By six bells, as the sun dipped toward the horizon, Nicholas stood at *Growler's* entry port in his full lieutenant's uniform, freshly brushed and immaculate despite the heat, which had mercifully begun to abate. A large boat from *Ocean* was making its rounds among the anchored ships, collecting captains one by one. From a distance, Nicholas could see it already carried a mix of passengers: a naval officer in blue and gold, along with several figures in civilian attire—men and women alike.

When the boat reached *Growler*, Nicholas descended the side ladder and took his place in the stern sheets, exchanging nods with his fellow officers. With *Lynx* still several miles ahead on station, Walsh was not present. Nicholas seated himself beside a tall, angular man in scarlet—Colonel Etherington, a Company officer returning to England after a long posting in Bengal. Opposite sat a red-faced, stocky lieutenant Nicholas did not immediately recognize.

"Lieutenant Cruwys, I presume?" the man said, offering a hand. "Rogers—now of the prize *Audacious*. Heard good things of your handling of the Frenchman, by all accounts."

Nicholas accepted the handshake with a polite nod. "We were fortunate to catch her unawares, sir. And my men acquitted themselves well."

The boat continued its circuit, pausing next for Commodore Hartley of *Salisbury*, then Captain Fenwick of *Thetis*, before making its way to *Ocean*. There it drew alongside a specially rigged accommodation ladder—more fitting for passengers than the usual side battens.

Ocean loomed above them, her immense hull rising sheer from the still water. The battle with the French seemed something of an unreality as she presented a picture of order and refinement, restored to her dignity in the idle calm.

As the boat came alongside, they were met at the accommodation ladder by Captain Hamilton, who greeted them with the composed affability of a senior East India Company officer.

"Welcome aboard, gentlemen," he called, his voice carrying the smooth authority of long habit. "You find us at liberty to entertain, thanks to this damnable calm. I'd sooner have a fair wind than a good dinner, but we must make the best of what Providence sends."

The quarterdeck had been transformed for the occasion. A broad awning cast shade across the space, beneath which a U-shaped table had been laid with fine linens, silver, and glass that caught the evening light. Servants in the Company's livery moved with quiet efficiency, setting decanters and arranging the final touches. Nicholas was struck, not for the first time, by the luxury that attended the Company's senior ranks. The porcelain bore the Company arms in gold and cobalt, and the crystal had a cut as fine as any in Bond Street. A light breeze had sprung up at last, bringing welcome relief from the day's heat.

Gathered about the periphery were passengers from across the convoy: Company officials returning home from long tours, merchants and factors with fortunes made in the East, and several ladies in fine muslin and silk, bringing a touch of civilian elegance to the otherwise masculine world of sail.

"Ah, Cruwys! A pleasure to see you again."

Nicholas turned to find Mr. Carlisle approaching, looking much as he had during their last conversation—impeccably dressed, quietly composed. At his side stood Caroline, equally poised, though perhaps a shade paler than she had been in the immediate aftermath of the battle.

"Mr. Carlisle. Miss Carlisle," Nicholas said with a bow. "I'm delighted to see you both."

"The pleasure is ours, Lieutenant," said Carlisle, his tone warm. "I understand you've been given command of the captured brig—a well-earned honour, I should say."

"Only temporarily, sir, as prize master. But yes, I have the privilege of commanding her for the voyage to Cape Town."

Caroline Carlisle's gaze met his with a directness that momentarily caught Nicholas off guard.

"We observed your vessel from *Ocean*'s quarterdeck this morning, Lieutenant. She has a most graceful bearing on the water. I should think you must be very proud to command her, even temporarily."

There was something in her manner—a quiet intensity, or perhaps a subtle warmth—that suggested more than casual interest. Nicholas found himself responding to it instinctively.

"I am, Miss Carlisle. She's a fine sailor. I count myself fortunate to have her, however brief the commission."

"Sometimes the briefest experiences are the most significant," she said, her voice pitched just low enough that he had to lean slightly closer to hear her. "And the most memorable."

Before Nicholas could frame a reply, they were interrupted by the arrival of a tall, aristocratic gentleman whose immaculate attire and languid bearing marked him as a man accustomed to attention. Perhaps five and thirty, with well-bred features and the poise of rank, he moved with the confidence of someone for whom precedence was never in question.

"My dear Caroline," he said, inserting himself into their conversation with polished ease. "You must introduce me to your naval friend."

Caroline's expression tightened by the smallest degree at the familiar use of her name, but her manners remained impeccable.

"May I present Lieutenant Nicholas Cruwys, currently commanding the prize brig *Growler*. Lieutenant Cruwys, may I make known to you the Earl of Pemberton, Lord Ashton, lately His Majesty's Special Envoy to the Governor-General's Council in Bengal, now returning to England after a most distinguished service."

Lord Ashton extended a hand. His grip was firm, his gaze frankly appraising.

"Charmed, I'm sure. One hears a good deal about your engagement with the French privateer. Most commendable, for an officer of your..." he paused, his eyes narrowing slightly, "experience."

Nicholas inclined his head. "Naval service often demands such decisions, my lord. Any officer in my position would have done the same."

"Modesty becomes a naval officer," Ashton observed, his smile not quite reaching his eyes. "Though I understand from Captain Hamilton that your actions went well beyond mere duty. Boarding an enemy vessel requires both courage and judgment. Still"—he sipped from his glass—"I find it remarkable how fortune may elevate a man so quickly, merely through the chance of capturing a prize. The Admiralty courts are generous in their valuations these days, so I hear from those who concern themselves with such matters."

The implication—that Nicholas's motives might be more mercenary than martial—was deftly delivered. He felt a flush of irritation, but his reply was measured.

"His Majesty's Navy exists to protect British interests, my lord. Prize money, while welcome, is incidental to that duty, and is shared amongst all of the ships present."

"Oh, quite, quite," said Ashton, flicking a hand as though brushing lint. "Duty, of course—always. Still, one ought not overlook the value of even a temporary command. Especially for an officer so... junior in his progress. We all must begin somewhere."

The pause before "junior" carried more sting than the word itself, a reminder of the vast social gulf between a lieutenant and a peer. Caroline's expression remained composed, though Nicholas noted a slight tension in her posture as Ashton's hand came to rest lightly on her arm, a gesture that suggested both protection and possession.

"I believe Lady Pemberton was hoping for your company before we sat down, my dear," Ashton continued, his tone softening. "She has arranged the seating with her usual attention to proper precedence."

The message was clear. Their conversation had reached its appointed end, and Caroline was expected elsewhere. She hesitated only a moment, her eyes meeting Nicholas's with a look that might have been regret, or simply civility.

"Of course," she said, her social mask now firmly in place. "Lieutenant Cruwys, it has been most enlightening to hear of your experiences. Perhaps we shall have further opportunity for conversation during our passage to England."

"I would welcome it, Miss Carlisle," Nicholas said, bowing with the formality the moment required.

As the others moved off, Mr. Carlisle leaned toward him slightly, voice pitched low.

"You must forgive Lord Ashton," he said. "His position in government—and his family name—have not accustomed him to contradiction. And I fear he's developed certain expectations regarding my daughter that have not been sufficiently discouraged."

Nicholas, who had been watching Miss Carlisle's retreating figure with mixed feelings, turned with a flicker of surprise. "Expectations, sir?"

"Nothing formal," Carlisle said. "But he is a widower of some years' standing, and his attentions to Caroline were marked during his time in India, though he travels home aboard another ship. His sister,

Lady Pemberton, acts as his hostess and has made it clear the match would meet with her approval."

He paused, a note of paternal concern audible beneath his usual reserve.

"Caroline, for her part, has shown no particular encouragement. But in our position..." He trailed off.

Nicholas understood. Despite their fortune and Carlisle's status as a senior director of the Company, they remained firmly within the mercantile class. No amount of rupees could purchase what Lord Ashton's title conferred. An alliance with the Earl of Pemberton—landed, titled, and well connected—would open doors otherwise barred forever.

It struck Nicholas with some irony that, in certain circles, his own modest Devon background, though lacking an estate, might carry more social weight than even the wealthiest merchant's fortune. The *Cruwys* name, ancient if not powerful, would still be recognised in drawing rooms that might never admit a Company man, however rich. It was a distinction that had felt meaningless during his years in the Pacific—but one that remained stubbornly real.

"I see," he said carefully. "Miss Carlisle seems quite capable of making her own decisions in such matters."

Carlisle gave him a sharp look. "Indeed she is. Perhaps too capable at times. But enough of personal matters. I believe Captain Hamilton is signalling for us to take our places for dinner."

The gathering moved toward the tables, where place cards had been arranged with the careful attention to rank and precedence that East India Company officers understood instinctively. Nicholas found himself seated near the foot of the table, as befitted his junior status, between a Company surgeon named Hillyard and a merchant's wife, Mrs. Tennyson, whose husband had remained aboard their own ship with a troublesome case of gout.

From his position, Nicholas could observe the company entire. Captain Hamilton, as host, occupied the head of the table, with Lady Pemberton—severe of aspect and unbending of spine—on his right as the senior lady present. Caroline Carlisle sat to his left, reflecting her status as an unmarried gentlewoman of good family. Lord

Ashton had been placed beside Lady Pemberton, while Commodore Hartley, as senior naval officer, took the seat beside Miss Carlisle. The captains of the other ships were arranged by seniority and interspersed with the more prominent passengers.

Nicholas noted that Lady Pemberton kept a watchful eye on Caroline's interactions, particularly whenever Lord Ashton's attention strayed too visibly in her direction.

The dinner was a remarkable display of the Company's resources. The first course offered turtle soup from a catch the day before, followed by fish curried in the Bengali style, spiced enough to tantalize, without overwhelming English palates. Then came fowl prepared in several ways: capon in wine sauce, roasted quail, and a turkey dressed with herbs Nicholas could not name but found excellent.

The main course brought a saddle of mutton, a haunch of venison preserved in *Ocean*'s ice house, and a glazed ham dressed with cloves and honey. These were accompanied by vegetables grown in deck pots—an indulgence permitted only to captains and Company grandees—and preserved fruits that brought a welcome freshness after weeks at sea.

Wine flowed liberally throughout: clarets of distinction, madeira richened by its equatorial voyage, and a potent arrack punch laced with lime, sugar, and spice for those inclined to bolder drink.

Conversation at Nicholas's end of the table remained general— voyage progress, weather, and carefully edited tales of life in India fit for mixed company. Mrs. Tennyson proved a lively presence, full of Calcutta anecdotes delivered with a wit sharp enough to entertain, but never quite stray into scandal.

"Lady Bingham was quite put out when Lord Ashton began to show marked attention to Miss Carlisle," she confided in a low voice, nodding toward a floridly dressed woman further up the table. "She had her hopes pinned on a match with her own daughter, poor thing. But he's never shown the slightest interest, despite her maneuverings."

Nicholas, who had been watching Ashton's manner with Caroline, noted the proprietary way the older man leaned in, occasionally touching her arm to emphasize a point. Caroline's manner remained polite, but a certain stillness in her posture suggested discomfort.

"Miss Carlisle seems... reserved in her response," he said carefully.

"Oh, any girl with sense would be," Mrs. Tennyson replied. "He's wealthy and well-placed, yes—but his first wife's situation was not altogether happy, or so one hears. And he's fifteen years her senior, at the very least."

Before further comment could be made, Captain Hamilton rose and lifted his glass.

"Gentlemen—and ladies," he said, bowing slightly to the female guests, "I give you His Majesty, King George."

All stood. "The King," they intoned, before drinking.

Commodore Hartley followed: "The Navy, the Army, and our honoured allies," which drew another round of raised glasses. Further toasts ensued: to the East India Company, to swift passage, to the memory of those lost in the French engagement—and, at last, from Lord Ashton himself, delivered with a faintly patronising smile:

"To our gallant young officers, whose courage in the face of the enemy does credit to their service."

Nicholas drank the toast with less enthusiasm than the rest, hearing clearly the condescension under the polish.

As the meal concluded and the company dispersed into smaller conversational groups, Nicholas found an opportunity to approach Caroline Carlisle, who had stepped away from the gathering to admire the sunset. The western sky was painted in deep bands of gold and crimson, the sea below catching the colours in muted reflection.

"A magnificent evening," he said, coming to stand beside her at the rail. "Though I confess I would trade it for a fair wind toward the Cape."

She smiled, the sunset brushing her profile with gold. "Even sailors must occasionally pause to admire beauty, Lieutenant. Or has the sea made you impatient with anything that stands still?"

"Not all," he replied, holding her gaze a moment longer than propriety might strictly allow. "Some things reward patient contemplation."

A faint colour rose to her cheeks, but she did not look away.

"You spoke, in Bombay, of the difficulty of returning to civilization," she said. Her tone was thoughtful rather than merely polite. "Have you found the transition easier with time?"

The question surprised him, not because it was inappropriate, but because it showed she had truly listened. There had been moments—particularly in his early return to uniform—when he had doubted his ability to readapt to the rigid hierarchies and layered decorum of European society, after years in the comparative simplicity of the islands.

"It becomes easier," he said. "Though there are times when I find our customs... constraining."

"Such as formal dinners aboard East Indiamen?" she asked, the corners of her mouth lifting slightly.

"Perhaps," he said, matching her tone. "Though I wouldn't discount the effort required to serve turtle soup and fresh vegetables at sixteen degrees south."

That earned a soft laugh. "No indeed. Captain Hamilton manages his ship admirably. Though I suspect that this evening, Lady Pemberton ensured proper forms were observed, despite our surroundings. She is rather... particular."

"So I've observed," Nicholas replied, noting that the lady in question was casting a glance in their direction, thin-lipped with disapproval. "I suspect our conversation may be nearing the limit of what she considers appropriate for an unmarried gentlewoman."

Caroline's expression wavered, somewhere between amusement and resignation.

"Perhaps I ought to return you to more suitable company, before your standing suffers irreparable harm."

"Perhaps you should," she said, though not with any great enthusiasm.

As they turned to rejoin the others, she added, more quietly, "I hope we may continue our conversation another time, Lieutenant. Our exchanges—both in Bombay and this evening—have been most... illuminating."

"It would be my pleasure, Miss Carlisle," Nicholas said, bowing slightly.

The evening concluded shortly afterward, with the captains returning to their ships as the last light faded. As Nicholas settled into the boat beside Commodore Hartley, the older officer gave him a speculative glance.

"Made a conquest among the Company passengers, have you, Cruwys?" Hartley asked in a low voice that would not carry to the others.

"Hardly, sir," Nicholas replied. "Merely a civil conversation with Miss Carlisle, whom I had met in Bombay and aboard *Ocean* after the action."

"Hmm." Hartley's grunt was noncommittal. "She's a fine-looking young woman, and her father is one of the Company's most successful merchants. But Lord Ashton seemed rather proprietary in his manner toward her. A man of his influence could make life difficult for a junior officer, if he chose."

Nicholas stiffened slightly. "I would never presume beyond the bounds of propriety, sir."

"I'm sure you wouldn't," Hartley replied, his tone suggesting the matter was closed. "In any case, we'll likely have wind by morning. The glass is falling slowly, and there's a certain feel to the air that suggests a change. Once we're underway again, social complications will be the least of our concerns."

True to Hartley's prediction, dawn brought a freshening breeze from the south, rippling across the sea and filling the waiting sails. Signal flags rose on *Salisbury*, and the convoy began to move again, resuming its orderly progress toward rounding the Cape. *Growler* took up her station with practiced efficiency, her crew responding to the changing conditions with the smooth coordination that spoke of growing confidence in themselves and their young commander.

Nicholas, standing on the quarterdeck with the morning sun warming his shoulders, felt a curious mixture of emotions—satisfaction at his ship's performance, anticipation of the challenges ahead as they approached the notoriously difficult waters around the Cape, and beneath these professional concerns, a lingering awareness of Caroline Carlisle's intelligent gaze and perceptive questions.

In the days that followed, the convoy made steady progress southwest, the largely favorable winds driving them onward. The weather held fair for the most part, though they encountered periodic squalls typical of these waters—brief but violent storms that swept across the ocean with little warning, requiring swift action to reduce sail before the full force of the wind struck. Nicholas noted with pride that his crew's response improved with each such incident, the men working together with increasing coordination and anticipation.

As they approached the Cape, the character of the sea changed noticeably. The long, rolling swells of the open ocean gave way to shorter, steeper waves, driven by the complex interaction of currents around the southern tip of Africa. The skies, too, became more variable, with cloud formations building and dispersing with remarkable speed, painting the horizon in dramatic patterns of light and shadow.

It was on a clear morning, as they sailed close-hauled on the larboard tack with a brisk southwesterly wind filling their sails, that the cry came from the masthead:

"Land ho! Three points off the starboard bow!"

Nicholas, who had been reviewing the ship's log in his cabin, came on deck at once, telescope in hand. From the quarterdeck, he could just make out a faint smudge on the horizon, barely distinguishable from the clouds that hovered above it.

"The Cape, sir," confirmed Williams, who had joined him at the rail. His weathered face was thoughtful in the twilight, his own glass trained on the distant shore. "Right where it ought to be. A fine sight, is it not? I've rounded it a dozen times, and that view never fails to impress."

Nicholas nodded, still studying the landfall through his glass.

"We should pass the headland tomorrow and make False Bay, with Table Mountain beyond," Williams went on. "They say when the cloud settles on the mountain like a tablecloth, it's a warning of foul weather. But as far as I can see, she's clear as crystal."

He paused, then added with quiet satisfaction, "God willing, we'll round the Cape while this weather holds, and by tomorrow we should be anchoring in Table Bay."

CHAPTER ELEVEN

The morning sun crested the jagged silhouette of Table Mountain, casting long shadows across Table Bay as *HMS Lynx* led the convoy into harbour on June 12, 1780, forty-two days after departing Bombay. Nicholas stood on the quarterdeck, watching as the distinctive geography of the Cape unfolded before them—the flat-topped mountain rising abruptly from the interior, flanked by Lion's Head and Devil's Peak like patient sentinels, with the whitewashed sprawl of Cape Town nestled at their feet.

It had been over three and a half years since he had last seen this view, from the deck of *Resolution* in November 1776, sailing outbound on Cook's expedition, *Discovery* in company, his head full of youthful expectation and an untested officer's sense of certainty. The harbour looked much as it had then: broad and sheltered, offering safe anchorage to ships that had survived the long, punishing run around the Cape. The Dutch East India Company's establishment still dominated the waterfront, its clean façades and red-tiled roofs orderly in the morning light, a reminder of over a century of colonial enterprise.

But for Nicholas, it marked something more. The Cape was the last edge of the old world—or the first edge of it, depending on one's direction. For years he had lived in longitudes where European power thinned into rumour: the outer islands, the blue-gold arcs of Polynesia, the lean uncertainty of far-off stations. This place—this headland—meant re-entry. The Atlantic lay beyond: narrower, charted, and more closely watched. With it came a return to

Admiralty eyes, to influence and consequence, to the remembered strictures of European society.

He found he was not entirely sure how he felt about it.

The usual harbour traffic continued uninterrupted: merchant vessels loading and discharging, fishing boats returning with their morning catch, and the occasional Dutch East Indiaman preparing for the long voyage back to the Netherlands. A Dutch warship, a trim 50-gun ship of the line—rode at anchor near the shore, maintaining the regular Dutch naval presence that had long been standard at the Cape.

"Table Bay hasn't changed much since my last visit, sir," Williams remarked as they approached their designated anchorage. "Same mountain, same Dutch efficiency. The holding ground's fair enough, but it can turn treacherous in winter when the north-westerlies come down. We've made it in good weather."

Signal flags rose aboard *Salisbury*. The East Indiamen were directed to anchor in the established commercial anchorage, while the naval vessels were assigned berths by the Dutch authorities farther from shore.

As *Growler* made her way toward her allotted position, Nicholas studied the town with a fresh eye. The Dutch colonial architecture stood out, whitewashed walls, high gables, and red-tiled roofs in orderly rows, the grid of streets radiating from the Castle of Good Hope, the pentagonal fortress that dominated the waterfront. He noted the signs of a quiet, disciplined colony: ships riding calmly at anchor, quay labourers moving in practiced rhythm, Company flags snapping over the warehouses. It felt, in its way, more settled than anything they had seen in months. A gateway between worlds. Europe ahead; the long arc of empire behind.

"Signal from *Salisbury*, sir," reported Midshipman Foley. "All captains to report aboard in one hour."

"Acknowledge the signal, Mr. Foley," Nicholas replied, his thoughts already turning to the diplomatic considerations their arrival might entail.

The Commodore's conference aboard *Salisbury* revealed the delicacy of the situation ashore. Gathered in the great cabin were the five captains of the escort, the six East Indiaman masters, and the senior British official at the Cape—a trade agent named Thomas Pringle, who maintained the Crown's commercial interests at this vital waypoint on the route to India.

Pringle was a spare, precise man, his careful manner honed by years of negotiation in a foreign port. As glasses were handed round, he outlined the political landscape with professional clarity.

"Gentlemen, your arrival comes at a time of growing strain between Great Britain and the Dutch Republic," he began, his thin fingers tracing idle patterns on the polished table. "Though we are not formally at war, relations have deteriorated markedly since the American rebellion began. The Dutch have maintained a policy of armed neutrality which, in effect, has benefited our enemies, particularly through the use of St. Eustatius by American privateers."

Commodore Hartley inclined his head. "We're aware of the broader situation, Mr. Pringle. Our immediate concern is to secure provisions and effect repairs sufficient to continue our passage to England."

"Provisions will be available through the established merchants," Pringle said. "Fresh water, food, and common stores pose no difficulty. Naval repairs, however, present complications."

He leaned forward, his expression carefully composed. "Governor van Plettenberg remains outwardly neutral, but he is under instruction from Batavia—that is, from the Dutch East India Company headquarters. While he welcomes your convoy, especially in light of visible battle damage, he has been directed to limit any assistance that might be construed as bolstering British military capacity."

Hartley frowned, the creases in his weathered face deepening. "That places us in a tight spot. *Thetis* and *Audacious* both need further work before we risk the open Atlantic."

"I understand, Commodore," Pringle said with genuine sympathy. "But I must stress the diplomatic sensitivity of your position. While there has been no breach of relations, tempers have frayed. Commodore Fielding's interception of a Dutch convoy in the Channel last January was seen in The Hague as a violation of neutral rights. More recently, the Dutch States General have been openly debating whether to join the League of Armed Neutrality proposed by Russia, which directly challenges our policy on neutral shipping."

He paused to polish his spectacles, then replaced them with care. "They have also refused to honour their treaty obligations to Britain, claiming this is an offensive, not defensive, war. That argument has not met with favour in London."

"The situation is plain enough," Hartley said. "We can expect limited official help. How long may we remain in harbour before our presence becomes diplomatically awkward?"

"Governor van Plettenberg has authorised a three-day stay," said Pringle. "It is shorter than the customary week granted to squadrons in peacetime, but not so brief as to give formal offence. I advise keeping strictly to that window."

"Three days," Hartley repeated, considering. "It will have to suffice. Captain Fenwick, Lieutenant Rogers, you'll manage with what your own crews can do. Mr. Pringle, are we permitted to shift men between ships?"

"Yes, Commodore. The restrictions apply only to Dutch assistance, not to internal arrangements among your own vessels."

"Very good. We'll begin reassigning our artificers at once. Lieutenant Cruwys, your people have shown themselves capable. Spare what skilled men you can—one or two of your sailmakers and a carpenter if he's strong."

"Aye, sir," Nicholas replied, already weighing which of his limited crew could be spared without impairing his own readiness.

The meeting concluded with Hartley's final instructions: maintain cordial but minimal contact with Dutch authorities, complete all provisioning and repairs within the allotted time, and avoid any behaviour that might be construed as reconnaissance or provocation.

As the conference dispersed and Nicholas prepared to return to *Growler*, a notion began to take shape. Their stay at the Cape would be brief, but perhaps not so brief as to preclude one carefully arranged meeting. Before departing *Salisbury*, he approached Commodore Hartley with a request that, while uncommon, fell within the latitude of professional courtesy.

"Sir, with your permission, I would like to extend an invitation to Mr. Carlisle and his daughter to visit *Growler* tomorrow afternoon. As representatives of the East India Company, their perspective on Dutch trade practices may be of some value, and..." He paused. "Mr. Carlisle expressed interest in *Growler's* handling, at the time of her capture."

Hartley studied him a moment, his expression unreadable. "A reasonable civility, Lieutenant. Permission granted. But let us keep our attention fixed on departure."

"Yes, sir. Thank you."

As the boat carried him back across the harbour, Nicholas found his gaze drawn toward *Ocean*, lying quiet in the harbour's light swell. He wondered if Caroline had seen their arrival, if she too felt that same taut intermingling of anticipation and constraint that had coloured their single shared dinner since Bombay. Her father's intentions, his own modest station, the grim arithmetic of prospects and politics—all of it formed a tangle too dense to cut, yet somehow irrelevant in the face of what had passed between them.

Upon returning aboard, Nicholas turned immediately to the matter of reorganising his crew. He selected the most able of his sailmakers and a pair of reliable shipwrights to assist aboard *Thetis*, along with a work detail of ten seamen. With those assignments settled, he drafted a note to Mr. Carlisle—formally worded, carefully composed.

> *Growler, at anchor*
> *Cape Town*
> *Monday, the 12th inst.*
>
> *Mr. Carlisle,*
>
> *Sir—*
>
> *I trust this note finds you in good health and spirits. With your indulgence, I venture to extend a small invitation which I hope may prove agreeable.*
>
> *If your time permits, I should be honoured to welcome you and your daughter aboard Growler tomorrow afternoon, to observe, at your leisure, the principal qualities of a French-built vessel*

now in British hands. The ship having been recently fitted and brought to order, her lines and rig may be of passing interest, particularly as they differ somewhat from those of our native construction.

Pray do not feel any obligation should other engagements prevent your attendance. I remain, as ever,

Your obedient and faithful servant,

Nicholas Cruwys
Lieutenant, Commanding H.M. Schooner Growler

The phrasing was deliberately neutral. He entrusted its delivery to Midshipman Foley, who departed promptly in the ship's boat.

Nicholas then turned to the business of the ship. He reviewed the provisioning lists for the morning's shore parties, conferred with his bosun over the state of the casks and slings, and began the draft of his readiness report for Commodore Hartley.

That evening, as the sun sank behind the bulk of Table Mountain and the light steeped the bay in shifting bands of gold and violet, a boat from *Ocean* arrived alongside. It bore a note from Mr. Carlisle, courteously worded:

Cape Town
Monday afternoon

Mr. Carlisle presents his compliments to Lieutenant Cruwys, and begs to express his appreciation for the kind invitation extended.

He and his daughter will do themselves the pleasure of coming aboard Growler at two bells in the afternoon watch, weather and tide permitting.

With all good wishes for the success of her present commission, he remains

Your obedient servant,
Edward Carlisle

Nicholas read it twice, his expression carefully held, though a faint smile tugged at the corner of his mouth. He summoned Monsieur Leclerc, who had long since assumed the role of unofficial steward, having managed the remains of the French captain's private stock with quiet efficiency.

"Monsieur Leclerc, we will have guests aboard tomorrow afternoon. Mr. Carlisle of the East India Company and his daughter. I would like to offer them a meal that reflects well on *Growler's* capabilities. What might we provide from our stores?"

Leclerc received the question with the gravity of a Frenchman who understood that at sea, food and hospitality were no small matters. "The ship's stores are limited, monsieur—but not without possibility. If your boat party ashore tomorrow morning might procure certain items: some fresh Cape vegetables, a few chickens, perhaps even a small haunch of venison, should the market oblige—I could prepare a meal that would not disgrace the occasion."

"You would cook it yourself?" Nicholas asked, surprised.

Leclerc permitted himself a slight smile. "Before I was a sailing master, monsieur, I trained as a cook. It is not unusual in the French service for officers to begin in more modest roles. I have retained the skill, though I've had little opportunity to practise it aboard *Growler*. Consider it my contribution to diplomacy."

There was a glint behind the courtesy. "Besides, I have observed that good food smooths difficult conversation, and perhaps your meeting with Mademoiselle Carlisle and her father may benefit from such… lubrication."

Nicholas raised an eyebrow at the man's perceptiveness, faintly discomfited by what the Frenchman might have seen, and what he had not yet acknowledged himself.

"Very well," he said. "I'll see the provisioning party instructed accordingly. Kindly provide a list."

The morning broke clear and sharply cold, the air bearing that distinctive crispness peculiar to the South African winter. Nicholas rose early and completed his rounds before the day's work commenced in earnest. He handed Leclerc's shopping list to Midshipman Foley and the purser leading the provisioning party, along with a small purse of silver dollars from his own funds to cover the special items.

As the boat pulled away for shore, Nicholas found himself unusually attentive to the state of his ship. *Growler* was already maintained to exacting standards, but today he ordered an additional polishing of the brass, a fresh holystoning of the decks, and particular attention given to the captain's cabin, where they would dine.

To the quiet puzzlement of the crew, he also ordered the sea cocks opened and a bucket of vinegar poured down into the bilge, a practice more common when newly out of port. The pumps were manned promptly, and by midday, the ship bore a more agreeable air. LeClerc said nothing, though he couldn't quite hide is quiet amusement.

At precisely two bells in the afternoon watch, a boat from *Ocean* came alongside. Nicholas stood at the entry port as Mr. Carlisle ascended the accommodation ladder with the dignified caution of a man more accustomed to merchantmen than warships. Behind him came Caroline, ascending with unhurried grace despite the constraints of her dress. She wore a gown of deep green that complemented her fair hair, which had been drawn back with simple elegance beneath a modest winter hat. As she reached the deck, her eyes met Nicholas's with a warmth that exceeded the formality of their greeting.

"Lieutenant Cruwys," Carlisle said, returning Nicholas's bow. "Most kind of you to extend the invitation."

Then, after a pause and a glance at their surroundings, he added, "Or rather—I believe I should say Captain, under the circumstances."

"You are generous, sir," Nicholas replied with a trace of amusement. "And very welcome aboard *Growler*."

Caroline stepped forward, offering her hand with composed ease. "Captain," she said, her smile quiet but unmistakable. "We're honoured."

"My daughter and I have been curious about your prize since the action," Carlisle continued. "A French-built vessel, is she not?"

"Indeed, sir," Nicholas said, gesturing toward the quarterdeck. "Launched at Cherbourg in '78—designed for speed and weatherliness. If you'll allow me, I'd be pleased to show you her qualities."

"We should be delighted, Captain," Caroline said. "I've developed a certain interest in naval architecture over the course of this voyage. The differences between warships and merchantmen are not only instructive, but rather striking."

Nicholas felt a flicker of pleasure at her words, though her poise made it difficult to say whether the interest was genuine or politely assumed. He led them aft to begin a carefully plotted tour, starting with the quarterdeck. He described the rig, the helm, the design of the French-built hull, how she pointed high to windward, how her balance under sail made her quick in stays.

Carlisle listened attentively, his questions practical and revealing: cargo capacity, complement, and the maintenance advantages of a copper-sheathed hull.

Caroline's attention, though quiet, was of another sort. She listened but also observed, not only the ship but Nicholas himself. There was a clarity in her gaze that unsettled him; she was not merely admiring a vessel, but measuring something less visible.

When they reached the bow, momentarily apart from her father—who had paused midships to examine the guns—she spoke in a lower voice.

"Your command suits you, Captain," she said, meeting his eyes. "There's a steadiness in you that wasn't quite there when we met in Bombay."

The remark surprised him. "Command changes a man," he said, struck by how precisely she had named something he had only recently begun to admit.

"As do all significant experiences," she replied. Her gaze drifted out over the anchored shipping. "I wonder what changes England will bring, for any of us."

Before he could answer, Carlisle rejoined them, his eye drawn to the clean lines of the cutwater. "A fine design," he said, running a practised gaze along the forward curve. "Built for speed. I daresay she cuts the water like a blade."

"Just so, sir," Nicholas replied, stepping back into the role of host. "In a fair wind she'll outpace most ships of her class, and she holds her wind better than many square-riggers."

They continued below: the gunroom, the tight but orderly galley where Leclerc was hard at work, and finally the captain's cabin, prepared for the meal. A small brazier had been brought aft, and its coals lent a modest warmth. A spirit-lamp had been lit for the coffee, giving off just enough warmth to take the edge from the southern wind.

The table had been laid with care: silver and porcelain salvaged from the French captain's stores, a clutch of fresh flowers in a weighted vase, and the broad stern windows framing Table Mountain in late afternoon light.

"Remarkable," Carlisle said, taking his seat. "One would hardly think this a ship of war. It has something of a gentleman's yacht."

"We make what use we can of circumstance, sir," Nicholas replied. "The arrangement is owed to Monsieur Leclerc, our sailing master—and former adversary—who has taken it upon himself to act as steward today."

As if summoned, Leclerc entered bearing the first course: a soup of Cape vegetables, lightly seasoned and finished with a dash of local white wine. He described its contents with quiet pride, presenting each element with the assurance of a man who remembered finer kitchens.

"Monsieur Leclerc was a prisoner when *Growler* struck her colours," Nicholas explained as the Frenchman withdrew. "He gave his parole, and has since become an invaluable part of our company. His knowledge of the ship has been... extensive."

"Pragmatic of you," Carlisle said, sampling the soup. "The French have always understood that some skills transcend politics. This, for instance"—he lifted his spoon again—"would do no dishonour to any table in St. James's."

The meal continued in easy stages: a local fish dressed with a light sauce, a roast of Cape venison with herbs native to the mountain foothills, and finally a dessert of preserved fruits—fig, apricot, and citrus—arranged with quiet elegance. Conversation flowed easily, touching on Bombay, their observations of the Cape, and the voyage yet to come.

Nicholas noted the gradual easing in Carlisle's manner as the meal progressed. The merchant and Company director had arrived with a degree of reserve—proper, slightly remote, touched perhaps by paternal caution. But by the dessert course, he had grown more animated, offering dry observations from his years in the East Indies, many of which elicited a flicker of amusement from his daughter. The resemblance in their humour was striking.

Caroline, too, seemed more at ease in the warmth of the cabin. Her natural intelligence and composure, often muted in formal company, now found clearer expression. She spoke of her impressions of Cape Town from a brief shore excursion that morning, remarking on the differences between Dutch and British colonial architecture, and the ways in which each empire adapted its habits, or failed to, to foreign climates.

As they sat over a final glass of wine, Carlisle shifted the conversation toward Nicholas's own unusual service.

"Your time with Captain Cook must offer a singular perspective on these colonial outposts, Captain," he said. "You've seen the Pacific, India, now the Cape, not merely as a passing observer, but as someone who, I gather, has lived among native peoples as well."

Nicholas inclined his head, somewhat surprised by the interest. "It does alter one's view, sir. Each European power imposes itself differently—and yet nearly all, I think, fail to see what is in front of them."

"In what sense?" Caroline asked, her eyes alight with curiosity.

Nicholas considered. The subject was not without its hazards. "Take the Dutch here: the colony is cleanly laid out, the defences well-sited, the gardens mathematically ordered to provision passing ships. But their success, such as it is, comes from enforcing a system upon the land, not from understanding the people already living upon it. They impose order without interpretation."

Carlisle's brow furrowed, not in disagreement, but in thought. "A fair point. Still, I suspect the commercial imperative drives much of that—the need for predictable output and steady supply."

"Undoubtedly, sir," Nicholas said. "Commerce shapes empire more profoundly than most politicians care to admit."

Caroline leaned forward slightly. "You speak as though you admired the native approaches, Captain. Many would regard such accommodation as weakness, or even failure."

Her tone was mild, but Nicholas sensed the weight behind it. It was not merely curiosity; it was the kind of question that tested character.

"I found wisdom in perspectives not my own," he replied. "Not all that is unfamiliar is inferior. Nor all that is familiar, superior. Captain Cook understood that balance. He prized local knowledge without compromising naval discipline. It served him well. Until—"

He stopped, the memory not one easily voiced.

"Until the Sandwich Islands," Carlisle said gently. "A bitter end to a remarkable career. Perhaps a reminder that understanding has its limits."

"Perhaps," Nicholas said. "But having known him, it's difficult to say what truly passed without being there oneself."

The conversation lingered in that vein—philosophical, reflective. Carlisle spoke of India, of his early postings, and the Company's uneasy alliances with local rulers. He had seen not only trade but also diplomacy and tension, and in his remarks there was a candour that spoke to long observation.

Throughout, Nicholas remained aware of Caroline's attention. She listened not merely with interest, but with intent, her questions deft, her silences equally so.

As the afternoon light began to turn amber with the approach of evening, Carlisle glanced at his watch and shifted in his chair.

"We've trespassed on your hospitality rather longer than intended, Captain. Most gracious of you to host us so fully."

"The pleasure has been mine, sir," Nicholas replied. "Good company is a rare thing at sea."

They rose together. Leclerc appeared to clear the remnants of the meal, accepting Carlisle's compliments with a modest bow.

"It was my honour, monsieur. A small reminder of civilisation amid our duties."

They emerged onto the deck. The sun hung low over the Atlantic, casting golden light across the harbour. Shore boats criss-crossed the anchorage as the rest of the convoy took on supplies, the bustle of imminent departure well underway.

"Captain Cruwys," Carlisle said as they reached the entry port, "I must thank you again. Our conversation has been... instructive." He paused. "We would be pleased if you would dine with us aboard *Ocean* tomorrow evening, as a return for your kindness. Captain Hamilton has also invited Lord Ashton, and several other officers from the convoy are expected."

The mention of Ashton caught Nicholas slightly off guard. He glanced toward Caroline, whose expression betrayed nothing.

"I would be honoured, sir—though I must confirm with Commodore Hartley that my duties permit."

"Of course. Naval obligations first, naturally. But if you're able, we shall expect you at six bells."

He extended his hand. Nicholas took it with the appropriate firmness.

Caroline stepped forward, her bearing a touch more formal than before. "Thank you for a most instructive afternoon, Captain. Your views on these matters have given me much to consider."

As Nicholas took her gloved hand, he noted a brief pressure—subtle, but deliberate.

"The education has been mutual, Miss Carlisle. I hope we may continue it."

He helped her down the ladder with measured formality, conscious of Carlisle's gaze, and of the line between propriety and feeling. As the boat pulled away toward *Ocean*, Caroline turned once to look back. The gesture was brief, but unmistakable.

Nicholas remained at the rail until the boat reached *Ocean*, its oars dipping rhythmically in the amber light. Only then did he turn, to find Williams standing quietly nearby, his expression composed in deliberate neutrality.

"The shore party reports all provisions aboard, sir," Williams said. "Fresh water, vegetables, and meat. Enough for twelve weeks at full issue."

"Very good, Mr. Williams. Have the watch schedule prepared for my review, and inform Midshipman Foley I wish to speak with him about tomorrow's duties. I'll need to determine whether I can accept an invitation aboard *Ocean* tomorrow evening."

"Aye, sir." Williams hesitated, then added with careful detachment, "The Carlisles seemed to enjoy their visit, if I may say so."

Nicholas allowed himself a faint smile. "They did indeed. Mr. Carlisle has a depth of insight not always apparent from his commercial exterior."

"And Miss Carlisle?" Williams asked—an innocent enough question on its face, though his tone held the faintest shade of knowing.

"A young woman of marked intelligence and discernment," Nicholas replied, his tone properly measured despite the warmth the name invoked. "Her father is fortunate in his travelling companion."

Williams gave a neutral nod, accepting the response without comment. "Will there be anything further, sir?"

"Not at present. Carry on."

Left alone once more at the rail, Nicholas looked out across the anchorage. *Ocean* lay bathed in the last of the sun, her rigging etched against the goldening sky. Around her, the harbour was busy with boats and movement—shouts carrying faintly across the water, the scent of pine and salt mingling on the wind.

He rested his hands lightly on the rail, thoughts turning inward. The visit had gone well, perhaps better than he dared admit. Yet the situation remained complex: his command temporary, his future uncertain, and his growing regard for Caroline at once unwise and irresistible. The invitation presented both challenge and opportunity. Lord Ashton's presence would undoubtedly sharpen the atmosphere, yet the chance to see her again—to find, perhaps, a moment of honest conversation behind the screen of form—was too valuable to refuse, if duty allowed.

He resolved to make it possible.

The following day, the 14th of June, the convoy stirred with increased urgency. Shore parties returned with the last of the stores, rigging crews completed their splices and knotwork, and the carpenter's hammers aboard *Thetis* and *Audacious* rang with determined haste. Nicholas oversaw the return of his borrowed hands from *Thetis*, their efforts having helped make possible at least a partial restoration of her injured masts. It was good work, but both frigates would still require proper refitting once they reached English yards.

By mid-afternoon, having confirmed with Commodore Hartley that he might be spared, Nicholas turned his attention to the evening ahead. He dressed with care—his best uniform coat, linen crisp, boots polished to a high shine. It was not merely a social call, and he treated it accordingly. The invitation offered a rare moment: a chance to speak with Caroline under the protection of civility, to continue a conversation not quite begun, and perhaps, to learn where he stood.

As Williams supervised the preparation of the boat that would carry Nicholas to *Ocean*, Leclerc appeared beside him, arms folded and expression composed.

"If I may speak freely, Captain," he said in his careful English, "Monsieur Carlisle appears to hold you in some esteem. Not every Company official extends so personal an invitation to a junior officer."

Nicholas adjusted his sword belt, glancing toward the anchored *Ocean*. "Perhaps he appreciated our earlier conversation. Mr. Carlisle strikes me as a man who values independent thought."

"Perhaps," Leclerc allowed. "Or perhaps he sees something that reaches beyond current rank."

Nicholas gave him a look, but the Frenchman offered only the faintest of smiles and withdrew. Before Nicholas could reply, Midshipman Foley approached to report that the boat was ready.

With a final check to his coat and sword belt, Nicholas descended to the waiting boat, aware that the evening ahead might demand care and discretion of a different sort.

The dinner aboard *Ocean* proved as finely orchestrated as he had expected. Captain Hamilton had arranged the gathering in his broad day cabin, the table laid for twelve: Nicholas, Lord Ashton, several senior East India Company officials, and the captains of two other Indiamen. Among them was Mrs. Willoughby, a Company widow returning from Calcutta—silver-haired, shrewd-eyed, and possessed of that particular poise found in women who had weathered much and wearied of little.

Caroline was seated between Lord Ashton and the captain of *Fortitude*—a deliberate choice that placed her directly across from Nicholas. He found himself between Mrs. Willoughby and a merchant named Peterson, whose conversation, though brisk and commercially minded, proved tolerable enough. The seating had been arranged with precision: ample opportunity to observe, little chance for direct exchange.

Lord Ashton carried much of the table's conversation. He had the bearing of a man long familiar with authority—well-featured, dark-haired, composed to the point of precision. His manner was assured without overreach, polished without pretence. There was a quiet control in him, as if certainty were not a manner but a discipline.

He spoke fluently on European politics, naval disposition, and the East India Company's prospects in the coming months. The Dutch, he predicted, would soon abandon neutrality; the League of Armed Neutrality would give them cover, and Britain would be forced to act. His tone was that of a man unbothered by doubt, or accustomed to making doubt irrelevant.

"The Cape," he observed, "is no longer merely a watering station. Its position is strategic. Whoever holds this place holds the hinge of the eastern trade."

The Company men nodded, their expressions ranging from approval to studied neutrality. Nicholas listened, offered a few remarks when prompted, but remained mostly silent. Across the table, Caroline was composed and inscrutable, engaged in the conversation, but offering no particular signal to any party. Once or twice, their eyes met; each time, she looked away first, though not abruptly.

"The situation grows increasingly untenable," Ashton pronounced as the soup course was served. "The Dutch refusal to honour their treaty obligations while simultaneously providing support to the American rebels cannot be tolerated indefinitely. I have it on good authority that Lord North's government is considering more aggressive measures."

Captain Hamilton nodded gravely. "Such developments would significantly impact our commercial operations in the East. The Dutch control crucial waypoints along our trade routes."

"Indeed they do," Ashton agreed, his tone suggesting superior knowledge. "Though perhaps not for much longer. There are discussions in certain circles about potential actions against Dutch possessions should diplomacy fail."

Throughout this exchange, Nicholas noted that Carlisle remained thoughtfully silent, his expression revealing nothing of his opinions on the matter. Caroline, too, observed the conversation with careful attention, though occasionally Nicholas caught her glance shifting to him—a brief moment of connection amid the general discussion.

When the conversation eventually turned to the convoy's journey thus far, Nicholas found himself drawn in more directly.

"Lieutenant Cruwys," Lord Ashton said, his tone carrying a hint of genuine interest beneath the surface courtesy, "you had the opportunity to command the captured French vessel for some weeks. Tell us, how does French naval construction compare to our own? One hears such varied reports about their capabilities."

The question seemed designed to draw Nicholas into the conversation while reaffirming the social dynamics at play—Ashton demonstrating his willingness to engage a junior officer while maintaining his position of authority.

"French naval architecture has certain distinctive qualities, my lord," Nicholas replied with professional composure. "*Growler* exemplifies their approach, built for speed and manoeuvrability, though perhaps less durable in heavy weather than comparable British vessels."

"Interesting," Ashton mused, swirling the wine in his glass. "One might draw parallels to the French national character itself, brilliant in favourable circumstances, less reliable when truly tested." He smiled slightly, clearly pleased with his own wit, though the expression held a certain self-awareness that softened what might otherwise have seemed condescending.

Several of the Company men chuckled appreciatively, but Nicholas noted that Carlisle remained expressionless, his attention seemingly focused on his meal. Caroline's slight frown suggested she found Ashton's remark less amusing than the others had.

"Naval design reflects many considerations beyond national character, my lord," Nicholas said carefully. "Strategic priorities, available materials, intended usage—all shape a vessel's qualities. The French emphasize speed because their naval strategy often relies on commerce raiding rather than fleet engagements."

"A diplomatic response, Lieutenant," Ashton observed with a thin smile. "Though I suspect your recent experiences commanding a French vessel may have softened your perspective. Extended exposure to foreign ways can sometimes blur one's natural loyalties."

The implication was subtle but clear, a reference not merely to *Growler* but to Nicholas's years in the Pacific, and perhaps a suggestion that his time among non-European cultures had left him ideologically suspect. It was not a direct insult, but it grazed the edge.

Before Nicholas could respond, Carlisle intervened.

"On the contrary, Lord Ashton," he said, his tone mild but with an underlying firmness that commanded attention. "I find that men who have experienced other cultures often develop a keener appreciation for British virtues, having seen the alternatives directly rather than through hearsay or prejudice."

Caroline's eyes brightened at her father's intervention, though she maintained her composure. "Indeed, Father. I found the Lieutenant's observations about Dutch approaches at the Cape, compared with our methods in India, most illuminating." She turned to Nicholas with a warmth that seemed genuine—though he was increasingly aware that, in this world of Company politics and aristocratic ties, very little was as simple as it appeared.

Ashton inclined his head, conceding the point without yielding the ground. "Perhaps so. Though I maintain that certain British qualities—honour, steadiness, loyalty—are innate rather than comparative. One either possesses them or one does not." His gaze rested briefly on Nicholas, then returned to Caroline. "Just as some possess a natural refinement that no experience or education can bestow."

There was a beat of silence—small, deliberate.

Mrs. Willoughby, who had until now contented herself with a second helping of rice pudding, set down her spoon with careful poise.

"Well," she said lightly, "I've known any number of men with refinement by birth—though far fewer who managed to keep it through travel, temptation, or a posting in Madras."

The silence that followed was brief, but exact. One of the Company men stifled a chuckle. Ashton offered a smile that did not reach his eyes.

"Touché, madam," he said smoothly. But his tone had cooled by a half-degree.

Nicholas, repressing a smile, met Mrs. Willoughby's gaze across the table. Her expression remained demure, but the glint behind it was unmistakably allied.

As the dinner concluded and the company moved to the stern gallery for brandy and conversation, Nicholas found himself momentarily alone with Caroline. She had stepped toward the broad windows to observe the scattered lights of Cape Town now twinkling in the darkness, and Nicholas approached with careful propriety, maintaining a respectful distance as he joined her in admiring the view.

"A beautiful sight," he remarked quietly. "Though not so dramatic as the harbour at Bombay."

"Each has its own character," she replied. "The Cape has a kind of austere beauty—the mountain rising sheer from the water, the oceans converging below like a footnote."

She turned slightly, her voice softening. "I thought you bore Lord Ashton with admirable restraint. He can be... exacting, when he chooses."

Nicholas kept his tone even. "His strategy was familiar. Your father's timing was well judged."

"My father sees more than many credit," she said. "He prefers judgment to display. Not a trait always welcomed in our circles."

There was a quiet depth to her manner in that moment, a withdrawal of surface grace that revealed something still and thoughtful beneath. For a breath, Nicholas felt himself seen not as a guest or officer, but as a man measured on different terms.

Before he could reply, Carlisle approached, his manner relaxed but deliberate.

"Lieutenant, admiring the Cape by night?" he asked lightly. "A fine vantage. The view repays attention."

"Indeed, sir," Nicholas replied. "I had remarked to Miss Carlisle on the singular nature of the landscape."

Carlisle nodded. "Remarkable—and, I'm told, soon to be behind us. Captain Hamilton informs me the convoy is to weigh anchor at first light tomorrow, weather permitting."

"So I understand. Our work aboard *Growler* is nearly complete, and the wind is holding westward."

Carlisle studied him for a moment. "Lieutenant, might I impose on you for a brief word before you take your leave? There are some questions—trade routes, points of passage—on which I would value your perspective. Your experience is wider than most."

The request, coming here and now, surprised Nicholas. "Of course, sir. As you wish."

"Excellent. Captain Hamilton has kindly made his smaller day cabin available for private discussions." He turned to his daughter. "Caroline, my dear, Mrs. Willoughby was hoping to consult you. Something about her impressions of Calcutta."

Caroline inclined her head with composed grace. "Of course, Father." Then, turning to Nicholas: "Lieutenant Cruwys. As always."

Nicholas bowed slightly. "Miss Carlisle."

She withdrew without haste, her bearing smooth, her thoughts unreadable. He followed Carlisle toward the cabin, aware that the next conversation might be the more delicate of the evening.

Carlisle led Nicholas into the smaller day cabin, empty and illuminated only by the soft glow of a single lantern. He closed the door and gestured to a chair before taking a seat himself behind the captain's desk.

"I'll come directly to the point, Lieutenant," he said without preamble. "I've observed your interactions with my daughter, since Bombay, during our mid-voyage dinner, aboard your ship, and again this evening."

Nicholas maintained his composure despite the sudden acceleration of his heartbeat. "Sir?"

"You needn't affect ignorance. I may be a merchant by profession, but I've negotiated too many complex agreements not to recognise when something is forming, especially when it goes unspoken." His tone was not hostile—merely direct. "My daughter finds you... interesting. Intellectually, certainly. Perhaps more."

The candour of the remark took Nicholas slightly aback. Convention urged evasion, but Carlisle's manner made it clear he had no interest in polite deflections. Nicholas, after a moment's thought, answered plainly.

"Mr. Carlisle, I hold your daughter in the highest esteem. Her intelligence, her dignity, her perspective on the world—these are qualities I deeply admire. Under different circumstances, I might speak more openly. But I am fully aware of the realities that stand between us."

"And what realities are those, in your view?" Carlisle asked, his voice even.

"I'm a junior officer with no fortune and no connections. My command of *Growler* is temporary. On our return to England, I expect to be reassigned, most likely in a subordinate role. Your daughter is the heir to a major mercantile house—and, as I understand it, being considered by a man of title. The disparity between us is not a matter I take lightly."

Carlisle nodded slowly, his eyes fixed on Nicholas. "A fair accounting. Though I wonder if it is complete."

He studied Nicholas for a moment, not unkindly, but intently. "Lord Ashton is a man of consequence. His name opens doors that even Company gold cannot. I would be dishonest if I said that was of no interest."

Nicholas inclined his head. "I understand, sir."

"I believe you do," Carlisle said. "But understand this as well: Caroline is not merely an heiress, nor a suitable match to be negotiated. She is a person of rare perception and independence—traits that do not always find easy company with status."

Nicholas said nothing, listening.

Carlisle stood and walked to the stern windows, the lights of Cape Town dim in the glass. "Her mother had those same qualities. She came from modest means, a clerk's daughter in Madras. I had ambition, not fortune. Her father thought I was beneath her."

He paused. "She said fortune was no measure of a man. And she was right."

He returned to his seat. "It made for a marriage I never once regretted."

Nicholas remained quiet, aware this was no ordinary conversation.

"Caroline presents herself as society expects," Carlisle said. "But that is only a facet—not the whole. You may have noticed."

"I have, sir."

Carlisle gave a faint smile. "Good. Then I needn't say more on that point."

He shifted back to a more practical tone. "Your own path has been far from ordinary. Midshipman under Cook, cast away in the Pacific, living among islanders, in command of a French prize—all before your majority. You are twenty, I believe? The same age as Caroline."

"Yes, sir."

"You've seen more than most men twice your age, and, more to the point, you've taken the measure of it. That is not common. I value it."

Nicholas inclined his head. "You are kind, sir."

"Not kind," Carlisle corrected him. "Observant. My business is judgment, Lieutenant, of men as well as markets. You've shown steadiness, discretion. That counts."

He tapped the desk lightly with his fingers. "What are your intentions, on your return to England?"

"To report to the Admiralty and resume duty, as directed."

"And beyond that? You hope for further command?"

"Naturally, sir. Though such hopes rest on many things—patronage, vacancies, the fortunes of war."

Carlisle nodded, his expression unreadable. "The Navy is an honourable calling. *Cruwys of Morchard*, if I am not mistaken? Old Devon blood."

"Yes, sir. My uncle holds Morchard still—the family seat these six centuries past. My father is his youngest brother, and I the second son."

"Then I imagine your upbringing did not tend toward trade."

"No, sir. It did not."

Carlisle looked out through the stern windows, where the last of the light hung faintly over the harbour. "Still. War unsettles every course. Even merit can founder in the wake of another man's influence."

He turned back. "Over the years, I've known officers—honourable men—who, having served with credit, chose another track. Some found in trade, or in the Company, not only advancement but a steadier footing. Regular pay. A fixed port. The means to build a life not always subject to the lottery of a list."

Nicholas remained silent, attentive.

"I'm not proposing anything," Carlisle continued, his tone gentling. "Nor questioning your present course. Only observing that such paths exist. And that, for certain men, they have proved a foundation—establishment, investment, a household of one's own. The Navy may offer honour, but seldom ease."

He paused.

"The Company values officers who think beyond the manual, who understand both command and context. You've seen more of the world than most, Mr. Cruwys. And you have made sense of it. That is not nothing."

Nicholas met his gaze. "That is generous, sir. I'll consider it, when the time is right."

"Good," said Carlisle. He rose then, and with him, the moment shifted. His manner softened by half a degree. "That is all. No proposal, no design, merely this: that steadiness and sense deserve their due, if a man can see his opportunities clearly."

He extended his hand. Nicholas took it, firm and steady, without undue ceremony.

"Thank you, sir. For your candour."

"In business," Carlisle said, "candour prevents expense. In life—well, it saves worse things."

As they moved to rejoin the others, Carlisle added one final note.

"Caroline sees the world clearly. She always has. She plays the part that's expected, but she does not mistake it for truth. I advise her, but I do not choose for her. If you believe her interest in you is conventional, you misread her."

Nicholas said nothing, but the words struck with clarity. He followed Carlisle back into the lighted gallery, the weight of the conversation settling not as pressure, but as possibility.

As they returned to the main cabin where the other guests were gathered, Nicholas found his thoughts unsettled by the implications of their conversation. Carlisle had made no explicit proposal—no promise, no guarantee—yet the signal was unmistakable. He did not regard Nicholas's interest in Caroline as either presumptuous or unwelcome. More than that, he had gently gestured toward a possible path, one that might allow Nicholas's professional future to align, however improbably, with his personal inclinations.

The remaining hour passed in a blur of polite conversation and formal farewells. Lord Ashton continued to dominate the proceedings with practiced ease, his manner toward Nicholas a precise calibration of aristocratic condescension: not openly hostile, yet never truly engaged. Caroline maintained her composed dignity, her speech and gestures impeccably correct. But Nicholas, watching closely, caught her gaze returning to him in unguarded moments, a quiet attention that spoke more than courtesy allowed.

When the time came for his departure, Nicholas made his farewells to Captain Hamilton and the assembled company. Carlisle shook his hand with a firmness that conveyed more than politeness, something closer to recognition, or measured approval.

Caroline offered her gloved hand with impeccable propriety.

"Safe travels, Lieutenant," she said. The words were entirely correct. Her eyes were not.

"If we meet again in Luanda," Nicholas replied, his tone even, "I shall count the weeks well spent."

She inclined her head—no more than courtesy required—but the faintest suggestion of a smile touched the corner of her mouth, and was gone.

As his boat pulled away from *Ocean* toward the waiting *Growler*, Nicholas turned to look back at the Indiaman's illuminated stern windows, considering the unexpected shape the evening had taken. Carlisle had offered no endorsement, no alliance—but something had shifted. The merchant's reserve had yielded, ever so slightly, to something more personal. It was not approval, exactly. But it was not dismissal. And in a world of measured men and tacit understandings, that alone was meaningful.

Lord Ashton remained a formidable rival, with advantages of birth and position Nicholas could not touch. Yet Carlisle's quiet frankness—his evocation of Caroline's mother, of judgement and choice—suggested that such advantages were not, in themselves, sufficient.

The Cape wind had turned sharp. Nicholas drew his coat close as *Growler* drew near, the lights on her quarterdeck steady in the dark. There had been no mention of replacing him. In their brief final meeting, Commodore Hartley had offered quiet praise for the state of the ship and crew, noting the improvement in *Growler*'s gunnery and drill. So Nicholas remained in command, not by oversight, but by tacit approval.

As he climbed aboard *Growler* and returned Midshipman Foley's salute, Nicholas felt the familiar pull of discipline settle into place. His present duty was clear: to bring his ship safely home. But beyond that, beyond the wind and swell, a different sort of possibility had begun to take shape, unconfirmed, unofficial, but real.

The convoy departed Cape Town on the morning of the 16th of June, 1780, precisely as scheduled. The weather proved favourable, with a steady southeasterly breeze driving them around the Cape of Good Hope and into the Atlantic proper. *Growler* took up her assigned station, her crew working with the quiet efficiency that Nicholas and Williams had cultivated, and which could only be sustained aboard a happy ship, where discipline was neither too lax nor overly strict. In this, Nicholas had drawn much from both Cook and Walsh: the goal was not simply order, but effectiveness. An efficient ship, after all, was a fighting ship.

As the distinctive silhouette of Table Mountain receded astern, Nicholas stood on the quarterdeck, his glass occasionally trained on *Ocean*, sailing near the centre of the convoy formation, again in the windward of the two columns. Somewhere aboard, Caroline Carlisle might be watching *Growler* in turn, maintaining, despite distance and decorum, the quiet connection that had taken shape between them.

Williams appeared at his side, his practical voice drawing Nicholas back to the immediate.

"Course is set northwest by north, sir. Wind steady out of the southeast. The glass is rising."

"Thank you, Mr. Williams," Nicholas replied, lowering his glass.

The convoy made steady progress northward and as May turned into June the African coast lay somewhere to the east, out of sight; they stood far enough offshore to catch the southeasterly trades—those broad, dependable winds that had carried countless ships along the western coast of Africa toward home.

Nicholas stood again on *Growler*'s quarterdeck, watching as the first gold light touched the sails of the convoy strung across the morning sea. The East Indiamen held formation with ponderous grace, their massive hulls ploughing the swell with measured purpose. *Salisbury* kept her position to windward, her fifty guns a sober declaration of strength, even at this far remove from home waters. *Lynx* ranged ahead, her sleek hull vanishing and reappearing with each long roll of sea.

The two weeks since departing the Cape had proved both challenging and rewarding. At times, contrary winds had driven against the northbound current, raising sharp, breaking waves. Squalls had struck hard on several nights, forcing the convoy to reform after scattered ships were driven off station. With only partial repairs achieved at the Cape, *Thetis* and *Audacious* had taken the worst of it—their jury-masted rigs groaning under the strain, with *Audacious* now trailing behind, her officers in constant anxiety over the safety of her spars.

Growler, by contrast, had borne the conditions well. Her tight hull and lively helm rode the sea with a suppleness that even Leclerc, never effusive, had acknowledged.

"She likes these waters, monsieur," the Frenchman had observed one evening, as they shared the last of the captured Bordeaux in Nicholas's cabin. "A good vessel knows her way home, even under a different flag."

Now, with the Cape well behind them and the trades still firm, the log showed nearly eight hundred miles covered in the past week alone—a notable feat for a convoy maintaining formation, particularly given the impairments of two of its escorts.

Williams approached, touching his hat in his customary quiet way.

"Southeasterly still, sir. Fresh and regular. The glass is high and holding steady."

Nicholas nodded. They were making for Portuguese Angola. The Portuguese colony served as a vital allied waypoint for vessels plying the long route between the Cape and Europe, its deep harbour at Luanda offering shelter, fresh water, and provisions to friendly ships navigating the African coast. More importantly, it was the first of the designated rendezvous points where the requested additional escort might join them, and where more thorough repairs could be made to the two crippled frigates.

"Signal from *Salisbury*, sir," reported Midshipman Foley, who had been observing the flagship through his glass. "General course alteration, two points to starboard."

"Acknowledge the signal, Mr. Foley. Helm, bring her two points to starboard."

As *Growler* answered her helm, Nicholas considered the reasoning behind the adjustment. The new heading would take them closer to the African coast, likely to hasten their approach to Luanda. At this stage, the Commodore must be keenly aware of the risks of encountering French or Spanish ships as they moved north, especially with the escort reduced to only *Salisbury* and two small warships in full fighting condition.

By noon, the convoy had steadied on its new course, the ships maintaining formation with practised precision. The day passed without incident, the steady trades carrying them northward as they had countless ships before. Two days later, at first light, the low shape of the African coast appeared on the horizon, a long, dark swell of land that gradually resolved into detail. Signal flags broke out from *Salisbury*, ordering the convoy to prepare for entry and anchorage.

By mid-morning, they were inside the great bay of Luanda, the sea much calmed under the shelter of the sandbar that protected the harbour. As they drew closer, Nicholas made out the features of the port: a substantial colonial settlement rising in tiers along a crescent-shaped shoreline. The São Miguel fortress commanded the heights, its whitewashed walls and red-tiled roofs vivid under a clear blue sky. Below, the town spread outward in a neat grid—European in origin, adapted to African heat, with wide verandas and high-ceilinged buildings designed to catch the breeze.

Already at anchor were several vessels: two Portuguese warships—a frigate and a sloop—flying their distinctive ensigns in the morning air; three Portuguese merchantmen, likely involved in the slave and ivory trades that underpinned the colony's economy; and most notably, a Royal Navy post ship—*HMS Mercury*, a sixth-rate of twenty-four guns, flying the signal for dispatches on board. The convoy entered harbour with the Commodore's ship firing the salute, answered by the guns of São Miguel. As the echo of the last gun rolled across the water, the ships moved to their stations.

The East Indiamen were brought in close to shore, where their deep draughts would still find holding but gain the most protection. *Salisbury*, *Growler* and *Lynx* anchored farther out, in a line ready to use springs on their cables to bring their broadsides to bear, should the harbour entrance need defending. *Thetis* and *Audacious* were positioned for easy access by boat and ready to be quickly warped alongside the quay for repairs.

As anchors splashed and cables rumbled through the hawseholes, Nicholas studied the activity ashore. News of their arrival had travelled fast. Boats now came off from the stone jetty—colonial officials in dress uniforms, merchants eager to trade, locals simply curious about the new arrivals.

"Signal from *Salisbury*, sir," reported Foley. "All captains to report aboard at two bells in the afternoon watch."

Nicholas acknowledged the signal and turned to Williams. "Have the boat prepared to take me across at the appointed time. I'll be in my cabin finishing the log."

The meeting aboard *Salisbury* proved brief but significant. Commodore Hartley informed the assembled officers that, following consultation with Captain Fenwick of *Thetis* and Lieutenant Rogers of *Audacious*, he had resolved to remain at Luanda for one week to complete essential repairs to both vessels.

"The jury masts have served their purpose in bringing us thus far," Hartley said, "but neither ship is fit to face a serious blow in her current condition. The Portuguese authorities have granted us access to their naval yard, including the use of their quay and shears. Suitable timber is available, and we have enough skilled men among our own crews to shape and step proper masts, if we set to the task in earnest."

He paused, his expression sober. "Furthermore, as you are aware, this is the first rendezvous point specified in the dispatches sent overland from India. The 12th of July is the final date by which any reinforcements might be expected to arrive here. Given the value of this convoy, we shall remain until the fourteenth, before proceeding, weather permitting."

He then turned to address the captains of the East Indiamen. "Gentlemen, your passengers may go ashore during our stay, but I caution that while accommodation in the European quarter is adequate, the tropical climate and local conditions may prove taxing to those unaccustomed to Africa. The Governor has kindly offered the use of several official residences for any ladies among your company, and there are suitable lodgings for gentlemen within the Portuguese quarter."

Captain Hamilton of *Ocean* spoke up. "I believe Mr. Carlisle has already made arrangements through his agent for accommodation for himself and his daughter. Lord Ashton, too, has contacts among the Portuguese merchants, I understand."

Hartley nodded. "Very good. That simplifies matters."

He then turned to the next item of business. "Now, as to the schedule of repairs..."

The discussion that followed was detailed and practical—dividing labour, allocating timber and carpenters, and setting a strict watch rotation to ensure the convoy's defence even while at anchor in friendly waters. Nicholas listened attentively, reporting on *Growler*'s condition when asked, but otherwise observing the decorum expected of a junior officer among more senior men.

As the discussion drew to a close, Hartley turned toward Nicholas. "Lieutenant Cruwys—*Mercury* is taking on water and will sail again on the afternoon tide tomorrow with her dispatches to India. While Captain Collyer sailed with no word of reinforcements for the convoy, and cannot be delayed, he has agreed to sit a lieutenant's board before he departs. You will report aboard *Salisbury* at two bells in the forenoon watch tomorrow for examination."

Nicholas met his eye and gave a steady nod. "Aye, sir."

Hartley offered no further elaboration, but the nod he gave in return carried the weight of quiet approval.

As the meeting concluded, Hartley addressed one final matter.

"The Governor has invited all captains and senior officers to dine at the *Palácio do Governador* tomorrow evening. I need hardly add that it is both a diplomatic necessity and a social obligation. Portugal remains our ally in this conflict, and we rely upon her goodwill for shelter along this coast. I expect all of you to attend."

He paused, giving the room a measured look.

"And gentlemen—let us remember that we are in friendly but foreign waters. I expect strict decorum from all liberty parties. Let no man confuse hospitality with licence."

That evening, Nicholas remained in his cabin long after the lanterns had been trimmed, reviewing in quiet detail the matters likely to be raised the next day. He opened his worn copy of *Hamilton Moore's Treatise on Navigation* and laid it alongside the ship's recent log, cross-referencing entries—wind bearings, soundings, lunar calculations—until the familiar rhythms calmed his thoughts.

He had nothing to fear, and yet the weight of formality pressed on him. The board was not merely a test of knowledge but a reckoning, a line drawn between promise and commission. His chart table was cleared of all but the French sextant and his journals. He polished the instrument slowly, almost absently, as he reviewed knots, rigging, sail plans, gunnery protocols, and the endless refinements of command. Not merely how to reef a topsail, but when to order it, and why.

Leclerc appeared at the door with two tin cups and the ship's last decent bottle of Cape wine.

"I take it we are not celebrating just yet, monsieur?" Leclerc asked, smiling faintly.

Nicholas accepted the cup. "Not quite. I thought I'd remind myself I still know the difference between a well-faked line and a death warrant."

Leclerc chuckled. "You've kept men afloat on worse."

Nicholas gave a rueful smile. "Let's hope the examiners aren't too particular about frayed edges."

The morning air was already thick with heat as Nicholas stepped into *Growler's* gig. The sea was calm, the harbour still. He wore his best uniform, coat brushed, linen fresh, logbooks and sextant secured in a leather case at his feet.

Aboard *Salisbury*, he was received with formality and escorted aft to the great cabin, where the examining board awaited. The long table had been cleared except for a chart, dividers, and a volume of the *Naval Instructions*. Through the stern gallery windows, pale light fell in measured slants across the floor.

Seated at the table were Commodore Hartley; Captain Fenwick of *Thetis*; and Captain James Collyer of *Mercury*. Collyer was younger than Nicholas had anticipated, perhaps only two or three years his senior—tall, fair-haired, and faultlessly turned out. His manner was quiet and observant, with the slightly amused reserve of a man accustomed to being listened to. His pale grey eyes showed curiosity more than judgment, and something in his stillness suggested he rarely needed to ask the same question twice.

Hartley opened the session.

"Lieutenant Cruwys, you are called before this board for examination, to confirm the acting commission granted by Admiral Hughes. You are aware of the procedure?"

"I am, sir."

"Very good. Captain Fenwick?"

Fenwick gestured toward the chart. "Mr. Cruwys, if you please—plot your course from Bombay to the Cape, noting your estimated positions and prevailing winds."

Nicholas opened his logbook and did so with quiet assurance. He marked their passage past the Laccadives, the shifting winds near Mauritius, the Mozambique Channel, and the squalls off Sofala. His tone remained even. He cited soundings, corrections, and the bearing of the wind on each leg of the voyage.

Questions followed: on rigging, on the manning and layout of *Growler*'s battery, convoy signalling under poor visibility.

Commodore Hartley then asked about powder rationing on extended passage (Nicholas couldn't be sure if he detected a certain ironic tone), then about prize procedure, and the conduct of a crew in heavy weather. Nicholas answered clearly, drawing on recent experience rather than textbook cases.

At last, Collyer stirred.

"I understand," he said, "that you were separated from Captain Cook's expedition in late 1777?"

"Yes, sir. I was assigned to chart the reefs and approaches off Bora Bora. A storm drove our native craft eastward and were carried into the Tuamotus."

"And from there?"

"We made landfall on Anaa, then worked our way to Tahiti. I completed the voyage to Bora Bora and spent over a year there—surveying and completing my survey per Captain Cook's orders.

"You were not detained"

"No, sir."

Collyer's eyes narrowed slightly—not in suspicion, but with interest. "Then you remained by choice."

"There was no better alternative. *Resolution* had long since departed, and no British vessel was expected."

Collyer gave a small nod. "And you travelled next to Samoa?"

"Yes, sir, again by a native craft. Then joined Captain Silva's ship."

"Ah. The Portuguese gentleman—formerly a privateer, now attached to the Goa run. You served under him?"

"No sir, I was a paying passenger. But I did assist when needed—in heavy weather, when under attack. I repaid his advanced funds, and, in return, he brought me to Macau."

Collyer steepled his fingers. "And what was your view of him?"

Nicholas paused. "Able. Opportunistic. Not overly troubled by flags or tariffs. But he kept his word. And I learned a good deal—of both sailing and negotiation."

Collyer's tone remained neutral. "And of the islanders? Their habits. Their... morals."

Nicholas met his eye without hesitation. "They govern differently. But there is order. I would not call them lawless."

Hartley gave a deliberate cough—not disapproving, but decisive. Collyer leaned back slightly and said no more.

The questioning resumed. Fenwick asked about gunnery: number of rounds, hit percentage, reload intervals. Nicholas replied: thirty-four rounds in nine minutes, four hits to the enemy's mizzenmast, steering compromised. *Growler* had carried only six-pounders; carronades were not mounted.

Hartley inquired about discipline aboard ship, the management of prize crews, and how Nicholas had maintained cohesion with a mixed complement. Nicholas answered plainly.

Collyer posed one final question.

"You're entering a shoaled anchorage from the northeast with a falling tide. Wind fresh from the southeast that backs northeast. You're less than three cables from a sandbar and dropping fast. What do you do?"

Nicholas replied without pause. "Veer the best bower. Back the foretopsail to check her headway. Stand by to kedge astern. Send a boat to windward with a line if time permits. Otherwise, strike yards, shift weight, and prepare to lighten."

Collyer said nothing, but gave a slight nod.

Hartley closed the *Naval Instructions*. "That will do, Mr. Cruwys. You will remain aboard. The board will confer and render its decision."

Nicholas saluted and was shown down to the gunroom, where a steward brought him coffee and left him to his thoughts.

He sat alone at the long table, the light from stern windows playing across the deckhead. A few of *Sutherland's* officers came in and out but they left him to his devices. Around him, the usual sounds of the ship, boots overhead, a voice raised briefly amidships, then quiet again.

From the great cabin above came the low hum of voices. And then—unexpectedly—a ripple of laughter. Hartley's voice. Fenwick's. Collyer's not clearly distinguishable.

Nicholas kept his posture, but his thoughts turned inward. The examination had been fair. His answers, sound. Yet he knew—as he always had—that his path through the Service would never be quite conventional. He was not the man anyone had expected: not just a Cruwys of Devon, but the officer who had once spoken Polynesian on the quarterdeck of a Portuguese brig.

There would always be questions. Always the quiet turn of the head. Always the second glance.

He folded his hands on the table and waited.

The sound of approaching boots roused Nicholas from his thoughts. A knock at the gunroom door followed.

"Lieutenant Cruwys," said the first lieutenant. "The board requests your presence in the great cabin."

Nicholas rose, adjusted his coat, and followed the officer aft.

The cabin was much as he had left it. Hartley sat as before, his hands folded before him. Fenwick leaned back slightly, a faint trace of weariness in his expression. Collyer stood now, hands clasped behind his back, his gaze level and unreadable.

Hartley spoke.

"Lieutenant Cruwys, this board finds your conduct, seamanship, and professional knowledge fully satisfactory. Your commission is confirmed, with unanimous consent."

Nicholas inclined his head. "Thank you, sir."

"You may rejoin your ship. A formal copy will be sent for your records. The Admiralty will receive the endorsement through proper channels."

Nicholas gave a quiet, correct bow. "Aye, sir."

Hartley's voice softened by a fraction. "Well done, Mr. Cruwys."

As Nicholas turned to go, Collyer offered a slight nod, not warm, precisely, but respectful. It was the acknowledgment of a peer. Nothing more was said.

Nicholas stepped back into the corridor, the door closing behind him with a soft click.

He was a confirmed lieutenant now, not acting. His duties were the same, but the confirmation brought a quiet satisfaction.

Just before noon, Nicholas was rowed ashore for the first time in the *Growler*'s gig. The landing at Luanda proved straightforward: well-kept stone steps rose from the water to a broad quay flanked by warehouses and customs houses. Portuguese officials moved among them with the crisp efficiency of a long-settled colonial administration.

After completing his formal call upon the Portuguese naval commander, Nicholas took time to explore the European quarter, curious about this outpost that linked Portugal's empire with the coasts of Africa and the trade routes beyond.

The upper town bore all the familiar forms of imperial presence: arcaded avenues, baroque churches, and square-faced government buildings that might have passed for Lisbon in miniature. But as he walked westward, the city's character began to shift. The avenues narrowed. The traffic thickened. The sounds of trade grew louder and more immediate. Turning a corner, Nicholas found himself at the edge of Luanda's infamous slave market.

The sight stopped him where he stood.

In a wide square ringed by trading houses and counting rooms, hundreds of captives stood or crouched in rows, grouped by age, sex, and what the traders deemed "quality." Some were bound in coffles, others merely ringed by guards with muskets and whips. All bore the marks of captivity: iron collars, raw wrists, the blank stare of stunned endurance.

European buyers in pale linen coats moved among them with idle curiosity, inspecting teeth, limbs, and posture as though judging livestock. Portuguese clerks oversaw the exchanges, noting names and amounts, collecting taxes with practiced detachment. Armed sentries patrolled the edge of the square. Nearby, African middlemen—traders from the interior kingdoms—haggled with their Portuguese counterparts in a coarse hybrid of languages, gesturing toward the captives with the brisk efficiency of men selling grain.

Nicholas stood transfixed by the sheer weight of it. He had spent years in the Pacific among Polynesians, who carried themselves with a grace and freedom that had never struck him as more exceptional then now. The contrast could not have been sharper: dignity erased, humanity made into stock.

A merchant approached, mistaking his uniform for interest.

"The Captain has an eye for quality, yes?" the man said in heavily accented English. "These Mbundu—very clever. They learn quickly. Make excellent house boys. Or perhaps something stronger, for the plantations?"

Nicholas recoiled. "I am not here to purchase slaves," he said, his voice flat.

The man smiled, unoffended. "Of course. But the Captain should understand, these are not innocents. Tribal enemies capture them. If we do not buy, they may be killed. The trade saves more than it harms."

Nicholas said nothing. He had heard such arguments before, couched in terms of necessity, inevitability, even mercy. They had the tone of justification without the substance. The fact remained: men, women, and children were being transformed into cargo.

As he turned to go, his eye caught a newly arrived group—perhaps thirty in number, thin and footsore from the march. Many bore fresh lashes or scabbed wrists. Their heads had been shaved, their markings burned or scraped away, their garments replaced with coarse rags. It was not only bondage but erasure: culture, name, and kin stripped clean, the better to price what remained.

Nicholas left the square with a heaviness that no architecture could dispel. Whatever else Luanda was—fortified, efficient, decorous in its facades, it rested, here, on suffering.

Later that afternoon, as he completed the arrangements for supplies to be delivered to *Growler*, Nicholas found himself walking along one of the main avenues of the European district. His steps slowed as he recognized a familiar figure on a balcony above—Caroline Carlisle, her fair hair and pale blue dress instantly distinctive against the whitewashed building. She stood gazing out toward the harbour, apparently unaware of his presence below.

For a moment, Nicholas simply watched her, struck anew by her quiet grace. Something about her composure, the thoughtful set of her features as she looked toward the distant ships—stirred a depth of feeling that caught him. Since losing Atea, he had guarded his heart carefully. There had been commercial arrangements during the long months aboard Silva's ship, and the one brief, unsought encounter with Helena Montague in Calcutta, but nothing that touched the core he had sealed away. Yet Caroline had somehow slipped past those defences, awakening emotions he had believed dormant.

She turned her head and saw him, her expression shifting in an instant from contemplative to luminous. The smile that lit her face held no artifice, no calculation—only genuine pleasure at the sight of him. She raised a hand in greeting, the gesture somehow more intimate than its simplicity suggested.

Nicholas removed his hat and bowed, propriety satisfied by this public exchange. To his surprise, Caroline gestured toward the entrance of the building, clearly inviting him to call. After a moment's consideration, he decided to accept. As a ship's captain—albeit a temporary one—he could properly pay his respects to the daughter of a Company director, particularly one whose acquaintance he had already made.

The house proved to be one of Luanda's better residences, maintained by a Portuguese merchant for the use of distinguished visitors. An African servant admitted Nicholas and led him to a sitting room on the upper floor, where Caroline awaited him.

"Lieutenant Cruwys," she said as he entered, rising from her chair with a smile that carried genuine warmth. "What a pleasant surprise to see you ashore."

Nicholas bowed formally, maintaining the appropriate distance between them, though it required more conscious effort than he'd expected. "Miss Carlisle. I hope I find you well after our passage around the Cape."

"Very well, thank you, though I confess I shall be glad of a week on solid ground. *Ocean* weathered the journey admirably, but there were moments when I wondered if we would ever see calm seas again." She gestured toward a chair. "Please, be seated. My father is meeting with the Portuguese merchants but will return shortly. I'm sure he would be pleased to see you."

Nicholas took the offered seat, acutely aware of her presence across from him. In the privacy of the sitting room, without the formal distance of a shipboard dinner or a public promenade, he found himself noticing details he had overlooked before—the light gloss of her hair in the afternoon light, and her eyes: deep green, but not simply so—they held the faintest glint of amber when the light struck obliquely. "You've secured comfortable lodgings," he said, striving to keep the conversation on neutral ground despite the unexpected intensity of his reaction to her presence.

Caroline smiled, a hint of something knowing in her expression. "Father has correspondents everywhere, Lieutenant. He arranged these quarters months ago, in anticipation of our stop here. He believes in leaving as little as possible to chance—especially when traveling with a daughter in foreign territories."

She paused, then tilted her head just slightly. "And really, must it be Lieutenant now? After the battle aboard the *Ocean*? I believe we agreed on first names Nicholas—in private, at least."

She coloured slightly, Nicholas hesitated, then gave a slow nod. "We did . . . Caroline."

There was a pause—no more than a breath—but in it something shifted. The sound of his name on her lips, spoken without rank or formality, struck him with quiet force. It was not forward, not improper—yet it startled him in its intimacy. When he answered her in kind, the name felt oddly unfamiliar in his mouth, as though it belonged to a language he had once known but seldom spoken.

Her directness, so different from the careful idioms of English drawing rooms, reminded Nicholas pleasantly of their earlier meetings. There was intelligence in her, yes, and restraint—but something else as well: a freedom of manner that left him slightly off balance in a way he had not thought unwelcome. And more than that, he was beginning to suspect he understood far less of her true thoughts than he had once presumed.

"And where are you staying, Nicholas? Surely, as a captain—even a temporary one—you're entitled to lodgings ashore?"

"I remain aboard *Growler*," Nicholas said. "Naval regulations require captains to sleep aboard, even in port, absent permission. Besides, prize vessels need constant supervision. And I've grown accustomed to my accommodations there. As you may recall from our dinner in Cape Town, the French captain had excellent taste in furnishings."

This drew a genuine laugh from Caroline. "How very practical of you—to commandeer not just his ship but his comforts. I hope you've been enjoying his wine cellar too."

"I confess I have," Nicholas replied. "French officers appear to provision themselves rather better than we do. Though in fairness, I've shared the bounty with my officers—and my guests," he added, "rather than keeping it all for myself."

Their conversation continued easily, touching on their experiences since rounding the Cape, observations about Luanda, and thoughts on the remaining journey to England. Nicholas found himself relaxing in her company, the rigid formalities that typically governed such interactions softening in this quiet setting.

Caroline leaned forward slightly, her expression growing more serious. "I noticed you returning from the direction of the commercial district earlier. Did you...?" Her question trailed off, but her meaning was clear.

Nicholas nodded grimly. "I encountered the slave market. A disturbing sight."

"Horrific," Caroline agreed, her eyes darkening with visible distress. "Father's business took us past it yesterday. I've never seen anything so heartbreaking, so fundamentally wrong. The way they were examined, as if they weren't human at all…" She shook her head, unable to continue.

Her response surprised Nicholas. Many Europeans, even those uncomfortable with slavery in theory, accepted it as a necessary element of colonial commerce. That Caroline appeared genuinely affected by what she had witnessed suggested a compassion and clarity of judgment that set her apart.

"In the Pacific," he said quietly, "among the islanders where I lived, such treatment would be incomprehensible. They have their conflicts, certainly, but to reduce a person in that way—to erase name, kinship, selfhood—that would be alien to them."

Caroline's eyes widened slightly, her attention sharpened. "Was it very different from our world?"

"In many ways, yes," Nicholas replied, surprised by his own willingness to speak of it. "Their social structure, their sense of status—it bears little resemblance to ours. They live with a kind of dignity that doesn't depend on rank or artifice."

"It sounds almost utopian," Caroline said thoughtfully. Then, after a pause: "One hears stories of Tahiti." A flush rose to her cheeks. "About the women, I mean…"

Nicholas was briefly taken aback. She sat watching him, her head tilted slightly, the question clearly more than idle curiosity.

"Many of the stories are true," he said, careful in his reply. "They are affectionate, and free in certain ways we are not. But that doesn't mean the feelings are shallow. I left someone there. It meant more than I expected."

Caroline's expression shifted not startled, not hurt, but quietly acknowledging. After a moment, she seemed to draw a breath and turn a corner in the conversation.

"I understand there's to be a dinner at the Governor's palace this evening," she said, with an ease that felt slightly rehearsed. "Father and I have been invited, along with Lord Ashton and several others."

"Indeed," Nicholas said. "The Governor has included the convoy's captains. I expect it will be a formal affair."

Caroline's tone shifted slightly. "Lord Ashton has offered to escort us. He's been most attentive here—he even secured the colony's best carriage."

The implication was clear enough. Nicholas felt a sharp twist of something he preferred not to name.

"His lordship is most considerate," he said, keeping his voice even.

Caroline regarded him for a moment, her gaze perceptive as ever. "He is attentive," she acknowledged. "Though not always in ways I might prefer." She hesitated, then added, "At least Lady Ashton is indisposed this evening—or claims to be—and will not be joining us. Her presence can be... fatiguing."

That last comment, lightly offered, stayed with him. There was more beneath the surface—of Caroline's position, of the pressures surrounding her, than he had fully understood.

Before Nicholas could respond to this rather revealing statement, the door opened to admit Mr. Carlisle, who stopped short at the sight of a naval officer in his sitting room. Following close behind was Lord Ashton, whose aristocratic features froze momentarily in barely concealed displeasure.

"Lieutenant Cruwys," Carlisle said, his tone polite but edged with surprise. "An unexpected pleasure."

Nicholas rose at once and bowed. "Mr. Carlisle, Lord Ashton. I was conducting business ashore and happened to see Miss Carlisle. I hope you'll forgive the informal nature of my call."

"Indeed," Ashton said before Carlisle could reply, his tone carrying a faint condescension. "How fortunate for us all that your naval duties brought you to this particular street. One might almost suspect Providence of arranging such a coincidence."

The implied rebuke hung in the air, but its impact was softened by its pettiness. Carlisle cast a sharp glance at Ashton, clearly displeased by the breach of hospitality.

"My daughter's acquaintances are always welcome in my home, Lieutenant," he said firmly, moving to the sideboard to pour port. "Particularly one to whom we owe a debt of gratitude for his conduct during the engagement with the French." He handed glasses to Ashton and Nicholas. "Besides, I've been hoping for an opportunity to discuss the convoy's schedule with one of the naval officers. How long do you anticipate we'll remain in Luanda?"

Nicholas accepted the glass with a nod. Carlisle, he noted, had deliberately redirected the conversation to neutral ground. "The current plan is to depart on the 14th of July, sir, assuming repairs to *Thetis* and *Audacious* are completed as scheduled. We're also awaiting word on possible reinforcements from Gibraltar or home waters."

"A week or more ashore will be most welcome," Carlisle said, sipping. "Though I don't envy you naval officers the return to shipboard life after such comforts."

"The service adapts us to such transitions, sir," Nicholas replied.

Ashton gave a thin smile. "How fortunate for you, Lieutenant. Adaptability is indeed a useful trait, for those whose circumstances are... changeable." His gaze flicked toward Caroline. "Those of us with more established positions must consider permanence and stability in our arrangements."

Caroline's expression tightened, though only slightly. "I've always thought that excessive concern with stability can lead to stagnation, Lord Ashton. The most interesting people I've met are those who've seen other worlds."

Ashton's smile remained fixed, though a muscle twitched in his jaw. "A charming sentiment, my dear, though perhaps more suited to novels than to the practical considerations of life. Wouldn't you agree, Carlisle?"

Carlisle, clearly wishing to avoid the undertow, cleared his throat. "There's wisdom in both. Stability provides the foundation for prosperity; perspective helps guard against complacency." He turned to Nicholas. "Will you dine with us, Lieutenant? We're taking a light meal before the Governor's reception this evening."

Before Nicholas could answer, Ashton interjected smoothly. "I'm sure the Lieutenant has duties to attend to. Naval responsibilities are demanding, are they not? We shouldn't detain him."

The dismissal was clear. Nicholas saw Carlisle's brief frown, and the flicker of irritation in Caroline's eyes. But he also knew when withdrawal was the wiser course.

"Lord Ashton is correct, sir," he said. "There are matters aboard *Growler* that need tending before tonight's gathering. But I thank you for the invitation and look forward to seeing you this evening."

He bowed to the room, his eyes meeting Caroline's a moment longer. The look they shared held too much for words, regret, interruption, and something deeper neither dared claim aloud.

"Until this evening, then," she said softly.

As Nicholas stepped back into the hall, he felt Ashton's cold gaze following him—watchful, proprietary. The encounter had made one thing plain: whatever he and Caroline might feel, the structures surrounding them would not yield easily. The simplicity he had known with Atea, the natural ease of connection in the Society Islands, now seemed a distant clarity. In its place stood the layered theatre of European society, where meaning lay as much in what was unsaid as in what was spoken, and where affection must navigate a tangle of appearances, obligations, and control.

The carriage that conveyed Commodore Hartley, Captain Walsh, and Nicholas to the *Palácio do Governador* that evening was less grand than whatever conveyance Lord Ashton had no doubt secured, but it served its purpose. The route took them through the heart of Luanda's European quarter, past imposing churches and administrative buildings, toward the Governor's residence, which stood on a rise overlooking the harbour.

The *Palácio* was an imposing structure, a blend of Portuguese colonial architecture and practical adaptation to tropical heat. Built around a central courtyard with a fountain, its thick stone walls and high ceilings offered natural cooling, while covered verandas on the upper floors caught what breezes the season allowed. Guards in colonial uniform stood at attention at the gate, and liveried servants guided guests toward the reception hall.

The Governor, Dom António de Almeida, received his guests in the entrance hall—a distinguished man in his early sixties whose formal dress and upright bearing spoke of a life in Portugal's imperial service. Beside him stood his wife, Dona Maria, a woman of quiet elegance whose Lisbon refinement lent grace to this distant post.

Nicholas surprised the Governor by addressing him in Portuguese. *"Excelência, é uma honra estar em sua presença. Agradeço a hospitalidade de Portugal neste porto amigável,"* he said. His accent was imperfect, but clear.

De Almeida's brows lifted in mild surprise. "You speak our language, Lieutenant? That is most unexpected."

"Only a little, Excellency," Nicholas replied, shifting back to English. "I picked up some during my time in the Pacific, where I encountered Portuguese traders. I've had little practice since."

"Even so, it is most gratifying," the Governor said, his manner warming. "Few British officers trouble themselves with our tongue. You must tell me later how you came to learn it in such distant waters."

Similar introductions followed, but Nicholas received a welcome warmer than his junior rank might typically invite, thanks to his linguistic gesture. Within, the *Palácio* proved unexpectedly opulent: European furnishings, chandeliers, and art that testified to Portugal's reach—Dutch paintings, Chinese porcelain, and African carvings displayed side by side in imperial confidence.

The company was larger than Nicholas had anticipated. Beyond the convoy's officers and East Indiamen passengers, de Almeida had invited senior Portuguese officials, the Catholic bishop, several local merchants, and the captains of other vessels presently in harbour—including *Mercury*. The result was a gathering of some fifty, reflecting the converging interests of naval power, commerce, and colonial administration.

He spotted Caroline almost at once, her figure distinct among the assembled guests. She wore a gown of pale yellow silk, and her fair hair was arranged in a style that managed to be both current and well-suited to the heat. Her father stood beside her, deep in conversation with a Portuguese merchant, while Lord Ashton loitered nearby, his aristocratic bearing and immaculate dress marking him out, as ever, as a man of station.

Protocol prevented Nicholas from approaching her directly without a pretext, so he circulated through the room, exchanging polite remarks with several of the guests, and—briefly—with Captain Collyer, who greeted him with a quiet nod of recognition. Collyer's reserved expression gave nothing away, but his eyes registered the moment.

All the while, Nicholas remained aware of Caroline's position, watching as Ashton lingered near her, occasionally placing a hand on her arm or leaning in with quiet remarks. Each such gesture struck him with unexpected force, sharp, unwelcome, and increasingly difficult to ignore.

It was not until dinner was announced that Nicholas found himself in proximity to the Carlisles. The seating had been arranged with meticulous regard for rank and precedence: Governor de Almeida at the head, Commodore Hartley at his right, and others spaced accordingly. Nicholas, as a junior commander, was seated near the centre—directly opposite Caroline, her father positioned further up the table where Lord Ashton also near the Governor in deference to his title.

The placement was a godsend, affording Nicholas and Caroline the chance to speak out of the immediate hearing, if not view, of either her father or Lord Ashton. As the first course was served—a soup of local vegetables seasoned with European spices, paired with a delicate Portuguese white—Nicholas ventured a quiet opening.

"Miss Carlisle, I trust Luanda is proving more hospitable than you feared?"

Caroline gave a slight nod, her expression unreadable for a moment. "In some ways, yes. It's a strange thing, though—how quickly a place can feel familiar, if your thoughts are occupied."

There was a pause as she lifted her wine glass, then set it down without drinking. "I've been thinking," she said quietly, "about what you told me earlier. About how people live differently—not just materially, but inwardly. I keep returning to that."

When Nicholas hesitated, she went on, her voice still low. "You speak of your Pacific experiences with a certain restraint, Lieutenant. Is it difficult to reconcile those years with your present circumstances?"

The perceptiveness of her question caught him off guard. Few had considered the personal weight of his journey, focusing instead on its exotic detail or strategic consequence.

"At times," he admitted. "The Pacific taught me many things that have no place in naval service—or in English society."

"Such as?" she asked, her green eyes meeting his with unexpected directness.

Nicholas paused, aware of the setting despite their lowered voices. "Different understandings of human connection, for one. The islanders form relationships based on affinity rather than convention or advantage."

Something shifted in Caroline's expression, a flicker of recognition, perhaps, or something more deeply felt. "How refreshing that must have been," she said, her tone suggesting she understood more than his words alone conveyed. "To be valued for oneself rather than one's position or prospects."

The comment carried an undercurrent Nicholas could not immediately place, something personal beneath the observation. Before he could respond, she continued, her tone subtly changed.

"I imagine you found the women there quite different from European ladies," she said, watching his reaction carefully. "In their expectations, and their freedom to choose."

The question might have seemed casual, but there was a quality in her voice—especially after their conversation that afternoon—that suggested more than curiosity. Nicholas found himself studying her again, attuned now to implication.

"They are more direct in expressing both interest and disinterest," he replied. "One always knows where one stands. European forms often seem designed to obscure rather than clarify true feeling."

A small smile touched her lips. "How diplomatic, Lieutenant. Though I suspect the differences go beyond mere expression." Her gaze held his, unhurried. "Do they form attachments based on genuine affinity rather than prescribed roles?"

"Often, yes," Nicholas said, sensing the edge of a boundary not often crossed in polite company. "They choose partners by inclination, without much concern for what others might think suitable."

"How liberating that must be," she said. There was no irony in her tone, only quiet wistfulness. "To choose based on one's heart rather than society's expectations." Her eyes met his again, steady. "Some of us find European conventions equally... constraining, in ways that few would understand."

Before Nicholas could decipher this somewhat astonishing reply, the Portuguese official beside her turned with a question about the East India Company's operations in Calcutta. She responded with perfect grace, as though the moment between them had never occurred. But Nicholas was left with the unmistakable sense that something had.

Later, as the fish course was cleared, Caroline's hand brushed his as she reached for her wine glass. The contact was brief, possibly accidental—yet it sent a jolt through him that felt vastly out of proportion. Her eyes met his, and he saw in them a flash of recognition: not surprise, but shared awareness. Whatever had passed between them was real. And it was not yet finished.

Nicholas was careful to maintain propriety in both manner and subject, aware that they were under observation—not only from Caroline's father and Lord Ashton but from the assembled company, many of whom would note, and possibly comment on, any behaviour that strayed beyond the bounds of acceptable interaction. Yet within these constraints, he found himself drawn to Caroline's mind and perspective in a way that transcended mere attraction.

Carlisle, looking up from his meal and glancing down the table, was suddenly struck by what seemed almost a glow between his beloved daughter—whose beauty was undeniable—and the young officer. He couldn't but recognize they made a striking couple. Cruwys was a fine-looking lad, tall and broad-shouldered, with his dark hair setting off an intelligent face, deeply tanned, with that faint scar across his left cheek. And he sensed the interest—and at this moment, the apparent happiness—of Caroline around Nicholas.

As he turned thoughtfully back to the other guests, the Governor caught his eye, nodded toward the couple, and raised his glass slightly before drinking.

As the dinner progressed through its multiple courses, Nicholas became aware of Lord Ashton watching their interaction with growing displeasure. Though too well-bred to show open irritation, the aristocrat's expression darkened whenever Caroline's attention lingered too long on Nicholas—which was increasingly often. At intervals, Ashton would attempt to reclaim her focus with some carefully chosen remark, a tactic that succeeded only partially and briefly.

"Do you hunt, Lieutenant Cruwys?" Ashton called down the table during a lull, his voice pitched to draw polite attention. "We maintain excellent coverts in Wiltshire. Nothing quite like the chase to reveal a man's true character."

The question was plainly intended to emphasize the differences between them, this casual reference to inherited estates a reminder of the gulf that separated a peer of the realm from a naval officer of uncertain fortune.

"I've had little opportunity for such pursuits, my lord," Nicholas replied evenly. "Naval service allows little time for sporting pleasures."

"A pity," Ashton said. "Though I suppose shooting at Frenchmen provides its own form of entertainment."

Several of the Portuguese officials looked uncomfortable at this offhand reference to warfare, but Dom António de Almeida intervened smoothly.

"I've observed in my years of hunting, my friends," he said, "that the most respected sportsmen know when to hold their fire. The thrill lies not merely in pursuit, but in the artful restraint that elevates sport above mere predation. And at the dinner table, as in the field, the finest exchanges are those in which we circle ideas rather than people."

He turned toward Ashton with a faint smile. "Wouldn't you agree, my lord, that there is more satisfaction in the elegant give and take than in the final capture? After all, we hunt game in the forest so that we might practice civility in our homes."

Ashton went pale at the rebuke, but said nothing. A diplomatic murmur rose across the table as the conversation turned, gracefully but firmly, toward the philosophical intersections of war and sport, drawing in several of the more reflective guests.

Nicholas, hard-pressed not to smile, caught the glance exchanged between Captain Walsh and Commodore Hartley—one of mild, detached amusement.

Throughout the remainder of the meal, Nicholas became increasingly attuned to the subtler dimensions of Caroline's conversation and manner. She engaged brilliantly with the topics around her—trade relations, colonial governance, even military strategy—displaying a breadth of knowledge uncommon for a woman of her age and station. Yet beneath that polished fluency, he sensed currents of thought and feeling held deliberately in reserve.

When the conversation turned to marriage customs in different cultures, prompted by an elderly Portuguese lady across the table, he noticed how Caroline's animation dimmed. Her responses grew more cautious, more conventional, as though reflex had replaced conviction. Only when a young Portuguese woman spoke of her unmarried aunt, a respected botanist, did Caroline's true interest visibly rekindle.

"How admirable," she said with unexpected warmth. "To dedicate oneself to scientific study rather than conventional domesticity must require considerable courage."

"Indeed," the young woman replied. "Though *Tia Luisa* claims it's merely selfishness—she says she could never share her life with someone who didn't understand her deepest nature."

Something in the remark seemed to strike a chord in Caroline, though she quickly guided the conversation back to safer ground. Nicholas, watching her closely, found himself wondering how much of what he thought he knew of Caroline Carlisle reflected her true self, and how much was practiced accommodation—an elegant mask worn with the ease of long habit.

After dinner, as was customary, the ladies withdrew to the drawing room while the gentlemen remained for port and political discussion. Nicholas joined a group of Portuguese merchants intrigued by his earlier use of their language. He conversed with them in halting Portuguese, supplementing when needed with English. The effort was well received. Governor de Almeida, observing from a short distance, remarked to Commodore Hartley on the diplomatic instincts of the young officer.

Nicholas was deep in discussion of coastal currents with a Portuguese captain when a servant approached, bowing slightly.

"For Lieutenant Cruwys, sir."

Nicholas took the folded paper with a murmur of thanks and opened it discreetly. The message was brief and unsigned:

> *The garden offers a fair view of the harbour lights. Perhaps you might comment on its arrangement before rejoining the company?*

The handwriting was elegant but purposeful—a hand trained for letters, not display. He recognized it at once as Caroline's, having seen her making notes in a small book during their conversation earlier that day.

He pocketed the note carefully, continued his conversation for a few minutes more, then made a casual excuse to step outside for air.

The evening was pleasantly cool after the day's heat, a breeze carrying unfamiliar scents from the hedges and vines beyond. Lanterns had been set along the central paths, casting pools of golden light that marked the way while leaving the garden's farther corners veiled in shadow.

Nicholas stepped out with deliberate calm, his gait unhurried, his bearing formal enough to appear casual. He followed the primary path away from the house, moving toward a terrace that offered the view mentioned in the note. As he approached, he saw her standing there, her pale blue gown almost silvery in the combined light of the lanterns and the rising moon.

Caroline stood at the edge of the terrace, one hand resting lightly on the stone balustrade, her face turned toward the harbour. She turned at the sound of his approach, and her expression eased at once—clear relief, quickly composed.

"Lieutenant. I feared my note might have been intercepted, or misunderstood."

"Neither, it seems," he replied, moving to stand beside her at the balustrade, though with enough space between them to satisfy propriety should anyone be watching. "Though I confess some surprise at receiving it."

Caroline gazed out toward the harbour, where the lights of the anchored ships formed a quiet constellation against the dark sweep of the Atlantic. "I wished to speak with you away from the constraints of the dinner table, and from Lord Ashton's constant surveillance. There are things that cannot be said in such settings."

"A risky proposition," Nicholas observed mildly. "Your reputation—"

"Is of less concern to me than it perhaps ought to be," she said, a trace of frustration in her tone. "At least here, so far from the drawing rooms of London and the people who delight in judgment."

Nicholas studied her profile, struck by how the moonlight drew out the clarity of her features—the high cheekbones, the straight nose, the determined line of her mouth. There was a tension in her bearing that suggested inner conflict, a struggle between outward composure and private conviction.

"Something troubles you, Caroline," he said, not as a question but as a quiet assertion.

She was silent for a moment, her fingers curling lightly around the stone balustrade. "I find myself at a crossroads, Nicholas. One that few would understand." She turned to face him fully, her eyes searching his with unusual candour. "What did you feel, when you realized the Pacific offered ways of living so different from everything you had been taught to think proper or natural?"

The question caught him off guard.

"Confusion, at first," he said. "Then a kind of liberation. The recognition that so many of our certainties are nothing more than conventions—learned habits, not truths."

"Yes," she murmured. "Liberation. That's precisely it." She looked out again toward the dark water. "I don't know what my father said to you in Cape Town, but I believe he means to accept Lord Ashton's proposal on my behalf when we return to England."

The words, spoken with quiet directness, struck Nicholas harder than he expected. He had observed Ashton's attentions, understood the logic of such a match—but hearing it stated so plainly brought a jolt of something much deeper: not surprise, but pain.

"I see," he said, working to keep his voice neutral. "And yet... are you certain? He gave me to understand the matter was still... fluid."

"I see," Caroline repeated, her tone unreadable for a moment. Then it softened into something more reflective. "To my father, Lord Ashton offers all the things money cannot buy: a title, political standing in a world that requires more than commercial success. In return, he receives a substantial dowry, a young wife, and the prospect of an heir his first marriage did not provide."

A note of bitterness entered her voice, but faded quickly. "My father means well. He truly believes Ashton would be a suitable match: respectable, secure, socially correct. What he does not understand is that I want something else."

"And what is that?" Nicholas asked gently.

She met his gaze, her expression raw beneath its control. "Genuine connection. The freedom to be fully myself with another person." Her voice dropped. "I've had glimpses of such connection, rare moments where I felt truly seen and understood." She blushed slightly, "With a companion in Calcutta. And perhaps…" she paused, visibly gathering herself, "with you. In our conversations."

The admission hung in the air between them, both unmistakable and deliberately unqualified. Nicholas sensed that she had spoken something carefully guarded—something offered at cost.

Caroline was silent for a moment more, then said quietly, "I cannot say more about Calcutta, not now. But I wondered about you. You made mention of someone earlier, when we spoke at the house."

Nicholas hesitated, then said, "Yes, I was with her in the Pacific for just over a year." His voice caught. "She died, fourteen months ago. But not before she taught me what it meant to be chosen without condition."

He looked down briefly, then met Caroline's eyes.

"Such connections are rare indeed, Caroline," he said. "And precious, when found."

"Yes," she agreed, her eyes steady on his. "And nearly impossible to reconcile with the life that awaits me as Lord Ashton's countess. A life of faultless propriety and quiet performance, where the self I most value must remain forever hidden."

Nicholas felt a rising empathy—for her position, yes, but also for the deep resonance it struck with his own experience: the feeling of living between identities, of never fully belonging to either.

"What will you do?"

"For now—delay," she said, with a flicker of determination. "My father won't act until we're home. Once there, I'll have to find a way to persuade him that status isn't everything. It won't be easy. Ashton is persistent, and Lady Ashton is... tireless in his cause."

"Caroline," he said softly, his voice unsteady, "I wish I could offer—"

Voices from the house interrupted. Nicholas released her hand at once and stepped back, putting space between them. Caroline moved to a nearby flowering shrub, bending slightly as if examining its scent.

Moments later, two Portuguese officials stepped out onto the terrace, deep in conversation about trade quotas and customs duties. They nodded to Nicholas in passing, giving no sign of noticing either him or the young woman nearby.

When they had moved on, Caroline returned briefly to the balustrade, now at a polite remove.

"We should return separately," she said, composed once more. "I'll go first. Wait a few minutes before following."

"As you wish," Nicholas said, understanding exactly why.

She turned to go, then paused. "Nicholas, our convoy remains here for another week. I expect we'll have further opportunities to speak—though perhaps not so privately."

She held his gaze a moment longer. Then, without another word, she vanished into the lighted path, leaving Nicholas alone with the scent of the garden and the anchored ships beyond—silent silhouettes against the Atlantic night, sentinels of duty and distance, and of everything that might yet divide them.

The next days passed in a blur of activity, with repairs to *Thetis* and *Audacious* proceeding at remarkable pace under Commodore Hartley's close supervision. Portuguese shipwrights worked alongside British seamen, their shared knowledge of wood and water transcending language. New masts were shaped from African timber, rigging reworked, and damaged planking replaced. By the fourth day, both vessels showed substantial improvement, though much remained to be done.

Nicholas divided his time between supervising routine work aboard *Growler* in preparing for the next leg to England, and fulfilling various responsibilities ashore. The Portuguese naval authorities had proved notably cooperative, granting access to stores and facilities with little obstruction. That goodwill stemmed partly from the longstanding Anglo-Portuguese alliance, but also, it seemed, from Nicholas's conduct at the Governor's dinner, which had left a favourable impression among the colonial officials.

In the course of these days, he encountered Caroline on three occasions: once at the harbour master's office, where she accompanied her father; once at a small reception hosted by the British consul; and once, quite by chance, in the botanical garden of the European quarter, where each had sought respite from the afternoon heat. These meetings were necessarily brief and conducted with proper decorum, but each deepened the sense of understanding between them. Their conversation remained outwardly conventional, yet carried an undercurrent of unspoken feeling—acknowledged silently, if never declared.

On the morning of the fifth day, as Nicholas stood on *Growler*'s quarterdeck overseeing the loading of fresh provisions, the lookout's cry broke across the morning air.

"Sail ho! Four sail to the north-west!"

Nicholas climbed to the maintop, and raised his glass, scanning the distance where the lookout had pointed. At first he saw only the shimmer of the sea, but then—rising on the swell—four ships came into view, sails white against the morning sky, moving in close formation.

Signal flags lifted aboard *Salisbury*, ordering captains to their ships and placing the convoy on alert. Within the hour, the incoming vessels had drawn close enough to be identified: a 64-gun ship of the line bearing a rear admiral's flag, accompanied by three frigates, all flying the British ensign. Beyond that, details were still indistinct.

"It seems our reinforcements have arrived after all," Williams remarked, standing beside Nicholas. "Just two days before our planned departure."

Nicholas nodded, relief tempered by a quiet unease. The arrival this force would certainly improve the convoy's security—and put it beyond the reach of any but the largest enemy force—but the presence of a rear-admiral would also alter the command structure. His own position, always provisional, might soon be redefined.

By mid-afternoon, the four ships had entered the harbour and anchored with precise naval efficiency. The 64-gun ship—a smaller third-rate ship of the line, which Nicholas now identified as *Centaur*—took station near *Salisbury*, while the three frigates— *Juno*, *Alarm*, and *Lowestoffe*—anchored in a defensive arc that effectively surrounded the convoy. Boats were immediately lowered, and a flurry of communication began between the newly arrived vessels and those already in harbour.

Nicholas watched as the Commodore—now again simply Captain Hartley—was rowed across to *Centaur* to report to the rear admiral. Even at this distance, the formality of the reception was evident: sideboys lined up, bosun's pipes shrilling, marines presenting arms as Hartley was received aboard with all the ceremony due his rank.

Two hours later, signals from *Salisbury* ordered Nicholas and the other captains of the original escort force to report aboard at once. When he arrived, he found the cabin filled with a faint but unmistakable tension. Captain Walsh was already present, along with Captain Fenwick of *Thetis* and Lieutenant Rogers of *Audacious*. All wore expressions of carefully contained concern.

"Gentlemen," Hartley began as Nicholas took his seat, "as you've observed, we have been joined by Rear Admiral Sir Thomas Ames, with a squadron out of Gibraltar. The Admiral has reviewed our situation and issued new orders that will affect each of us. He asked me to convey them to you, along with his admiration and appreciation for the work done in bringing this convoy safely here from Bombay."

Nicholas felt a prickle of unease at Hartley's tone. It seemed odd that the Admiral had not summoned them himself, but there was little to be read from that alone.

"The convoy will continue to England as planned, departing on the 14th of July," Hartley went on. "However, there will be changes to our command structure and assignments."

He turned to Walsh. "Captain, *Lynx* is restored to her original mission of carrying dispatches with all possible speed. She is to depart immediately for Gibraltar and then to England, carrying dispatches from India and the Company, and now also from the Admiral and from me. You will not wait for the convoy, which is now considered adequately protected."

Walsh gave a crisp nod. "Aye, sir. When are we to depart?"

"Tomorrow morning with the tide," Hartley replied. "The dispatches are being prepared now and will be delivered to you by evening."

Nicholas listened with growing apprehension, sensing the shift about to come.

Hartley turned to him.

"Mr. Cruwys, I regret to inform you that you will be superseded in command of *Growler*. The Admiral has appointed Lieutenant Frederick Graves—currently serving on his staff aboard *Centaur*—as prize master for the remainder of the journey to England, and provisionally as Master and Commander."

The words landed with quiet finality. Nicholas had known, of course, that his command was temporary. But the manner of its ending—abrupt, impersonal, unaccompanied by even the formality of a meeting—cut more sharply than he expected.

More than that, he realised with sudden clarity: he would be departing with *Lynx*, leaving Caroline behind with the convoy... and with Ashton.

"I understand, sir," he said, his voice level.

Hartley hesitated, as though bracing himself.

"You are to return to *Lynx* as third lieutenant," he said. "Lieutenant Chester is reassigned to her, effective immediately. The Admiral has released additional officers to *Thetis* from *Juno* and *Lowestoffe*, and felt it appropriate to return Chester to his former berth."

A pause followed—brief, but heavy.

"It was not my recommendation," Hartley added.

Walsh's jaw tensed, but he said nothing.

Nicholas nodded, adjusting inwardly to the fresh blow. "Understood, sir. When am I to relinquish command?"

"This afternoon. Commander Graves will come aboard at four bells in the afternoon watch to take formal possession. You are to report to *Lynx* by the end of the dog watch."

Nicholas inclined his head. "Very well. I'll have all logs and accounts prepared for Commander Graves's review."

"See that you do," Hartley said. Then, after a pause: "You've handled temporary command admirably, Mr. Cruwys. This decision reflects protocol, not any failing on your part."

Nicholas gave a small, professional nod. But as he stood, he felt the sharp edge of it nonetheless.

Later that day, as Nicholas supervised the final preparation of *Growler*'s logs and accounts, a boat approached carrying Commander Graves—already, even in this distant port, wearing the uniform of his new rank. As he stepped aboard, Nicholas observed him with professional interest.

Graves was perhaps twenty-four, with the confident bearing of a man accustomed to preferment. His uniform was immaculate; his manner brisk but not discourteous.

"Lieutenant Cruwys," he said, touching his hat in salute. "Commander Frederick Graves, here to assume command of His Majesty's Ship *Growler*."

Nicholas returned the salute precisely. "Welcome aboard, sir. The ship is ready for your inspection."

The handover proceeded with formal efficiency. Nicholas guided Graves through the vessel, introducing him to the officers and men, noting the ship's particular handling characteristics, and finally presenting the logs and accounts for signature. Throughout, both men maintained a professional detachment—though Nicholas could not help the quiet pang that came as he watched another man take possession of the ship he had brought through storm, action, and repair.

"You've kept her in excellent condition," Graves remarked as they concluded the tour in the captain's cabin—no longer Nicholas's domain. "The Admiral mentioned she was taken during a convoy engagement. A fine piece of work."

"The credit belongs as much to the men as to me," Nicholas replied. "They performed admirably under difficult circumstances."

Graves nodded, apparently satisfied. "I understand you're to rejoin *Lynx* for the passage to Gibraltar."

"Yes, sir. We depart tomorrow morning."

"Well, I wish you a safe voyage," Graves said, extending his hand in a gesture that felt genuinely collegial. "Perhaps we shall meet again in England."

Nicholas shook it. He bore no grievance toward Graves himself; the man had merely stepped into an opening created by a system that favored timing over merit.

"I look forward to it, sir."

His personal belongings had taken only minutes to pack: the books, instruments, and clothing he had brought aboard, along with his sword and pistols, and the French sextant and navigation tools. The remaining items and furnishings that had belonged to the French captain he left behind—properly, he felt they belonged to the ship.

His parting words to the crew were brief but sincere, expressing his appreciation for their discipline, courage, and camaraderie, and his confidence in their future under new command.

The boat that ferried him to *Lynx* felt strangely silent. His chest of belongings rested near his feet—compact, weathered, and a reminder of how little he truly possessed after years at sea and long separation from home.

As *Lynx* drew nearer, he straightened his shoulders out of habit rather than conviction. The uniform still fit; the salute would still come. But something in him had shifted. This was not failure—he knew that—but neither was it triumph. It was merely the familiar pattern of European life reasserting itself: preferment, patronage, appearance above merit. And he was beginning to understand, with a cold clarity, how easily one could be passed over by the world one served too well.

Captain Walsh received him on deck with characteristic directness. "Welcome back, Mr. Cruwys."

"Thank you, sir. It's good to be back."

He knew he should feel gratitude for returning to a ship and captain he respected, yet all he could think about was what—who—he would be leaving behind. The sudden departure meant he would have no chance for a proper farewell to Caroline, no opportunity to explain his feelings or understand hers more fully. The realization left him with a hollow ache that no naval duty could immediately dispel.

Later that afternoon, Walsh surprised him with a summons to dine privately in the captain's cabin that evening. As Nicholas came into the gunroom, having changed for dinner, he found Harrington seated alone at the table. The second lieutenant looked up.

"Settled back in Nicholas?" Harrington asked, his tone deliberately casual yet unable to entirely mask a note of genuine concern.

"More or less," Nicholas said. "Though I confess it feels strange to be back in these quarters."

Harrington nodded, a flicker of understanding in his expression. "Few things alter a man more than command. Even a brief taste leaves its mark. I never mentioned it, but—two years ago—I was sent prize master aboard a large French merchantman we took off Crete. Only two weeks or so, but I remember it still." He hesitated, then added, "Many officers in your position might nurse a grievance at being superseded. Your composure does you credit."

Nicholas was surprised by the frankness. "Graves had the advantage—time in rank and a voice near the admiral. The service has its own order."

"It does," Harrington said. "Though I'll say nothing of Graves, I will say more broadly that order doesn't always serve judgment as it should."

He paused. "I spoke to Captain Walsh before the admiral's decision was final. Said I thought you ought to continue with *Growler* to England."

Nicholas looked at him. "I'm grateful, Henry."

"It wasn't a kindness," Harrington said. "I said what seemed plain. As the then first lieutenant. He smiled sardonically. "You handled her well, and not many could have done so in your place."

His expression softened slightly. "The sea has its own ways of instructing a man—some of them quieter than the quarterdeck."

He rose, setting aside a folded chart. "But the captain is expecting you, and I doubt he means to dine alone."

Then, with no change of expression, he extended his hand—without ceremony, but with meaning.

"The Navy has its disappointments, Nicholas. But sometimes, given time, it answers back."

Nicholas took the offered hand, sensing they had crossed into a quieter solidarity—not yet close friends, perhaps, but something more than merely officers sharing a deck. As he made his way aft to the captain's cabin, he carried that moment with him.

"You seem remarkably composed for a man who has just been relieved of his first command," Walsh observed, as they shared a bottle of claret over a simple but well-prepared meal of fresh fish and local vegetables.

Nicholas considered his response. "Disappointment serves no purpose, sir. I knew the command was temporary, and while I'd hoped it might continue to England—or beyond—the service has taught me to accept such changes with equanimity."

Walsh studied him over the rim of his glass. "A diplomatic answer. The truth, I suspect, is rather more complex."

"Perhaps, sir," Nicholas acknowledged. "But dwelling on personal feelings won't alter the admiral's decision."

"No, it won't," Walsh agreed. "Though you might be interested to know that before superseding you, the admiral inquired quite thoroughly into your conduct, both in the action against the French and in your handling of *Growler*. Captain Hartley spoke well of you."

That gave Nicholas pause. "I'm grateful for the confidence, sir."

"Don't mistake me, Mr. Cruwys. The outcome was inevitable. Commander Graves is the admiral's nephew, and part of a prominent naval family. There were rumours before we sailed that his uncle—Admiral Thomas Graves—stood well with the Admiralty as a likely appointee for command in America."

Nicholas nodded. The revelation of the family connection explained much, though it did little to ease the sting. Nepotism was hardly new. That Graves had been granted a command over more senior officers merely underscored Nicholas's own lack of influence.

Walsh continued, "I'm glad you understand. But the fact that inquiries were made at all suggests your actions have not gone unnoticed. Graves may have the advantage of name and placement, but you've begun to build something harder to earn—a reputation."

He leaned forward slightly, his tone thoughtful. "The service has changed since your time with Cook. The excitement of discovery has been replaced by the demands of war. In those days, exploration captured the Admiralty's imagination. Now, survival commands its attention."

He refilled their glasses. "But even in war—perhaps especially in war—the Navy needs men who've seen beyond Europe. The Pacific has shaped you. That may yet prove valuable to England, though not, perhaps, in the way you first imagined."

Nicholas was struck by the quiet force behind the words. He had always respected Walsh as a sailor, but had not expected such reflection from a man he'd thought principally direct.

"Thank you, sir," he said. "I'll try to remember that."

"See that you do," Walsh said. Then, with a return to his usual tone: "And I'll say one thing more, Mr. Cruwys—and I say it from regard. A young officer in your position would do well to fix his thoughts on duty. This life is not well suited to permanent attachments—certainly not at your age, and perhaps not at all before post rank."

He paused, then added more briskly, "Now, I expect you to resume your duties as third lieutenant with the same diligence you showed in command. We have a fast run ahead of us, and I intend to make Gibraltar inside the admiral's thirty-day estimate."

"Aye, sir."

As Nicholas returned to his cabin, his mind was unsettled. Walsh's candour had taken him by surprise, and he knew real regard had been offered behind the formality. Yet his thoughts turned inevitably to Caroline. *Lynx's* departure—and his own sudden removal—meant he would have no chance for a proper farewell. By the time she learned of the change, they would already be at sea.

The knowledge hollowed him. Whatever Walsh might say about attachments, the ache was real, and it deepened by the hour.

He sat at his small desk, considering whether to write her a note. But what could he say? That in the span of a few brief encounters, she had awakened feelings he had believed permanently dormant after Atea's death? That despite all the practical impossibilities, he had begun to imagine a future in which their paths might somehow align?

Such declarations would be premature, improper, and—under the circumstances—cruel.

His reverie was interrupted by a soft knock at his cabin door. Opening it, he found Midshipman Foley standing outside, a sealed note in hand.

"A boat just came alongside, sir," Foley explained. "The messenger asked that this be delivered to you personally."

Nicholas took the note with a quiet word of thanks, then closed the door and broke the plain wax seal. The single sheet contained only a few lines, written in a hand he knew at once:

I have learned of your departure tomorrow.
If you walk along the eastern quay at first light, you might encounter someone taking the morning air before the day's heat makes such exercise impractical.
A coincidence, perhaps—but sometimes fate arranges such meetings for those who seek them.
—C.

He read the note twice, then folded it carefully and placed it inside his journal. The invitation was clear, yet written with enough ambiguity to withstand scrutiny. Caroline had found a way to arrange a final meeting—a chance to say what could not be left unsaid.

He slept little that night, his mind full of what the morning might bring. When the first grey light began to filter under his cabin door by way of the gunroom skylight, he rose and dressed with care, then made his way quietly to the deck. Lieutenant Harrington was already there and nodded as Nicholas approached.

"The captain said you might request a boat," he said, with studied casualness. "He left word that you were to be accommodated, provided you return within the hour."

Nicholas offered a dry smile of his own, unsurprised by Walsh's omniscience. "I'll be back well before then."

The eastern quay was deserted at this early hour, the first golden light just beginning to touch the upper stories of the warehouses and merchants' offices that lined the harbour. Nicholas walked steadily along the stone pavement, the only sounds the gentle lap of water against the quay walls and the distant calls of seabirds. The air was still fresh; the day's heat not yet begun. A light mist hung over the harbour, softening the outlines of the anchored ships.

He had nearly reached the end of the quay when he saw her.

Caroline stood alone in a pale apricot morning dress, her golden hair covered by a light shawl. She was gazing out at the harbour, where *Lynx* was visibly preparing for departure, her crew already at work on deck.

Nicholas approached quietly. She turned at the sound of his footsteps, and smiled—a smile so unguarded, so luminous, that it made his chest tighten.

"Lieutenant Cruwys," she said, her voice pitched just right for any who might overhear. "What a fortunate coincidence to encounter you here."

"Indeed, Miss Carlisle," he replied, playing the fiction. "I came to take a final look at Luanda before our departure."

They stood side by side at the quay's edge, maintaining a proper distance, both facing the harbour as if admiring the view. For a moment, neither spoke. The weight of all that could not be said hung gently in the space between them.

"I heard of your change in assignment," Caroline said at last, her voice low but steady. "I'm sorry you were replaced in command of *Growler*. It seems a poor reward for having captured her in the first place."

"Naval service often operates on considerations beyond merit," Nicholas replied lightly. "Commander Graves will make a capable captain, I'm sure."

She turned slightly, studying his profile. "You accept it with remarkable grace."

"What choice do I have?" He shrugged. "And returning to *Lynx* is no hardship. She's a fine vessel with an excellent captain."

"Still, to leave so suddenly…" Her voice softened. The words contained more than their surface.

Nicholas glanced toward a narrow passage between two warehouses, sheltered from view. With a quick look to be sure they were unobserved, he gestured subtly. "Walk with me a moment?"

Something flickered in Caroline's eyes—hesitation, perhaps—but also that spark he had come to admire. She nodded once.

They moved toward the passage at a measured pace, still maintaining the appearance of casual civility until they were out of sight. The sounds of the harbour faded behind them.

"Nicholas, I had to see you," she said, her voice dropping the fiction entirely. "When I heard about your orders... I couldn't bear the thought of your sailing without a proper goodbye." Her eyes searched his face. "But I shouldn't have come. It's madness."

She didn't move.

"Do you regret it?"

"No." One word, and it held all the weight they had left unspoken.

Nicholas knew he should keep his distance. But the years at sea, the months spent among people with different codes of conduct, had taught him that courage came in many forms—not all of them martial.

"Caroline," he said—her name a confession. "I may never see you again."

"Don't say that," she replied, fierce now. "This war can't last forever."

"Even so. The sea is vast. And there's your father. And Ashton." He hesitated. "I cannot leave without saying the truth."

Her breath caught.

"Then tell me," she said, stepping closer. "Or better yet, show me."

He did.

Their lips met—gently at first, then with a depth born of separation already begun. Caroline's arms slid around his neck. His hands found the small of her back, her jaw. For a moment, they existed only in that narrow strip of shade.

When they parted, Caroline's cheeks were flushed, her eyes clear. And yet something flickered there—a quiet complexity. A knowing.

"I won't apologize," she said, adjusting her shawl.

"Nor should you," Nicholas said. "Not for something true."

She reached into her pocket and withdrew a small package, wrapped in silk and tied with a ribbon.

"Nicholas," she said, using his name again. "For your journey. But please—don't open it until you're at sea."

He took it. Their hands touched and lingered.

"I shall treasure it. Whatever it is."

Voices from the quay intruded. Caroline stepped back with practiced composure, though her lips were still slightly reddened from their kiss.

"I should go," she said, the warmth in her eyes not yet faded. "And you have a ship waiting."

"Caroline, I—"

She laid two fingers gently on his lips.

"Not now, Nicholas. Not yet. Perhaps when we next see each other."

He nodded.

"Write to me," he said, "even if there's no answer."

She didn't reply—only turned, and walked back through the passage.

Nicholas waited until she had gained a proper distance before emerging. By the time he reached the quay, she was already a figure near a waiting carriage. He paused as he saw her father—distinct, unmistakable—handing her up into it.

The carriage pulled away. Nicholas stood there, watching it vanish into the brightening light.

What they had shared had been real. But so was everything that still stood between them.

He felt the shape of it in his chest, not sorrow, exactly. But the hollow weight of something not yet lost, and not yet his to claim.

Nicholas returned to the waiting boat, the small package secure in his pocket. Whatever the future held, whatever Caroline's true feelings might be, he had experienced a connection that transcended the conventional. That knowledge would accompany him across the leagues of ocean that lay ahead, a private truth as precious as the token she had entrusted to him.

As *Lynx* weighed anchor an hour later, her sails filling with the morning breeze, Nicholas stood on the quarterdeck, eyes fixed on the receding shoreline, watching until the last rise of Luanda disappeared below the horizon. Only then did he return to the privacy of his cabin, where he unwrapped Caroline's gift with deliberate care.

Inside the folds of silk lay a small silver case—oval, finely worked, the surface engraved with a subtle geometric pattern. It rested cool in his hand, heavier than he expected, and finely made.

He pressed the clasp and opened the lid.

Along the inner rim, a narrow band of inlaid ivory framed the image set within.

Behind protective glass, a watercolor miniature—of Bora Bora, not Caroline. Her own likeness would have been too personal, too declarative. Instead, the painting showed the island's high peak rising above the lagoon, rendered in delicate, confident strokes. He recognized the view at once—from one of his own sketches, given to her father during their meal abord *Growler*.

She had painted it herself. He had no doubt of that.

Inside the lid, engraved in small, careful script:

> *Islands of memory anchor us through life's storms.*
>
> C.C. July 1780.

He closed the case slowly, the latch giving a faint click as it shut.

Nicholas held it for a long moment in his hand, then wrapped it again in the silk she had chosen and placed it deep in his sea chest, beneath his spare coat and the oiled canvas bag that held his most private effects.

By noon on the 21st of July 1780, *Lynx* was well clear of the coast, her sails drawing clean as she turned northwest into open water. Ahead lay Gibraltar—over fifteen hundred leagues distant. Behind, the continent faded into haze. And somewhere behind that, in a different world, Caroline Carlisle had watched his ship depart.

CHAPTER TWELVE

The morning of the 12th of August 1780 found *Lynx* cutting through Atlantic swells under a sky of flawless blue, her sails drawing perfectly in a steady northeasterly breeze. Captain Walsh stood on the quarterdeck, his compact figure silhouetted against the horizon as he watched the morning sun glint on distant sails, three merchantmen bound southward off the larboard beam, their identity still uncertain at this range.

"Deck there! Sail ho, two points off the starboard bow!"

Less than an hour later as the ships courses drew together, Nicholas raised his glass toward the new sighting. After three weeks of solitary sailing since leaving Luanda, any encounter merited careful attention. The French and Spanish navies prowled these waters with increasing boldness as the war expanded across the globe.

"Mr. Cruwys, your assessment?" Walsh called, his tone carrying the familiar sharpness that demanded precision.

Nicholas steadied himself against the ship's motion, focusing his glass with practiced ease. The distant vessel resolved gradually, three masts, her sail plan distinctive, her lines unmistakably military.

"Frigate, sir. Approximately a league distant." He paused, studying the set of her sails. "I believe she's British, sir. Her cut is familiar."

Walsh moved to join him, extending his own glass. After a moment's observation, he nodded. "Indeed. *Minerva*, I shouldn't wonder. Thirty-two guns, Captain Harris. She was at Gibraltar when we departed for India."

The identification proved accurate. Within the hour, the frigate had closed sufficiently for signals to be exchanged, confirming her identity as *HMS Minerva*, three days out from Gibraltar on patrol southward. Although carrying dispatches, she hove to, and Captain Walsh ordered a boat prepared, and with a last glance at Nicholas as watch officer, departed to meet with Captain Harris.

"She's a fine-looking ship," remarked Harrington, who had appeared at his side. "Newer than most in the Mediterranean squadron."

"Indeed, sir" Nicholas agreed. "Built '78 at Woolwich, if I recall correctly. One of the first with copper sheathing from the start."

"You've a good memory for ships."

Harrington's gaze was appraising. "Twenty ships of the line at Gibraltar when we left, plus frigates and smaller vessels. The

Spanish have been blockading since last summer. Should make for an interesting arrival."

Nicholas nodded, understanding the implication. Their return to Gibraltar would not be the peaceful conclusion to their voyage that some might have expected. The great rock fortress, Britain's sentinel at the entrance to the Mediterranean, had been under siege by Spanish forces for over a year. While naval supremacy allowed the garrison to be supplied, the situation remained precarious.

"At least we're bringing good news," Nicholas said. "News of the successful convoy and the capture of two French warships should be welcome."

Walsh returned an hour later, his expression thoughtful as he climbed back aboard *Lynx*.

"Captain Harris confirms the Spanish blockade continues," he announced once he had gathered his officers in his cabin. "Ten Spanish ships of the line maintain station in the Bay of Algeciras, with frigates patrolling further out. However, as we heard at the Cape, Admiral Rodney relieved the garrison in January with a substantial convoy and defeated a Spanish squadron in the process. Supplies are adequate for the moment."

He unfolded a chart of the approaches to Gibraltar, spreading it across the table. "Our orders remain unchanged," Walsh continued. "We are to proceed to Gibraltar, delivering our dispatches before continuing to England. However, Captain Harris advises that we traverse the Straits at night to avoid the Spanish patrols."

Three days later, as Nicholas stood on *Lynx*'s quarterdeck supervising the midshipmen during their noon sights, the masthead lookout hailed, "On deck, sail ho! Four sail two points on the starboard bow!"

At a gesture from Walsh, Nicholas slung his telescope and climbed swiftly to the maintop. He moved with the ease of long habit, his hands sure on the shrouds, his feet in the ratlines, his balance unthinking—he had grown used to the heights in his earliest days at sea, when the masthead was both duty and refuge. There was a clarity aloft, a solitude he valued: the wind sharper, the world laid out cleanly beneath.

Settling himself, he raised his glass and scanned the horizon. For a moment, he saw only the empty sweep of the Atlantic, but then, as the ships rose on a swell, they came into view—four large vessels in line ahead, their sails billowing white against the blue.

Sliding down the backstay, he landed lightly on deck and reported, "Four ships of the line, sir. Appear to be ours—three seventy-fours and a sixty-four. Westerly course."

Walsh gave a slight nod, the flicker of approval passing across his features. "Well, well. A tidy squadron."

Later, after signals confirmed the ships were friendly, Harrington and Nicholas stood side by side, each preoccupied, but comfortable in their shared silence—a marked change from the formal reserve of their early days aboard *Lynx*.

"I've been meaning to ask you," Harrington said at last, his voice pitched for Nicholas alone, "about your reckoning methods, when conditions prevent precise sights. I've seen your figures in the navigation log. Your estimates tend to prove unusually consistent once conditions improve."

It was a straightforward question, offered without condescension, and Nicholas appreciated it as such. "I use the Admiralty's standard forms, but also some techniques I learned in the Pacific. The island navigators adjust instinctively for a vessel's motion. Applied to our dead reckoning, those corrections seem to narrow the margin of error."

"Fascinating," Harrington said, his usual reserve giving way to clear interest. "Would you show me? I pride myself on accuracy, but there's something in your approach that's worth studying."

"I'd be happy to," Nicholas replied, surprised, and pleased.

"Excellent," Harrington said, allowing himself a slight smile. "Tonight perhaps, after the evening watch. I've a bottle of Madeira still sound from Bombay. Seems the right accompaniment."

They reached the Straits two nights later, having maintained steady way despite variable winds. Nicholas stood the middle watch as *Lynx* slipped between the ancient boundaries—Gibraltar to larboard, the darker mass of North Africa to starboard. The night was clear, the quarter moon giving just enough light to navigate by, while still offering a measure of concealment.

He had never passed through the Straits before. Cook's expedition had sailed directly from England to the Cape without touching the Mediterranean. Now, as he watched the Rock loom larger, he felt a curious tightness in his chest. More even than the Cape, Gibraltar marked his return to European waters. The Pacific, Tahiti and Bora Bora, Atea, the long arc across the Indian Ocean—all of it felt impossibly far behind, like a dream losing colour upon waking.

Yet Caroline's gift was with him still. The small silver case remained in his coat pocket, its weight a private anchor. He had taken to carrying it during his watches—not as a talisman, but as a kind of bearing. At night, when the cabin was dark and the sea whispered, he would open it and study the painted image within, letting memory rise.

Sometimes he saw Atea and Bora Bora. The lagoon at dusk; their laughter; the hush of the surf's voice on the reef as the sun slipped down upon another of those seemingly endless days of contentment. For a year they had lived beyond the reach of time or care, the days flowing uncounted, unmarred—until the end came, sudden and complete. Both had been under twenty, and it seemed, looking back, as though on those distant South Pacific shores they had slipped the world's grasp for a little while—into something older, more whole. Now, the memory receded—not gone, but turning slowly to amber, made more remote with each passing month, and with each bitter— or indeed merely ordinary—encounter with life. And with its fading came a quiet certainty: that such grace would never be granted twice.

Other times, it was Caroline's voice he heard—measured and wholly self-possessed, or the feel of her hand as she passed him the wrapped case, her fingers cool against his own, or of their kiss and embrace as they parted. His time with her belonged to something else entirely: not a vanished paradise, but a worldly future not yet made. Where Atea had met him in joy and instinct, Caroline engaged him in intellect and precision. She asked questions without preamble, listened without filling the silence, and expected him to answer without evasion. With her, he found himself reaching beyond the confines of duty and naval discipline—toward something more considered, more examined. It surprised him how both women—both moments—could inhabit the same small silver object she had entrusted to him: one holding all he had lost, the other all he might yet become.

Dawn broke as they approached Gibraltar, the eastern sky ablaze with colour that gradually revealed the vast limestone promontory. The Rock rose over 1,300 feet from the sea, its near-vertical faces imposing even at a distance. At its summit and on its flanks, Nicholas could just make out gun emplacements and fortifications—centuries of military effort etched into stone. The town of Gibraltar nestled at the western base, protected by walls and bastions. Despite the early hour, the harbour bustled with activity: warships at anchor, supply vessels loading and unloading, boats moving with the precise choreography of naval routine.

Across the bay, farther west, lay the Spanish mainland and the town of Algeciras. Through his glass, Nicholas could see the Spanish fleet at anchor—ships of the line flying the red-and-gold ensign of Spain, a visible reminder that the siege was no formality.

Lynx anchored in Rosia Bay, the protected anchorage south of the main harbour. Almost at once, a boat approached from shore carrying a lieutenant from the Port Admiral's office, requesting Captain Walsh's immediate presence.

"Mr. Cruwys, you'll accompany me," Walsh said as he prepared to go ashore. "Bring the dispatch case. Mr. Chester—see to the ship's needs. I'll arrange fresh water and provisions after I've reported to the Admiral."

The pull to shore in gave Nicholas his first close view of Gibraltar. Evidence of the siege was everywhere—expanded fortifications, new gun positions, military camps in places that had likely once been gardens or public squares. Soldiers in red and blue moved briskly along the waterfront. Civilians passed among them with the air of people who had grown used to war.

The Port Admiral's headquarters stood in a broad stone building near the dockyard. Royal Marines snapped to attention as Walsh and Nicholas approached. Inside, clerks and officers moved briskly through narrow corridors until they were shown into a spacious office overlooking the harbour.

Rear Admiral Sir Thomas Eldridge, newly appointed to the Gibraltar station, was a man in his mid-fifties with the weathered look of one who had spent much of his life at sea. His manner was brisk but not unfriendly.

"Captain Walsh, welcome to Gibraltar. Your timing is fortunate—we've had no direct news from India since the last courier brought word of your convoy's departure."

Walsh bowed slightly. "Thank you, Admiral. May I present Lieutenant Nicholas Cruwys, formerly of *Resolution* under Captain Cook, now serving as my third lieutenant."

Eldridge's brows rose at the name. "Cook's expedition? I was sorry to hear of his fate. A tremendous loss to the Service. I've heard scattered reports from merchants—*Resolution* and *Discovery* seen at the Cape some months ago, but nothing since. Of course, they're not fast ships, and I daresay they've taken some wear."

"Indeed, sir," Nicholas said, feeling the familiar pang at any mention of Cook.

"Lieutenant Cruwys was separated from *Resolution* before Captain Cook's death," Walsh explained. "Shipwrecked in the Society Islands, and only recently returned to the service—via India."

"Extraordinary," Eldridge said, turning his full attention to Nicholas. "We'll have to hear that tale in full, Lieutenant. But first—your dispatches?"

Nicholas stepped forward and presented the sealed leather case, which contained official correspondence from Admiral Ames, Commodore Hartley, Governor Hornby, Admiral Hughes, and senior officials of the East India Company. Eldridge broke the seals and began scanning the contents with the practiced efficiency of a man long accustomed to absorbing vital information quickly.

"Excellent news about the convoy," he said after a few moments. "The capture of two French warships will be well received at the Admiralty—especially now."

He looked up, his tone sharpening. "You should know the situation here has changed since your departure. Spain entered the war last June, as you may have been informed before sailing. The Dutch have not yet declared war, but the situation grows more precarious."

Walsh nodded. "Aye, sir. Captain Harris of *Minerva* mentioned as much."

"Indeed. Our boarding of neutral vessels carrying naval stores to French ports—technically legal under treaty—has provoked formal protest. The Russians have proposed a League of Armed Neutrality, and the Dutch may well join it. Should that happen, we'll face a broader coalition, and our naval forces are already stretched."

Eldridge turned to a large map of Europe and the Atlantic displayed on the wall. "Currently, the Channel Fleet under Admiral Darby is maintaining a precarious blockade of Brest. Admiral Rodney commands in the Leeward Islands, where he is engaged with the French under de Guichen. Meanwhile, we maintain a constant watch here against the Spanish, who would dearly love to recapture Gibraltar."

This strategic overview, delivered with professional clarity, painted a sobering picture. Britain, traditionally dominant at sea, now found itself fighting to maintain control of vital shipping lanes against multiple opponents.

"And Canada, sir?" Nicholas asked, thinking of Cook's original mission to find the Northwest Passage.

"Holding, though precariously. Quebec remains in our hands, but American privateers harass our supply lines. General Clinton maintains New York, but the situation in the southern colonies is fluid." Eldridge sighed, the weight of global conflict evident in his bearing. "Not the empire you left behind in '76, Lieutenant."

Eldridge glanced toward the window, where the Rock loomed in sunlight above the anchorage.

"There are signs," he said quietly, "that something larger may be in motion. Spanish activity at Algeciras has increased—more troops, more floating batteries under construction. And French engineers have been observed in consultation with their staff."

He tapped a finger lightly on the edge of the dispatch case. "We cannot be certain of their intentions, but intelligence suggests a coordinated assault may be planned before autumn."

Nicholas listened in silence, aware that this was the edge of a far more complex war.

The admiral returned to his desk, shuffling through the dispatches once more. "Captain Walsh, *Lynx* will be required to proceed to England as soon as reprovisioning is complete. The Admiralty must receive these dispatches without delay. I'll provide additional correspondence regarding the situation here for delivery to Lord Sandwich."

"Aye, sir. We can be ready to sail within forty-eight hours."

Eldridge nodded approvingly. "You've made very good time from Luanda. Come to dinner tonight at the Governor's. Both of you."

As Walsh and Nicholas exchanged a glance, the admiral added something that made Nicholas's heart skip.

"Incidentally, Captain Trevenen was asking after any word of *Resolution*. I believe he has a nephew who was a midshipman aboard her. You may wish to contact him."

Nicholas felt a surge of surprise—and something else, warmer and less easily named.

"Captain Matthew Trevenen, sir? Indeed I do. He's the reason I joined the Navy. His ship was in Plymouth when I visited with my father, and he showed me *Pallas*, his frigate at the time. I've not seen him since before joining *Resolution*. His nephew James and I entered the Academy together, and joined the expedition side by side."

"Well," Eldridge said, mildly amused, "he's risen in the world since then. Commands a seventy-four now—*Thunderer*—and has distinguished himself in several actions. Good family, the Trevenens. Old naval stock. I shall inform him of your arrival. I imagine he'll wish to speak with you."

The Governor's residence stood along Main Street—a substantial building whose elegant façade masked the military headquarters that occupied much of its interior. Nicholas arrived promptly at seven, freshly bathed and dressed in his best uniform. Captain Walsh was already present, deep in conversation with Admiral Eldridge and several army officers, their red coats providing a splash of colour amid the prevailing naval blue.

"Ah, Mr. Cruwys," Walsh said as Nicholas approached. "Allow me to present you to Governor Fenwick."

George Augustus Fenwick, Governor of Gibraltar, was a spare, upright man in his sixties whose military bearing remained evident despite his civilian dress. A veteran of several campaigns, he had earned a reputation for both strategic brilliance and humane leadership during the ongoing siege.

"Lieutenant Cruwys, welcome," the Governor said. His Scottish accent, though softened by years of English service, remained distinct. "Admiral Eldridge tells me you served with the unfortunate Captain Cook. A great loss to navigation."

"Indeed, sir—though I was separated from the expedition before his death."

"So I understand. A remarkable journey you've had. You must tell us more over dinner."

The gathering was smaller than Nicholas had expected—perhaps twenty guests in all, mostly senior naval and military officers, with a few civilians from Gibraltar's permanent administration.

Lady Fenwick, the Governor's wife, was a formidable Scotswoman whose talents had clearly been turned to maintaining standards of civility under siege. When Nicholas complimented the meal—remarkably varied given the circumstances—she smiled with cheerful defiance.

"We manage tolerably well, Lieutenant," she said. "The Spanish blockade is not so effective as they might wish, and Admiral Rodney's relief earlier this year resupplied us admirably. Besides"—with a glint in her eye—"a Scottish household wastes nothing. Siege or no siege."

Throughout the meal, conversation ranged from military affairs to the state of London society to the war's progress in North America. Captain Walsh answered most of the questions concerning India—naval logistics, convoy organization, and the East India Company's shifting priorities, but Nicholas was drawn in as well, particularly when discussion turned to the French presence in the Indian Ocean and conditions at Calcutta. His remarks—carefully phrased and offered with appropriate modesty—were well received, especially by the younger officers and colonial officials eager for a more immediate perspective on distant waters.

As the dinner concluded and guests began to withdraw, Governor Fenwick sought him out again.

"I understand from Captain Walsh that you'll be sailing for England within days," he said. "When you reach London, you'll find it changed. The war has tested not only our arms but our institutions, and the patience of the people. Keep that in mind when you report to the Admiralty."

"I will, sir. And thank you for your hospitality."

"Good voyage, Lieutenant. Britain needs her seasoned officers now more than ever."

Nicholas left the Governor's residence with these words echoing in his mind. The weight he carried had shifted subtly. It was no longer just about a posting, or dispatches, or a commission. He was returning to a country fighting not only for its empire—but, in some deeper sense, for its place in the world.

He slept fitfully that night, his dreams a confused jumble of images: Atea standing on a beach in Bora Bora; Caroline looking back from a departing boat; Cook on the quarterdeck of *Resolution*; and, strangest of all, himself in captain's uniform, commanding a ship whose name he could not read, sailing into waters cloaked in fog and shadow.

Dawn found him already awake, standing on *Lynx*'s quarterdeck as the first light touched the summit of the Rock. The harbour was coming to life—boats moving between ships, sentries changing on the batteries, fishermen setting out despite the risk of Spanish patrols.

"Early riser, Mr. Cruwys?" Walsh emerged from below, looking rested and alert despite the previous evening's engagements.

"Yes, sir. I was observing the harbour defences."

Walsh nodded. "Impressive, aren't they? The Spanish have been trying to crack this nut for over a year. Gibraltar may be the most heavily fortified position in the world."

They watched as a gun crew drilled below, their movements practiced and deliberate, the rhythm of siege life reduced to routine.

"The admiral has confirmed we sail tomorrow," Walsh added. "First light, weather permitting. The harbour master has been instructed to prioritise our provisioning."

"Very good, sir. I'll ensure everything is properly stowed."

"And I understand Captain Trevenen has invited us to dine aboard *Thunderer* this evening?"

Nicholas was surprised Walsh already knew of the invitation, which had arrived by boat just after dawn.

"Yes, sir. Captain Trevenen was kind enough to invite us both. I intended to request permission this morning."

Walsh's expression was unreadable. "Permission granted. Trevenen is a respected senior post-captain, and not far from his flag. His interest in you is... notable. Indeed," Walsh said evenly. "An officer's connections often shape his career as much as his competence. Trevenen's support could mean a great deal."

As dusk approached, Nicholas prepared for dinner aboard *Thunderer*. The ship of the line lay anchored near the harbour mouth, her broad beam and towering rigging casting a long shadow across the water. At seventy-four guns, she represented the backbone of the Royal Navy—powerful enough to stand in the line of battle against the most powerful enemy vessels, yet agile enough to operate independently on extended station.

The boat ride across gave Nicholas time to reflect. Captain Matthew Trevenen had been a figure of near-mythic stature in his childhood: tall, broad-shouldered, with the wiry strength and unselfconscious authority that seemed to run in the family. Their first meeting in Plymouth—when the captain had shown a curious eleven-year-old around his frigate, *Pallas*—had left an impression that had never faded. Now, nearly ten years later, Nicholas was returning as an officer in his own right.

As they neared *Thunderer*, Nicholas studied her with professional appreciation. Despite the strain of blockade duty, she was immaculate: her black and yellow sides freshly painted, rigging newly blackened. The figurehead—a warrior hurling a thunderbolt—stood proud at the bow.

"Impressive vessel," Walsh said beside him. "Trevenen runs a tight ship, by all accounts."

The reception as they came aboard was formal and correct. The bosun's pipes shrilled, marines presented arms, and the officer of the watch greeted them with due ceremony. They were escorted below to the great cabin, its broad stern windows framing the harbour and, beyond it, the Spanish coast.

Captain Matthew Trevenen stood waiting—a tall, broad man in his late forties, his frame still strong, though silver now showed at the temples. His face, lean and weathered, bore the stamp of command without ostentation. There was an ease in his bearing—a balance of physical presence and calm authority—that Nicholas remembered from childhood. He wore his uniform not as display, but as second skin.

"Captain Walsh," Trevenen greeted, extending his hand. "Welcome aboard *Thunderer*. I appreciate your indulging my invitation on such short notice."

Walsh shook the offered hand with appropriate deference to the senior captain. "The honour is mine, sir."

Trevenen acknowledged the compliment with a slight nod before turning his attention to Nicholas. For a moment, he studied the younger man with an intensity that seemed to peel away the years, seeing beyond the lieutenant's uniform to the boy he had once briefly encountered. He saw a confident young lieutenant, nearly as tall as himself, who nevertheless carried an air of experience and gravity beyond his twenty years.

"Lieutenant," he said finally, his voice carrying the distinctive Cornish lilt that time and service had not entirely erased. "You've grown somewhat since we last met in Plymouth harbour. Though I'd have recognised you nonetheless—you have your grandfather's bearing, the old squire."

"Captain Trevenen," Nicholas replied, deeply moved by this recognition. "It's an honour to meet you again after so many years. Your example was instrumental in my decision to join the service."

A smile briefly transformed Trevenen's stern features. "So I understand from my nephew James. He wrote to me from the Academy that Richard Cruwys's younger son had joined him there, inspired by a ship tour I scarcely remembered giving. The responsibility weighs heavily in retrospect."

His tone was dry, but there was genuine warmth beneath it, the satisfaction of a senior officer seeing the fruits of casual mentorship years later.

"Please, gentlemen, be seated," Trevenen continued, gesturing toward a table already set for dinner. "We have much to discuss, and I am aware you sail on the morning tide, so we will combine conversation with sustenance."

The dinner itself proved excellent despite the limitations imposed by the siege. Trevenen, like many senior captains, maintained his own cook and had clearly devoted considerable resources to ensuring his table reflected his status. The wine was of particular quality—French vintages that had likely been captured from enemy vessels, now served with ironic appreciation to British officers.

Conversation initially followed the expected pattern—professional discussions of the strategic situation, the Spanish blockade, and the broader war effort. Walsh and Trevenen exchanged observations on naval tactics and fleet dispositions with the ease of experienced officers, while Nicholas contributed when appropriate, conscious of his junior status yet included by Trevenen's occasional direct questions.

It was only after the main course had been cleared and port circulated that Trevenen steered the conversation toward more personal matters.

"So, Nicholas," he said, leaning back slightly in his chair, "Tell me of your time with my nephew aboard *Resolution* under Captain Cook. A remarkable expedition by all accounts, though with a tragic conclusion."

"Yes, sir," Nicholas replied. "James and I were midshipmen together. He was an excellent officer—quick-witted and naturally skilled at languages, which proved invaluable during our interactions with the Pacific islanders."

"He wrote to me of your separation from the expedition," Trevenen continued. "He was most distressed you had been left behind to survey Bora Bora and subsequently lost contact with the ship. You may not know that after the storm that struck following your departure from Tahiti, Cook took *Resolution* to Bora Bora to search for you, and sailed the waters between the islands. Though finding no trace, he and James maintained hope that you might have survived."

"I heard later from the islanders that *Resolution* returned to Bora Bora," Nicholas said quietly. "But I never knew how thoroughly they searched."

There was a long silence. This revelation touched Nicholas deeply. He had often wondered how his disappearance had been received by his shipmates, particularly by Captain Cook and by James, who had been his closest friend aboard. That Cook had searched for him even more diligently than he supposed rekindled and deepened the sorrow about Cook's death. The older men watched the emotions play across his face gravely.

"James was kind to remain concerned, sir. Our friendship at the Academy and aboard *Resolution* was significant to me. We were in sight of Bora Bora when the storm struck and the pahi canoe carrying myself and the quartermaster who was my companion, Markham, was blown eastward as far as the Tuamotus. All but two of the native crew survived, however, and after repairs we sailed back to Tahiti, learning then that the expedition had sailed only a few weeks before. Have you news of him? Or of *Resolution* and *Discovery*?"

Trevenen's expression grew somber. "I received a letter from James sent from the Cape of Good Hope on a ship just sailing as he arrived several months ago. He and the expedition are still at sea. *Resolution* and *Discovery* were continuing their journey home, but of course are not the swiftest vessels. James was well, though deeply affected by Cook's death."

Trevenen took a sip of port before continuing. "The news of Cook's death caused quite a stir in London when it reached us. The circumstances, combined with reports of the new discoveries in the Pacific and along the Northwest coast, these matters have captured public imagination despite the ongoing war."

Walsh, who had been listening with interest, spoke up. "Do you anticipate Midshipman Trevenen will receive advancement upon his return?"

"I would expect so," Trevenen replied, with a hint of family pride. "The Admiralty generally recognizes the service of officers on such significant voyages. James's skills and experience should position him well."

The conversation continued, shifting to Nicholas's own remarkable journey—from the Society Islands through his time with the Portuguese trader Silva, his service in India, and the eventful voyage home, including the capture and command of *Growler*. Trevenen listened with genuine interest, occasionally asking incisive questions that revealed his own extensive experience in distant waters.

"You've had an education few officers receive, lieutenant," he observed as Nicholas concluded his account. "The true measure of an officer is forged through experiences, adaptation to unexpected circumstances, leadership under pressure, exposure to different worlds and ways of thinking."

Nicholas acknowledged this with a nod. "Yes, sir, the Pacific taught me lessons no textbook could contain, sir. As did my time aboard Silva's trading vessel."

"Ah yes, the Portuguese trader." Walsh's eyes took on a knowing glint. "Your facility with the sword and pistol, skills apparently honed during that period, were demonstrated admirably during our engagement with the French privateers." He turned to Trevenen, "His boarding of the enemy vessel was executed with particular skill, I must say."

"So I understand from Admiral Eldridge's summary of your reports. You did the lieutenant a great honor in trusting him with command of *Growler* at such a young age. A trust it seems he repaid well." Trevenen studied Nicholas thoughtfully. "Which brings me to a matter I wished to discuss. Your imminent return to England presents certain considerations for your future career."

Nicholas felt a flicker of surprise at the directness of the approach—particularly with Walsh present.

"The Admiralty will naturally take interest in your experiences with Cook's expedition," Trevenen continued. "Your observations of Pacific navigation, island cultures, and the charts you've preserved—they hold scientific and strategic value well beyond your personal narrative. How you present that information may influence what follows."

"I intend to report fully and honestly, sir," Nicholas said carefully.

"As you should." Trevenen leaned forward, his tone shifting. "But you should also understand the political context awaiting you. Lord Sandwich, one of the principal patrons of Cook's voyages, remains First Lord—but his position has weakened. The war has broadened beyond initial expectations, and with the probable loss of America, questions of naval leadership now echo in Parliament."

Walsh nodded. "The political winds in London shift with every dispatch from America or the Indies. Today's sound decision becomes tomorrow's miscalculation when fortunes change at sea."

"Precisely." Trevenen's expression grew more serious. "In such a climate, your association with Cook's final voyage—a mission that captured the public imagination before war overtook such ambitions—may carry weight. It distinguishes you from the countless lieutenants whose service, however honourable, lacks such connection. And for now—though this may soon change—it calls back to what the Navy, the Government, and the country once celebrated."

Nicholas saw what was being offered: that his past might be positioned not only as experience, but as capital. A way to distinguish himself in a crowded field.

But something in him resisted.

"Sir, with respect, Captain Cook valued accuracy and service above advancement," he said. "I'd not wish to dishonour his memory by seeking advantage from our association."

Trevenen's features softened slightly. "Well said, Nicholas. And precisely the sentiment I'd expect from one who sailed with him. But there's no dishonour in ensuring your work is seen. Cook himself knew the value of having his discoveries recognised and recorded."

His tone turned more paternal.

"When you reach London, call on Sir Joseph Banks at the Royal Society. He sailed with Cook on the first voyage, and his interest in Pacific navigation remains strong. Your account of the Society Islands and their techniques would interest him, and his influence is not inconsiderable, in scientific or naval circles."

"I shall do so, sir," Nicholas replied, recognising the counsel for what it was: wise, and meant in true regard.

Trevenen stood, went to his desk, and returned with a sealed packet.

"This contains letters of introduction—to Sir Joseph, and to Admiral Keppel, who now sits on the Board. They may be of use when you arrive."

Nicholas accepted the packet with surprise—and gratitude. "Thank you, sir. This is most generous."

"It is no more than is due. The service needs officers who have seen past the narrow rim of Europe. The world is changing, Nicholas And the next century will not be shaped by those who never left Portsmouth."

As the evening drew to a close, Trevenen suggested a brief walk on *Thunderer*'s upper deck. The night air was pleasantly cool after the warmth of the cabin, and the lights of Gibraltar glittered against the looming shadow of the Rock. The three officers stood at the rail, gazing toward the Spanish coast, where the occasional flicker of campfires marked the positions of the besieging forces.

As they made ready to depart, Trevenen drew Nicholas slightly aside, speaking in a lower tone that would not carry to Walsh, who was engaged in conversation with *Thunderer*'s first lieutenant—an old acquaintance.

"I've watched your progress from a distance, Nicholas," he said, the return to first name marking a shift to something more personal. "When you came aboard *Pallas* in Plymouth, I saw something in your manner—a quality of attention, of genuine curiosity about the sea—that suggested promise. James's letters from the Academy, and later from *Resolution*, confirmed that impression. I was relieved to learn you survived and had returned with such credit."

Nicholas was deeply moved to learn that Trevenen had followed his career. "I'm honoured by your attention, sir. Your example that day in Plymouth truly did set my course."

"We never know when a small gesture may shape another man's path." Trevenen smiled faintly, the lines at the corners of his eyes deepening. "Remember that as you rise in the service. The midshipman observing you today may command a fleet tomorrow."

As Nicholas and Walsh returned to their boat, the older captain's parting words stayed with him:

"Safe voyage, Lieutenant Cruwys. I expect we shall hear more of your career in the years to come."

The ride back to *Lynx* was quiet, each officer absorbed in his thoughts. Only as they neared the ship did Walsh speak.

"You've made a powerful friend in Captain Trevenen," he observed, his tone even. "Such connections can prove invaluable in our service—particularly for officers without substantial family influence."

"His interest was unexpected, sir," Nicholas replied honestly. "I would never have presumed on so brief a childhood acquaintance."

Walsh studied him in the darkness. "I suspect it's more than that. Trevenen sees quality where it lies. That's the mark of a senior officer worth the name. His patronage is not lightly given, nor should it be lightly regarded."

As Nicholas stepped back aboard *Lynx*, his mind was full of crosscurrents. The unexpected connection with Trevenen offered prospects he had never imagined, yet brought with it a sense of obligation. What had been, only hours before, a solitary return to England now carried the weight of expectation, and the quiet knowledge that being seen meant being measured.

The wind had held steady, and *Lynx* surged westward up the Channel under full topsails, her hull alive with motion and purpose. Portsmouth lay no more than a day ahead.

The voyage from Gibraltar had been remarkably swift—twelve days since clearing the Straits under cover of darkness on the 29th of August 1780, their dispatches safely aboard, and the Spanish blockade evaded without incident. Nicholas had stood the middle watch that night, and the sight of the Rock by moonlight remained etched in memory.

His thoughts had grown heavier with each degree of latitude. The Straits, the Bay of Biscay, and now the Channel, each nautical milestone brought him closer to a future he could not clearly envision. Gibraltar had not lacked for news. The officers and officials he'd met ashore had painted a vivid picture of Britain's embattled position. Admiral Eldridge, Governor Fenwick, and others had spoken openly: of the siege, of French and Spanish threats, of the widening conflict in India and the Americas, of strained alliances and uncertain futures. Nicholas had absorbed it all in silence—and had come to understand that he felt no desire, nor capacity, to turn away from the Navy. Not when Britain stood imperiled on so many fronts.

The morning sky broke golden behind them, gilding the sails and drawing shouts from aloft as land was sighted, a low green smudge to the north that slowly resolved into the familiar contours of the Isle of Wight. England, at last.

Captain Walsh appeared on deck, his compact figure radiating the quiet confidence that had defined his command throughout their long passage. He stepped over to the first lieutenant.

"A fair landfall, Mr. Chester," Walsh remarked. "We've made good time from Gibraltar."

"Indeed, sir. Twelve days is remarkable for this season."

Walsh nodded, eyes on the approaching coast. "The dispatches we carry will be welcome at the Admiralty. The safe arrival of our convoy, despite French interference, proves we still command the sea lanes that matter."

By noon on September 10th, the masts of the dockyard came into view, and *HMS Lynx* rounded to her anchorage. Portsmouth lay sprawling before them, the beating heart of His Majesty's Navy. Forests of masts filled the harbour, their spars etched against the pale sky like the lattice of some immense machine. Ships of the line rode high at their moorings; brigs and cutters darted between, while the cries of stevedores and the shrill calls of bosuns' whistles rang out from the jetties. The air reeked gloriously of tar, rope, smoke, and salt—each scent a note in the great maritime chord of empire.

Nicholas surveyed the scene with mixed emotions. Over three years had passed since he had sailed from Plymouth aboard *Resolution*, full of youthful excitement and naval ambition. Now he returned not merely changed, but defined: by shipwreck, by command, by loss, and by encounters that had expanded his understanding of duty beyond charts and signal books.

He knew now that his heart, his loyalty, and his ambition lay within the service. The Navy had claimed him utterly, not by coercion, but by revelation. And yet even as that clarity settled in him, his thoughts turned to Caroline: to her courage, her restraint, and the brief depth of feeling they had shared. Whatever paths awaited, he would carry that memory forward, not as a burden, but as something deliberate, and still unfinished.

CHAPTER THIRTEEN

On the evening of the sixth day in port, Harrington invited Nicholas to join him for dinner at the Three Crowns, a respectable establishment favored by naval officers that stood a comfortable distance from the more riotous environs of the Point. The invitation represented a subtle shift in their relationship, no longer simply the second and third lieutenants of the same vessel, but two officers whose shared experiences had fostered a deeper connection.

The Three Crowns offered private dining rooms for officers of sufficient rank, and it was in one such chamber, paneled in dark wood and lit by beeswax candles, that Harrington and Nicholas found themselves seated before a table laid with roast mutton, new potatoes, and a bottle of surprisingly good claret.

"To successful voyages," Harrington proposed, raising his glass once they were settled.

"And safe returns," Nicholas added, completing the toast.

They drank, and for a moment silence hung between them—not uncomfortable, but weighted with the unspoken understanding that their service together was likely approaching its end.

"Walsh received word this morning," Harrington said at last, confirming what both had anticipated. "Orders are expected within days. The admiral's secretary was unusually forthcoming—apparently our report on the French privateers collaborating directly with naval vessels in joint command has generated interest at the Admiralty."

Nicholas nodded, unsurprised. It was a dangerous development.

"The Navy needs commanders who can think independently," Harrington continued, studying Nicholas. "Your capture of *Growler* after Hargrove fell—that wasn't merely following orders. It was genuine initiative, as were many decisions made while separated from Walsh's immediate command as part of the convoy escort."

"You would have done the same," Nicholas replied, uncomfortable with praise that seemed to elevate his actions above those of his fellow officers.

Harrington smiled slightly. "Perhaps. But I've had the advantage of years you haven't, time to observe, to learn the unwritten codes of naval service. You've compressed that learning into months, while simultaneously adapting to European ways after years in the Pacific. It's rather remarkable when one considers it objectively."

Nicholas was struck by the perception in Harrington's assessment. The second lieutenant had always maintained a certain reserve, his aristocratic background occasionally creating distance between them. Yet beneath that polished exterior lay a keen observer of character, one who had apparently been taking Nicholas's measure throughout their service together.

"I've learned as much from watching you and Captain Walsh as from any of my experiences abroad," Nicholas said honestly. "The way you maintain discipline without resorting to extremes, how you balance the Navy's demands with the men's needs, these are lessons no island navigation could teach."

"Naval service is its own peculiar world," Harrington agreed, "with customs as rigid and intricate as any society ashore. Speaking of which—" he paused, refilling their glasses, "—my family keeps a house in London, in Grosvenor Square. Not grand by some standards, but comfortable enough. Should your orders take you to the capital, you would be welcome to stay rather than wasting your pay on lodgings."

The offer caught Nicholas by surprise. While friendships between officers were common, such hospitality extended beyond the usual professional courtesy.

"That's most generous," he said carefully. "Though I wouldn't wish to impose."

"Not at all. The house stands empty most of the time except for the servants. My father visits when Parliament sits, but that's not until November. My mother and sisters remain in Sussex until the Season. You'd be doing the staff a service by giving them something to occupy their time." Harrington's tone was light, but the offer itself reflected genuine regard.

"Besides, I expect London may be something of a shock after your travels. Having a familiar face—or at least a reliable address—might prove useful."

"Then I accept with gratitude," Nicholas said, recognizing the practical wisdom in Harrington's suggestion. "Though my orders remain uncertain."

"Not for much longer, I suspect. There was another piece of gossip from the admiral's secretary—apparently I'm to be promoted to Master and Commander, with *Falcon*, an 18-gun sloop currently finishing repairs at Chatham, as my first independent command." Harrington's expression remained controlled, but there was no mistaking the satisfaction in his eyes.

"Congratulations," Nicholas said warmly, raising his glass. "Most well-deserved. *Falcon* will be fortunate to have you."

"We'll see how fortunate she feels after meeting the French," Harrington replied with characteristic dry humor. "The Channel is lively these days, with privateers off Cherbourg and Calais growing increasingly bold."

The remainder of their dinner passed in comfortable conversation—discussions of naval strategy, reminiscences of their voyage from India, and occasional diversions into matters of mutual interest outside the service. Nicholas found himself appreciating anew the quiet competence that had made Harrington such an effective second and first lieutenant, and understanding how those same qualities would serve him well in command.

Three days later, Captain Walsh summoned Nicholas to his cabin, where several official documents lay spread across his desk.

"Ah, Mr. Cruwys. I've just received confirmation of my new appointment." He indicated one of the papers. "Post-captain, with command of *Triton*, a 28-gun frigate currently completing construction at Sheerness. After some weeks of leave I will take command to oversee her final fitting-out and select her officers."

"Congratulations, sir," Nicholas said sincerely. "Most well-deserved."

Walsh inclined his head in acknowledgment. "The service rewards results, Mr. Cruwys—as you'll discover. Which brings me to your situation." He picked up another letter. "The Admiralty has taken note of your experience with Cook's expedition and your subsequent journey. They are particularly interested in your observations of the Society Islands and the navigational techniques you recorded."

"I see, sir," Nicholas said, uncertain where the conversation was leading.

"You are to report to the Admiralty in London without delay," Walsh continued, consulting the letter and handing Nicholas a sealed packet. "These are your orders. I understand—unofficially—that several members of the Board wish to speak with you directly regarding your observations."

Nicholas accepted the orders with a mixture of anticipation and unease. An interview at the Admiralty could lead in many directions, a new assignment, certainly, but of what nature?

"Thank you, sir. When am I to depart?"

"Tomorrow's morning post-chaise would be advisable. The dispatches we carried have already stirred interest."

Walsh paused, then added with his usual precision, "I have included my own report on your service aboard *Lynx*, and your conduct during the engagement with the French. It speaks favorably of your judgment and capability—particularly in your command of *Growler*."

The following morning, as he prepared to depart, Harrington met him on deck.

"Remember my offer regarding the London house," he said, pressing a letter and a small brass key into Nicholas's hand. "This will introduce you to Morley, the butler. He'll see to your needs."

"You're most kind," Nicholas replied, genuinely moved by his fellow officer's generosity.

"Kindness has little to do with it," Harrington countered with a slight smile. "Naval officers must look after one another. The service is hard enough without adding unnecessary discomforts. Besides, you'll need a respectable address when you meet with the Admiralty. It creates a certain impression."

Nicholas recognized the practical truth in Harrington's assessment. In the Navy, as in society at large, appearances mattered, not merely in the sense of personal vanity, but as indicators of reliability and standing.

"I shall report on London's current state when you arrive," Nicholas promised. "Though I confess I've never visited the capital before."

"Never?" Harrington seemed genuinely surprised. "Then you're in for an education. London is a world unto itself, one that operates by rules as intricate as any you encountered in the Pacific, though considerably less logical at times."

Nicholas took a post-chaise to London that morning, wincing at the expense—nearly £2, an extravagance for a lieutenant's modest means, but necessary given the urgency of the Admiralty summons or the journey. The coach would make the seventy-mile journey in a day and a half, changing horses at regular intervals.

As the coach rolled forward, Nicholas found himself entering a world entirely new to him. He had visited Plymouth and Portsmouth, of course, but London was quite a different matter. The naval towns were familiar as variations on a theme—the harbour, the dockyard, and the streets of taverns catering to sailors. But London, he knew, was the great metropolis, the center of an empire. Having never seen it, he felt a twinge of uncertainty, a sensation uncomfortably reminiscent of his first days among the Tahitians, when cultural bewilderment had threatened to overwhelm him.

The journey itself proved instructive. As they passed through Hampshire and Surrey, the post-chaise traversed a landscape far removed from the islands of the Pacific or the colonial outposts of India. Here was England—its patchwork of hedged fields, its ancient villages with square-towered churches, its coaching inns and toll gates, all speaking of a civilization whose roots ran deeper than anything he had encountered in his travels. By comparison, the Portuguese settlement at Luanda had seemed like a tenuous European foothold in a vast, indifferent continent.

The coach stopped at small posting houses along the route, where passengers might refresh themselves while horses were changed. At each stop, Nicholas found himself studying his fellow travelers— merchants, country gentlemen, clergymen, occasional army officers—observing their manners and dress with the same attentiveness he had once applied to understanding native customs. It struck him that after nearly four years abroad, he would need to reacquaint himself with the subtleties of English society, particularly the rarefied world of London that he would soon enter.

The sprawl of London announced itself long before they reached its center. First came outlying villages, then suburbs, each merging into the next until the coach was rattling through narrow streets flanked by buildings that blocked out the sky. The sheer scale of it all took Nicholas's breath away—the endless rows of houses, the press of humanity, the dizzying variety of shops and trades being plied in the open. Nowhere in his travels had he seen anything comparable.

Bombay, for all its teeming energy, had lacked this architectural density, this sense of a human settlement compacted by centuries of growth.

Nicholas peered through the coach window at streets clogged with traffic—curricles and hackney coaches jostling with drays and carts, sedan chairs weaving between, and pedestrians of every description thronging the narrow footways. Gentlemen in powdered wigs and silver-buckled shoes strode past chimney sweeps covered in soot; elegant ladies in hooped skirts stood at shopfronts while beggars huddled in doorways nearby. Street vendors hawked their wares in singsong cadences that reminded him, oddly enough, of Tahitian chants, though their words offered hot pies and oysters rather than tales of ancestral heroes.

The smells were overwhelming: horse dung and coal smoke, roasting meat and human waste, perfume and unwashed bodies, all mingling in a pungent symphony that was London's own peculiar fragrance. Above it all hung a haze that softened outlines and dimmed the late afternoon light, a mixture of fog and coal smoke that he would soon come to recognize as the city's perpetual shroud.

They arrived at the Bull and Mouth Inn near St. Paul's as dusk was falling. Oil lamps and candles were being lit in shop windows, creating pools of golden light amid the gathering gloom. Nicholas settled his fare and immediately directed the porter to arrange a hackney coach to transport him and his sea chest to Grosvenor Square, where Harrington's family home awaited. No sense delaying when a comfortable lodging had been so generously offered, and besides, Harrington had been right—a respectable address would serve him well when presenting himself to the Admiralty.

Harrington's London home proved to be a substantial townhouse of pale Portland stone, its façade distinguished by tall sash windows and a porticoed entrance. Nicholas paid the hackney driver, approached the glossy black front door, and knocked with the brass knocker shaped like a dolphin—a subtle reference to the family's naval connections.

The door was opened by a dignified man in his fifties, immaculately dressed in the manner of a superior family servant. Nicholas presented Harrington's letter, explaining who he was. The butler—

Morley, as Harrington had named him—received this information with perfect composure, neither surprised nor particularly impressed, but rather with the air of a man for whom accommodating naval officers was a routine part of his duties.

"Lieutenant Harrington informed us by letter, sir, when you first arrived in port," Morley said, directing a footman to carry Nicholas's sea chest. "We have prepared a room in the east wing. If you would follow me."

Nicholas understood then that Harrington had foreseen his recall to London, and felt even more grateful. It suddenly occurred to him that Walsh too may have had a hand in this—not merely for Nicholas's sake, as he now had to admit to feeling somewhat overwhelmed by London, but also so that Nicholas might reflect well on the ship when called to the Admiralty.

He found himself ushered into a household that operated with the precision of a well-handled ship, each servant knowing their station and duties without apparent need for direction. The house itself was a revelation—not ostentatious like some aristocratic residences, but furnished with the quiet luxury of old money. Polished oak paneling, Turkey carpets, family portraits in gilded frames, and furniture whose quality spoke of generations of careful acquisition rather than fashionable excess.

His room proved to be a spacious bedchamber with adjoining dressing room, furnished with a four-poster bed, a writing desk by the window overlooking a small garden, a comfortable armchair, and a wardrobe large enough to accommodate ten times the modest contents of his sea chest. A fire had been lit in the grate, taking the early autumn chill from the air, and fresh linen lay on the turned-down bed.

"Dinner is served at seven, sir," Morley informed him. "Would you prefer to dine in your room or in the small dining room?"

Nicholas, momentarily overwhelmed by this sudden transition from naval austerity to domestic comfort, chose the latter option, feeling that a solitary meal in such spacious accommodations would only emphasize his status as an interloper.

"Very good, sir. Timms will attend you should you require assistance with your toilet. The household maintains Lieutenant Harrington's custom of informal dress for dinner when no guests are present."

That evening, Nicholas dined alone in what Morley had termed the "small dining room," a chamber that could comfortably seat twelve, with windows overlooking the square and walls adorned with paintings of naval engagements. The meal, served with quiet efficiency by a footman, consisted of clear soup, roast fowl, vegetables from the family's country estate, and a tart of late summer fruits, accompanied by wines from a cellar that clearly contained vintages far superior to those he had encountered in naval service.

As he savored this unexpected luxury, Nicholas reflected on the curious path that had led him from the simple abundance of Bora Bora to this bastion of English aristocratic life. In both places, he found himself navigating cultural codes not entirely his own—accepted but not quite belonging, aware of subtleties that marked him as different from those born to such surroundings.

After dinner, he had mentioned to Morley his intention to report as ordered to the Admiralty the next day. The machinery of Harrington's household had stirred into motion with quiet, almost alarming precision.

He was woken in the morning not by bell or voice but by the gentle clink of porcelain as a tray was set beside the bed. Hot water had been drawn; his linen was pressed; his uniform coat, brushed and set out with gloves and cravat, awaited on a valet's stand he had not noticed the night before.

Before breakfast, a bath—full, steaming, and faintly scented—had been prepared, followed by a shave conducted not by Nicholas himself but by a visiting barber summoned, apparently, for the purpose. One of the footmen, a youth of enviable composure, offered advice on hackney routes to Whitehall, delivered in tones worthy of a master of ceremonies.

Nicholas submitted to it all with a mixture of gratitude and disbelief. He wondered, not for the first time, what the staff imagined of this naval lieutenant suddenly lodged in the east wing. A cousin fallen on hard times? A promising godson? A debt Harrington had finally decided to repay?

He could only hope that, when he reached the Admiralty, he might seem as well turned out as Harrington's household believed he ought to be.

The Admiralty building in Whitehall presented a façade of imposing Georgian symmetry, its Portland stone colonnade flanked by wings that extended back from the street. Above the entrance, a pediment displayed maritime symbols of Britain's naval power—anchors, ropes, and tridents arranged in classical composition. Guards in the scarlet coats of the Marines flanked the entrance, standing impassive despite the occasional drizzle.

Nicholas ascended the steps, feeling a curious blend of anticipation and trepidation. Here, in this building, decisions were made that affected the course of empires and the lives of countless seamen. Here, the movements of fleets were plotted, careers were made or broken, victories celebrated, and losses assessed with the dispassionate calculation of national interest.

The orders had been clear enough, but Nicholas still found them difficult to reconcile with custom. A lieutenant, summoned directly to the Admiralty, to be interviewed not by secretaries or flag captains, but by the Lords themselves, was almost unheard of. Even officers with far longer records, with battle honours or family names, might serve years before such an audience. The Navy was not a democratic institution. It ran on influence, seniority, and the slow accrual of notice. That a young officer with no powerful connections should be called in this way struck Nicholas as improbable. He suspected—correctly—that it was not only his record, but the lingering mystique of Cook's expedition that had stirred interest at the highest level.

Inside, Nicholas presented his reporting orders to the clerk. He was directed to a waiting room where several other officers already sat: a post-captain with the dark complexion of a man recently returned from the West Indies or another tropical station; two commanders engaged in low conversation; and a lieutenant whose arm was supported by a sling, perhaps the result of recent action. None acknowledged Nicholas beyond the briefest nod. Each man was absorbed in his own affairs and calculations.

After an hour's wait, a clerk appeared and conducted Nicholas to a small anteroom, where another, more senior clerk requested his journals and charts, along with any letters of introduction he might carry. Nicholas produced the documents, including the charts in Silva's metal tubes, and Captain Trevenen's sealed letter to Admiral Keppel, which the clerk accepted with noticeably increased interest.

"These are your original observations from the Society Islands?" the man asked, examining the carefully preserved pages with quick, professional movements of someone who handled important documents daily.

"Yes, sir," Nicholas replied. "My journals and charts from the time spent on Bora Bora and other islands. I've maintained and expanded them during my journey back to England, adding observations I made while with a Portuguese trader and later in India."

The clerk nodded, his interest clearly piqued. "These include notes about navigation techniques not covered in Captain Cook's previous accounts. Wait here, please."

Two hours passed. Nicholas had resigned himself to the Admiralty's notorious capacity for delay when a young lieutenant entered briskly and said, "Mr. Cruwys? You will come with me."

He was led not to a clerk's chamber, nor an interview room, but—to his quiet astonishment—to the Admiralty boardroom itself: the sanctum where the Lords Commissioners met to determine the fate of fleets and empires.

The ceiling soared to a breathtaking height, its barrel-vaulted expanse divided into elegant panels by ornamental bands of guilloche pattern. Tall sash windows with internal shutters lined the right hand wall—their lower panels closed against the rain, the upper panes admitting a diffuse gray light, the glass still bearing the slight distortions of hand-blown manufacture.

To his left a fire below the marble mantlepiece opposite the windows, and above the mantel was the boardroom's most curious feature: a brass windvane, connected through the ceiling to the weathercock on the roof. Its indicator needle turned gently, responding to the capricious London wind, silently informing the Lords of the wind's direction—knowledge that might decide when fleets could sail, or when enemies might approach. The surrounding paneling was elaborately carved with depictions of naval instruments.

The wall were mostly paneled in dark oak except for some areas of deep blue, and were adorned with portraits of admirals who had shaped Britain's maritime supremacy: Hawke at Quiberon Bay; Anson, who circumnavigated the globe in *Centurion*; Vernon, the hero of Porto Bello; and Russell, victor of La Hogue. Between them hung large-scale charts of the Navy's principal theatres: the Channel approaches, the Mediterranean basin, the West Indies, the Indian Ocean—all framed in oak. Smaller maps showed strategic harbours and anchorages. In one corner stood a massive terrestrial globe, its surface marked by discoveries and claims inked in different hands over the past half-century.

A great mahogany table dominated the centre of the room, its polished surface reflecting the warm glow of beeswax candles set in silver holders, each engraved with the Navy's fouled anchor. Three men sat in high-backed red leather chairs—their silhouettes framed in soft light from a silver candelabrum of imposing height, crafted to commemorate the Peace of Utrecht nearly seventy years earlier.

Mr. Stephens, the First Secretary of the Admiralty, who had followed Nicholas into the room, now stepped forward to stand beside him, clearing his throat with the practiced discretion of a man whose entire career had been built on perfect protocol. Dressed in court black with a crisp cravat and modestly silvered waistcoat, Stephens exuded the self-effacing authority of a man who had navigated decades of Admiralty affairs without once raising his voice above a murmur.

"My lord, gentlemen," Stephens announced in measured tones, "I have the honour to present Lieutenant Nicholas Cruwys, formerly of His Majesty's ship *Resolution* under Captain Cook, subsequently of His Majesty's sloop *Lynx* under Captain Walsh. Lieutenant Cruwys comes before this body by special summons to report upon his observations of native navigation in the Pacific islands."

Stephens then proceeded with the necessary formalities.

At the far head of the table, beneath a particularly grand portrait of King George III in naval uniform—painted after the King's review of the fleet at Spithead in 1773—sat the First Lord himself: John Montagu, Earl of Sandwich.

"Lieutenant Cruwys, I have the honour to present the Right Honourable John Montagu, fourth Earl of Sandwich, First Lord of the Admiralty."

Sandwich was not what Nicholas had expected. Rather than the inflated figure of caricature and rumour, he beheld a man of middling height and unremarkable build, his face lined by long service in government and the cares of a war now entering its fourth year. His complexion was sallow; his lips, pale and thin; but his eyes—grey, hooded, and penetrating—missed nothing. His wig was powdered without extravagance, his claret coat finely cut but devoid of display. Nicholas bowed deeply, as protocol demanded. Sandwich acknowledged him with the slight inclination of the head that was all a First Lord might extend to a lieutenant without patronage.

"To his lordship's right," Stephens continued, "Vice-Admiral George Darby, Commander-in-Chief Channel Fleet, First Naval Lord of the Admiralty."

Darby, newly appointed both to command the Channel Fleet and to the Admiralty Board, was dressed in full flag officer's uniform: dark navy coat with gold braid worn neat, white facings, and the understated lace befitting a man of precise habits. He appeared to be about sixty, his face pale and sharply lined, with eyes the pale grey of distant weather and just as difficult to read. He inclined his head slightly—less a courtesy than a professional recognition—and Nicholas felt the appraisal behind it. Darby's reputation in the service was that of one of its most seasoned and competent admirals, inclined more to caution than aggressive tactics, with cool judgment and unflinching standards.

"Mr. Alexander Dalrymple," Stephens went on, "of the East India Company and lately chief cartographer to this office."

Dalrymple, looked up from the folio he had been leafing through— one of Nicholas's own journals, by the look of the ink—and gave a courteous, precise nod. He was a man in his fifties, stocky and pale-complexioned, with a nose slightly too long and a mouth prone to compression when deep in thought. His hair, thin and worn close, bore only a trace of powder. Though dressed in plain dark coat and linen, there was an energy to him that belied the sedateness of his appearance, a keen, slightly irritable intelligence that had produced many of the Admiralty's most useful charts, even if his manner had sometimes strained official patience. That he was seated here, given no formal position but every measure of influence, spoke volumes.

"And of course," Stephens concluded with brisk modesty, "you are already acquainted with myself, Mr. Philip Stephens, First Secretary."

With that, he stepped quietly aside and took his place at the special recess built into the end of the great mahogany table—a cut-out portion designed specifically to accommodate him and his papers. The custom-built section, with its tier of drawers resembling a desk, allowed him to sit almost embedded within the table itself, perfectly positioned to record the Board's decisions. Before him lay a sheaf of memoranda, a sanded inkwell, and a bound folio awaiting the day's proceedings. His quill, already poised, made no sound as the silence settled around the table.

Nicholas stood before them, conscious suddenly of his provincial background, his unconventional career path, and the three years that had separated him from the ordinary progression of naval advancement. He maintained the stance of a professional naval officer—back straight, hands behind him, chin level—yet felt the weight of their combined gaze as a tangible force.

"Lieutenant Cruwys," said the First Lord, examining him with the penetrating gaze that had assessed a generation of naval officers from midshipmen to admirals, "we have reviewed your journals with considerable interest. Your observations on Pacific navigation techniques are particularly noteworthy."

"Thank you, my lord," Nicholas replied, keeping his composure despite the unexpected presence of such senior figures.

"We see you've brought a letter from Captain Trevenen of *Thunderer*," Sandwich continued. "He writes separately as well, regarding your meeting in Gibraltar. He speaks highly of your capabilities, and suggests your experience might be of use in Mediterranean operations. He also mentions you were aboard *Resolution* when his nephew joined Captain Cook's expedition."

"Yes, my lord. James Trevenen and I served together as midshipmen. Captain Trevenen was exceptionally kind in Gibraltar—offering both counsel and letters of introduction." Nicholas felt a rush of gratitude that Trevenen had indeed followed through on his word.

"Captain Trevenen's judgment carries weight with this Board," Darby remarked. "As does Captain Walsh's report concerning your conduct during the action against the French privateer, and your subsequent handling of *HMS Growler*."

"Vice Admiral Darby has several questions regarding your charts and the methods you describe," Sandwich continued.

Darby leaned forward slightly, his manner exacting but not unkind. "I've come up from Portsmouth specifically to consult with the Board on matters of navigation and seamanship," he said, adjusting his position in the chair. " Lord Sandwich was most insistent I hear of your findings personally. These sailing techniques you document—using swell patterns and star positions without conventional instruments—how reliable did you find them in practice? The Admiralty is particularly keen to understand any methods that might prove useful to our officers, especially given the challenges we face in distant waters."

Remarkably reliable, sir," Nicholas answered without hesitation. "The Pacific islanders have navigated vast distances for generations using these methods. I witnessed their effectiveness personally during journeys between islands where no land was visible for days at a time."

"And you mastered these techniques yourself?" Darby asked.

"To a degree, sir, though not with the same facility as those born to the tradition. But enough to understand their principles and application."

"Indeed?" said Dalrymple, tilting his head. His professional interest was evident in the sharpness of his gaze and the annotated folio at his elbow. "Can you be precise, Lieutenant? Such claims, while attractive, tend to suffer in recollection."

Nicholas answered without hesitation. "The crossing from Matavai Bay in Tahiti to the coast of Savai'i, in the Samoan group—some four hundred leagues—was made in twelve days, sir. Landfall was made within five miles of the navigator's predicted bearing, without the use of any European instruments."

Dalrymple's brows rose, and for a moment he said nothing. "Astonishing. The Royal Navy receives any number of accounts of 'intuitive' seamanship, most of them fit only for the Royal Society's fireplace. Yours may be an exception." Dalrymple gave a small nod, flipping a page in his notes.

For the next hour, Nicholas answered the panel's questions with clarity and precision, drawing on recollections that had been sharpened by long sea miles and longer reflection. He described the reading of swells and their patterns, the star paths used for navigation, the methods by which distant islands might be inferred from cloud formations or seabird movement. Throughout, he measured his responses carefully—mindful that too much enthusiasm might cast him as uncritical, or worse, sentimental, while too little would undermine the utility of what he had observed.

Nicholas found himself navigating a social and professional environment as challenging in its way as any Pacific reef passage. The precise vocabulary, the subtle gradations of emphasis, the unspoken hierarchies of influence and interest, all required careful reading. He was reminded of his early confusion with Tahitian social customs, except that here, the consequences of misreading the signs could affect his entire naval career.

Sandwich and Dalrymple exchanged occasional glances during the discussion of navigation principles that might hold military application in unfamiliar waters. Darby seemed most focused on Nicholas's brief command of *Growler,* watching him closely, as though weighing not just his words, but the character beneath them.

Near the end of the hour, Dalrymple tapped one of the bound journals with his forefinger. "These bearings," he said, with the air of a man observing something rare but not yet irreplaceable, "are taken with a consistency not often found in reports from the field. I have seen submissions from officers who fancy themselves surveyors, and their latitudes dance like fiddlers on a tavern table. But yours"—he glanced over his spectacles at Nicholas—"are not merely careful. They are repeatable. That, Lieutenant, is the only standard that matters."

Nicholas inclined his head, uncertain whether to offer thanks or refrain. Dalrymple gave a short huff of approval, or perhaps simple acknowledgment.

"Your charts, too," he went on, rapping the edge of one folio with a knuckle, "are cleanly laid out, well-graduated, and free of the ornamental nonsense that renders so many useless at sea. I should like to know who taught you to draw a coastline with restraint."

Nicholas, caught between modesty and pride, said simply, "I learned the practice under Captain Cook, sir."

"Then he taught you well," Dalrymple replied. "Your notes on landfall by swell convergence are particularly sound. The Royal Navy would do well to remember that the Pacific is not navigated by compass and gold braid alone."

There was a pause. Sandwich's fingers stilled on the arm of his chair; Stephens blinked but said nothing. Darby's face did not change, though his gaze shifted once to Dalrymple before returning to Nicholas.

"Lieutenant Cruwys," Sandwich said finally, "your account of these matters is most illuminating. Given your unique combination of experiences—both with Captain Cook's expedition and subsequently in the Pacific and Indian Oceans—we shall require further consultation with you."

Nicholas inclined his head, uncertain how to respond to such direct attention from the First Lord.

"You are to remain in London until further notice," Sandwich continued. "We may wish to interview you again once we have fully reviewed your materials. The clerk will record your lodging address. I suggest you also call upon Sir Joseph Banks at the Royal Society in the coming days—he has expressed interest in discussing your observations in greater detail."

"In the meantime," interjected Mr. Stephens, the First Secretary, "arrangements have been made for payment of your back wages and prize money due from the capture of the French vessels. You should present yourself to Mr. Hargreaves at the Navy Pay Office in Somerset House tomorrow morning."

Nicholas expressed his thanks, recognizing this as unusually prompt attention to a junior officer's financial affairs. Clearly his Pacific experiences had elevated his case beyond routine consideration.

"That will be all for now, Lieutenant," Sandwich concluded, already turning his attention to papers before him.

Nicholas bowed and withdrew, his head still ringing slightly from the scale of what had just occurred. He had stood before the highest naval authority in the empire, had been personally recognized by the First Lord, and had apparently impressed men whose decisions shaped Britain's maritime destiny. Yet he had received no specific orders, no clear indication of what might come next.

As he emerged into the corridor, the young lieutenant who had escorted him reappeared.

"The First Secretary suggests you establish a bank relationship while in London," he said, handing Nicholas a sealed note. "This introduction to Messrs. Coutts & Co. may prove useful when you receive your back pay. They have experience with naval officers' affairs."

Nicholas accepted the note, thanking the lieutenant. This was another indication that his case was receiving unusual attention. Naval lieutenants typically handled their modest finances without the services of a private bank.

Outside, the rain had increased, though passing sedan chairs and carriages moved through the damp with undiminished energy. Nicholas ignored the weather and walked slowly along Whitehall, absorbing the grandeur of government buildings that housed departments whose authority stretched from the Caribbean to the coasts of India and beyond. He felt a curious sense of dislocation— he was at once at the very center of British power and yet somehow peripheral to it, a lieutenant with exotic experiences but no immediate purpose.

The following day, Nicholas presented himself at Somerset House, a sprawling complex on the Strand that housed several government departments, including the Navy Pay Office. The building's classical façade and courtyard presented a stark contrast to the ramshackle establishments of the Strand, its architectural grandeur conveying the weight and permanence of administrative power.

Inside, corridors lined with clerks' offices formed a bureaucratic labyrinth through which Nicholas was guided to the office of Mr. Hargreaves, a thin, precise man whose fingers bore the permanent ink stains of his profession. Hargreaves consulted a ledger, verified Nicholas's identity, and with surprising efficiency processed the payment of his back wages—£58 7s 3d for his service since departing Calcutta—plus an initial payment of £43 12s for his share of prize money from the captured French vessels.

"The final prize money may take some months to process," Hargreaves explained, pushing a form toward Nicholas for his signature. "The Admiralty Court must assess the value of the captured vessels and their contents, then calculate each officer's proper share according to rank and role. But given the special interest in your case, this advance has been authorized."

Nicholas signed where indicated, acutely aware that the sum now being handed to him—over a £100, represented more money than he had ever possessed at one time. For a lieutenant accustomed to living on five shillings a day, such a sum offered temporary but welcome financial security.

From Somerset House, Nicholas proceeded to the banking house of Coutts & Co. on the Strand, where the First Secretary's introduction secured him an interview with a junior partner. The bank's interior spoke of discreet wealth—polished wood paneling, Turkey carpets underfoot, and clerks working with quiet efficiency at high desks. Nicholas, still in uniform, felt the eyes of several clients assess him as he was shown to a private office at the rear.

"Lieutenant Cruwys," the banker said, reviewing the Secretary's note. "We would be pleased to establish an account for you. Coutts has a tradition of serving naval and military officers, particularly those with unusual financial circumstances: irregular prize payments, extended service in distant waters, that sort of thing."

The meeting proceeded with surprising smoothness. Though Nicholas's means were modest by the bank's usual standards, the Admiralty's interest in his case clearly carried weight. Papers were signed, and Nicholas departed with a small leather-bound passbook recording his newly established account, and the comforting sum of nearly £200 made up of both the new admiralty draft and most of the money he had left from his trading days and the back payment authorized by Admiral Hughes in Calcutta.

The following days passed in a curious blend of waiting and activity. Nicholas called at the Royal Society as suggested, presenting his letter of introduction from Captain Trevenen. Sir Joseph Banks received him with genuine enthusiasm, peppering him with questions about Tahitian botany, social customs, and navigation techniques. Banks's own Pacific experience during Cook's first voyage gave him a framework for understanding Nicholas's observations that most Londoners lacked.

"You must dine with me next week," Banks insisted as their discussion concluded. "I have a small circle of natural philosophers who would be fascinated by your account of island navigation. The astronomical implications alone merit further investigation."

Nicholas accepted the invitation, aware that such connections might prove valuable regardless of his naval future. Yet as he made his way back to Grosvenor Square, he found himself increasingly conscious of the strange limbo in which he existed—neither fully employed nor officially on leave, awaiting an Admiralty decision that might arrive tomorrow or not at all.

In the evenings, he worked on expanding his journals, recording details of his Admiralty interview and his impressions of London with the same careful attention he had applied to Pacific phenomena. Occasionally, he would remove Caroline's miniature of Bora Bora from its box, studying the delicate brushwork that had captured the island's distinctive peak rising from its lagoon. *Islands of memory anchor us through life's storms.* The inscription seemed increasingly prescient as he navigated the unfamiliar social currents of the capital.

London itself revealed new facets daily as Nicholas explored its extent. Unlike Portsmouth or Plymouth, with their singular focus on maritime life, the capital encompassed every dimension of British ambition. The contrast between wealth and poverty struck him forcibly: elegant carriages rolling through Mayfair within sight of the squalid rookeries of St. Giles; shops displaying luxuries from across the empire while beggars huddled in doorways; coffee-houses where merchants and politicians discussed affairs of state while street children peered hungrily through windows steamed by conversation and spilled tea.

He found himself regularly drawn to the river, where the familiar rhythms of maritime life offered a kind of constancy amid the bewildering breadth of the metropolis. The Thames teemed with craft of every description—lighters and barges, wherries and ferries, coastal traders and deep-water merchantmen—all plying their trade along the great liquid highway that was London's lifeblood. Watching the watermen thread their way through the traffic, Nicholas felt a quiet kinship with their practised seamanship, a wordless fraternity that endured beyond uniform, class, or station.

As September gave way to October, Nicholas found himself unprepared for the deepening chill of the English autumn. The mornings brought a biting cold that penetrated his naval uniform—designed more for the tropics, and his breath formed clouds in the air as he walked London's streets. After nearly three years in tropical climates, from the Society Islands to India, his body had grown accustomed to constant warmth. Now, the returning cold seemed to reach into his very bones—a physical reminder of how long he had been away, and how thoroughly he had adapted to distant shores.

One particularly raw morning, as Nicholas returned from a walk along the river, Morley met him in the entrance hall with a letter bearing the Admiralty seal.

"This arrived by messenger just after you departed, sir," the butler said, presenting the envelope on a small silver tray.

Nicholas broke the seal and found a brief note from Mr. Stephens, the First Secretary, informing him that further interviews regarding his Pacific observations would be scheduled in approximately two weeks' time. In the interim, he was to remain in London, available for consultation if required. The note concluded with a phrase that both reassured and unsettled him: "Your future appointment is under active consideration at the highest levels."

That evening, as Nicholas sat before the fire in his room, contemplating this latest communication, a commotion in the entrance hall drew his attention. Voices, footsteps on marble, the unmistakable sound of chests being set down, these familiar noises brought him to his feet just as Morley appeared at the door.

"Commander Harrington has arrived, sir," the butler announced, with the first hint of genuine warmth Nicholas had yet detected in his professional manner. "He asks if you would join him in the library when convenient."

Nicholas found Harrington standing before the fireplace in the library, still in his travel clothes but looking remarkably fresh despite the journey from Portsmouth. A decanter of brandy and two glasses had already been set out on a small table nearby.

"Ah, Nicholas! There you are," Harrington greeted him, his manner reflecting the slight but unmistakable shift that had occurred in their relationship since Nicholas had accepted his hospitality. "I see you've settled in. Morley tells me you've been a model guest—unlike some of my school friends, who apparently use the house as if it were a tavern whenever my father is away."

"Your generosity has been invaluable," Nicholas replied with genuine gratitude. "I'd be significantly poorer if I'd been paying for lodgings all this time."

Harrington waved this aside as he poured two generous measures of brandy. "Nonsense. It's what any sensible officer would offer a shipmate. Besides, the house requires occupation to remain properly alive. Too many of these London residences stand empty and neglected while their owners retreat to the country."

He handed Nicholas a glass. "I've received my confirmation—Commander Harrington, with orders to take *Falcon* as soon as she completes her refit at Chatham. I'll be there for perhaps a month overseeing the work, but I've a week's liberty first." His eyes gleamed with the particular satisfaction of an officer receiving his first independent command. "I thought we might celebrate properly while I'm in town."

Nicholas raised his glass in salute. "To Commander Harrington and *HMS Falcon*—may she bring you glory and prize money in equal measure."

They drank, and Harrington settled himself into one of the library's worn but comfortable leather chairs.

"Now, tell me of your adventures in the metropolis. Have the Lords of the Admiralty recognised your worth?"

Nicholas described his interview, the unexpected presence of the First Lord himself and of Vice Admiral Darby, and the subsequent meetings with Banks and various officials. Harrington listened with genuine interest, occasionally asking perceptive questions about the political dimensions of these encounters.

"They're keeping you in reserve," he concluded, after hearing about the most recent message. "The mention of 'highest levels' suggests Sandwich and Darby are involving themselves in determining your next posting. That's uncommon for a lieutenant without significant family connections."

"Uncommon, and a little unsettling," Nicholas admitted. "I'd rather have clear orders than this state of uncertainty, even if the alternative meant immediate service abroad again."

Harrington nodded. "The Navy teaches us to value clarity of purpose above all else. London, by contrast, thrives on ambiguity and deferred decisions." He studied Nicholas. "I notice you're still wearing your tropical-weight uniform. Have you ventured into the realm of London tailors yet?"

Nicholas glanced down at his coat, suddenly aware of how it differed from the more substantial wool of Harrington's own. "I haven't given it much thought," he confessed. "Though I admit I've found the autumn chill rather penetrating after years in warmer climes."

Harrington set down his glass with sudden decisiveness. "Then that shall be our first order of business tomorrow. You need proper clothing for an English winter—both naval and civilian. A lieutenant who has caught the Admiralty's eye should present himself accordingly."

The following morning found them on Savile Row, where Harrington led Nicholas to a discreet establishment whose clientele included naval officers of sufficient means to command bespoke tailoring. The proprietor, Mr. Holcroft, received them with professional deference, paying particular attention to Harrington, whose family had evidently patronised the establishment for generations.

"Commander Harrington, a pleasure as always," Holcroft said, bowing slightly. "My congratulations on your promotion. Your father's last visit mentioned it might be forthcoming."

"Thank you, Holcroft. I've brought Lieutenant Cruwys, recently returned from extended service abroad. He requires a complete wardrobe suitable for English weather—two new winter-weight uniforms, civilian attire for various occasions, and a proper greatcoat. The lieutenant has served with distinction, but he's been in tropical climates for some years and finds himself unprepared for a London autumn."

Holcroft's practiced eye took Nicholas's measure—not merely his physical dimensions, which he noted with professional precision, but his bearing, the way he stood, the quality of his current coat. Nicholas found himself subjected to the same quiet scrutiny he had once applied to Tahitian canoe hulls or the rake of a mast.

"If I may suggest: a superfine wool for the uniforms, warmer than your present cloth, but preserving the dignity of naval appearance. For civilian wear, perhaps a blue broadcloth coat, buff waistcoat, and grey breeches—those would suit the lieutenant's colouring. And of course, a substantial boat cloak against the worst weather." Holcroft's tone was deferential, but his recommendations were made with the quiet confidence of a man whose judgment was rarely questioned.

What followed was an education in the arcane world of London gentlemen's clothing. Fabrics were examined, styles discussed with reference to current fashion—though never straying into the excessive ornamentation favoured by certain circles—and decisions made about buttons, pockets, linings, and facings with the precision of a ship's carpenter planning a delicate repair. Through it all, Harrington guided Nicholas with the ease of one well-versed in this aspect of upper class life, but never once made him feel provincial for his unfamiliarity.

"Consider these essential tools of your profession," Harrington said quietly, as Nicholas winced at the total being entered into Holcroft's ledger. "Just as a good sextant is worth its price for accurate navigation, proper attire ensures you're judged on your merits, not your appearance."

Nicholas nodded, recognising again how Harrington's privileged understanding of English society constituted a different form of navigation, one no less valuable to an officer seeking advancement. The sum was substantial, nearly £20 for the full order, but his recent payment from the Navy Pay Office made it possible without hardship.

"The uniforms and greatcoat will be ready within three days, sir," Holcroft promised. "The civilian attire by the end of the week."

Their next stop was a bootmaker of similar quality, where Nicholas was measured for a pair of sea boots suitable for winter service, and a pair of dress boots for wear in town. These, too, represented a considerable investment, but one that Nicholas understood would serve him well in the years to come, whatever orders next came down from Whitehall.

The following evening, Harrington announced his intention to introduce Nicholas to one of London's better clubs. Not the rarefied establishments restricted to aristocracy or political grandees, but one frequented by naval officers of sufficient standing and gentlemen with interests in maritime affairs.

"The Anchor and Crown admits officers of lieutenant's rank and above," Harrington explained as their carriage made its way through streets shrouded in fog. "Founded by captains who served under Anson during his circumnavigation. Less exclusive than White's or Brooks's, but more dignified than the taverns near the Admiralty. You'll find the conversation informative, and the company generally worth cultivating."

The club occupied a handsome building just off St. James's Street, its entrance marked only by a discreet brass plate bearing its name. Inside, a hushed atmosphere of masculine comfort prevailed: leather chairs arranged in conversational groupings, walls lined with nautical paintings and charts of historical significance, and a pervasive scent of tobacco, wine, and beeswax polish. A fire burned in a substantial hearth at each end of the main room, driving back the autumn chill.

Harrington was greeted by name by the steward, who escorted them to a table in a well-situated corner from which they could observe most of the room while conducting their own conversation in relative privacy. Wine was brought without being ordered—a Bordeaux of excellent quality that Harrington explained was the club's standard offering, imported directly from France during peacetime and procured through more circuitous routes during current hostilities.

As they settled in, Nicholas became aware of the room's occupants, perhaps twenty men in total, ranging in age from their own early twenties to white-haired veterans of wars long past. Most wore civilian dress, though with the unmistakable bearing of military or naval men; a few in naval uniform, with the odd marine officer as well. The conversations around them touched on topics both familiar and novel to Nicholas: naval deployments in the West Indies, the strategic implications of Spanish involvement in the war, commodity prices affected by privateering, and London political gossip that threaded through it all.

"Captain Williams over there," Harrington said quietly, indicating an older officer in conversation with two civilians near the fireplace, "commanded the frigate *Tartar* during the Seven Years' War. Took three French prizes off Brest in a single engagement. Now advises merchant houses on naval protection for their convoys. The gentleman to his left is something in the diplomatic service, attached to our embassy in Madrid before the war."

Nicholas found himself newly attuned to these overlapping spheres of influence—naval officers whose experiences shaped policy, diplomats whose negotiations redirected deployments, merchants whose trade routes helped determine strategic priorities. It was a microcosm of the broader system within which his own career existed.

"Ah, Pryce is here," Harrington remarked, nodding toward a man in his thirties who had just entered. "Navy Office—procurement.

Knows more about the timber shortage than anyone in London. I should introduce you, he might have insights into whether your Pacific observations are likely to result in a specific posting."

Before Harrington could signal to his acquaintance, a distinguished older officer approached their table, his gaze fixed on Nicholas with evident interest. Both men rose instinctively.

"You must be Lieutenant Cruwys," the gentleman said without preamble. "I recognised you from Admiral Darby's account." He extended his hand—a courtesy, but one delivered with the assurance of rank. "Admiral of the Blue Sir George Pocock, KB. Retired service."

Nicholas took the offered hand, bowing slightly. "An honour, sir," he said, still a little taken aback by the directness.

"You've caused quite a stir at the Admiralty, young man," Pocock continued, drawing up a chair without waiting for invitation. "Not every day a lieutenant reports to the Board with observations that catch Sandwich's personal attention. Both the First Lord and Admiral Darby mentioned your case to me over dinner last week."

Nicholas glanced at Harrington, who looked as surprised as he felt.

"Sir George commanded in the East Indies before the Seven Years' War," Harrington said quietly. "He defeated the French squadron off Cuddalore, and again near Pondicherry."

"Ancient history now," Pocock replied with a dismissive wave. "But I maintain certain connections at the Admiralty. Your Pacific navigation techniques have generated considerable interest, Cruwys. There's talk of incorporating some elements into the training of selected officers."

The conversation that followed ranged widely across naval matters, with Pocock revealing himself both knowledgeable about current deployments and candid in his opinions of various commanders. Nicholas soon found himself drawn into a discussion of comparative navigation techniques—European precision instruments versus Pacific observational methods—that attracted the attention of several nearby members, who gradually joined their circle.

As the evening progressed, Nicholas became aware that he was being evaluated not merely on his technical knowledge, but on his manner, his ability to hold a position in debate without appearing dogmatic, to speak with assurance while deferring appropriately to senior officers. It was, he realised, another form of examination—no less consequential than his interview at the Admiralty.

By the time they departed, Nicholas had made the acquaintance of several influential figures, including two serving captains, a senior administrator from the Navy Board, and a Member of Parliament who sat on the committee with responsibility for naval appropriations. Harrington, observing his friend's measured navigation of these social currents, nodded approvingly as their carriage bore them back toward Grosvenor Square.

"You handled yourself well," he said. "Pocock rarely engages with officers below post rank, yet he sought you out. That suggests your name is being discussed in circles that matter."

"It's disconcerting to be the subject of such attention," Nicholas admitted. "Especially when I remain uncertain of my next assignment."

"Welcome to the Navy's particular form of purgatory," Harrington replied, with a wry smile. "Combat is straightforward by comparison—you face the enemy, you fight, you win or lose. But advancement? That requires navigating shoals invisible to the untrained eye, with currents that shift according to political winds in Whitehall."

Nicholas's thoughts increasingly turned to the East India convoy. By his calculations, they should have arrived in the Channel—*Ocean* with Caroline aboard, and Lord Ashton no doubt at her side at every opportunity. Soon, perhaps, he would receive some word from the Admiralty regarding his next appointment. Until then, he continued to learn the complex social currents of London, aided by Harrington's guidance and bolstered by the growing circle of connections that might, in time, shape his naval future as significantly as any skill in seamanship or gunnery.

Harrington departed for Chatham after a week's leave, where *HMS Falcon* awaited his attention. Two days later as the late afternoon light faded and Nicholas dressed for dinner, he was interrupted by a knock at his door. Morley entered, his customary reserve slightly softened by what appeared to be genuine respect.

"Lieutenant," he said, presenting a calling card on a silver salver, "a visitor has asked to see you. She waits in the small drawing room."

Nicholas glanced at the card:

Miss Caroline Carlisle, Ocean House, Portland Place.

His heart quickened as he descended the stairs, adjusting his uniform coat with unconscious precision. The East India convoy must have arrived, though he had heard no official word. Caroline, here in London, seeking him out at Harrington's family home—the implications swirled through his mind as he approached the drawing room door.

She stood by the window, gazing out at the square, her figure silhouetted against the fading winter light. Her dress was of deep blue wool—practical yet elegant—with a fur-trimmed pelisse draped over her shoulders against the London chill. Her fair hair was arranged more simply than he remembered, though no less becoming for its lack of elaboration.

"Caroline," he said softly as he entered.

She turned, her face illuminated by a smile that sent a jolt of recognition through him. For a moment, neither spoke, the silence charged with all that had passed between them, and all that remained unresolved.

"Nicholas," she replied at last, her voice steady, though her eyes betrayed deeper emotions. "You look well. London seems to agree with you."

"The convoy has arrived?" he asked, moving toward her while maintaining a proper distance.

"Three days past. We docked at Greenwich on Monday. Father has taken a house in Portland Place—he's named it Ocean House, after the ship. It appears he intends a more permanent presence in London than in years past." She paused, studying him with those perceptive green eyes. "I persuaded him that courtesy required we inform you of our arrival without delay."

The arrival at Greenwich made perfect sense. The deepwater port below the city had long served as the preferred landing for East India Company vessels. It offered the dock facilities and warehouses needed to unload the valuable cargoes that filled the Company's holds, while still allowing convenient access to the commercial heart of London.

"I'm grateful," Nicholas said, aware of how formal they sounded—like players reciting lines, when what he truly wanted was to close the distance between them and take her hands in his. "The voyage from Luanda was uneventful, I hope?"

"Reasonably so. We encountered a storm in the Bay of Biscay that delayed us, but nothing to match our adventures with the French privateers." A flicker of shared memory passed between them. "Lord Ashton proved an attentive companion throughout when there was visiting between ships. He has been most persistent in his attentions."

The mention of Ashton hung in the air like a challenge, or perhaps a warning. Nicholas felt the familiar twist of jealousy at the aristocrat's name, though he kept his expression neutral.

"I understand he has significant estates," he replied, testing the waters of her meaning.

"Indeed. Three thousand acres in Wiltshire, a house in St. James's Square, and connections throughout government," Caroline said, her tone matter-of-fact rather than impressed. "He makes no secret of his intentions regarding me."

Before Nicholas could respond, she changed tack. "But I didn't come to discuss Lord Ashton. I wanted to see you. To know how you've fared since our parting. Father mentioned you'd been summoned to the Admiralty. Has there been a decision regarding your next posting?"

"Not yet, though I expect news soon. I was received by the First Lord and Vice Admiral Darby at the Admiralty. He heard himself adopting the same careful neutrality, as if they were acquaintances exchanging news rather than two people who had shared soul-stirring kisses on a distant African quay.

"I'm glad," she said simply. "Your work deserves recognition."

A silence fell between them, weighted with all that remained unsaid. Nicholas studied her, sensing a tension beneath her composed exterior, a subtle guardedness that hadn't been present in Luanda.

"Caroline," he said finally, unable to maintain the pretence of casual conversation, "in Luanda, before we parted—"

"Nicholas," she interrupted gently, her voice soft but tinged with resolution, "we should speak plainly. What passed between us in Luanda was real. But we both know the realities we face here in England differ greatly from those in distant ports."

"My feelings haven't changed," he said quietly.

"Perhaps not," she acknowledged, meeting his gaze directly. "But circumstances have. We are in London now, where other considerations apply. My father's position, your naval career, Lord Ashton's suit—none of these can be dismissed with a wave of the hand."

Nicholas felt a chill that had nothing to do with the weather. "Are you saying what we had was only a diversion for the voyage? Something to be forgotten now that we've returned to society?"

"No," Caroline said, and for a moment the composure slipped, a flash of pain crossing her features. "Never that. But I must be practical, Nicholas. There are aspects of my situation—of myself—that you cannot fully understand."

"Then help me understand," he urged, taking an instinctive step toward her.

She moved back slightly, preserving the distance between them. "I cannot. Not now, perhaps not ever." Her voice was calm, but firm. "It would be best for both of us if we acknowledged the impossibility of continuing as we began in Luanda."

The words struck him with physical force. "You cannot mean that."

"I must," she said, her eyes bright with unshed tears despite the steady tone. "Lord Ashton's offer provides security and position that align with my father's expectations and my own... needs. Your path lies elsewhere, Nicholas, with the Navy, with the achievements that await you."

"Caroline—" he began, but she raised a hand to stop him.

"Please," she said. Her composure wavered, then returned. "This is difficult enough without prolonging it. I valued our time together more than you may ever know. But it belongs to Luanda, to the convoy, to a world apart from this one."

She turned toward the door, pausing as she passed beside him. The scent of jasmine lingered about her—a trace of India, of Africa, of memory.

"I wish you every success, Lieutenant Cruwys," she said formally, though her voice caught slightly on his name. "Perhaps, in time, we might meet again, as friends."

She departed without another word.

Nicholas remained motionless, staring at the closed door. The drawing room, moments ago charged with possibility, felt suddenly cold.

He was still there when Morley discreetly appeared to light the lamps against the gathering darkness, the butler's face revealing nothing of his thoughts regarding the brief visit or its apparent conclusion.

That night, Nicholas slept little, his mind replaying Caroline's words, searching for meanings beneath the surface, for explanations beyond the obvious interpretation of a woman choosing security and position over uncertain attachment. Yet he also felt anger, and something deeper: a disillusionment that cast shadows across his thoughts, colder and more enduring than grief.

In the stillness of his chamber, with London's muffled sounds filtering through the windowpanes, Nicholas found himself thinking of Atea. The memory came with startling clarity—her face smiling in the sunlight of Bora Bora, her movements as graceful and natural as the sea itself, her laughter untouched by artifice. What they had shared, despite their youth and her cultural distance, had been genuine in ways that now seemed impossible in his world.

There had been no calculations of advantage or position, no questions of lineage, no consequences to weigh—only the clean, bright recognition of one soul in another's presence. In that simplicity, there had been a deeper kind of paradise, one that transcended even the supreme physical beauty of the island itself.

He felt a sudden, sharp awareness of what had been lost—not only Atea herself, taken by fever after her injury on the reef, but the very possibility of love unclouded by social concern. The drawing rooms of London, the careful maneuvers of courtship, the strategic alignments of marriage—they seemed hollow echoes of something he had once known and could no longer find.

He rose and went to the window, looking out at the moonlight gleaming on the wet cobblestones below. A new cynicism settled over him—not theatrical, but real—a quiet hardening of something that had remained vulnerable despite all he had seen and experienced. If Caroline, who had seemed to understand him better than anyone since his return, could retreat behind social calculation so completely, what genuine connections could he hope to form in this world of appearances and advantage?

For the first time, Nicholas fully grasped that his journey had not merely carried him across oceans, but across ways of being, and that returning to England meant accepting certain constraints he had once left behind. His naval duty remained clear, his ambition intact, but something essential had altered in his view of the society to which he had returned.

Dawn found him at another window, watching the first pale light gather along the rooftops of Mayfair. Whatever private disquiet he felt regarding Caroline, it must not be permitted to trespass upon the conduct of his duties. A naval officer learned early to divide the inward from the outward—to set the heart to one side, if need be, and proceed. That habit of mind had served him well from Tahiti to Calcutta; it would serve him here in London.

The Viscount Westborne, Harrington's father, arrived at the Grosvenor Square house in late October as Parliament prepared to reconvene, bringing with him the particular atmosphere of aristocratic politics that characterised his circle. A tall, austere man with the same aquiline features as his son, the Viscount carried himself with the self-assurance of one who had advised and shaped policy across multiple ministries. As a former Secretary at War and a respected voice in the House of Lords, his influence extended into various departments of government.

Upon meeting Nicholas—of whom he had heard through his son's letters—the Viscount had studied him with the composed scrutiny of one long practiced in the quiet art of discernment. After a moment, his expression eased, and he declared himself satisfied that his son's hospitality had been extended to "a gentleman of intelligence, evident steadiness, and—if I am not mistaken—the blood of a good West Country house." It was not lightly said. The compliment, offered with measured warmth, reflected a mind that respected breeding, certainly, but placed higher store in the bearing of the man himself. There was no hauteur in it, no affectation, only the plain courtesy of one who knew both the weight and the welcome of such acknowledgment.

"My son writes that you've caught the Admiralty's interest, Lieutenant," the Viscount remarked over dinner on the evening of his arrival. "Not a common thing for a young officer to accomplish without considerable assistance—or considerable substance."

"I've been fortunate in my opportunities for service, my lord," Nicholas replied, aware of the careful pitch required in such company.

"Fortune," the Viscount said, "tends to favour those who've made themselves useful in inconvenient places." He sipped his wine with deliberate calm. "Henry speaks well of you, and he is not often wrong in such matters. I trust your time in the Pacific hasn't led you into the more romantic errors currently in vogue—visions of untouched paradise and primitive virtue."

"The islanders have their own virtues and failings, my lord, much like any people," Nicholas replied. "Their navigation skills are remarkable, their social structures complex in their own terms. But I harbour no illusions about Eden."

It was the correct reply—well-measured, serviceable. But even as he said it, the truth pressed inward. He knew now that Bora Bora had indeed been Eden—not in fable, but in fact. A place of extraordinary beauty beyond anything he had seen or even heard rumour of: the green flanks of its volcanic peaks rising sheer from the sea, crowned with cloud; the blue lagoon luminous as blown glass; coral gardens drifting like smoke beneath water so clear it seemed not to exist. The air fragrant with breadfruit and frangipani; the breeze always moving, always warm, always salt-soft. It was a world unhurried, held in a stillness not of idleness, but of perfect balance.

In Atea's presence—her laughter, her calm, the way she moved through that world—he had known a kind of life that asked nothing of him but attention. Not idleness, but grace. A paradise, until her fall on the reef—and the sickness that followed, swift and senseless, leaving the world outwardly unchanged, yet altered beyond repair.

And he knew now, too, that it would not endure even for the islanders themselves. More ships would come over the horizon—French, English, Spanish—like storm-clouds gathering beyond the reef. Perhaps not for several years. But they would come. The wider world would not leave such a paradise untouched.

The thought carried a weight he seldom gave voice to: not guilt, exactly, but a quieter sorrow—that he had seen something fleeting and near-perfect upon the earth, and that even in its noblest purposes, exploration bore a cost.

The Viscount gave a faint nod, apparently pleased. "Good. The service has too many theorists already. Practical men are rare enough—and necessary, especially now."

These occasional encounters with Lord Westborne provided Nicholas with unexpected insight into the political dimensions of naval affairs. The Viscount's observations—never careless, and seldom idle—offered glimpses into the workings of influence beneath the visible surface. His assessments of ministers and admirals, delivered with the calm authority of a man accustomed to shaping outcomes quietly, revealed the delicate balance of patronage, ability, and necessity that governed both political and naval advancement.

"Hood is gathering influence," the Viscount remarked one evening in mid-November, standing by the library fire. "Sandwich recognises his capabilities, though their temperaments differ. Consider how political necessity elevated Darby to the Channel Fleet command just this past August—when Geary resigned and Barrington declined the post, Sandwich needed someone reliable, if not brilliant. Darby's appointment was born of expediency rather than exceptional merit, but he has proven steady in these few months of command." He paused, studying the flames. "If I were a young officer with recent distinction, I would pay attention to Hood's movements. His star is rising, and he does not forget the names of those he finds useful. Unlike Darby, whose command stems from political necessity, Hood's influence grows from demonstrated ability and aggressive action."

Such comments, while never explicitly directed at Nicholas as advice, nonetheless contained information that might prove valuable in navigating his own uncertain future. He filed them away carefully, alongside the growing store of observations about London society that might one day prove useful.

On a particularly bitter morning in late November, as the first hints of snow swirled through London's streets, Nicholas received a note from Sir Joseph Banks requesting his presence at the Royal Society that afternoon. The message conveyed an unusual urgency that piqued his curiosity.

Upon his arrival at the Society's imposing quarters, he was immediately ushered into Banks's private study, where the naturalist awaited him, surrounded by stacks of papers and specimen cases.

"Ah, Cruwys! Excellent timing," Banks greeted him, rising from behind his desk with surprising agility for a man of his substantial build. "The most extraordinary news has arrived. *Resolution* and *Discovery* have returned to England—they docked at the Nore yesterday morning. Cook's journals and scientific materials arrived here only hours ago."

Nicholas felt a surge of complex emotions—joy at the safe return of his former shipmates, renewed grief for Cook, and intense curiosity about their discoveries since his own separation from the expedition.

"James Trevenen?" he asked immediately, thinking of his friend. "Is there word of him?"

Banks nodded, understanding the question's importance. "Lieutenant Trevenen is well, from all reports. He was appointed acting lieutenant after Cook's death, a promotion since confirmed by the Admiralty. The ships were commanded by Captains Clerke and Gore after Cook's loss, though Clerke himself died of consumption during the voyage. They completed extensive exploration of the North

Pacific and confirmed there is no practical Northwest Passage, just as Cook suspected."

This information came as both relief and confirmation. Though he had learned some information, Nicholas had long wondered about the details of the expedition's fate after his separation, and the knowledge that they had fulfilled their mission, despite the tragedy of Cook's death, brought a sense of completion to a chapter of his life that had remained unresolved.

"There's more," Banks continued, his enthusiasm bubbling through his usually composed demeanor. "Your journals and observations from Bora Bora have been compared with the expedition's subsequent findings in the Society Islands. Captain King specifically mentions your work in his supplementary journals, confirming the accuracy of your navigational observations and cultural documentation. More significantly, he confirms the instructions given to you by Cook, and the regard in which you were held by him, particularly in matters of survey and coastal work. Your reputation at the Admiralty is likely to benefit considerably from this independent verification."

Nicholas recognized the name immediately—Lieutenant James King had served as one of Cook's officers and, following the deaths of both Cook and Captain Clerke, had taken command of *Discovery* for the final portion of the voyage. Known for his scientific mind and precise observations, King's validation carried significant weight.

This was indeed significant news. The parallel observations made by the expedition after his departure would validate his own records in a way that no personal testimony could achieve. Such confirmation, coming through official channels from fellow officers of unquestioned standing, would eliminate any lingering doubt about the reliability of his accounts.

"Furthermore," Banks added, lowering his voice slightly as if sharing a confidence, "I understand from Lord Sandwich's secretary that the First Lord has taken particular interest in your case, especially now that Cook's final reports have arrived. You may expect a summons from the Admiralty within days."

Nicholas departed the Royal Society with his mind awhirl, walking through London's darkening streets barely conscious of the biting cold. The return of *Resolution* and *Discovery*, the confirmation of his work, the prospect of a new appointment—these developments converged to suggest that his period of uncertainty might soon conclude.

True to Banks's prediction, a messenger arrived at Grosvenor Square the following morning bearing the Admiralty seal. The note inside requested, though such requests carried the weight of commands, Nicholas's presence at the Admiralty at eleven o'clock the next day. The formal wording gave no indication of the meeting's purpose, though the signature of First Secretary Stephens suggested its significance.

He dressed with particular care in his new winter-weight uniform, noting how the superior cloth and cut lent him a more substantial presence than the tropical-weight garments of his earlier years. Harrington's insistence on proper London outfitting now seemed prescient rather than merely practical.

The morning was crisp and clear, a rare respite from the city's usual November murk. Nicholas arrived at the Admiralty precisely at the appointed hour, his composure restored, though his heart remained heavy from the evening before. The same young lieutenant who had escorted him previously appeared once more, this time conducting him not to an anteroom or clerk's office, but directly to the Admiralty boardroom.

The boardroom hadn't changed since Nicholas last stood within its panelled quiet—the same high windows looking out onto Whitehall, the same polished table reflecting the fire that burned beneath the marble mantel. But now there were only three men seated there: Lord Sandwich, at the head beneath the portrait of King George, Vice Admiral Darby, and Secretary Stephens. Their expressions revealed nothing, but the very sparseness of the gathering lent it a greater weight than any formal assembly.

"Lieutenant Cruwys," Sandwich said, gesturing to a chair opposite Darby. "Join us, if you please."

Nicholas took the indicated chair, acutely aware of the singular nature of the moment—a lieutenant, scarcely confirmed in his rank, seated alone across the table from the First Lord of the Admiralty and one of the Navy's most esteemed flag officers, commanding the Channel Fleet and a member of the Admiralty Board. That he had been invited to sit, rather than stand to attention, spoke with quiet force as to what might follow. It conveyed not ease, but significance. Beneath his outward composure, a sharp current of anticipation stirred, one he mastered with the habitual economy of expression the service demanded. To betray eagerness would be worse than to feel none at all.

"Your appearance has improved since our last meeting," Sandwich observed with characteristic directness. "The benefits of proper London tailoring, I presume?"

"Yes, my lord," Nicholas acknowledged. "Commander Harrington was kind enough to direct me to appropriate establishments."

"Henry Harrington has his father's good judgment," Darby remarked. "The Viscount mentioned you were staying at their house. A valuable connection, Lieutenant."

Nicholas inclined his head, recognising the underlying current in Darby's words. The Admiralty was aware of his social affiliations as well as his professional record.

"We've reviewed the journals and dispatches brought back by *Resolution* and *Discovery*," Sandwich said, his tone sharpening into its habitual clarity. "Your observations regarding the Society Islands are confirmed in every significant aspect. Captain King speaks in your favour—strongly—and Captain Cook's own remarks are especially noteworthy. In fact, he wrote a letter recommending your promotion should you return, or be found."

The words struck deeper than Nicholas expected. For a moment, he could not speak. Cook's voice—calm, exacting, rarely given to praise—echoed in his memory, and he felt a tightening in his chest. That such a man had committed his regard to paper, and that it had survived him, meant more than Nicholas could easily say.

"I am honoured to know it, my lord," he said quietly, steadying his voice.

"Furthermore," Darby added, "your subsequent experiences—both among the islanders and during your passage through the East Indies—represent an uncommon education for a naval officer. Your conduct in command of the *Growler* demonstrated an ability to apply those experiences in the King's service."

Nicholas listened, the shape of what was to come forming slowly but clearly.

"The war has entered a critical phase, Lieutenant," Sandwich said, leaning forward slightly. "The situation in the American colonies remains unresolved, and our conflicts with France and Spain now threaten British interests throughout the Atlantic and Caribbean. Admiral Rodney has returned to the West Indies with reinforcements, tasked with defending our holdings and disrupting French operations."

Nicholas stood composed, listening. He had not been told to expect an appointment—nor dared imagine anything beyond continued half-pay or perhaps a billet in some minor sloop.

"Your orders are being prepared," Sandwich continued. "You are appointed second lieutenant aboard *Triton*, a new 28-gun frigate nearing completion at Sheerness. She will join the Channel fleet under Admiral Darby."

A pause, deliberate and unhurried.

"Captain Walsh requested you by name. He has expressed confidence in your discretion, and in your ability to learn quickly. That confidence is not widely given."

"I am grateful, my lord," Nicholas said, his voice neutral.

"You may find Channel service tedious," Sandwich allowed, sitting back. "But the discipline of a larger ship—under a captain such as Walsh—will prepare you for better things. Endure the dull parts, Mr. Cruwys. That is where most men fail."

As the meeting concluded and Nicholas rose to depart, Darby offered a final observation.

"Lieutenant Cruwys, this appointment carries little glamour and less reward. But it does carry scrutiny. The Channel is unforgiving in its own way—monotony breeds error."

He adjusted a paper on the desk, then looked up again.

"Captain Walsh requested you. That weighs more with me than any examination result. He does not flatter, and he does not tolerate fools."

"I understand, sir," Nicholas replied. "I will do my utmost to prove worthy of the trust."

Darby gave a slight nod. "Cook saw something in you worth developing. I see the same promise—though still unproven in squadron conditions. The French may oblige us soon enough. Be ready to justify your name in the logbook as well as on the muster roll."

"You are to report to *Triton* no later than the fifteenth of December," Secretary Stephens added, reaching for the next folio. "Until then, you are on leave."

Nicholas bowed, took his leave properly, and stepped out into the low grey of Whitehall—where the wind off the river smelled of hemp, wet stone, and woodsmoke. It was not the appointment he had allowed himself to hope for in sleepless moments: no staff posting, no dispatch command, no swift path to a name in the Gazette. *Triton* was solid, yes, and he knew he still had much to learn from Walsh, but tied to the Channel—where the winds were bitter and the chances few.

Caroline was gone, though only now did the fact seem to settle fully.

He walked westward, slowly, hat brim low. There was work ahead, and he would do it; but for now, London felt like the shell of something grand, hollowed out and cold inside.

Nicholas determined to use the three weeks of leave to visit his family in Devon, even if briefly. He had last seen them when the family had visited Plymouth as a farewell shortly before *Resolution* had sailed in July of 1776.

Two days before his departure from London, Nicholas received word that *Resolution* and *Discovery* had arrived at Portsmouth for final debriefing and Navy Yard work. Determined to reunite with his old shipmate, he decided to keep the Devon visit short and then travel to Portsmouth to see James Trevenen.

The three days spent at the house in Cathedral Yard in Exeter had been illuminating—not for what occurred, but for what did not. He did not visit Cruwys Morchard itself. The estate belonged now to his cousin—the current squire, eldest son of his father's elder brother—who maintained the property with formal efficiency and no particular interest in a naval lieutenant with only a distant and unlikely claim on the entail.

His father, whose world extended little beyond the county's boundaries, had received his seafaring son with genuine affection but limited comprehension of all Nicholas had seen. The books were still arranged in the same order on the same narrow shelves. His father's life had long been measured in title deeds, judgments, and the quiet clarity of a well-reasoned argument.

His elder brother, now also practising law in Exeter, had inherited their father's careful temperament. He asked after Nicholas's travels with courtesy but little curiosity, listening to edited accounts of Pacific islands and naval service with the polite detachment of a man trained to observe, not to engage. He remarked, without irony, that the Admiralty was said to suffer from a want of efficient clerks.

"You seem changed, Nicholas," his mother had observed quietly as they walked in the garden on his final morning. "There's a certainty about you now—a way of seeing beyond what's immediately before you."

"The world is larger than I once thought," he had replied simply.

"And Devon smaller?" she asked, with gentle perception.

"Not smaller, Mother. Just one part of a greater whole."

He had departed with the quiet awareness that while Devon would always be his origin, it was no longer his true home. The naval service, with its global reach and varied demands, had become his proper sphere, a realisation that brought both clarity and a touch of melancholy. The gulf between his experiences and his family's understanding was not merely geographic but fundamental to how they perceived the world and their place within it.

The reunion occurred on *Discovery*, where James had remained as part of the skeleton crew overseeing the ship's final disposition. The years had matured his friend—the lanky midshipman Nicholas remembered had filled out into a lean, confident officer whose weathered face and steady gaze spoke of all he had witnessed since their separation.

"Nicholas!" James exclaimed, embracing him with genuine warmth that transcended naval formality. "By God, it really is you. When Uncle Matthew wrote from Gibraltar that you'd appeared like a ghost from the Pacific, I could scarcely believe it."

"The ghost has substance enough," Nicholas laughed, returning the embrace. "And you—a confirmed lieutenant now. Well deserved, from all accounts."

They retired to a small dockside tavern where naval officers gathered, securing a table that offered some privacy for their conversation. There, over ale and a simple meal, they exchanged their parallel journeys. Nicholas spoke of his experiences in the Society Islands, his time with Silva, and his eventual return via India; James recounted the expedition's continuation to Hawaii, the tragedy of Cook's death, and the voyage's final arc through China and home.

"Strange to think," James observed as their conversation deepened, "that while we were turning north through the Pacific, you were still somewhere among the islands—or already adrift on another course entirely. The world seemed impossibly vast when we departed Plymouth, yet somehow our paths have reconverged."

"The Navy ensures that," Nicholas replied. "All journeys lead back to Portsmouth or Plymouth—if you're flying a British ensign."

James studied his friend thoughtfully. "You've changed, Nicholas. Not just in the obvious ways—we've all aged beyond our years at sea—but in how you see things. There's a depth to your perspective that wasn't there before Bora Bora."

"Living among the islanders changes one's understanding of what is fixed, and what is merely convention," Nicholas said. "As does being cast entirely on one's own resources."

"I believe it," James said. "After Cook fell in Hawaii, I experienced something similar—though less prolonged. Forced to reconsider everything I thought I knew about leadership and human nature." He paused, then added with quiet certainty, "He would be proud of you, Nicholas. Of what you've become."

That simple statement, delivered without embellishment, affected Nicholas more deeply than elaborate praise might have done. Coming from someone who had remained with Cook until the end, it carried a weight that validated his own journey in unexpected ways.

"And now second lieutenant on a new frigate," James continued, raising his glass in salute. "A remarkable appointment. It may be the Channel Fleet, but you're likely to see action of some kind."

"And you?" Nicholas asked. "What comes next for Lieutenant Trevenen?"

"A new appointment soon, I hope. Uncle Matthew has suggested I might benefit from Mediterranean service—Malta or Gibraltar, perhaps. But first, I'm to assist with the official account of our voyage. Captain King has primary responsibility, but additional officers are needed for verification and detail."

They parted with the promise to maintain correspondence—two friends whose vastly different journeys had nonetheless prepared them for the challenges that lay ahead in a navy at war across multiple oceans.

On his return to London on the 5th of December, Nicholas found Henry Harrington had returned for a few days from *Falcon*. That evening, in the study they spoke of their orders. It was too early to call for lamps, but the fire alone could not quite hold the corners. Henry, seated in the worn leather chair beside the hearth, stirred his brandy absently while Nicholas stood by the window, watching the haze of chimney-smoke drift east across St. James's Park.

"Report by the fifteenth. She's still completing at Sheerness."

Henry made a soft sound in his throat—agreement, or resignation. "You'll freeze your teeth out before February."

Nicholas gave a small, dry smile. "Quite possibly."

There was a pause, filled by the fire's shifting hiss. Henry glanced toward the papers on the desk—one of them, a note in Walsh's severe, upright hand.

"I thought—" Henry began, then stopped. "Well. One always thinks of the Indies, doesn't one? Dispatches, signals, a sudden vacancy. Something with consequence."

Nicholas turned from the window. "So did I," he said, quietly.

Henry nodded once and reached for the decanter. "*Triton's* no disgrace. Frigate service's a step up in the line. And Walsh has never asked for anyone, as far as I know."

"I know," Nicholas said. He sat at last, folding his hands over one knee. "I do know. It's only—"

He trailed off, unsure of what it was. Only not what he had imagined. Only cold, and grey, and far from any prize court or dispatch. Only service.

Henry understood. He refilled his glass, then Nicholas's.

"You'll do the work," he said. "And be seen doing it. That's what matters."

Nicholas nodded. The fire crackled softly. Outside, the light was going fast. There would be letters to write, and a coat to have altered.

"Strange to think," Nicholas said, swirling his glass, "that while we were charting the North Pacific, the foundations of the Empire were shifting beneath us."

"The Navy has never failed in its essential duty," Henry replied. "The Channel is secure. No enemy fleet has threatened our shores—not in a century."

"No," Nicholas agreed. "But the war has changed. If France and Spain ever learn to fight in concert…"

"They won't," Henry said, not lightly, but with the certainty bred into men who grew up in Admiralty houses. "Different systems. Different tempers. They'll never coordinate as we do. Still, that's why the West Indies matters. If Rodney and Hood can bring de Grasse to action and cripple the French fleet there, well, then the rest can be managed. Even the colonies."

Nicholas nodded, feeling how far his world had opened, how what had once been a series of isolated commands and charts had become part of something vast and shifting.

At length, Henry sat back and said, "I'll most likely be in the Channel as well. *Falcon's* not built for grand manoeuvres. Escort work. Patrols. Maybe a brush with the Brest squadron if the weather favours us."

He spoke without complaint, but something in the pause gave Nicholas pause.

"You sound almost disappointed."

Henry smiled faintly. "Not disappointed. A command is a command. But your path… it's been uncharted from the start. You've made your own bearings. That's rarer than people admit."

Nicholas looked down at his glass, unsure what to say. He had been many things—lucky, out of place, briefly lost—but rarely had he thought of himself as free.

Henry lifted his glass again. "To the next time we meet—on land or at sea. Preferably with a post-captain's commission and a French prize under tow."

"To that day," Nicholas agreed, grateful for the friendship that had taken root between them, despite the difference in their origins.

Five days before his scheduled departure for Sheerness, as Nicholas was finalising his arrangements, a letter arrived bearing the Carlisle trading company seal. He opened it with a surge of hope that quickly faded as he recognised Edward Carlisle's handwriting rather than Caroline's.

Ocean House, Westminster
10th December, 1780

Lieutenant Nicholas Cruwys, R.N.
London

Sir,

News of your appointment to His Majesty's Ship Triton has lately reached me by way of Admiralty circles. Permit me to offer my sincere congratulations on this responsible and creditable posting, which I understand to be a reflection of the confidence placed in your conduct and abilities by those best situated to judge them.

I take the liberty of inviting you to dine at Ocean House on the evening of the 11th instant. There are matters relating to current activity in the Channel—particularly with regard to convoy organisation, marine insurance, and the increasing presence of neutral tonnage—which may be of professional interest to an officer newly assigned to that station. While the paths of commerce and naval service do not always converge, there are occasions when a shared understanding may serve the broader interest of the Crown.

Miss Caelisle sends her compliments and joins me in this invitation, though she regrets that a prior engagement with Lord and Lady Ashton will prevent her from attending the dinner itself.

I remain, with the highest consideration,
Sir,
Your most obedient and humble servant,
Edward Carlisle

Nicholas read the note twice, uncertain how to interpret its purpose. Caroline's "prior commitment" with Ashton suggested her decision had indeed been made, yet the invitation itself indicated that Carlisle maintained an interest in their connection—now reframed in purely professional terms. After brief consideration, he penned an acceptance, recognising that whatever his personal disappointment, Carlisle's knowledge of Channel conditions might prove useful.

Ocean House proved an elegant townhouse in the fashionable Portland Place development—not as grand as Harrington's family mansion in Grosvenor Square, but substantial and tastefully appointed in a style that spoke of merchant wealth rather than inherited position. Nicholas arrived precisely at the appointed hour, determined to maintain professional composure despite the emotional undercurrents of the visit.

Carlisle received him in a study whose furnishings reflected both his commercial interests and personal refinement—rosewood bookshelves filled with leather-bound volumes, a substantial desk bearing maps and ledgers, and discreet displays of Asian antiquities acquired during his years in the East. The merchant appeared genuinely pleased to see Nicholas, greeting him with the warm handshake of a man who valued directness in business and personal matters alike.

"Lieutenant—or should I say, Lieutenant Cruwys of *HMS Triton*," Carlisle said, his voice carrying the same measured authority Nicholas remembered from their conversations in Bombay and aboard the *Ocean*. "A sound appointment. Walsh does not suffer mediocrity, and your name has been mentioned in certain quarters with increasing frequency."

"It was not what I had anticipated," Nicholas acknowledged, accepting the glass of excellent Madeira Carlisle offered. "But Captain Walsh requested me specifically. I am told the assignment will offer scope for development under more exacting conditions."

"Indeed," Carlisle replied, gesturing Nicholas to a comfortable chair near the fire. "There is no better tutor than necessity, and the Channel—dreary as it may be—is a crucible of exactitude. One cannot pretend in the Downs."

Their conversation held to a professional register as Carlisle spoke of recent developments in coastal shipping and the convoy structure—concerns about neutral carriers out of the Baltic, rumours of French interest in the Isles of Scilly, and the rising cost of marine insurance that reflected the general sense of anxiety. Nicholas listened attentively, noting the breadth of Carlisle's knowledge and the precision of his sources; whatever his official standing, the man knew how commerce moved, and who might be quietly steering it.

When the servants announced dinner, Carlisle led him to a dining room whose dimensions and furnishings reflected the same understated prosperity as the rest of the house. The table was set for two—confirming that Caroline's absence was no matter of timing or traffic, but a deliberate absence. Nicholas had prepared himself for that reality, but the confirmation struck with more weight than he expected.

"You report to Sheerness next week, I believe," Carlisle said as they began the meal—a carefully prepared but unshowy menu of English dishes, plainly seasoned and handsomely served.

"By the fifteenth," Nicholas said. "She is still taking on stores. I am to join Captain Walsh and assist with crew arrangements."

"A post of quiet importance," Carlisle remarked. "The Channel offers few prizes these days, but reputations are still forged there—often more honestly than abroad."

The conversation continued over several courses, measured and intelligent, with little ornament. It was only when the servants had withdrawn and the port stood uncorked between them that Carlisle, as was his way, turned gently but directly toward matters of a more personal nature.

"You may be wondering about Caroline's absence this evening," he said, studying Nicholas.

"Miss Carlisle mentioned certain... reconsiderations when she visited me at Viscount Westborne's house," Nicholas replied carefully. "I understood her to mean that our acquaintance would necessarily assume a more formal nature now that we have returned to England."

Carlisle's expression revealed both sympathy and measured appraisal. "Caroline's situation is more complex than you might appreciate, Lieutenant. Her decision regarding Lord Ashton's suit represents practical considerations beyond mere social advancement."

Nicholas maintained his composure despite the painful subject. "Miss Carlisle is not obliged to explain her decisions to me, sir. Our acquaintance, while valued, was brief and conducted under unusual circumstances."

"Indeed," Carlisle acknowledged, seeming to weigh his next words carefully. "Yet I believe you deserve some context, given the genuine connection you formed during our voyage. What I am about to share is offered in confidence, as one gentleman to another."

Nicholas nodded, uncertain where this might lead but unwilling to refuse any insight into Caroline's apparent change of heart.

"My daughter possesses exceptional qualities—intelligence, perception, character—that exceed the limited expectations society places on women of her station," Carlisle began. "From childhood, she has exhibited interests and capacities that conventional female education cannot satisfy. In India, as my business partner in all but name, she found scope for these capabilities. London offers far fewer such opportunities."

He paused, studying the ruby depths of his port. "Lord Ashton, for all his aristocratic assumptions, recognises these qualities in her. His first marriage was conventional, arranged for land and lineage. He has told me quite directly that in Caroline, he seeks a partner of intellect and understanding, one capable of engaging with the political and diplomatic circles he inhabits."

"That speaks well of his discernment," Nicholas said, masking his inner turmoil. "Miss Carlisle deserves nothing less than full appreciation of her abilities."

Carlisle's gaze sharpened. "There is more to it than that. Caroline's nature is... unconventional in certain respects. During our years in India, she formed a particular attachment—to the daughter of a senior Company official. A friendship of unusual depth and, I believe, of uncommon devotion."

The statement lingered in the air, its implications suspended in the hush between them. Nicholas felt—not surprise—but a quiet resolution, as though a series of dissonant notes had at last found their chord. He recalled facets of Caroline's manner that had long resisted interpretation: her reflexive reserve, her oblique allusions to "different understandings," the warmth that surfaced only after a certain guard had been lowered.

"I see," he said softly. And he did. In Tahiti and Bora Bora he had witnessed forms of affection that bore little resemblance to English convention. Attachments flowered there with unembarrassed frankness, and in directions that would have drawn censure in London. Yet they were met with a kind of tranquil assent—accepted, not excused—as natural, even honourable.

Atea had spoken of such things without the least apology. *"The sea has many currents,"* she had said, her voice as matter-of-fact as the tide. *"One follows where they lead."*

Carlisle, still watching him, said after a pause, "Do you indeed?" His tone held a trace of relief, shaded by caution. "Many gentlemen of our society would greet such a confidence with... discomfort. Or worse."

"In the Pacific," Nicholas replied, "I saw that human attachments take many forms. It broadened my view—though not my own inclinations. What seemed to matter most in those waters, was the honesty between the parties. The rest... belongs to custom, not principle." He paused, steady. "My regard for Caroline remains unaltered."

Carlisle was silent for a moment longer. Then: "She believed you might understand. It was one reason, she said, she was drawn to you—beyond the more obvious accord of mind and temperament."

"And Lord Ashton?" Nicholas asked, the question arising from practical concern.

"Is a man who has learned the limitations of conventional arrangements," Carlisle confirmed. "Ashton's first marriage taught him the misery of a union without genuine companionship. He seeks in Caroline a partner who will engage with his intellectual and political world, while maintaining the social appearance necessary for his position. Their understanding includes certain... accommodations regarding private matters."

The implications, though unspoken, were clear enough. Ashton offered Caroline not merely wealth and position, but a framework in which she might pursue her own happiness in ways that England's rigid proprieties would never publicly acknowledge. It was a pragmatic arrangement—one that merchants like Carlisle, accustomed to the complex negotiations of distant markets, might comprehend better than idealists or moralists.

"I appreciate your candour, sir," Nicholas said after a moment's reflection. "Few fathers would discuss such matters with a man in my position."

"Few fathers have daughters like Caroline," Carlisle replied with a trace of pride beneath his practical tone. "Or find themselves speaking to officers whose experiences extend beyond European shores."

"Your appointment to *Triton* under Captain Walsh speaks strongly, Lieutenant. The Channel is not where reputations are burnished quickly, but it is where judgement is tested, and seen. Advancement may come more slowly there—but it comes more securely, and with fewer illusions." Nicholas recognised the shift. For the rest of the evening, their conversation returned to matters of trade, naval operations, and Britain's global position.

As he rose to depart, Carlisle offered a final observation. "Caroline values your understanding, Lieutenant. She asked me to convey that, should circumstances permit, she would welcome a correspondence during your deployment—on matters of mutual intellectual interest, naturally."

"I would be honoured," Nicholas replied, understanding this offer for what it was: a gesture of parting, and of grace.

Carlisle extended his hand. "Safe voyage, Lieutenant Cruwys. Britain needs officers of your calibre in these uncertain times. I expect we shall hear of you."

Nicholas stepped out into the cold night air, the sound of hoofbeats fading along Portland Place. The conversation lingered in his mind—not only what had been said, but what it revealed: about Caroline, about himself, and about the world he had left behind in the South Seas.

He had not understood everything then. He doubted he did even now. But he had learned to recognise sincerity, and to honour it—even when it came in unfamiliar forms.

The next morning, Nicholas departed London for Sheerness, his sea chest loaded aboard the northbound mail coach, Harrington's house and its quiet order already receding into memory. There was nothing to detain him in town, and no reason to delay. The journey gave him time to reflect on all that had transpired since his return to England—the Admiralty's attention, his appointment to *Triton* under Captain Walsh, and, not least, the final and unspoken conclusion of his connection with Caroline Carlisle.

Her father's revelations had transformed his understanding of her actions, replacing perceived rejection with comprehension of the complex realities she navigated. In a society that offered women few paths beyond conventional marriage, Caroline had found an arrangement that might accommodate her true nature while providing the protection of aristocratic position. Nicholas could not begrudge her this pragmatic choice, even as he felt the loss of what might have been between them under different circumstances. Yet even so, Nicholas felt a new cynicism about European women and society—for he knew that in Polynesia, he and Caroline might have lived a different life, and been happy.

CHAPTER FOURTEEN

A thin sleet rattled against the quarterdeck awning as *Triton* warped into Portsmouth on the 14th of November 1781, the wind blowing foul from the south-east and bringing with it a stink of wet rope, coal dust, and anchorage filth. Though less than a year old and under a taut captain, she was streaked with salt, and her timbers groaned with the familiar complaint of ships long kept at sea without relief. The men went about their mooring stations with the grim economy of the well-drilled but ill-rested.

Nicholas stood aft, his greatcoat stiff with salt, and watched the grey outlines of Portsea emerge through the weather—a skyline of chimneys and signal masts, tanneries and tavern roofs. He had thought Sheerness bleak when they departed in March after final fitting out; Portsmouth, seven months and another winter later, looked no kinder.

Triton had brought in the Lisbon convoy—five sail of merchantmen, ragged and late but intact. The return leg had been no better: French chasse-marées had shadowed them in the Bay, though they'd kept their distance; a gale off Ushant had parted the line and lost them two days; and one merchant captain, grown feverish, had very nearly put his brig on the Goodwins through sheer confusion. It had not been glorious service, but it had been done.

They were to refit, take on provisions, and—if rumour was to be trusted—receive new orders. Something abroad. Something sharper than the endless grey tread of the Channel.

Nicholas turned from the rail as the bosun's pipe sounded from the waist. The hands were already preparing to lower the launch.

Nearly a year since he had jointed *Triton*. And still second lieutenant. Still here.

But he no longer thought it bitterly. Not after what he had learned under Walsh.

The ship's first lieutenant, Mr. Conyngham, was Walsh's creature to the bone—stolid, pale-eyed, and dry as a biscuit. They had served together in *Cyane*, and Conyngham had the air of a man who had long since chosen efficiency over affection. He neither hindered nor helped Nicholas, but observed him closely and judged him fairly. In its way, that too had been a form of education.

A shout from forward; the heave of line; the cable creaking in the hawse. *Triton* was in.

The Channel was behind them. For now.

That evening, with the wind still moaning low through the shrouds and the quarterdeck watch stamping their feet for warmth, Nicholas was summoned below. The steward, appearing wordlessly at the wardroom door, offered no hint of mood or urgency—only, "Captain's compliments, sir."

Walsh's cabin was dim but orderly, the stove lit, the charts rolled and stowed, a single decanter on the sideboard left unopened. The captain was seated at his writing desk, coat off but neckcloth still knotted, his expression as unreadable as ever. He gestured Nicholas to shut the door.

"I've just come from *Britannia*," Walsh said without preamble. "Admiral Darby has issued our orders. *Triton* is to undergo brief overhaul—stores, gunnery, copper touch-up where needed—and sail in three weeks to reinforce Admiral Hood in the Leeward Islands."

Nicholas inclined his head. "Yes, sir."

"There's more," Walsh said, tapping a sealed paper on the desk. "Lord Sandwich has written to Darby asking for officers suitable to serve as junior flag lieutenants in the Caribbean. Hood's staff is expanding; they've lost one man to illness, and another is due to take a cutter. Darby recalled you from the Admiralty interviews last winter, and—upon my agreement and my report—has put your name forward."

Nicholas said nothing. It did not seem quite real yet.

"You'll transfer to Hood's staff upon our arrival and rendezvous with *Barfleur*," Walsh went on. "Until then, you remain with me. But you are to report to London for a private briefing at the Admiralty, no later than the twenty-fifth. You are to return to *Triton* by the first of December."

A pause followed—deliberate, not unfriendly.

"You've acquitted yourself well, Mr. Cruwys," Walsh said. "I don't propose to repeat it, so you may remember it now."

Nicholas drew a breath. "Thank you, sir. I'll do my best to repay the confidence shown."

"I've no doubt you will. That'll be all."

Nicholas rose, bowed slightly, and withdrew, the latch catching behind him with a quiet click. The companionway smelled of cold metal and worn varnish. Above, the bells were striking.

Nicholas left *Triton* the following morning, the official letter from Admiral Darby tucked safely among his orders, and a curious lightness in his chest that he had not expected. The journey to London was long and damp—coaches delayed by half-flooded roads, inns crowded with staff officers on leave and minor clerks escaping the coast. But he scarcely minded the discomfort. A year before, he had left the Admiralty with quiet disappointment, assigned to *Triton* rather than the staff post he had dared not name aloud. Now, by Walsh's hand and Darby's recognition, he had come round to it at last—and with experience enough behind him to feel he had earned it.

He reported to the Admiralty on the twenty-second, and the meetings were brief, formal, and carefully noncommittal. Hood, it was made clear, would determine his exact duties in theatre. Still, the commission stood: he was to serve on a flag officer's staff in a campaign of real consequence. For the first time in months, he allowed himself a measure of quiet pride.

The Harrington residence in Brook Street received him with its usual order and reserve. He had spent the past few days there in a state of pleasant suspension—walking the park in the mornings, attending to the necessary correspondence, and rehearsing, in his head, what might be expected of a flag lieutenant in the Indies.

On the evening of the 25th of November, Nicholas returned to the Harrington residence where he to find the house in unusual commotion. Viscount Westborne had arrived unexpectedly from Parliament, and Henry Harrington had travelled from Chatham upon receiving an urgent summons from his father. As Nicholas entered the drawing room, he found both men engaged in hushed but intense conversation.

"Ah, Nicholas," the Viscount said, looking up as he entered. "You've heard the news, I presume? It's all over London now."

"News, my lord?" Nicholas asked, immediately sensing the gravity of the situation.

"Yorktown," Henry Harrington said, his usually composed features tight with concern. "Cornwallis has surrendered to Washington and the French. The dispatches arrived this morning on *Rattlesnake*."

The words struck with physical force. General Cornwallis's army had been Britain's principal force in the southern colonies—the cornerstone of strategy in that theatre. His capitulation represented not merely a military setback but potentially a decisive turning point in the entire American war.

"The details are still emerging," Viscount Westborne continued, gesturing for Nicholas to join them, "but the broad strokes are clear enough. Cornwallis was besieged at Yorktown by Washington's army and French forces under Rochambeau. Meanwhile, the French fleet under de Grasse prevented our navy from reaching him by sea."

"How bad was it?" Nicholas asked, accepting the glass of brandy that Henry silently offered him.

"Nearly seven thousand men surrendered," Henry said quietly. "The entire southern army—with all its artillery, baggage, and supply. I spoke with a midshipman from *Rattlesnake* this afternoon. He said our troops marched out with colours cased while the band played *The World Turned Upside Down*."

The Viscount's expression was grave. "I've just come from an emergency session of the Lords. North's government is in chaos. The opposition is already calling for immediate peace negotiations."

Dinner that evening was a somber affair. The Viscount had invited several political associates to join them, and the conversation inevitably centered on the implications of Yorktown for Britain's broader strategic position.

"It's the naval dimension that concerns me most," remarked Admiral Middleton, a friend of the Viscount's and the Comptroller of the Navy. As head of the Navy Board since 1778, Middleton oversaw all naval expenditure, shipbuilding, and dockyard administration, while the Board of Admiralty handled operational command. The stern, meticulous Scotsman had already made his mark implementing innovations like copper sheathing of ship's hulls, but now faced his greatest challenge. "The French fleet's role at Yorktown demonstrates what many of us have warned about for years—we can no longer maintain naval supremacy in all theaters simultaneously."

"Six years of war have stretched us too thin," Viscount Westborne agreed. "The fleet is undermanned, ships are deteriorating faster than the yards can repair them, and now we face France, Spain, and the Dutch Republic simultaneously. The American colonies may prove to be merely the first domino to fall."

"What of the West Indies, sir?" Nicholas asked, thinking of his imminent deployment with Hood.

Admiral Middleton looked at him sharply. His reputation for being demanding and detail-oriented was immediately apparent. "You're joining Hood's squadron, I understand?"

"Yes, sir. We sail on the 7th of next month."

"Then you'll be at the center of what may well be the decisive campaign of this phase of the war," Middleton said, speaking with the authority of a man who controlled the Navy's administrative machinery. "With America effectively lost—though few will admit it openly yet—the West Indies become our most vulnerable and valuable overseas possession. The sugar islands alone generate more revenue than all thirteen American colonies combined. Hood and Rodney must hold them at all costs."

"Parliament will never approve peace terms that surrender the West Indies," the Viscount added. "Jamaica, Barbados, Antigua—these are considered essential to British commercial interests in a way the American colonies were not."

Later that night, long after the final glass had been taken and the guests had withdrawn, Nicholas remained in the drawing room, seated slightly apart from the dying fire. The voices from dinner still echoed faintly in his mind—Westborne's clipped analysis, Henry's frown of consternation, the low murmur of names and ministries passed like counters across the table. But now the house had settled into its night-time hush, that curious stillness peculiar to London's older quarters, where time itself seemed to breathe more softly. In the embers and silence, the conversation assumed a different weight—less immediate, more enduring. And for the first time in days, Nicholas allowed himself to consider not only what had happened, but what lay ahead.

As the evening progressed, Nicholas had observed the shifting currents of opinion around the table. The initial shock of defeat was giving way to a more calculated assessment of Britain's remaining strategic options. The American conflict might be lost, but these men of power were already looking ahead to how Britain might salvage its position in the global struggle against France and Spain. Nicholas understood that while the Admiralty would determine the fleet's operational movements, it would be Middleton's efficient management of the Navy Board that would determine whether ships like his own would have the supplies, repairs, and support needed for the coming campaign.

Barfleur awaited, and with her, Rear Admiral Hood's squadron and the coming campaign in the West Indies—a proving ground for everything he had become since first stepping aboard *Resolution* as a wide-eyed midshipman. The words settled over Nicholas like a sudden shift in wind. A staff appointment with one of the Navy's most respected admirals, aboard a ship of the line, in the decisive theatre of war—such a position was not given lightly.

The personal costs of the journey were real: partings that could not be undone, a love that could not survive its return to England. But in their place remained something harder to define and more enduring—a way of seeing, of judging, of being.

He had lived by other winds and under other stars. What he carried now was not merely knowledge, but measure. And in the long rhythm of the sea, he understood, that was a kind of command.

The End.

Author's Note

This novel is a work of fiction, though it draws upon the historical fabric of the late 18th century with care and, I hope, fidelity. Many of the events, settings, and figures within—including the third voyage of Captain James Cook, the operations of HMS *Resolution* and *Discovery*, and the cultures of the Society Islands—are grounded in the documented accounts of the period, particularly those kept by Cook himself, by Lieutenant James King, and others in the expedition.

Nicholas Cruwys is an imagined officer, but his training, duties, and experiences reflect those of real midshipmen and commanders in His Majesty's Navy during the 1770s and 1780s. The Royal Naval Academy at Portsmouth, the surveying methods employed aboard Cook's ships, and the Pacific navigation traditions of Polynesian seafarers have all been portrayed as accurately as sources permit.

Atea and her kin, are fictional, but their world—its language, navigation, and cosmology—is drawn from historical accounts, chiefly those recorded during the first and third of Cook's Pacific voyages. The Tahitian language has been rendered sparingly, and where used, adapted to pronunciation conventions familiar to English readers of the era.

Above all, this is a tale of invention built upon a scaffold of truth. I have tried to honour both: the lived world of those who served at sea during a turbulent and brilliant age, and the quiet transformations that mark a young man's coming of age.

Any errors or oversights are mine alone.

Printed in Dunstable, United Kingdom